"Breanna."

Royce drew her to her feet, tilted up her chin with his forefinger. "Answer my question. Do you want me?"

"It's not fair of you to ask me that," she murmured. "Not when I'm foxed."

"You'd never answer me if you weren't."

She couldn't deny the truth of that. "You're right." Stunned, she watched her own gloved fingers reach up, trace the hard curve of his jaw. "I wouldn't answer it. I also wouldn't do this." Her fingertips brushed his lips as she'd longed to do before, felt their warmth even through her glove. "Let me ask you the same question, my lord."

"Royce," he corrected, his voice even huskier than it had been before. "And go ahead."

"Royce. Do you want me?"

Sparks glittered in his midnight eyes. "Yes, I want you. You have no idea how badly. More than I realized. Much more than I should." He turned his lips into her palm. "Does that answer your question?"

Mutely, she nodded.

He kissed the pulse at her wrist. "Then answer mine."

"*The Theft* is a book to be savored and enjoyed by all.... Brava, Ms. Kane, for creating yet another wonderful story to tug at our heartstrings, bring a chuckle to our lips and a smile to our faces."

—CompuServe Romance Reviews

THE MUSIC BOX

"*The Music Box* is a trip into Wonderland, full of adventure and mystery with a magical romance to warm readers' hearts!"

—*The Literary Times*

"Breathtakingly brilliant! Andrea Kane ... has taken intrigue and passion to new heights."

—*Rendezvous*

"Ms. Kane's mystery/romance will ... bring a sparkle of love and laughter to your life."

—*Bell, Book & Candle*

"Ms. Kane has worked her special magic with this delightful story.... *The Music Box* is simply enchanting. Don't miss it!"

—CompuServe Romance Reviews

THE BLACK DIAMOND

"Andrea Kane is the reigning queen of prize-winning historical romance. *The Black Diamond* is a beautiful tale of love, an exciting tale of adventure, and an adrenaline-pumping rush of nonstop action."

—Painted Rock.com

"Andrea Kane is a 'diamond of the first water' in the galaxy of historical romance stars."

—*Romantic Times*

Books by Andrea Kane

My Heart's Desire
Dream Castle
Masque of Betrayal
Echoes in the Mist
Samantha
The Last Duke
Emerald Garden
Wishes in the Wind
Legacy of the Diamond
The Black Diamond
The Music Box
"Yuletide Treasure"—Gift of Love Anthology
The Theft
The Gold Coin
The Silver Coin

Published by POCKET BOOKS

For orders other than by individual consumers, Pocket Books grants a discount on the purchase of **10 or more** copies of single titles for special markets or premium use. For further details, please write to the Vice President of Special Markets, Pocket Books, 1230 Avenue of the Americas, 9th Floor, New York, NY 10020-1586.

For information on how individual consumers can place orders, please write to Mail Order Department, Simon & Schuster Inc., 100 Front Street, Riverside, NJ 08075.

ANDREA KANE

THE SILVER COIN

SONNET BOOKS

New York London Toronto Sydney Tokyo Singapore

An *Original* Publication of POCKET BOOKS

A Sonnet Book published by
POCKET BOOKS, a division of Simon & Schuster Inc.
1230 Avenue of the Americas, New York, NY 10020

Copyright © 1999 by Andrea Kane

ISBN: 0-671-03409-X

First Sonnet Books printing September 1999

10 9 8 7 6 5 4 3 2 1

SONNET BOOKS and colophon are trademarks of
Simon & Schuster Inc.

Front cover illustration by Lisa Litwack
Tip-in illustration by Gregg Gulbronson

Printed in the U.S.A.

To my own grandfather, whose special feeling for me is enduring, and whose belief in family inspired the character and strength of Breanna's and Anastasia's grandfather. Like the late viscount, my grandfather continues to watch over us, with a love and pride that will live on forever.

1

She was going to die.

It was only a question of when.

He sat calmly at a far corner table of the London coffeehouse, sipping his tea and gazing out the window as he contemplated the busy cobblestone streets. London looked the same as always. It was chillier than when he'd left, with winter closing in. The fog had transformed from a clammy blanket to a raw mist—a mist that thickened as it mingled with the puffs of cold air emerging from the mouths of scurrying patrons and plodding horses. Everyone seemed in a hurry, including the shopkeepers who stepped outside in rapid succession, glancing about for any last-minute customers, then locking up for the day. One by one, they turned up their collars and hurried home to their waiting families.

How touching.

How convenient.

The throngs of people, while providing an interesting scene for an early evening diversion, made it easy to remain unnoticed. He'd intentionally picked this coffeehouse—one whose customers were primarily artists and authors, none of whom would have the slightest idea who he was. So he remained, a solitary gentleman enjoying his solitary late-day tea.

And if, by chance, one of his colleagues happened to wander in, spot him at his corner table, that colleague would doubtless offer his greetings, inquire where his lordship had been, and learn about his prolonged business trip abroad.

Given his status and position, his explanation would be accepted without question or doubt.

Ah, anonymity. It came in many forms, each one of them satisfying indeed.

He set down his cup, tugging his gloves more snugly into place and studying his cloaked hands—his right one, in particular. The German physician had been remarkably skilled, he mused, turning his palms up, then back down again. Same size. Same shape. Right down to the tapered fingers. With his gloves in place, it was impossible to tell that his right forefinger was a mere replica of what it had been. Oh, it couldn't bend at the knuckle, of course—wood never did—but he had no cause to bend that forefinger anyway. Not anymore. Now he had a substitute: his middle finger—a trigger finger impeccably trained, ready to perform on command. He also had a new weapon, one fashioned especially for him, made by the same craftsman who'd designed and constructed the original. Both weapons were unique. But this new version was a stunning, one-of-a-kind achievement. Mastering it had taken every ounce of his skill and concentration, given his physical impediment. But master it he had—as brilliantly as he'd mastered its predecessor—and almost as quickly.

Yes, the weapon—and the proficiency to use it—had been acquired within a month of leaving England. But conquering the pain—*that* had taken every day of the three long months he'd been away.

Still, it would surge to life, sometimes so acutely he nearly screamed aloud. It would never truly leave him. That he knew. Not even for a day.

But it also wouldn't stop him.

Nothing would.

As if to taunt him, the front door of the coffeehouse opened, admitting a cold blast of December air. He winced as the chilling wind shot through the room, found him in his corner, and set off the throbbing in his hand. Gritting his teeth, he waited for the worst of the pain to subside, bitterly acknowledging that the winter months were going to be excruciating. Cold intensified the dull ache that gnawed relentlessly at him, sharpening his agony with a piercing stab.

He had no choice but to endure it.

Damn the winter.

Damn the pain.

And damn Breanna Colby.

He finished his tea, cursing silently as the hot beverage did nothing to warm away his agony. A drink. That's what he needed. A good, stiff drink to dull the throb.

Tossing some coins on the table, he left the establishment, shoving his hands in his pockets as he made his way through the tangle of people to the nearest tavern.

Inside, it was dark and smoky, but he paid little attention to his surroundings as he ordered a brandy. He tossed it down in three gulps.

The liquor worked wonders, burning through his

system and making its way to the raw nerve endings at his knuckle.

When all this was over, he vowed, he'd spend winters somewhere warm, somewhere where the pain was bearable. There he could live in seclusion. There he could savor his victories.

Especially the one hovering just ahead—his ultimate triumph and long-awaited revenge. Doing away with that miserable bitch who'd done this to him, condemned him to three months of agony and a lifetime of physical torment.

She'd pay for each and every day he suffered, each and every night he'd awakened, drenched in sweat, pain spearing through his hand, shooting up his arm. Oh, yes, she'd pay. First, by watching her precious cousin die at her feet, then by waiting, wondering, when the bullet meant for her would find its mark.

It wouldn't be immediate. Oh, no, it would be prolonged. Torturing her had to be savored. He had to terrorize her to the point where she'd be crazed with fear.

Until she realized, with a final surge of panic, that she couldn't escape him.

Until she understood he never failed, never missed his mark.

Until she knew it would take one bullet, and one bullet alone, because he never needed a second.

And until she knew that he was watching her, toying with her, deciding when and where to end her wretched life.

Oh, Lady Breanna Colby, by the time I kill you, you'll beg to die.

And die you will.

2

Kent, England

The grounds of Medford Manor were alive with the sounds of activity, as a large crowd of workmen hammered and sawed, moving about the shell of what was becoming an elegant house—one that stood directly across the grounds from the existing one.

Bricklayers stood on scaffolding, spreading mortar and laying the final bricks of the structure, while carpenters hoisted up beams and rafters, nailed them into place. Stonemasons were constructing the marble fireplaces that would stand in each of the numerous bedchambers and meticulously shaping the stones that would define the sculptured footpaths and entranceway steps.

Breanna eyed the scene from thirty yards away, folding her arms across her breasts and nodding definitively.

Anastasia and Damen's home was well under way.

It hadn't been an easy feat to accomplish—not given the speed with which they wanted everything done. For starters, Breanna had sped up the process by doing a few quick sketches—based on what she knew of her cousin's tastes and what she suspected of Damen's—the week before their wedding. She'd showed the sketches to the soon-to-be newlyweds— and gotten their instant and unconditional approval.

Then again, Breanna had reflected with a smile, they were so absorbed in each other, she doubted they'd even studied her sketches. In fact, they'd probably have made a fuss over them even if she'd flourished pictures of a giant chamber pot and enthusiastically heralded them as sketches of their new manor—a manor that was destined to be the most exquisite home in all of England.

Ah, love.

Well, Stacie and Damen were more than entitled to that love. Lord knows, they'd been to hell and back waiting for the day they could wed. And it had come—a perfect day that united a perfect couple. As for the sketches—it didn't matter whether they'd truly seen them or not. Breanna's instincts told her they'd be pleased.

That very day, she'd taken action. The best architects had been hired, as well as the finest craftsmen, with the understanding that the Marquess and Marchioness of Sheldrake's home was to be completed as quickly as possible without compromising quality.

Everyone had taken that order to heart and, within days, plans had been drawn up. Those plans were approved on the day before the wedding—by Breanna. *That* she'd only agreed to do after Stacie had all but begged her. It seemed the bride-to-be was far too excited to sit still and look at drawings, and besides, she'd added brightly, Breanna was the artistic one in the family. So didn't it make sense for her to look over the plans? Finally, Breanna had relented, and taken over the task herself. As a result, everything proceeded on schedule and, on the day Stacie and Damen left for their wedding trip, a work crew arrived at the site and construction began.

The way things looked now, the manor would be finished before the Season began in March.

And not a minute too soon, Breanna thought, smoothing her hair as she strolled through the gardens, watching the structure take shape. Damen had made it abundantly clear that he intended to fill that house with children—as soon as nature permitted. Knowing Damen and Stacie ... well, Breanna wanted this house ready.

She fingered the folds of her mantle, nodding her approval as she angled her head this way and that, watching the manor take on detail and dimension. Nothing too elaborate. Just a roomy, airy, lovely home, filled with light and love.

Especially love.

She smiled, thinking with more than a little excitement that Stacie and Damen should be returning from the States any time now. They'd been away nearly three months, and Stacie had promised they'd be back for Christmas.

The wedding trip had been an exciting one, according to the letters Breanna had received. Fidelity Union and Trust—Stacie and Damen's bank—had opened its doors in October and was already thriving. Judging from the newspaper clippings Stacie had included with her letters, the bank was the financial triumph of Philadelphia, a perfect merging of the Lockewoods and the Colbys. Enough so that the new Mr. and Mrs. Lockewood weren't needed at all, and could spend their entire time enjoying Philadelphia, attending an occasional party, or in utter seclusion.

Breanna's smiled widened as she pondered all Stacie had said—and all she hadn't said. She'd written pages and pages on how wonderful it was to share with Damen the city in which she'd lived for ten years, the people, the sites. But she'd said suspiciously little about the secluded aspects of the trip.

It didn't take a scholar to figure out why. Given the passion that sizzled between Stacie and Damen . . . well, suffice it to say that it was good there hadn't been *too* many parties for them to attend. She doubted they would have had the strength to walk, much less dance.

In any case, Christmas was now only a few weeks away. And, since Stacie always kept her promises, she and Damen would already be on their way home. Breanna could hardly wait to see her—and to see her face light up when she beheld her soon-to-be-completed house.

The first step of their grandfather's dream.

Breanna's gaze lifted to the heavens, and she could almost feel her grandfather's reassuring presence. How overjoyed he'd be—Stacie and she sharing the grounds of Medford Manor, giving birth to their children here. It was precisely what he'd want, the lasting bond between the Colbys that he'd prayed for when he'd gifted her and Stacie with their coins.

The realization never failed to bring tears of joy to her eyes.

Breanna turned toward her own house—the house she shared only with her staff since that dreadful day in August when Bow Street had taken away her father, locked him up in Newgate.

Even now, the events of that day made her ill, just as her father's crimes made her shudder. He was a cruel and unforgivable man, and whatever small amount of feeling she'd held for him had been extinguished when she'd learned what he'd done—*and* what he intended to do. She'd closed off his room the morning after his arrest, a tacit sign to the servants that he was no longer part of her life.

They'd followed her lead, said nothing despite the lurid articles carried by the newspapers—articles that described the full extent of the Viscount Medford's unscrupulous dealings and his lifetime incarceration for attempted murder.

No words were necessary, not between Breanna and the beloved staff who'd raised her. They'd gone through the same gamut of emotions she had, at least with respect to the shock and horror. As for the sorrow and the shame, those were hers alone to bear. He'd been, after all, only their employer, while he was *her* father. It had taken her some time to come to terms with that, but it was behind her now, and the emotional scars would heal.

In the meantime, she was free—free from her father's menacing presence. It was as if a great weight had been lifted from her shoulders, allowing the real Breanna to emerge in an unencumbered way she'd never believed possible, and for that her staff cheered silently beside her. They were, after all, truly her family—the only real family she'd ever had, except for her beloved cousin Anastasia.

Reaching the manor, Breanna paused, seized by the sudden urge to celebrate. For the first time ever, life seemed perfect, rife with promise. Stacie was happily married and on her way home, a holiday season loomed ahead—filled with house parties and laughter—and she herself had a full life to lead. One she'd tentatively but successfully initiated as soon as the trauma—and the scandal—of her father's arrest had begun to die down.

She'd been prepared to be ostracized. Most especially by the *ton*. But, to her surprise, people were more sympathetic to her plight than she'd realized, somehow coming to the conclusion that her only offense was being George Colby's daughter—a bitter twist of fate rather than a character flaw. One by one, callers began coming by; first, matrons whose kind hearts compelled them to soothe and comfort her. Then, their daughters—young women she'd met at the few parties she'd attended two Seasons ago.

And then, the major turning point had occurred. Lady Margaret Warner, who'd been affable toward Breanna since Anastasia's coming-out last summer, had come to call. Lady Margaret's visit was a signal to the inner circle of young noblewomen who followed her example—a signal that it was socially acceptable to associate with Breanna Colby. Tacitly, she instructed them to follow suit. They began visiting Medford Manor in a steady trickle—to gossip, yes, but eventually, upon learning of Breanna's artistic talents, to show her their needlepoints, to ask her opinion of their sketching. And, when she responded with warmth and encouragement, they began inviting her to their homes as well.

Breanna was amazed at her own transformation. In fact, she discovered she was not at all the loner she'd believed herself to be. Instead, she was hungry for companionship—companionship she could receive and reciprocate, now that her oppressive father was gone.

In no time at all, she had friends, homes to visit, events to attend. Her days were no longer spent in lonely isolation—arranging and rearranging her porcelain figures, sketching, and reading. Guests arrived several times a day, including even an occasional gentleman or two. No one particularly enthralling. Then again, she wasn't looking to be enthralled. All she wanted was a bit of youthful merriment: some conversation, a stroll, perhaps even a little flirtation; the very things she'd been denied.

So what if the gentlemen were a trifle bland, acceptable rather than exhilarating? Exhilarating had never been a trait she was attracted to, anyway. Stable, even-tempered, well-mannered—that was what she felt comfortable with.

Still, she *was* becoming a bit bored, feeling oddly restless these past few weeks.

Well, all that would vanish the instant Stacie returned.

Our house party, she thought suddenly, her foot poised on the first entranceway step. *The one Stacie proposed before she left.*

Excitement flared inside her. *How could I have missed this opportunity?* she mused, recalling her cousin's idea to celebrate both their comings-of-age with a gala party at Medford Manor. Stacie hadn't specified a date. Well, now was the perfect time. Stacie's twenty-first birthday had arrived in October, and her own had occurred just last week. Plus, the celebration could be not only in honor of their birthdays, but in honor of Stacie and Damen's homecoming. And it would herald the holiday season.

It was ideal. The more she thought about it, the more enthused she became. In fact, she'd sit down with Wells right now, begin a guest list. Invitations could be sent out in a matter of days. But would that be enough time, with Christmas a mere fortnight away?

Gathering up her mantle, Breanna scooted up the steps, bursting through the front door and colliding with Wells at his post.

"Oh, Wells, I'm sorry."

The butler straightened, smoothing his uniform and tossing her a look that was more amused than it was bothered. "It's quite all right, Miss Breanna. Although I must admit that, for a moment, I thought Miss Stacie had returned."

Breanna's eyes sparkled, and she laughed aloud. "Not yet. But any day now. That's why I was in such a hurry. Do you remember that house party Stacie and I toyed with having when she returned? What would you think about planning it now, and making it a homecoming, holiday, and birthday celebration all rolled into one? I know, I know," she rushed on, as Wells opened his mouth to reply. "It's not enough notice to give our guests. I should have done this sooner. But it completely slipped my mind. Perhaps if I hand-delivered the invitations myself, it would soothe enough feathers to make the party possible?" She shot Wells a hopeful look.

"I doubt it," he replied.

Her entire face fell. "Very well then. We'll host the party after the holidays."

"We'll do no such thing." Wells readjusted his spectacles. "Not after all the work we've done."

Breanna's brows drew together in puzzlement. "Pardon me?"

"Mrs. Charles and I. We waited until half of November was gone. When you didn't begin planning the party, we did. The guest list was completed by the first of December, and invitations went out last week. Mrs. Rhodes is hard at work on the menu, and I believe she and Mrs. Charles have hired the musicians as well. The day after Miss Stacie arrives home, you and she can pick out the fabrics for your gowns. They'll be ready within a week. Of course, anything I've forgotten, including any last-minute touches, will be left to the two of you."

Disbelief flashed across Breanna's face, and laughter bubbled up in her throat. "Would you care to tell me when this party will take place?"

"The twenty-eighth and twenty-ninth of December. That will give Miss Stacie and Lord Sheldrake plenty of time to arrive and settle in, and all of us a chance to enjoy a quiet holiday as a family before our guests descend upon us. It will also give you a chance to breathe before your stream of callers arrive on New Year's Day." Wells's lips twitched. "The same stream of callers that filled those rare hours when you weren't overseeing the building of Miss Stacie's new home. Why, it's no wonder you were too busy to remember your wish to hold this party—and to plan it."

Breanna stopped laughing only long enough to toss Wells a sheepish look. "You're right. And I'm sorry." She stood on tiptoe, kissed Wells's lined cheek. "You, my friend, have rescued me more times than I care to count. You're a constant source of amazement."

A corner of his mouth lifted as he took her mantle, hung it away. "You and Miss Stacie keep me young. Exhausted, but young." He turned back to her, growing sober. "However, there is one difference. Miss Stacie has found the future your grandfather prayed she'd find. She's happy, whole. But you—I worry about you, Miss Breanna. You're still searching. You rarely consider your own happiness. So it's up to me to do it for you."

"By happiness I assume you mean properly wed," Breanna noted dryly. She gave Wells's arm a squeeze. "Well, stop worrying. I barely give marriage a second thought."

"I know. That's why I worry."

She chewed her lip to keep from chuckling at his forlorn tone. "I hate to shatter your dreams, Wells, but if you've planned this party in the hopes that I'll meet my future husband there, you're bound for disappointment. I'm doubtless acquainted with all the guests you've chosen to invite. And, as I conjure up a memory of each one of them . . ." She wrinkled her nose. "Let's just say it's unlikely I'll be making any wedding plans this coming year." A sudden notion struck, and she arched a suspicious brow in Wells's direction. "I *do* know all our guests, don't I, Wells? You haven't arranged any chance encounters with potential suitors?"

He sighed. "Unfortunately, no. Although not for want of trying. It's just that all the eligible gentlemen I had in mind are unavailable; either because they're away or because they have the poor judgment to be involved with other women—women who are unquestionably less remarkable than you. However, I'm hoping that Lord Sheldrake will be able to suggest—"

"No," Breanna interrupted. "I don't want Damen playing Cupid."

"But—"

"Absolutely not." She gave a vehement shake of her head. The gesture loosened one of her smoothly coiffed auburn tresses enough to send it toppling to her neck—a condition she promptly rectified by tucking the tress back beneath its pin. "I'll leave my future to fate. And so will you," she added meaningfully.

Before Wells could further his argument, a knock sounded at the front door.

Breanna pivoted about, eyeing the door quizzically. "Are we expecting anyone?"

"Perhaps fate," Wells suggested wryly.

A grin. "Then by all means, let her in."

Wells complied, turning the handle and swinging the door wide.

A uniformed messenger stood on the step, turning up his collar against the winter chill. "I have a package for Lady Breanna Colby," he announced to Wells, gripping a box in both hands.

"I am she." Breanna stepped forward, accepting the package and examining it curiously. "I wonder who it's from," she murmured, waiting until the messenger had received his shillings and gone before investigating further.

"One of your suitors, perhaps?"

"I don't have any suitors, Wells," she corrected, wriggling the top off the box. "I merely have . . ." Her voice trailed off as she peeled back the paper, looked inside. "What in the name of . . ." She placed the box on a low table in the hallway, and lifted out two small dolls, both with red hair and green eyes. The dolls wore identical pale-blue day dresses. Each frock was torn in the same spot—on the left side of the chest— and was marred by a bright spot of what appeared to be red paint.

Red paint that looked for all the world like blood.

"Who sent these?" Wells demanded, scowling at the dolls.

A cold knot of dread was beginning to form in Breanna's stomach—a knot she couldn't explain but that tightened more with each passing second.

Her heart thudding faster, she reached back into the box, snatching up the small square note that had been propped against the dolls' heads so as not to go unnoticed.

She unfolded it, wetting her lips with the tip of her tongue as she steeled herself.

The words leapt out at her, and she read them twice, icy fear slashing through her in ruthless talons. "Oh my God." She dropped the note, all the color draining from her face as she backed away.

"Miss Breanna?" Wells was visibly alarmed. "What is it?" He picked up the card. Adjusting his spectacles, he read aloud, " 'Did you think I'd forget you? Never. It's retribution time. I'm back to even the score. One bullet. That's all I need. One for each of you. First your cousin, then you. Soon. So tremble, Lady Breanna. Tremble and wait.' "

3

"*T*ell me the entire story again. As calmly as possible."

Cecil Marks leaned against the desk, tugging at his scarlet waistcoat and trying to ignore the din taking place behind him as a group of thieves were dragged into the Bow Street office, struggling and swearing. He'd been a Bow Street runner for three years now, and he still preferred combing the streets for criminals to actually bringing them in and having to contend with the chaos. But given the recent murders that had occurred here in London and the investigation that had ensued—well, he had no choice but to stick close to the home office.

He glanced down at his writing tablet, then back at the white-faced young woman who stood before him, wringing her hands as her elderly butler tried to comfort her. This was the last thing he needed after the kind of day he'd had. He'd questioned a half-dozen suspects, pored over pages of facts—and he wasn't in any mood to soothe the fears of an overwrought woman.

Then again, Lady Breanna Colby wasn't just any woman.

A lady in the true sense of the word, she was. Marks remembered that from last time. And a real beauty, to boot. Hair like burnished copper and eyes like chips of jade. Delicate and, at the same time, almost regal. Marks recalled the way she'd watched him lead her father away, her head held high, her eyes bright with tears she refused to shed, grief and shame she refused to display. It was rare to meet a woman who possessed that much restraint, much less one who was emotionally strong as well as beautiful.

Yes, she was a survivor, all right. Except that right now Lady Breanna looked ready to come apart at the seams.

Marks could well understand why. Hell, he'd be unnerved, too, if he was in her place. The problem was, he had no time or resources to devote to her situation. Not when the whole matter boiled down to a mere threat.

"My lady," he replied, after listening to her second recounting of the story. "I know you're upset. But unless someone's actually tried to hurt you, my hands are tied. Unless, of course, there's something you haven't mentioned? Something more substantial this man's done? If so, tell me and I'll get right on it."

Breanna drew an unsteady breath. "That's just it. He hasn't actually *done* anything—yet. But it's clear he intends to."

"You say he sent you this package." Marks jerked his thumb toward his desk, where the opened box lay. "Those two dolls and a note."

"Not just two dolls," Breanna corrected. "Two disfigured dolls. And it's not just a note, sir. It's a threat. Surely you can see that."

Marks twisted around, examined each doll for the third time, then scanned the note. "I admit, whoever sent this is warped, even unbalanced. But as for proof that he's going to kill you—"

"Mr. Marks, please don't patronize me. You of all people remember what happened the night my father was arrested—or rather, *after* he was arrested."

Marks cleared his throat. "You're talking about that shooter."

"He wasn't just an arbitrary shooter. He was paid to kill Anastasia, hired by my father—through his informant—to do so. When I shot him in the hand before he could shoot Stacie, he bolted. Obviously, he realized he might be exposed, so he killed Mr. Cunnings—the one person who could identify him—then vanished."

"We *believe* he killed Cunnings," Marks amended, scratching his head. "The killer was never found, nor was any proof of his identity." Seeing the anguish on Breanna's face, he felt a pang of guilt. "But, yes," he conceded, "we're pretty sure Cunnings's murderer was the same man who took a shot at your cousin."

"And I maimed him."

Marks's lips thinned into a grim line. "I understand why you'd think this message was from him. Maybe it was. Fine, it probably was. The question is, what can we do about it? We couldn't find him three months ago. What makes you think it'll be any easier to find him now?"

"The fact that he's surfaced." Breanna gripped the folds of her gown between her fingers, an earnest pucker forming between her brows. "Sir, I don't work for Bow Street. I'm not presuming to tell you how to do your job. But isn't it possible this man dropped out of sight long enough, not only to wait for your inves-

tigation to die down, but to give his wound time to
heal? That he's only now able to resume his work?
His note certainly makes it sound that way."

"I agree. It does sound as if he was waiting to be up
to snuff before he contacted you. But that doesn't
mean he'll be any easier to catch than he was before.
Think about it, my lady. Paid killers don't operate out
in the open. Nor do they advertise in newspapers to
find clients." Marks flipped his notepad shut. "What's
more, they don't take jobs without monetary compensation—*major* monetary compensation. With your father in Newgate, no one's interested in paying this
assassin to kill you or your cousin. So why would he
take the risk? Why would he chance getting caught in
exchange for nothing? He wouldn't."

"My instincts tell me otherwise."

"No rudeness intended, my lady, but I'm in the
middle of some pretty ugly murder investigations. I
can't abandon those cases in favor of your *instincts.*"

Breanna made a frustrated sound. "I realize that.
I'm not asking you to abandon anything. I read the
newspapers. I'm aware of how busy you are. All I'm
asking is that you probe this matter a bit—perhaps
after hours." She pressed her lips together, squaring
her shoulders in that regal way she had. "I'm sorry if
that sounds presumptuous. But remember, mine isn't
the only life that's at stake. My cousin's is, too. I'm
sure her husband, Lord Sheldrake, would appreciate
any assistance you could provide in eliminating a potential threat to his wife."

Lady Breanna's pointed comment wasn't lost on
Marks. He knew damned well who the Marquess of
Sheldrake was, how prominent he was in London busi-
ness and society. He also knew he was the "Locke-

wood" of the House of Lockewood—the most influential merchant bankers in England, maybe even in the whole damned world. Not to mention that the House of Lockewood was the very place where Cunnings, Sheldrake's right-hand man, had been murdered. Murdered because he'd been instrumental in an ugly plot that sacrificed lives and undermined the marquess himself.

Yes, if the assassin truly had resurfaced, Sheldrake would definitely want him found, want all the loose ends of the nightmare tied up. Most especially because the assassin's target had been Lady Anastasia Colby, now the Marchioness of Sheldrake. And everyone knew how much Damen Lockewood adored his new bride . . .

Hell, Marks thought, eyeing Lady Breanna with a kind of grudging respect. This woman wasn't only resilient and beautiful. She was smart, too.

"All right." He gave a terse nod. "I'll do some checking—as much as I can given what's going on here. I'll start with the messenger service that delivered the package to your home. After that, I'll review the details of Cunnings's murder. Maybe I can turn something up."

His tone said otherwise.

"Perhaps if you speak to Mr. Cunnings's colleagues," Breanna suggested. "I know you did that right after he was killed. But that was three months ago. Maybe someone can provide you with new information. Who knows? It's possible one of Mr. Cunnings's less reputable associates—male or female—saw him with this man but didn't think anything of it at the time. Until now, when you mention that the suspect you're searching for dropped out of sight for the past several months and has only now resurfaced."

Marks arched a brow. "That's a bit far-fetched, wouldn't you say?" He averted Breanna's protest by holding up his palm. "I said I'll try. And I will. But I'm not promising anything." He shifted impatiently, eager to resume work on his current murder investigations. "Give me a few days, maybe a week. When I'm finished poking around, I'll ride to Kent, tell you what I've found out."

"Thank you, sir." Breanna gestured toward the desk. "Shall I leave the note and package with you?"

"Hmm? No. Take them with you. They'd probably get lost in the shuffle here. If I need to see them again, I'll let you know." Marks gave Lady Breanna what he hoped was a reassuring smile. "Go home now. And try not to worry. The chances are this madman got just what he wanted: he scared the wits out of you. And that will be that."

Across the street from Bow Street's office, the well-dressed man turned up his collar, moved casually away, and continued walking.

Excellent, he thought, a smug smile curving his lips. *She's gone to Bow Street. They can't help her, of course. They've got nothing. But she's frightened. Good. She has reason to be. And this is only the beginning.*

He rounded the corner and disappeared.

"I doubt Mr. Marks will help us much," Breanna commented a few minutes later, leaning her head wearily against the carriage seat. "I feel thoroughly patronized. Worse, I'm not even sure he believed me at all."

"Oh, he believed you," Wells returned in a tight voice. "Your situation is just not, in his opinion, a matter of urgency. He'll do what he can. If not for your sake, for Lord Sheldrake's." Pursing his lips, Wells added, "Miss Breanna, I held my tongue in there because my frustration would have done you more harm than good. But now that we're alone, I want you to know I don't intend to entrust your safety entirely to the Bow Street runners. Whether or not I'm overreacting, I plan to hire additional guards."

Grimly, Breanna nodded. "I think that's wise, particularly since there are so many comings and goings at Medford these days. With all the activity necessary to complete Stacie and Damen's new home . . ." A painful sigh. "For the first time, I'm relieved she's away. That means she's out of danger. Hopefully, Mr. Marks is right and this will all turn out to be nothing more than a scare. If that's the case, Stacie won't even have to know about it. She's so audacious, I shudder to think how she'd decide to handle things. And if he's wrong . . ." Breanna swallowed. "Let's just say that if he's wrong, if the assassin means to carry out his threats, there will be plenty of time to fill Stacie in when she arrives home. In the meantime, she can remain blissfully unaware."

Far away, on a ship bound for England, Anastasia Lockewood awakened with a start. Her eyes snapped open, and she sat up, perspiration breaking out on her brow.

"Sweetheart?" Damen shot up like a bullet. "Are you going to be sick again?" He swung his legs over the side of the bed, reaching for the chamber pot as he spoke.

"No." Anastasia waved the receptacle away, shuddering as she contemplated how many times she'd needed it on this trip home. "I'm fine. Really." She wrapped the sheet around her, drawing up her knees, and resting her chin atop them. "At least physically."

Relieved, Damen resettled himself beside her, smoothing back her hair and pressing his lips to her bare shoulder. "Then what is it?"

"I don't know." Anastasia frowned, staring about their modest cabin and wondering how many days it would be before they docked in London. "But I have the most uneasy feeling. Something's not right at home."

Scowling, Damen murmured, "With Breanna, you mean."

"Yes. With Breanna."

Damen nodded. He knew better than to question his wife's connection with her cousin. He'd seen first-hand how attuned to each other they were. They were more like sisters, twins in fact, than they were like cousins—in far more ways than merely their striking physical resemblance.

"We're almost home," he soothed. "Breanna must realize that. Maybe she's feeling the same restlessness you are. Maybe that's what you're sensing. After all, we have been away for months."

"I suppose so." Anastasia sounded distinctly unconvinced. "Breanna's probably anticipating our homecoming as much as I am." A pause. "Her birthday was last week," she continued, as if trying to persuade herself that Damen was right. "She's finally of age. I wonder if she's planning the party we talked about before I left."

"I'm sure she is. In fact, I'm sure she's exhausted. Between planning a house party and handling the initial construction of our home by herself—I'm sure she's counting the days until we're there to lend a hand."

"That's true." Anastasia relaxed a bit. "Even with the staff's support, she's doubtless buried in details, determined to oversee all the preparations herself."

"Um-hum." Damen slipped his arms around Anastasia's waist, laid a possessive palm on her still-flat abdomen. "On the other hand, maybe she senses you have an announcement for her."

His wife shot him a wry grin over her shoulder. "If so, she's probably lining the grounds with chamber pots. I can't seem to take ten steps without needing one."

"That's only because of the motion of the sea. The ship's doctor assured me the sickness will ease once you're home, with both feet planted firmly on land."

Laughter danced in Anastasia's eyes. "He would have assured you of anything to calm you down. You've interrupted him six times a day for reassurance that everything I'm experiencing is normal. The poor man probably bolts his door at night, for fear that you'll burst into his cabin and accost him with yet more questions about your pregnant wife."

Not the least bit contrite, Damen chuckled, tugging his wife down to his chest. "I'm allowed to worry. I'm a new husband *and* an expectant father. I'm also insanely in love with my wife—a wife who, for the past three weeks, has either swooned or been sick every time she's stepped out of bed."

"Then perhaps I should stay on it—or rather, in it." Her attention diverted by more scintillating matters, Stacie feathered her lips across her husband's chest, nuzzling his nipples as her fingers trailed down the hard planes of his stomach. She smiled as she felt his heart rate quicken. "After all, I'm fine when I'm re-clining. Better than fine, in fact." Her hand slid lower, found its goal, and her fingers surrounded Damen's erection, caressed him in light, teasing strokes. "So if you want me to feel better—"

"Say no more." Features stark with desire, Damen rolled her to her back, covered her mouth—and her body—with his. "You couldn't feel any better," he murmured huskily. "You already feel too damned good."

"Show me," she whispered, twining her arms around his neck.

Damen proceeded to do just that, breathing love words against her skin, into her lips, as he penetrated her slowly, exquisitely, melding their bodies into one.

Their lovemaking was as shattering as ever, per-vading every pore of Anastasia's body, touching every inch of her soul, leaving her weak, bonelessly sated.

But afterwards, wrapped securely in Damen's arms, sleep evaded her.

Unbidden, the uneasiness crept back, latching its disturbing tentacles into her mind. And, like the re-lentless queasiness that plagued her, it refused to be shaken.

Something was wrong, she concluded, stirring fit-fully on the bed.

Her gaze shifted to the cabin's tiny porthole, and she willed the winds to propel them swiftly to En-gland.

Breanna needed her.

She had to get home.

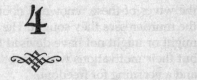

4

*T*he headline of *The Times* was quite disconcerting.

It seemed that, try though they would, Bow Street could not definitively prove who had killed two prominent noblemen.

Although, after carefully questioning dozens of people—servants and associates alike—they did have their theories.

This should be fascinating, he thought, settling back in his dining room chair and skimming the article beneath the headline.

His brows raised in interest as he read on.

While the murders were still unsolved, Bow Street had begun to alter their original theory that the crimes were linked, at least so far as sharing the same assailant. Instead, the police were now speculating that, while one crime probably inspired the other, the two murders had been committed by different killers. And not by two hardened criminals, but by two women, each with the same relationship to the victim *and* the same motivation to do him in.

Women?

Now that was an intriguing notion.

Leaning forward, he read on.

Evidently, Bow Street was coming to suspect that the wives of these renowned noblemen were, in fact, the murderesses they sought. The women in question might or might not have devised their plans together, but their motivations were doubtless the same: greed and a yearning for freedom.

He continued, almost laughing out loud as he followed Bow Street's reasoning.

The fact was that both wives had mysteriously disappeared at the same time their husbands had been shot. Initially, it was presumed that they'd been kidnapped. But now, more than a week later, no ransom notes had surfaced, nor had any trace of the women or their whereabouts been uncovered. So it was looking more and more like they'd killed their husbands, then run off, perhaps with other lovers, most likely taking with them some private source of wealth—be it cash or jewels—that no one other than they and their husbands knew about.

How clever, he thought, his teeth gleaming with amusement. *What would we ever do without Bow Street and their unmatched genius?*

The article concluded by assuring everyone that the authorities were hard at work, determined to apprehend the perpetrators.

What a waste of time, he reflected, folding the newspaper in half and placing it on the table. *Bow Street will never find them. No one will. They've vanished forever.*

He was just biting into his second scone when a knock sounded at the dining room door.

His butler entered. "Pardon me, m'lord, but a gentleman from Bow Street is here to see you. A Mr. Marks. He insists on speaking with you personally."

A flicker of apprehension—one he kept carefully concealed.

Slowly, he chewed and swallowed his food, then dabbed at his mouth with a linen napkin. "Does he now?" He rose, a frown creasing his brow as he smoothed his gloves into place. "Did he state what his business was?"

"Something about John Cunnings, sir. Apparently, the authorities are speaking to all his associates again. I have no idea why."

Ah, but *he* did know why. He knew precisely why.

Or, more specifically, *who*.

Breanna Colby.

"I see," he replied, his mind racing.

Marks's visit had to tie in to the trip Lady Breanna had made to Bow Street three days ago. The miserable bitch. She'd obviously accomplished more than he'd realized, done a better job of convincing the police to help her than he'd anticipated.

Still, this conversation had to be strictly routine. Bow Street had no evidence to link him to Cunnings—not then or now—and certainly none to link him to their current murder investigation. They were searching for runaway wives, for heaven's sake, not reputable gentlemen.

He'd do nothing to sway their way of thinking. Nor would he antagonize them. To the contrary, he'd be warm, gracious, utterly cooperative.

And Marks would leave no wiser than when he arrived.

Lady Breanna was another matter entirely. She had to be punished for her brazen act.

The very notion made excitement surge through his blood. He'd find a means of punishment that would intensify her fear beyond measure.

And, as a result, heighten his exhilaration even more.

"Sir?" the butler prompted. "What shall I tell Mr. Marks?"

"By all means, show him in," he replied graciously, clasping his hands behind his back. "I'll answer any questions he has."

And then I'll deal with the lovely Breanna Colby.

Four days later, Bow Street delivered its report.

Marks arrived at Medford just before lunch. He propped himself against the sitting-room door frame—a blatant indication that this wasn't going to be a lengthy visit—and relayed his findings to Breanna and Wells.

Thoroughly, meticulously, he read through the entire list of interviews he'd conducted, and their outcomes. He'd spoken with every conceivable one of John Cunnings's associates, from the women he'd squandered his illegally acquired money on, to the men he did business with, to his neighbors, to those few friends he had. No one knew anything about an assassin, nor did they know of anyone who'd want to kill Cunnings. In fact, they knew nothing more about Cunnings's illegal dealings than they had three months ago—which was nil, other than whatever they'd read in the newspapers.

Having concluded his report, Marks straightened and smoothed his scarlet waistcoat. "That's all I have, my lady." He shut his notebook. "Have you received any more threats?"

Breanna shook her head. "No."

"Then I'd say you're in no immediate danger. Nor is your cousin, Lady Sheldrake. Besides, the point is moot. We have nothing more to go on."

"But Mr. Marks—"

"I've done everything I can, my lady." His mouth set in grim lines. "I can't justify spending another hour on this—not with the current murder investigation I'm involved in. My suggestion is: be careful. Don't go out alone. Tell your cousin the same when she returns from her wedding trip. I noticed you hired some guards. Good idea. The more security you have the better. That'll scare this lunatic off—*if* he plans to carry out his threats. Which I don't think he will." With that, Marks tipped his hat. "Good day, my lady."

He crouched down in the bushes by the roadside, watching as Marks drove through the iron gates and curved onto the road leading away from Medford Manor.

Good. Bow Street's finished. She's on her own now. Which means I can strike whenever I wish. I won't rush it. The time has to be right . . .

It was two days later when the carriage bearing the Lockewood family crest turned off the road, heading toward Medford.

Inside the carriage, Anastasia frowned as the iron gates loomed into view—along with two burly men posted on either side.

"Who are they?" she demanded, scooting to the edge of her seat and eyeing them. "And why are they standing so rigidly at the gates—as if they're sentries?"

"I don't know." Even Damen looked perplexed, his brows knitting as one of the two men gestured for their driver to stop.

The driver complied, and the man approached the carriage.

"I'll need your names, please," he began, peering inside the window. "Then you'll have to wait to be announced . . . oh forgive me, Lady Breanna. I didn't know you'd gone out." He bowed, backed away from the carriage, and waved them on. "Drive right through."

"But I'm not . . ."

Damen stopped Anastasia with a gentle squeeze of her arm. "Thank you," he called to the guard, gesturing for their driver to continue on his way.

"Why did you silence me?" Anastasia demanded, turning to her husband. "He thought I was Breanna."

"I know," Damen responded. "I wanted it that way. It got us inside faster, without further explanation. The sooner we reach the manor, the sooner we find out what the hell's going on here."

Anastasia opened her mouth to reply, then gasped, her attention captured by another, far more enticing, sight. She pointed out the window as the carriage rolled down the drive toward the house. "Damen, look." Her eyes widened, and she stared at the graceful structure to their left, workmen swarming all around it. "That's our house—and it's already standing. Why, it's practically completed."

"I'll be damned." Damen shook his head in amazement, as stunned by the progress that had been made during their absence as was his wife. "Breanna must have had these people working day and night."

"*Breanna* must be working day and night," Anastasia amended. "If I know her, she's overseen all this construction herself. In fact . . ." She scrutinized the area carefully, searching until she saw the bright spot of burnished color that was her cousin's hair. "There she is!" She whipped around. "Dixon, stop," she instructed the driver.

The bewildered driver brought the carriage to a screeching halt.

"Take our bags to the house," Damen advised him, stifling a grin. "We'll follow on foot."

"Yes, m'lord." Dixon alighted, intending to properly assist his passengers, only to have Anastasia fling open her door, knocking him flat on his back as she leapt down from the carriage herself.

"Oh, Dixon, forgive me. Are you all right?" she asked anxiously, relief flooding her face as the driver squirmed to a sitting position.

"Fine, m'lady," he assured her, brushing dirt off his uniform.

"Thank goodness." She gathered up her skirts, looking like a thoroughbred at the starting gate. "Then if you'll excuse me . . ."

She didn't wait for a reply.

She took off at a run, shouting, "Breanna!" and waving her arm.

Damen swung down from the carriage, offering a hand to the half-crouched, half-sitting driver. "Don't be too hard on yourself, Dixon," he consoled, his lips twitching as he helped the still-dazed driver to his feet. "Keeping up with my wife is next to impossible."

"Yes, sir. Thank you, sir." Dragging his sleeve across his brow, Dixon stared after Anastasia's rapidly moving figure. Then, with a hard shake of his head, he jumped back into his seat and drove on.

Chuckling, Damen watched Stacie rush toward her cousin, shouting over the din and waving frantically.

Breanna glanced up, spotted her, and broke into an immediate run.

"Stacie!"

The cousins embraced, laughing as they broke apart, saw all the workmen gaping at them, and realized what a spectacle they were making.

"You're home. I can't believe it!" Breanna grasped Stacie's hands, surveying her from head to toe. "You look wonderful. Positively radiant. Marriage agrees with you." She glanced beyond Stacie and smiled as Damen approached them. "And here's the man responsible for your radiance. Welcome home, Damen."

"Breanna." He kissed her hand, then gave her a warm hug. "It's so good to see you."

"Home, indeed," Stacie piped up, moving excitedly about as she assessed the manor that was fast taking shape. "I can't believe what you've accomplished. My God, have you slept since September?"

A hopeful look lit Breanna's eyes—eyes that seemed unusually puffy, lined, with heavy dark circles beneath them.

For reasons of her own, she disregarded Stacie's question in lieu of her own. "Do you like it? I was half afraid you'd object to the artistic liberties I took. But you were so preoccupied before the wedding, and I couldn't get you to sit still and look at the sketches. And with winter nearly upon us, we had to lay the foundation right away. Either that or we'd have to wait until spring, which would mean your home wouldn't be ready until next fall. I couldn't bear having you in London until then. So I got things started. You'll do all the decorating yourself, of course."

"Of course *not*," Stacie corrected. "I have no talent at decorating, and you know it. I need your help— with every last piece of furniture." She gazed at the half-finished manor again, her eyes growing damp. "You did all this for us ... Breanna, what would I ever do without you?" She gulped back a sob.

Breanna blinked in surprise. "Stacie, you're crying. Why?"

"Because I'm touched. Because I'm so glad to be home. Because I missed you. Because I can't believe how much you took on while we were away. Be- cause—"

"That's not what I meant," Breanna interrupted, in- clining her head in puzzlement. "I know why you're happy. And I'm as thrilled as you—that you're home, that you like what I've done. But you never cry. At least you never used to."

"That was then," Stacie informed her ruefully, dab- bing at her eyes. "This is now. I seem to be doing a fair amount of crying these days. Crying and swoon- ing and retching. It's completely unlike me."

Their gazes met.

"You're with child." Breanna's words were a state- ment, not a question, and she seized Stacie's hands again, staring insightfully at the spot where her man- tle covered her abdomen, as if she could see through to the changes beneath. "I knew it. Oh, Stacie, I'm so happy for you." She hugged her cousin, then Damen, tears glistening on her own lashes. "I'm going to be an aunt. Not a second cousin, mind you, because as far as I'm concerned, you're my sister, not my cousin. So, this babe will call me Aunt Breanna." She grew se- rious for a moment. "Are you all right—you and the babe?"

"*We* are. But Damen's not." Anastasia shot her husband a teasing look. "He's been overwrought the entire trip home. The ship's doctor nearly tossed him overboard several times. Not to mention that the doctor was the first one to disembark when we docked. He nearly knocked down three elderly women in his haste to get away. By now, he's probably at some out-of-the-way alehouse, in a drunken stupor and planning how to avoid the House of Lockewood for the next six months."

Breanna laughed—a small, strained sound. "I'll take that as a warning. Wells will make sure Damen has a full snifter of brandy each night before bed to calm his nerves." Her expression grew hopeful. "That is, if you stay here. You will stay here, won't you? You won't go to London? I know it'll mean less privacy for you, but—"

"I've already sent our driver on to the manor with our bags," Damen interceded, dismissing her concern with a wave of his arm. "Knowing how much Stacie missed you, I'd never think of separating you two again. Besides, this way we can take over supervising the building of our home. Correction, *I* can take over supervising the building of our home. Stacie is to get no closer to the construction than we are now. Please, Breanna, I'm counting on you to keep an eye on your cousin during the hours I spend at the bank. I'll be forever in your debt."

Anastasia rolled her eyes. "I'm pregnant, Damen, not incapacitated. Fine." She held up her palm to ward off his tirade. "I'll be as docile as a lamb."

"That'll be the day."

"I'll take care of Stacie." Breanna smoothed her hand over her hair—and Stacie could have sworn her fingers shook. "You have my word, Damen. I'll never let any harm befall her. Never."

Breanna's oddly somber tone, her seemingly extreme reaction struck an uneasy chord in Stacie's mind. But before she could open her mouth to respond, her cousin had rushed on.

"I have so much to tell you," she declared, feeling Stacie's quizzical stare, and averting her gaze to avoid it.

Nonetheless, Stacie saw the worried shadow flicker across her face.

"We're hosting that party you and I discussed," Breanna informed her brightly. "Right here. The week after Christmas. Wells, Mrs. Charles, and Mrs. Rhodes planned the whole thing. It will be a holiday party, birthday celebration, and welcome home gathering all in one. I'm sure it will be the talk of the *ton*. In addition, we've also been invited to a dozen holiday parties elsewhere. Of course, you'll have to tell me which invitations you want to accept and which you don't—"

"Breanna." Stacie had had enough. This sort of aimless babbling was as unusual for Breanna as crying was for her. It was time to get to the bottom of this.

Silencing her cousin's chatter, Stacie lifted Breanna's chin and studied her—closely—for the first time. No, she hadn't imagined the dark shadows beneath Breanna's eyes, nor the strain tightening her face. And her cheeks, when she wasn't smiling, were pale.

"What's wrong?" Stacie demanded. "And don't tell me nothing. I won't believe you. I've had the oddest feeling for over a week now—like something ominous was going on here. Tell me what's happened."

Shoulders sagging, Breanna gave up the pretense.

"I prayed I wouldn't have to tell you," she said, lacing her fingers tightly together. "I prayed it would all be resolved by the time you got home. But it isn't. And now, there's a babe to consider . . . so you have to know."

"Know what?"

"A little over a week ago I received a package—a package and a note." A weighted pause. "They were a warning."

"A warning?" Stacie echoed. "From whom?"

"From the man Father paid to kill you."

"*What?*" Stacie blanched. "From that assassin who tried—?"

"Yes."

"How can you be so certain?" A muscle flexed in Damen's jaw. "What was in the package? What did the note say? What kind of warning?" Damen's questions sliced the air like a knife, and he slid a protective arm about his wife. "Breanna, I think you'd better tell us everything."

With a weary nod, Breanna did, eliminating none of the details, including the trip she'd made to Bow Street and the lack of information they'd turned up. "But I know in my gut it was *he* who sent them. I think Bow Street agrees, even if they've washed their hands of the matter."

"That explains the extra security," Anastasia concluded aloud. "*And* my uneasy feeling."

"Yes. Wells arranged for guards."

"How can Bow Street just dismiss such blatant evidence?" Anastasia asked, twisting around to gaze up at her husband.

"No crime has been committed," Damen returned

quietly, his forehead creased in thought. "Did they talk to the messenger who delivered the package?"

"Yes." Breanna nodded. "He had no contact with whoever sent it. The lad was given the box by his supervisor when he reported for work. And, according to the supervisor, the package was left, along with an envelope containing delivery instructions and a ten pound note, on his doorstep."

"Then Bow Street's exhausted their clues. Also, judging from the headlines of the newspaper we bought in London, they're consumed with this murder investigation." Damen pursed his lips. "There's got to be something we can do. And there is always the chance Marks is right—that this madman will stop his threats as quickly as he started them."

"You don't believe that," Stacie said quietly.

Soberly, Damen met her gaze, deliberately masking the full extent of his worry, yet unable to demean what they had together by offering her a barefaced lie. "No. I don't."

A heartbeat of silence.

Breanna drew herself up—a gesture that proclaimed she was battling her own fears, and determined to master them. "This is the first day I've ventured out since Mr. Marks delivered his report," she admitted. "I've been too alarmed and too preoccupied to go about my business. But when I awakened this morning, I made a decision. I refuse to become a prisoner in my own home—*again*. Father's gone. No one's going to do to me what he did.

"Besides," she continued, the edge in her tone softening, giving way to anticipation—and more than a touch of eagerness. "I was impatient to come out here and see how much work had been done on your home." She clasped Stacie's hands, hoping against hope that she and Damen might still salvage the pleasure of watching their new home take shape—a surprise she'd relished giving them long before the threatening package arrived. "Let's not let this ruin your homecoming. Come. I want to show you your new manor—or at least the portion of it that's completed."

"Of course." Anastasia tossed Damen a beseeching look—one that spoke volumes. She was asking him to grant Breanna the measure of peace she needed—for the moment. There would be plenty of time to dwell on the horrid possibilities suggested by the threatening package. But for now, it was time to savor the joys of being home. For all their sakes.

"All right." Damen's taut nod told her he understood, although he did pause long enough to scan the grounds with an unsettled eye. "But," he added, unable to totally dismiss the worry that still gnawed at him, "after that I want to inspect those dolls and read that note."

"Of course." Breanna agreed at once, more grateful than she was unnerved. "Oh, and Damen? If you could convince Wells that your being here means there's another strong and able-bodied man to see to our safety, I'd be forever in your debt. That poor man has taken on the roles of guardian, overseer, and sentry. I worry about his strength holding out."

"I'll talk to him the minute we get to the manor." Damen's lips thinned into a tight, unyielding line. "As for you and Stacie, nothing and no one will get near you. You can count on that." He cleared his throat, deferring this conversation for later. "Now, let's take a tour of our home."

He guided the two women forward, pausing only long enough to peer over his shoulder, his penetrating gaze raking the grounds in one more exhaustive sweep.

Other than the crew of workmen toiling in their immediate vicinity, everything seemed quiet.

Safe, he thought. At least for now.

5

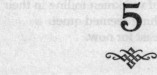

So this is Lady Breanna's bedchamber.

He smiled darkly, hovering near the doorway and
surveying the feminine decor.

Immaculate mahogany furniture. Canopied bed.
Pristine bedcovers. An array of tiny porcelain figures
decorating the nightstand, dresser, and fireplace mantel.

Orderly, delicate, and intact. Just like its owner.

She wouldn't stay intact for long.

He caught a glimpse of himself in the looking
glass, and smiled at the bizarre image he made.
Workman's clothes. They hardly suited him. Still, the
disguise had gained him entry to the estate. He'd
known today would be the day. The minute he heard
the gossip in London—that the Marquess of Sheldrake had returned from his wedding trip—he knew
she'd finally be leaving her sanctuary today. If only
to show the partially finished manor to the newly
married couple.

She'd surprised him by leaving the house early—

even before her cousin arrived. Evidently, she'd grown tired of being cooped up. Or perhaps it was that more than a week without threats had made her bold. Either way, she'd strolled across the grounds, venturing over to the construction site.

Giving him the perfect opportunity to lie in wait.

And then, when Anastasia and her new husband arrived, to do what he'd come here to do.

The ladder he'd taken from the shed had proved most useful. He'd propped it against the rear of the house—the side facing the wooded section of property—and climbed into a hall window on the second floor.

From there, he'd made his way to Breanna's room.

He rubbed his gloved palms together, moving slowly from the mantel to the dressing table. Idly, he fingered first one object, then another. He had to choose wisely. Something personal. Yet nothing she'd miss. Also, something intimate.

He lifted the silver-handled brush, then changed his mind. No. She'd notice that immediately.

The porcelain figures.

He prowled about the chamber, studying the dozens of tiny glass statues, wondering which would be least missed.

None of them fit that bill.

The lady was a collector. She obviously took great pride in her treasures. If any one of them disappeared, she'd realize it was gone.

No. It had to be something else.

He glanced into the modest sitting room beyond.

A sketchpad sat neatly on the desk, beside which lay a quill, some pencils, and a pile of papers.

She was a good artist, he mused, flipping through

the book. The sketches were all of rooms, all in different stages of completion. A bedchamber, with a large, four-poster bed. An impressive walnut library whose shelves were lined with books. A sitting room. A nursery. Each page contained notes on recommendations for carpets, drapes, paintings, and other personal touches, bearing in mind "Stacie's" favorite colors and textures.

Obviously, these were Lady Breanna's ideas for the manor being built across the way.

He shook his head, flipped the pad shut, and replaced it. Instead, he reached for the loose pile of papers alongside it.

Ah. Other sketches, ones that were far less defined than the first set. Clearly, these were abstract doodlings, done during thoughtful moments, then torn away as extraneous. A bouquet of flowers. A ship sailing the ocean. Snow falling around a manor, blanketing the grounds in white.

Lingering over the winter sketch, his eyes glittered triumphantly. The starkness. The long stretch of bare snow. Yes. This one would do quite nicely.

He folded the sketch, slipped it into his pocket. Swiftly, he rearranged the contents of the desk so they looked undisturbed.

Now for the intimate item.

For this, he needed something that would make her feel truly invaded. Invaded and, once he'd added his personal touch, terrified.

He didn't hesitate. Going over to the dresser, he eased open the drawers until he found what he sought.

A chemise. White. Unadorned and untainted.

Untainted—for now.

He stuffed the undergarment beneath his coat, then mindfully shut every drawer.

His job done, he slipped out of the bedchamber and retraced his steps: through the hall, out the window, down the ladder.

He returned the ladder to the shed, where he gathered up some tools—tools he had no idea how to use but that seemed functional enough for one who was supposedly building a house. After all, he had to look the part of a workman, in the unlikely event someone stopped him.

Keeping his step loose-limbed, he made his way through the wooded portion of the estate. Cap pulled low, he threw continuous sidelong glances to his right and left, ensuring he was alone.

He was.

This might be the last time he'd be able to enter the manor via this route, he reflected. Once his gifts had been delivered—clearly divulging his unwelcome visit—guards would doubtless be swarming the estate, posted on this section and *every* section, rather than just at the front gates as they were now. That diligent butler would see to it.

Ah, well. He had other means of entry. More traditional means.

Means Lady Breanna herself had offered him.

He'd just eased onto the main path and was about to head toward his concealed carriage, when he heard the voice.

"You there! What are you doing?"

He froze, his hand immediately slipping into his pocket, closing around his pistol.

Slowly, he pivoted about, keeping his head down—

low enough so his face remained hidden, but not so low that he couldn't see his potential adversary from beneath the cap's rim.

One glance told him that this stocky, uniformed person was not a workman.

Fine. That meant he wouldn't know anyone on the crew—a fact that might just spare his life.

Staring at the dirt, the assassin assumed the role his clothing proclaimed him to be. "I need a drink," he muttered. "I've been layin' bricks all morning."

"A drink?" Rather than sympathetic, the man sounded assessing. "It's scarcely mid-day."

An adversary with a conscience, he thought, fingers gripping the pistol more tightly. Not a promising sign.

Still, he'd make one last attempt.

"Yer right, sir." He took a half-step backward, appearing to retreat even as he purposefully kept his quarry in view. "I'll get back to work, get me ale at quittin' time."

He waited for a reaction, impatiently hoping the man would continue along, make this easy on both of them.

It didn't happen that way.

The man's eyes narrowed suspiciously. "You don't look too eager to go back. In fact, you look more like a fleeing thief than a thirsty workman." He stepped forward, his hand sliding to his pocket—and doubtless his weapon. "You're coming with me. We'll soon find out who you are."

"Now that's where you're wrong." Jerking up his head, the assassin simultaneously whipped out his gun—flourishing it before the other man could even begin to grope for his. "You *won't* find out who I am. No one will."

The guard's eyes darted from the assassin's face to his pistol, widening in fear as he realized he'd fatally underestimated his opponent.

A cry formed on his lips.

It was never uttered.

The single bullet penetrated his heart.

He was dead before he hit the ground.

Rather than feel relieved, the assassin felt a surge of annoyance. How irritating, he contemplated, eyeing the lifeless man crumpled at his feet. Now he'd have to dispose of the body *and* stage a reason for the shooting. After all, he couldn't have Bow Street discover the guard here, thus introducing the possibility that the murder was tied to Medford Manor—and to the package Lady Breanna had received. That might cause them to reopen her case.

No. He had to remove the body, place it elsewhere. Somewhere and in some manner that would provide an explanation as to why this man—one who happened to be on his way to do a guard shift at Medford Manor—would be killed.

But move it where? And why would someone kill this fellow in cold blood?

The answer was as obvious as it was ironic, because the victim himself had provided it.

A robbery.

He'd make it appear that the killing was the result of a theft, that the guard had resisted the bandit's demands—and paid for it with his life.

Swiftly, he glanced about, made sure he was still alone, undetected.

He was.

Further, the pounding and hammering, still reverberating from the construction site, was deafening enough to ensure that the sound of his gunshot had been drowned out—a lucky break, since the pistol crack would normally have been audible from this distance.

In conclusion, he had enough time to properly arrange things.

That determined, he crouched down, rifled the guard's pockets. The first thing he did was to confiscate the man's weapon. Just as expected, it was an average flintlock pistol. Unimpressive and unimaginative.

He spared it but one disparaging glance before shoving it into his own pocket, to be disposed of later. Then, he helped himself to the thin wad of pound notes and handful of shillings he found in the man's coat. He grimaced as he extracted a plain, well-worn timepiece. Cheap and tawdry. Ah, well. He'd bring it home and destroy it, so there would be nothing to trace back to him. True, it would be a nuisance. Still, it was a necessary nuisance, if he wanted to protect himself and convince the authorities that this murder had indeed been the result of a theft.

He tore the guard's coat in two spots, mussed his shirt and waistcoat. Minutes later, he dragged the body onto the path. He trudged the exact route the guard would have taken to reach his post, hauling the body a respectable distance before hiding it in the bushes on the roadside halfway between the rear portion of the estate and the front gates.

With a distasteful frown, he brushed dirt off his gloves, simultaneously retracing his steps until he reached the isolated spot where he'd left his carriage.

How irksome to have wasted his talents in so demeaning a fashion, he brooded, climbing into the driver's seat, taking up the reins, and guiding the horses onto the deserted path.

On the other hand, the guard seemed of good stock. True, not a member of the gentry, but not a gutter rat either. He had morals, dignity. He'd probably raised his children that way.

Perhaps he had a daughter. A daughter on the threshold of womanhood, maybe even a virgin. Now *that* might be worth looking into.

The assassin's irritation vanished. He'd have to find out the dead fellow's name, get some information on his background, his family. Then, he'd decide whether or not this was worth pursuing.

That line of thought reminded him that there was probably a message awaiting him from the Continent—a message whose contents he was eager to read.

He urged his horses into a trot.

Jamie Knox's body was discovered two hours later.

Known for his punctuality, Knox was missed within twenty minutes of the time when he'd been expected to report for duty at the front gates. And since he only lived a mile away and traveled to work by foot rather than by carriage, it seemed logical to send a groundskeeper to his cottage to find out what was keeping him.

His puzzled wife assured the servant that Jamie had left for work at the usual time. That fact aroused everyone's suspicions—enough to check out Knox's walking route more thoroughly.

It was one of the young gardeners who found him, coming upon Knox's lifeless body in a thicket of brush.

Wild-eyed, the lad backed away from the corpse, taking off for the front gates at a dead run. In a voice trembling with tears and dread, he blurted the situation out to the guards.

Pandemonium broke loose.

Breanna had just arranged for tea to be served in the sitting room, and Wells was congratulating Anastasia and Damen on becoming expectant parents, when the ruckus outside reached their ears.

"What on earth is going on?" Breanna murmured, moving aside the sitting-room curtain and peering out. She started. "Something's wrong."

She dropped the curtain, her face pale as she turned to Wells.

"I'll find out," he said at once.

"I'll go with you," Damen added quickly. He jumped up from the settee and followed Wells into the hall.

Anastasia and Breanna exchanged glances. Then, without a word, they left the sitting room, joining the men as they headed for the front door.

The pounding started before Wells could reach his post.

He hurried forward, flung open the door.

"What is it?" he demanded, meeting the grave stare of Albert Mahoney, the head of the security staff he'd personally hired to safeguard the estate.

"One of my guards," Mahoney replied, not mincing any words. "Knox. He's been killed. Shot to death."

"Oh my God." Breanna's hand flew to her mouth. "Here?"

"No, ma'am. On his way to work." Mahoney swallowed, turning to face Breanna with a tight, drawn expression. "From what we can tell, he was robbed. His money's missing. So's his timepiece. And, of course, his gun. He must have been grabbed from behind, which would explain why he didn't have a chance to draw his weapon. My guess is he fought back. And the thief shot him."

"How close to our gates?" Anastasia demanded. "Where exactly did you find him?"

Seeing Anastasia for the first time, Mahoney blinked, his head whipping from Anastasia to Breanna and back again.

"Mr. Mahoney, this is my cousin—the Marchioness of Sheldrake," Breanna managed, her voice shaky. "And her husband, Lord Sheldrake, head of the House of Lockewood. I'm sure you've heard of him."

"I have." Mahoney gave a half bow. "An honor to meet you both. Sorry it has to be under such grim circumstances."

"As are we," Damen replied.

"Speak freely, Mr. Mahoney," Breanna advised him. "Both Lord and Lady Sheldrake are aware of why you've been hired. They know the entire story, since it affects them, too."

"Very well." The guard nodded his compliance, turned to address Anastasia. "We found Knox in the bushes off the path leading to the manor—around the curve, about halfway between the rear of the estate and the front gates."

"And you say he was shot—by a thief." Damen frowned. "How do you know it was a thief?"

The guard gave an uneasy cough. "We don't *know* anything, not for sure. No culprit's been found. Still, Knox's valuables were missing. So my guess is, it was a thief. Unless you have proof that says otherwise."

"I don't." Damen raked a hand through his hair.

"No attempt was made to break into Medford Manor," Mahoney reminded him. "So I doubt it was the intruder we're guarding against."

"Unless the intruder never got a chance to break in because Knox scared him off first. Or unless he had no intentions of breaking in, but was just scrutinizing the estate, watching Breanna's comings and goings. There are a dozen 'unlesses.' But none of them is worth a damn. They're pure speculation—not enough to get Bow Street to ride out here, much less to take action." Damen began pacing about the entranceway.

Mahoney eyed him speculatively. "I've sent for a constable, sir. He'll take all the information and make arrangements for the body. If there's anything you think he should know—"

"No." Damen halted, gave a hard shake of his head. "There's nothing. Nothing but a bad feeling. And that's not evidence."

"No, sir, it's not." Mahoney cleared his throat. "If you'll excuse me, I'll get back to my post. I've got to calm everyone down, make sure the constable arrives—"

"Go." Damen gestured for the guard to leave. "Do what you have to."

"Did Mr. Knox have a family?" Breanna broke in, her fingers laced so tightly together, they ached.

"Yes, m'lady. A wife and two grown sons."

"His wife . . . she's been told?"

A terse nod. "Her sons live nearby. They'll help their mother out, to the best of their abilities, anyway. But they have families of their own and—"

"Tell Mrs. Knox we'll take care of her expenses," Breanna interrupted. "*All* her expenses, from a proper funeral to whatever she needs—clothing, food—anything. And please, tell her how sorry we are." With a choked sound, she averted her head.

"I'm sure she'll appreciate that. I know my wife would." Mahoney paused, staring down at the tips of his shoes. "Lady Breanna, if you'll forgive me for speaking out of turn, stop blaming yourself. Knox knew the risks of his job. We all do. Most of the time we beat the odds. But once in a while—we don't. The thief pulled the trigger, not you."

Unsteadily, Breanna nodded. "Yes . . . the thief."

A heavy silence descended.

"I'll be going now," Mahoney said at last. "If you need me, send for me."

Wells shut the door behind the retreating guard. "You don't think it was a thief," he said to Damen, a statement rather than a question.

Damen's stare was brooding. "If it was, his appearance was extremely coincidental, wouldn't you say?"

"Yes, I would."

Breanna spun around, faced the men. "You think it was . . . *he*. Well, so do I."

"I think it *might* have been he," Damen corrected her gently.

"If it was, his message is clear," Anastasia pronounced, worry glittering in her eyes. "He's showing us no guards can keep him away."

"Then we're prisoners." Twin spots of red stained Breanna's cheeks, and she looked almost as angry as she did fearful. "We can't go out, we can't protect ourselves . . ." She shot Wells a purposeful look. "We certainly can't have that party. It's too risky. We'll have to cancel it."

"Even if we do, that's still no guarantee we'll be stopping him from doing whatever it is he intends to do." Anastasia's palm drifted automatically to her abdomen as if to protect her unborn child from harm.

Damen followed her motion, and felt his gut clench. Perhaps they were all overreacting, letting their imaginations run wild. But for his family's sake, for the sake of his own peace of mind, he couldn't take that risk.

Abruptly, he made a decision.

"I've got to ride into Town." He reached for his topcoat.

"To Town? Why?" Quick as a wink, Anastasia was beside him. "Damen, what are you planning?"

He caressed her cheek, kissed the bridge of her nose. "I want to speak with someone. Someone I think can help us."

"Who?"

"Royce Chadwick." Damen shrugged into his coat. "You don't know him. He couldn't make it to our wedding; he was out of the country. But he's an old acquaintance of mine. We attended Oxford together. From there, he went on to the military. He was a brilliant strategist during the war with Napoleon. Since then, well, let's just say he's gone on to become the best at what he does."

"Which is?"

"He finds people—people who either can't or don't want to be found."

"Royce Chadwick," Wells repeated. "Isn't he the Earl of Searby's brother?"

"Yes. Although Edmund and Royce are about as alike as tea and spirits."

"Indeed." Wells was frowning now. "If gossip stands me correctly, the earl's brother is a reckless fellow—a bit *too* wild and daring."

Damen's lips curved. "Yes, Royce is not your staid ballroom type. He lives by his own set of rules. But he's incredibly shrewd, he's honest, and he's smart as a whip. And, as I said, he's the best man I know at finding people who have vanished—people even Bow Street can't find."

"Such as people who choose not to repay their loans?" Stacie guessed, astutely determining how Damen knew of this Royce Chadwick's work first-hand.

"Exactly." Her husband smiled, admiring her keen insights—insights he'd come to know and love. "He's done some fine work for me *and* my bank." Pausing, he framed Stacie's face between his palms, bent to kiss her shining crown of hair. "Stay put," he ordered. His glance lifted to include Breanna. "Both of you. In this case, it's better to be overcautious. Wells, don't let either of them out of your sight. I'll be back later today—with a plan."

6

Royce Chadwick lived and worked on Bond Street.

His home, which also served as his office, stood in a row of three-story, gated Town houses, all of which exuded an aura of understated wealth and power—an aura that both commanded a second look and, at the same time, demanded privacy.

A description one could just as easily ascribe to Royce.

He and Damen had met at Oxford. The two men had developed an immediate affinity for each other, despite the fact that their philosophies of life differed sharply.

Damen was a pragmatist. He met life head-on, confronted its challenges, and emerged from them wiser, surer, and farther along the path to his own success.

Royce created his own challenges.

Bold, defiant, he took on the world, unwilling to accept the status quo, loath to compromise. He lived on the edge, pushed the rules as far as they could go—and then some—a fact that nearly got him expelled from Oxford on more than one occasion by the narrow-minded administration who ran it.

But, damn, he was brilliant. Brilliant and, in his own way, honorable. True, he was unconventional, driven by demons he never discussed. And yes, he lived by his own code of conduct, conduct that too often got him in trouble. But he never used people, never took advantage of those less intelligent or weaker than he. On the contrary, he was a loner, relying upon his own ingenuity and cunning to get him what he wanted—partially because he was a man of integrity and partially because he refused to settle for the mediocrity offered by others. He probed, he challenged, yet he drew his own figurative line—a line he wouldn't cross to reach his ends.

In short, reckless or not, Royce Chadwick was a fine man—one Damen admired and, at the moment, needed.

Pulling his carriage alongside the house, Damen swung down, hastened up the steps, and knocked.

An older man with ice blue eyes, silver hair, and a cloaked expression answered the door. "Yes? Ah, Lord Sheldrake." His thin lips pursed so tightly they seemed to disappear into his face. "Forgive me, sir, I didn't realize you had an appointment."

"Don't apologize, Hibbert. I didn't."

Damen stepped into the entranceway, knowing he had his work cut out for him. Trying to talk his way past this man was akin to single-handedly taking on an army. Hibbert was more than Royce's butler, more even than his steward and his clerk. He was all three—*and* a veritable sentry who stood between his employer and the world. Plus, he was Royce's right hand, his advisor, ofttimes his eyes and his ears. Hibbert's distinguished, elderly appearance stood him in good stead when he was helping Royce gather information. No one suspected that beneath the aged, benign exterior lurked the intelligence, cunning, and agility of a fox.

"Is Royce home?" Damen demanded without preliminaries. "Because, if so, I need to see him. Now."

Hibbert arched a brow. "It's not like you to become overwrought, my lord."

"That's because I'm usually here because someone's threatening my money. This time someone's threatening my wife."

A sharp intake of breath. "I see." Hibbert studied Damen for one long, thoughtful moment. Then, he nodded. "Have a seat in Lord Royce's office. You know where it is. I'll see if I can free up some of his time."

"I'd appreciate that." Damen strode down the hall, turning into the cluster of rooms Royce used for his work. He stepped into the outer office, bypassing the settee and pacing over to the bookshelves. He tapped the volumes impatiently, not really seeing them, then walked over to the window and gazed out.

Damn, he hoped he was overreacting. Maybe it really had been a thief who'd killed Knox. Maybe it wasn't that demented assassin. Maybe the incident was totally unrelated to the package Breanna had received. Maybe neither she nor Anastasia were in danger.

Then again, maybe they were.

"Hibbert's right. You aren't yourself."

Damen turned, grateful as hell to see Royce Chadwick lounging in the doorway. "No, I'm not."

"Welcome home." The tall, broad-shouldered man straightened, folding his arms across his chest and studying Damen through penetrating midnight blue eyes that were so dark people often mistook them for black. "Congratulations, albeit belatedly, on your marriage. I'm sorry I missed the wedding. It couldn't be helped. I was halfway back from India." Royce ran a hand over his square jaw, missing nothing of his colleague's distress. "For a man who just returned from his wedding trip, you look wretched. Marriage too much for you?"

"Hardly." Damen wasn't in a lighthearted mood. "In fact, I'm beginning to wish that Stacie and I had never come home. She was finally safe. The biggest worry I had was seeing how weak she became after perpetually kneeling over the chamber pot—"

Dark brows shot up. "Kneeling over the chamber pot? Does that mean you have another announcement to make?"

"As a matter of fact, yes."

A low whistle. "I'm impressed. After only three months of marriage. No wonder you enjoyed your trip so much." Royce gave Damen a mock salute before moving into the room, crossing over toward the inner office and gesturing for Damen to follow. "Double my congratulations, then."

"Royce, we need to talk." Damen entered the room, shut the door behind him.

"So I gathered. Hibbert said it was urgent." All humor having vanished, Royce perched against the mahogany desk, turned his watchful gaze back on Damen. "He also said that it concerned your wife. Judging from your agitation, it must be serious."

"It is. At least I think it is." Damen paused, drew a slow breath to compose himself.

"Sit down. I'll get you a drink." Royce indicated the armchair by his desk, then went to the sideboard, poured two glasses of Madeira. "Here. Drink this. You obviously need it. Then, tell me what's wrong. I've never seen you so unnerved."

"I've never *felt* so unnerved." Damen tossed off the contents of the glass. "Then again, I've never cared as deeply about anyone as I do about Stacie. And now, with the babe on the way ..." His head came up. "Royce, I want you to find someone for me."

Royce's eyes narrowed. "Who?"

"That's the problem. I don't know. I don't know his name, where he lives, or what he looks like. I'm not even sure he's in England—although my instincts scream out that he is. All I know is that I need him found. Found and locked up."

Slowly, Royce sipped at his Madeira. If he was taken aback by Damen's request, he kept his surprise carefully hidden. "Start at the beginning. Not with what you *don't* know, but with what you *do* know. The circumstances that brought you here, the basis for your apprehension."

A terse nod. "I'm sure Hibbert told you who I had him checking into for me while you were in India."

"The Viscount Medford. Yes, he told me. He also told me that Medford owed money everywhere, to everyone. And that he was recouping it by involving himself in some pretty shady business dealings— shadier, as it turned out, than any of us realized. But Medford's in prison now. So he's hardly a threat." A heartbeat of a pause. "Does this have to do with what happened right after his arrest? That assassin Medford hired through Cunnings—the one who showed up at the docks to do away with your wife?"

"You heard about that, then."

"The minute I set foot on English soil. Does that surprise you?"

Damen shrugged. "Not really. Some things can't be kept quiet. Do you know all the details?"

"I asked a few questions at Bow Street. They filled me in. This paid killer aimed at your wife, but before he could shoot, he was maimed by her cousin. He fled the scene, stopped off at the bank to silence Cunnings—permanently—then vanished. Is that close enough?"

"All but the last. He didn't vanish—at least not for good."

Royce's glass paused midway to his lips. "He's back."

"It damned well looks that way." With that, Damen told Royce about the note and package Breanna had received, her subsequent trip to Bow Street, and the precautionary security Wells had hired. He concluded by relaying the news that a guard had been killed earlier today, describing where Knox had been when the alleged thief came upon him.

Royce listened intently, swirling the contents of his drink, his brow furrowed in thought. When Damen finished, he took a deep swallow of Madeira, then placed the glass on his desk. "I can see why you're worried," he said. "As for Bow Street, I wouldn't expect much help from them. They're up to their necks investigating the murders that are throwing the *ton* into a frenzy. Not to mention that you've given them no real proof to go on. Which doesn't mean the threat to your wife and her cousin isn't real, only that you can't count on Bow Street to hunt this assassin down."

Damen leaned forward. "I agree. The question is, can we count on *you* to hunt him down?"

Pensively, Royce rubbed the back of his neck. "This is an ugly situation, Damen."

"Since when has that deterred you? Usually, the greater the challenge, the more determined you are to go after it. Hell, this should really intrigue you—an unknown assailant, a crime that could happen anywhere, anytime. It's just the kind of danger you thrive on. So what's stopping you?"

"This crime involves lives. Lives of people you care about."

"That should motivate you, not frighten you off."

"I'm not frightened. I'm realistic. Locating a faceless, nameless assassin is not exactly my specialty."

"An assassin is nothing more than an exceedingly violent criminal. And understanding criminals' minds is precisely how you manage to track them down."

"The criminals I track have names and faces," Royce reminded him. "You're talking about something entirely different."

"Surely you've met men who enjoy killing. All those years in the military—there must have been some soldiers who actually enjoyed pulling the trigger."

In response, Royce's jaw set, his dark eyes glittering harshly. "I've met men who enjoy killing others *and* men who thrive on destroying others without actually killing them. And not just in the military. So, do I understand a mind like this assassin's? Yes. But you know the way I work, Damen. My tactics involve taking risks—big risks. I won't jeopardize your wife's life."

"Stacie's life is already in jeopardy."

Silence.

Damen slammed his glass to the desk. "Does this mean you refuse to help me?"

Royce studied the naked pain on his friend's face,

swore quietly under his breath—and relented. "No. I'll help you. I'll do as much as I can. As much as you'll let me," he amended. "You might not like my ideas, *or* my methods. Not when it comes to a matter this close to your heart."

"I'll take that chance."

Nodding, Royce rifled through some pages on his desk. "The other problem I have is that I'm in the middle of another case—one I took on weeks ago. I can't walk away from that."

"I wouldn't ask you to. Handle both cases at once. Set up an office at Medford if you need to. Bring Hibbert. I don't care. Just find this lunatic before he . . ." Damen bit off the rest of his sentence, too sickened to utter it.

"He's not a lunatic," Royce countered quietly. "Let's begin with that. At least not in the way you mean. He's unbalanced, yes, but he's very controlled, very methodical, very intelligent. He couldn't be a professional assassin unless he was. He's got to be thorough, well-organized, and have excellent timing. Which means his mind is quick, maybe even as quick as his pistol. To relegate him to the role of madman would be a grave error in judgment—one that could cost you dearly." Royce's lips pursed in thought. "I want to see that letter. And the dolls. I also want to talk to Lady Breanna, hear everything she remembers about the night her father was arrested, or rather, *after* he was arrested and the assassin showed up." A wary stare. "Tell me about her."

"Who? Breanna?"

"Yes. Is she fragile? Will I have an hysterical female on my hands? Is she a swooner, one who'll collapse each time I ask a question that triggers a memory? Or

is she a wailer, one who will drench three handker-
chiefs before I find out everything I need to?"

Despite the gravity of the situation, Damen couldn't
stifle a smile. "You don't have a very high opinion of
women, do you? Odd, considering, from what I've
seen over the years, they have a *very* high opinion of
you. They gravitate to you like flies to honey—until
you tire of them and move on."

"On the contrary, I have a very high opinion of
women. They're ideal companions—both in bed and
out—splendid conversationalists and, before you be-
rate me for not giving your wife the credit she's due,
occasionally fine business partners. In fact, I often
suspect that women are smarter than men—smart
enough to know that it's best to hide that fact from
our easily shattered self-esteem. But when it comes to
emotions, all that wisdom goes straight to hell. They
whine, they weep, they cajole, they pout. When that
happens, I become exasperated and walk away. I'm
not the comforting type. Nor the type who's easily
moved or manipulated. So I'm asking you, what is
Lady Breanna like? Particularly now, when she's
under duress?"

"She's a remarkable young woman," Damen
replied honestly. "She's been through a lot, particularly these past few months. Finding out what her father
was capable of, weathering the scandal that followed
his arrest—she's been astonishingly strong. I don't
think you have to worry about her weeping or
swooning. She's not inclined to do either."

"Good." That determined, Royce rose to his feet in
one fluid motion. "I'll ride to Kent with you, attempt
to make some sense out of this—at least enough to
keep your wife and Lady Breanna safe while we fig-

ure out who this killer is and when he's going to strike."

"How long can you stay?"

"Just overnight. I've got to get back here by tomorrow, tie up some loose ends. I promised Edmund I'd spend Christmas with him and his family. Then, if necessary, I'll return to Lady Breanna's estate. I take it you're staying there rather than here in Town?"

"Yes." A terse nod. "Christmas. I'd almost forgotten about it." Damen frowned, speaking half to himself. "Breanna wants to cancel her party."

"What party?"

"She and Anastasia both just turned twenty-one. They planned a party to celebrate that and the holidays."

Royce grew thoughtful. "Canceling it might be unwise."

"Why?"

"Let me read that note. Then I'll answer your question." Royce inclined his head. "When is this party scheduled to be held?"

"On the twenty-eighth and the twenty-ninth of December. But now, with Jamie Knox being murdered—"

"As I said, let me read the note. After that, we'll make a decision about the party." Royce gestured toward the door. "Go home to your wife. I'll fill Hibbert in, then follow in my own carriage."

"Fine." Damen stood as well, giving Royce a grateful look. "Thank you. I'm in your debt."

"Not yet you're not. If we figure out who this killer is, stop him from hurting anyone else—*then* you'll be in my debt."

7

The guard held up a commanding hand.

Royce reined his horses to a stop, waiting patiently at the gates of Medford Manor for the expected interrogation.

Two uniformed sentries approached his phaeton slowly, carefully, each of them keeping one hand inside his pocket, doubtless clutching his pistol lest it be needed. The first guard held up a lantern, using its light to better make out Royce's features in the growing darkness of the evening.

"Can I help you, sir?" he inquired, reaching Royce and staring him down with a hard, no-nonsense look.

Who could blame him, given that one of his men had been killed that very day?

"My name is Royce Chadwick. The Marquess of Sheldrake is expecting me."

The guard studied Royce for another moment—presumably matching his physical appearance to the description Damen had provided. Clearly satisfied with what he saw, he relaxed. "Yes, my lord, he is. Go right through." He gestured for the other guard to open the gates.

A minute later, the gates made a grating sound, and swung wide to admit Royce's phaeton.

Nodding politely, Royce led his horses on, guiding them down the long drive leading to the manor. He took the opportunity to look around, taking in as much of the scenery as twilight would permit.

He could make out the construction site, a broad area that would soon house what appeared to be an imposing dwelling. That would be Damen's new home, Royce reflected. Hibbert had reported to him that the marquess planned to move to his wife's family estate once their new manor had been completed. Evidently, the construction was coming along nicely. But it was far from finished.

Which meant that workmen would be coming and going from the grounds at an alarming rate. And that, in turn, meant the assassin could more easily find his way onto the estate, lose himself in a crowd of people.

The most logical thing for Royce to do was to shut down the construction—at least for now. On the other hand, he might be able to use that accessibility to Medford Manor to his advantage. He wasn't sure yet. But he wasn't ready to close any doors—not until he had every shred of information in his possession *and* the time to evaluate it.

Rounding the drive, Royce brought his phaeton to a stop, and swung down to his feet. He'd reviewed the details of the case with Hibbert before leaving London. Then, he'd mulled them over during his two-hour ride to Kent. The package Lady Breanna had received, the too-coincidental murder of the guard—the whole situation had a very unpleasant taste to it.

Instinct told Royce that Damen's worries were well-founded. The question was, could they find this animal, stop him in time?

Mounting the front steps, he knocked.

A distinguished older man with spectacles answered the door, and a look of consummate relief swept across his face as he scrutinized their visitor, determined who he was. "Lord Royce," he stated.

"Yes."

"Come in." The butler stepped aside. "My name is Wells. Lord Sheldrake's been expecting you. According to him . . . that is, I'm praying . . . truthfully, we're *all* praying that you can help keep Miss Breanna and Miss Stacie safe." Wells cleared his throat, abruptly remembering his place—and his composure. "Your room is already made up. I'll have a footman carry in your bags." He extended his hand to take Royce's topcoat.

"Thank you." Royce shrugged out of the thick wool coat, handing it over. He assessed the butler quickly, although little insight was needed to see that this man was loyal to the core, and deeply attached to the two grown women he still considered to be his young charges.

That would be an asset and a liability.

It meant that Wells could be counted upon for any and every form of assistance. He could also, however, be counted upon to let his feelings interfere with his objectivity.

And *that* could be a problem.

Then again, Damen suffered from the same affliction. He was so bloody in love with his wife, not to mention doubly protective of her now that she was pregnant, that it was dubious whether or not he could be counted upon to act with his customary pragmatism.

Which left the women.

Royce frowned. Lord help him if Damen's wife wasn't every bit as bold and strong-willed as he'd described her. And as for Lady Breanna, well, she'd better be more than remarkable. She'd better have the internal strength of a soldier about to march into battle.

"I'll show you to the sitting room," Wells was saying. "The family is gathered there. Lord Sheldrake thought you'd want to speak with them before you freshened up for dinner."

"He's right. I would."

Royce followed Wells down the hall, glancing about as he did.

Medford Manor was spacious and warm, an appealing combination of aged beauty and modern freshness. Twin staircases with curving, mahogany banisters, divided by a rich Oriental carpet, were accented with low tables filled with vases of holly sprigs and snowdrops and, hanging on the walls, intricate needlepoints depicting sunsets, children playing in the snow, and colorful gardens.

Interesting. It was as if several generations had had a hand in fashioning this place, each adding its own strokes to the canvas, yet together creating a painting that blended together as naturally as dawn and day.

He was growing more and more curious about the cousins he was about to meet. He knew little about them, other than the fact that they strongly resembled each other, and that Anastasia had been raised in the States—Philadelphia, if he correctly recalled. She must be extraordinary for Damen to have fallen so hard, so fast, not to mention brilliant for him to have entered into a business partnership with her—a partnership that, according to Damen, had been forged on his respect for Anastasia's business acumen rather than his personal feelings for her.

Where did Lady Breanna fit into all this? Royce mused. She *hadn't* been raised in America. She'd been raised right here, by a father who'd effectively sealed her off from the world, relegated her to the manor while he tried to manipulate her future in order to cling to his own. A father who'd turned out to be, not only a felon and a scoundrel, but a cold-hearted bastard who'd resort to murder to achieve his ends.

What effect had that had on her?

He was about to find out.

"Lord Royce has arrived," Wells announced in the sitting room doorway.

All three of the room's occupants rose.

"Royce, come in." Damen moved forward, his arm wrapped around the waist of a beautiful young woman with delicate features, jade green eyes, and auburn hair that tumbled, unbound, about her shoulders. "This is my wife, Anastasia."

Boldly, Anastasia Lockewood appraised Royce as he approached, kissed her hand.

"Lady Sheldrake. It's a pleasure."

"I'm happy to meet you, my lord," she replied, still studying his face. "I didn't even know of your existence until today. But, based on Damen's description of the investigations you conduct for him, I have the feeling you helped fit together the pieces to a very ugly puzzle several months ago that ended up saving my life. For that, I thank you."

Royce inclined his head with interest. A straightforward, candid woman—now *that* was refreshing.

"You're welcome," he responded with a hint of a smile. "But I'm afraid I can't take credit for the investigation you're describing. I was in India when Damen sought me out. My associate is the one who did the probing."

Damen's wife smiled, an open, infectious grin. "Then please thank him for me. As for you—your associate's skill speaks just as highly of you. After all, you chose him. And only the cleverest of businessmen are shrewd enough to ally themselves with equally clever partners. Just look at Damen."

A chuckle. "I see what you mean." Royce's gaze shifted, as a flash of color and movement from beside the settee caught his eye, drew his attention to the room's final occupant.

He found himself gazing at a woman who appeared, at first glance, to be a very close replica of Anastasia.

At second glance, he realized she was no replica, but an original.

Breanna Colby was a portrait come to life, all flawless lines and subtle hues—and yet, decidedly inaccessible.

She was nothing short of exquisite—a graceful, delicate, punch-in-the-gut beauty. True, her features were seemingly identical to her cousin's. Still, they were somehow different. Or perhaps it was the personality he could sense hovering behind the vivid coloring and fine features that made it so.

To begin with, Breanna's eyes, the same jade green as Anastasia's, were softer, more remote than her cousin's—as if she were guarding a part of herself she was reluctant to share, reserving judgment while letting you know you had to earn the right to be allowed in. Her expression was thoughtful, speculative, but carefully schooled. And her hair, that same glorious auburn color as Anastasia's, was upswept, perfectly arranged atop her head without a single strand mussed or out of place. She was lovely, proper, self-contained—a lady through and through.

Abruptly, Royce knew why Damen had said Breanna would never weep or swoon. This was a woman who kept her emotions in check. Her feelings, her thoughts, certainly her fears, would remain private, known only to her and to the select few she chose to trust.

He could even guess why.

She'd survived George Colby.

But he'd left his mark—in ways others could only imagine.

Yes, there was more to Lady Breanna than met the eye. *Much* more. Royce was willing to bet his life on it.

Damen cleared his throat, alerting Royce to the fact that he'd been staring. "Royce, may I present Lady Breanna Colby. Breanna—Lord Royce Chadwick."

"Lady Breanna." Royce said politely, bowing at the waist, then walking over to kiss her hand.

"Welcome to Medford Manor, my lord." Breanna's tone was measured, her voice soft, lilting. Whereas Anastasia's crisp English inflections had been muted by years in America, Breanna's speech was utterly precise, the epitome of refinement.

Royce's lips grazed her knuckles. "Your home is lovely."

"Thank you. Not only for the compliment, but for your kind intentions." She hesitated, then added, "I appreciate your riding out here so late in the day. Damen seems to think you can help us."

Royce straightened, one brow arching in question. "But you don't?"

She rubbed the folds of her lavender day dress between her fingers. "I'm not certain. It's not that I don't trust Damen's instincts. I do. It's just that—"

"It's just that I'm a total stranger and you're uncomfortable with me."

Surprise flashed in her pale green eyes, and she gave a self-conscious nod. "Exactly."

"I understand your reluctance. But, I assure you, I know what I'm doing. *How* I do it, now that's a different story. You might not care for my methods, especially since they can get a bit risky. What I suggest is this: let me take a look at the package and note you received, ask you a few questions. After dinner, we'll discuss my strategy. If you don't care for it, I'll leave."

"And we'll be right back where we started," Damen put in tersely.

Breanna gave a resigned sigh. "That's certainly true. Very well, my lord. We'll try it your way." She crossed over, retrieved a box from the end table, and brought it to Royce, shuddering with distaste as she handed it to him. "This is what he sent."

Royce opened the box, carefully examining each doll before replacing them, turning his attention to the note.

He read it through three times before lifting his head, meeting Breanna's anxious stare.

"Sit down," he advised, gesturing toward the settee. "I want to hear everything you remember about what happened the night your father was arrested. Beginning after Bow Street led him away."

Breanna inclined her head, frowning a bit. "Aren't you going to react to the dolls and the note?"

"Yes. *After* I've gotten all the facts. Now have a seat and tell me about your confrontation with this assassin." Royce glanced up, speaking to Anastasia and Damen as Breanna settled herself on the settee. "I want to hear the entire story from Lady Breanna's point of view. No interruptions. Once I've finished, I'll ask each of you if you remember anything different from or in addition to what she's said."

"In other words, keep quiet," Anastasia supplied.

Royce perched on the arm of the settee, folding his arms across his chest and turning his full attention to Lady Breanna. "Go ahead."

She wet her lips, lowering her lashes and staring at the rug as she mentally traveled back to the night in question. "The Bow Street runners led Father off. Damen, Stacie, and I stayed behind on the docks for a moment. I suppose we needed reality to sink in, to convince ourselves that the whole nightmare was truly over. I was weak-kneed with relief that Stacie was safe. She'd taken a terrible risk dragging that confession out of my father. Finally, we started to leave. Stacie walked first. Damen and I were right behind her. I got the oddest feeling . . ." She made a vague gesture with her hand. "I can't explain it. I just sensed a pair of eyes boring into me. I whirled around—and reached for the pistol I'd been carrying. That's when I saw him."

"You saw him," Royce repeated. "How clearly?"

"Not clearly at all. He was some distance away. It was late at night, and the fog was fairly thick. What I saw was the silhouette of a man, and the glint of his pistol. I saw him raise the pistol, aim in Stacie's direction. I knew exactly who he was, and what he intended to do. I had to stop him. So I shot. I scarcely remember that moment. All I remember is knowing I had to do something or he'd kill Stacie. There wasn't time to call out and warn her. There was only time to act. So I did."

"Then what happened?"

"He screamed. His pistol struck the ground. I heard it. He clutched at his hand. Then, he bent, groped for his gun. That was when Damen drew his own weapon. The killer turned, stumbled away. After that, the night literally swallowed him up."

"He never said anything? Never shouted anything at you?"

"No. I never heard his voice—other than the scream of pain."

"And his appearance? What can you remember about that?"

"Only that he was tall. And somewhat lean, in terms of his build. I couldn't make out his features, or even his hair color."

Royce stroked his chin thoughtfully. "And the only one who knew this killer's identity was John Cunnings. Unless . . ." A penetrating look. "You're sure your father couldn't shed any light on this? I understand that visiting him in Newgate would be unpleasant for you, but . . ."

To Royce's surprise, Breanna's chin came up, and she negated his statement with an adamant shake of her head. "No, my lord, you don't understand. And I don't mean how unpleasant it would be to brave Newgate. I mean how unthinkable it would be to face Father. However, that's irrelevant. Because I'd do precisely that—anguish or not—if I thought it would help. But it wouldn't. Father can't tell us anything. I know that firsthand. You see, Wells and I were in the

pub when my father met with Mr. Cunnings, instructed him to hire that killer."

"Were you?" Royce could feel his interest peak.
"You overheard their conversation?"

"Every word. My father pressed Cunnings about
meeting this associate of his. Cunnings refused. He insisted on being the sole contact. He said his associate
preferred it that way. No name was ever mentioned.
Whoever this gunman is, only Cunnings knew his
identity. Which is why Mr. Cunnings himself is now
dead."

"The assassin had to eliminate him. I agree."
Royce's fingers stilled against his jaw. "Let's get back
to this meeting between your father and Cunnings—
the one you overheard. Tell me what else Cunnings
said, besides refusing to divulge the killer's name.
What other specifics about him did he mention?"

Breanna knotted her hands in her lap. "Cunnings
said he'd known him for quite some time. He implied
that the man's accomplishments were impressive.
Cunnings assured Father that no matter where Stacie
was hiding, his associate would find her and kill her.
He described him as an expert tracker and an even
better shot. Oh—and he added that he was expensive.
Very expensive. The implication was that he was
worth it, that he was accomplished in his line of work.
Does that answer your question, my lord?"

"As a matter of fact, it does." Royce glanced down
at the note he still held, reread its message. Then, he
rose, lowering the piece of paper and leveling a grave
stare at Breanna. "This man is dead serious about his
threats, my lady. You were right to be afraid."

She flinched, but didn't look away. "I suspected as
much."

"I'm sure you did." Royce frowned, wishing he had a different evaluation to relay. He didn't normally experience personal feelings when it came to the people involved in his investigations. But in this case . . . hell, in this case, it was more than money or finding missing relatives that was at stake—it was lives. What's more, he couldn't help but admire the way Lady Breanna was holding herself together, especially since he'd just confirmed her worst fear: that she was the ultimate target of a killer. Her inner strength was remarkable. Yet, at the same time, there was something about her—something disturbingly vulnerable—that made Royce wish there were a way to spare her this ordeal.

But there wasn't.

The only way to maximize her odds of survival was to be as honest as possible, to let her know exactly what she was up against. And then to offer his services to protect her.

Roughly, he cleared his throat. "The only mistake you made was to assume the assassin would disappear from your life. He never would. His arrogance wouldn't let him. He believes he's superior, that no one can thwart him. You challenged that belief. Not only that, you had the audacity to maim him—who knows how badly. My guess is you put him out of commission for a while, which would explain his absence these past few months. He was probably nursing his wounded hand, recovering his marksmanship to its full potential. Now he's back. He's had months to harbor his rage and thirst for vengeance. He's determined to put you in your place, and punish you for what you did." A swift glance at Anastasia. "*After* he finishes the job he took on but never completed."

Breanna made a soft sound of surprise. "Are you saying he wants to hurt Stacie, not simply as retaliation against me, but to prove he's the ultimate master at killing people?"

A terse nod. "Not only killing people, but completing his assignments. He wants to prove to you, to the world, to himself, that he never fails. The marchioness represents a failed execution—his first, if I had to venture a guess. He won't leave a stone like that unturned."

Damen swore. "So the reason he's back—"

"Is to kill your wife *and* Lady Breanna. In that order." Royce didn't mince words. "But first, he wants to torment Lady Breanna. To make her feel the maximum amount of anguish and fear. That will restore the sense of power he feels he's lost."

Breanna came to her feet, and began moving restlessly about the room. "Tell me, my lord," she said at last. "Is there nothing we can do?"

Royce weighed his answer carefully. "In my opinion, the best way to hold him at bay, to keep him from striking while we figure out who he is, is to pointedly ignore him."

"I don't understand."

"He's expecting you to come apart at the seams. He can scarcely wait for that to happen, in fact. So you must deny him the satisfaction. You have to retain your composure at all costs, to pretend you're unbothered by his threats. You have to make him believe his actions aren't having the desired effect. That will force him to keep trying, which buys us more time. If he doesn't think he's successfully terrorized you—or terrorized you severely enough—he won't move on to the next step of his plan."

"Which is killing me," Anastasia clarified.

"Yes."

"There's only one problem with that, Royce," Damen inserted. "While I'm relieved as hell that it will deter him from coming after my wife, won't it make things worse for Breanna? Won't it infuriate him if she remains so totally unruffled, intensify his obsession to try—and succeed—in terrorizing her?"

Royce nodded. "Yes. He'll become bolder, more violent in his demonstrations. He'll also become angrier, more frustrated. The positive consequence of that is it might cause him to make a mistake." A weighted pause. "The negative consequence is that it will make him that much more dangerous. Especially to Lady Breanna, who's the main target of his rage. I won't lie to you. There's risk involved here—high risk. On the other hand, there's risk involved right now. A professional assassin is determined to murder these two women. The only way to eliminate the danger is to eliminate the killer. Which is just what I'm trying to do. Whether you choose to do things my way—that decision is yours."

Silence descended, suffocated the room like a heavy blanket.

Breanna was the first to speak.

"You said you'd discuss your strategy with us after dinner. Does that mean you have a specific plan in mind?"

"I have the first steps of a plan, yes."

"I'd like to hear it."

Royce pursed his lips, considering her request. As a rule, he never shared unfinished strategy with anyone other than Hibbert. But in this case, with both these women's lives at stake, didn't he owe them an explanation, if for no other reason than to let them make a decision as to whether or not they chose to put their safety in his hands?

"All right," he conceded. "But remember, I have yet to review everything we've just discussed. I also haven't heard Damen or your cousin's recollections of the night you shot the assassin. Further, I have some remaining questions. For example, we haven't even touched on the subject of the murdered guard. Some of the details of my plan won't be worked out until I'm satisfied I have all the information I need—*and* until you've decided whether you'll go along with my methods."

"Fair enough." Breanna smoothed a hand over her hair. "Putting those issues aside, tell us your ideas. Your *preliminary* ideas," she amended.

Anastasia interrupted with an exasperated sound. "You both act as if we have all the time in the world. How do you know this madman will be patient while you sort out your plan? Shouldn't we be *doing* something—*now?*"

Royce flashed Anastasia a tolerant look, unsurprised by her reaction. Having sized up Damen's wife, he'd guessed she'd be the impatient one, the one who was unwilling to wait. "I don't think our time is unlimited," he clarified. "But no, we shouldn't be doing something. Not unless it's the *right* something. If Lady Breanna takes my advice, stays calm and *outwardly* unbothered by what's happened thus far, it will buy us more than a week to close in on this man. I can almost guarantee it. The way his mind works—he won't kill until the stage is set precisely as he means it to be."

Breanna paced slowly about the settee as she considered his words. Then, she raised her head, regarded him through wary, questioning eyes. "You keep talking about my behaving a certain way, acting a certain part. You believe he's watching me."

"At every possible opportunity, and without alerting the guards—yes."

She paled a bit, but didn't flinch. "And how do I show him I'm unaffected by his threats?"

"You go on with your life—taking certain necessary but subtle precautions," he added. "You've already hired additional guards. Hire more. After all, a man was murdered just outside your estate. It's only natural for you to seek protection. Get Wells to situate guards all around the periphery of the estate. After that, go about your business."

This time it was Damen who reacted, tensing as if he'd been struck. "Go about her business?"

Royce's nod was definitive. "In a manner of speaking. Of course, it's expected that Lady Breanna will be distressed by the guard's death. No one will be surprised if, until the highwayman who's allegedly responsible is caught, she chooses not to leave the grounds. Also, it's assumed she'll want to spend time with her cousin, who's only just arrived home. The two women should stroll out to the construction site each day—with you at their sides, of course. After all, it is your house, too, that's being built. You'd obviously want to see it take shape."

"You don't think we should call a halt to the construction?"

"No. At least not yet. We don't want to take away every opportunity this assassin has to creep onto the grounds, and to blend in, undetected. The more rope we give him, the more likely he is to hang himself."

Damen started, swearing under his breath. "That's

insane. Now you're tempting fate to an absurd degree, Royce. I don't like it."

"I didn't expect you would," Royce replied calmly. "But that's how I'd handle things—*if* I end up handling things." He offered no further explanation. But it was clear that, unspoken or not, he'd demand absolute control if he were running this investigation, and that he wouldn't diverge from his rash tactics, despite Damen's objections. "In the meantime," he continued, "what my role would be over the next few days would be to check out as many local shops as possible, see if I can determine where those dolls were bought. *And* who bought them." A frown. "Although I don't hold out much hope. At least not initially. The assassin probably bought them far enough away so they couldn't be easily traced."

"What about extending your search?" Anastasia demanded.

"I will. After the holidays. Christmas is next week. It makes no sense to travel to shops that will be closed. And speaking of Christmas," Royce added, "the three of you should share a private family celebration." He paused, turned to meet Breanna's gaze. "And after your private celebration, you must hold your party, as planned."

Breanna's eyes widened, and she sucked in her breath. "You want the party to take place, in spite of the killer? Or maybe I should say *because* of him. You really do believe in taking risks, don't you, my lord?"

"I believe in outwitting my enemies. That involves taking risks."

"Risks?" Damen bit out. "You're not only inviting the bastard onto Breanna's grounds, now you're inviting him into her house."

"Maybe." Royce weighed that possibility carefully. "I suppose he could use the opportunity to slip by the guards and into the manor. But it's a hazardous step for him to take. He might sneak in to leave another of his gifts. But he wouldn't use the occasion to hurt Lady Breanna or your wife. Not with so many potential witnesses around. Such extreme carelessness would, in his mind, be unacceptable, beneath his level of genius." A defiant glint lit Royce's eyes. "Still, if he does slink into the ballroom or gaming rooms, I'll be ready for him."

"*You* will?" Breanna exclaimed, her delicate brows arching.

"Um-hum." Royce was as surprised as Breanna by the offer he'd just extended. He hated large house parties. They bored him. He hadn't attended one in years. An occasional ball or two during the Season, gambling at White's and at the more lucrative horse races—those were the extent of his social appearances. Yet, suddenly, he knew he'd made the right decision by opting to attend Breanna's party. It was the only way to keep things looking normal, while at the same time shielding Breanna and Anastasia from unwarranted danger.

"You've got to hold that party," he stated flatly. "Otherwise, the entire *ton* will be abuzz and the assassin will catch wind of the fact that he's unnerved you. Still, I'm not completely reckless. I realize you'll need protection. So consider that protection granted. I'll delay checking out the more remote shops about those dolls until after all your guests have left. Instead, I'll ride to Medford Manor in time for the festivities. If the assassin *should* show up—he'll be properly greeted."

"By you?"

A corner of Royce's mouth lifted. "I know it's boorish to arrive at a holiday gathering without an invitation. But, should you decide to retain my services, that's exactly what I intend to do."

"I see." Lady Breanna acknowledged his statement, and for the first time Royce saw a trace of humor light her far-too-serious eyes, warming them to a rich, shimmering jade. "Well, thank you for warning me."

He nodded slowly, feeling a keen surge of anticipation at the prospect of bringing down this killer and putting that luminous glow back in Lady Breanna's eyes. "You're welcome."

*C*hristmas morning—the perfect time to arrange a shipment.

An uncommon quiet settled over the London docks, the normal rush of activity suspended as workers joined their families to attend mass. Hoists and winches were silent, ships swayed lazily in the chilly waters with few crewmen aboard to attend them. Tiny snowflakes sprinkled about, covering the docks in a diaphanous veil of white and adding to the unnatural sense of stillness hovering over the Thames.

The assassin's footsteps echoed as he crossed the alley dividing the cluster of warehouses. He glanced about, smiling as he took in the deserted buildings and path, contemplated all the sailors and workmen now gathered in Church.

What a pity that they were ignorant of the brilliant strategy taking place just beyond.

He'd done a thorough job. Organized just the right crew to convey his cargo. Selected excellent merchandise. Readied the choice assortment without leaving a mark—*any* mark that might detract from their worth.

And made all the arrangements right out in the open, while the residents of London were deep in prayer.

The instructions to his men hadn't taken long. This was his regular crew—a crew that had worked for him in the past, and were far more afraid of him than they were of the authorities. Fear was a splendid motivator. It ensured loyalty in a way that even money could not. Because if there was one thing stronger than greed, it was the drive for self-preservation.

Everything was in place—at least for this crop of merchandise.

What a lovely New Year's gift his cargo would make for three fortunate gentlemen.

There would be another delivery sent on its heels. Plans were already in motion.

Yes, the week ahead looked promising indeed. Another target to hit, another shipment to begin arrangements for, and—most exhilarating of all—in four days a trip to Medford Manor.

A trip he'd counted on making with the utmost discretion. After all, there wasn't a prayer Lady Breanna would throw open her gates to hundreds of guests. Not now. Not after the dolls, the note, the guard. The party would, of course, be canceled.

But it hadn't been.

His anticipation faded, transformed to the anger that had been boiling inside him all week long, intensifying more with each passing day. He gritted his teeth, pondering the unexpected response—or rather, *lack* of response—Lady Breanna had displayed to last week's events. That maddening little bitch. Rather than quaking with fear, she'd spent her days strolling the grounds with her cousin and Sheldrake, laughing and chatting as if all was right with the world. Despite the fact that that guard was killed at the portals of her home, she *still* hadn't panicked, hadn't canceled her holiday gathering and locked herself in her house.

There was only one explanation that made sense, he reminded himself, resorting to the same logic he'd used all week to bring himself under control.

She hadn't made the connection.

It was more than plausible. After all, he *had* done an exceptional job of making the murder look like the work of a highwayman. She'd obviously believed his ruse, dismissed the incident as being unrelated to the package she'd received. Yes. That's what had happened. It made sense, not only in comprehending Lady Breanna's behavior, but Sheldrake's, as well. The marquess's mind was far too sharp not to have considered the possibility that the two incidents were related. And, given his romantic attachment to his wife, it was unthinkable he'd subject her to danger. Therefore, he must have examined the evidence and determined that whoever sent those dolls to Lady Breanna had not been the same person who killed the guard outside her estate.

The assassin's lips curved, his good humor restored.

How delightful. He'd outwitted the entire family.

More fools they.

Actually, he was wasting his time feeling angry. Because, disappointed though he was that Lady Breanna wasn't yet shivering with terror, he was equally pleased at what that meant for him. Now he could accomplish this next part of his plan with great ease. He wouldn't have to sneak into Medford Manor, or resort to forcible entry. He'd simply stroll through the front door, right along with the other guests, choose the appropriate moment to leave the gift he'd brought for her ladyship.

After discovering this memento, she wouldn't be laughing.

No, on the contrary, she'd be overcome with horror, gripped with fear. Any hopes she'd entertained that the dolls were an isolated incident, that the guard's death was a coincidence, that she was safe in her own home, would be dashed.

He could hardly wait to see the terror in her eyes.

A gust of wind struck him and he winced, fitting his gloves more snugly into place, then shoving his hands in his pockets. Damn, how he loathed the cold.

Almost as much as he loathed *her*.

It was fitting the two would come together; that she'd die during winter.

A twig snapped and, reflexively, he turned up his collar, pulled the brim of his hat lower, shielding his face from view.

An instant later, two people—a young man and an even younger woman—darted by, sparing him not even a second glance. Giggling, they darted into one of the warehouses, the heated look in the young man's eye revealing precisely what was going to occur inside that wooden shed. The lad paused, assessed the area—deserted but for the assassin's retreating figure—and, having ensured their privacy, shut the warehouse door.

The assassin kept walking, head lowered, feeling a pang of envy. Ah, the pleasures that young couple were about to enjoy.

It was times like these he missed Maurelle.

Just thinking of her made his pulse quicken in a way no other woman could begin to equal.

Even after all these years.

He could still remember the first time he saw her. It was a sultry summer evening more than fifteen years ago, and she'd been coming down the stairs of that dilapidated brothel right outside Paris. He'd been pacing back and forth just across the street—whether by chance or by fate—driven there by the internal demons that pumped through his blood. Restless, consumed by a lethal hunger only he understood, he'd been eyeing the brothel, trying to decide if sex would ease the yearnings pounding inside him.

That's when she'd emerged.

She was easily the most striking woman he'd ever seen—thick black hair, huge dark eyes, offset by the palest of skin, all crowning the most lush, desirable body any woman could boast. The instant he glimpsed her, all his inner turmoil had converged, slamming forcibly from his brain to his loins.

He'd paid for a full night. He'd used every minute of it. But when morning came, he was no more ready to say good-bye than he'd been twelve hours earlier. He wanted her again—and not only for a night. There was something insatiably exciting about Maurelle, something rich and dark and exhilarating that aroused him beyond bearing. Something that clawed inside him and drew him back to her side, night after night, week after week.

Perhaps it was because, even then, he recognized her as his equal.

She was his equal still.

A slow smile curved the assassin's lips.
Life had an ironic way of working out.

Royce couldn't hide his relief when the time finally came to leave his brother's estate. It wasn't that he didn't enjoy spending Christmas with Edmund and Jane. They were good, decent people—if somewhat dull—who tried their best to make him feel welcome. The highlight of the visit was romping about with their three sons: Thomas, William, and little Christopher. Thomas—actually Edmund Thomas, heir apparent to his father's title—was five years old, and far more interested in climbing trees than he was in acquiring the skills necessary toward being the Earl of Searby. William, four years old and no less energetic than his brother, kept dragging Royce off to play in the snow, pelting his uncle with snowballs. And Christopher, at just shy of two, was a virtual whirlwind of activity, toddling from room to room on his stubby little legs, sending vases and crystal crashing to the floor in his wake.

The hours spent with his nephews were a welcome reprieve for Royce. Frolicking about kept his mind off the two cases he was now working on—the one involving Viscount Ryder's missing illegitimate daughter, and the more recent one involving Lady Breanna Colby.

Both cases centered around women, and both were frustrating as hell.

Ryder was old, in broken spirits, and searching for an unacknowledged bastard daughter who had unexpectedly become his sole living heir. One short month ago, Ryder's son Nathaniel had succumbed to a severe bout of influenza, dying suddenly, unmarried and childless, leaving Ryder with no one to inherit the family name and title. The problem was that the aged viscount knew less than nothing about his illegitimate daughter, other than the fact that she'd been conceived in his home—the product of a torrid liaison with a fetching chamber maid who'd been discharged the moment she became with child—and born in the back room of a London workhouse. Glynnis Martin, the chamber maid in question, had sent word to him of the babe's arrival, adding that she'd named their daughter Emma, after her grandmother. Ryder had destroyed the note and never responded. As of now, he could remember no additional details surrounding the child's birth.

A pathetic lack of information, indeed.

As a result, Royce had nothing to go on—not a description or an address where he might find either mother or daughter. He'd gone straight to the workhouse where Emma had been born, knowing even as he did that it was an exercise in futility. Sure enough, the institution provided as few clues as he'd anticipated. The attendants there had seen dozens of bastard children brought into the world in just such a fashion and, as a result, kept no records of their whereabouts. One of the established matrons who'd been at the workhouse for more than two decades thought she remembered someone matching Glynnis Martin's description. If her memory served her correctly, the young woman in question had arrived at their doors some eighteen years ago, hugely pregnant, and given birth to an infant daughter. She'd sent a note off to the child's father and waited to hear from him. When she didn't hear, she became despondent. One night about a week later, she took the infant and disappeared.

Vanishing into anonymity.

Just like the assassin threatening Lady Breanna.

This new case bothered Royce even more than Ryder's did, no doubt because of the longstanding friendship and respect that existed between him and Damen. Royce felt doubly compelled to find a solution, to protect Damen's wife.

And to protect her cousin.

Both investigations were plaguing him, beating relentlessly at his brain.

Dashing about in the snow with three energetic nephews did wonders toward alleviating that.

It didn't, however, make being at Searby any easier.

Then again, that house held nothing but dark memories for him—memories that no amount of revelry could erase.

So, it was with a great deal of relief that, on the day after Christmas, he bid Edmund and his family goodbye and took his leave.

He and Hibbert—who traveled with him to Searby—stopped in London overnight; long enough to gather up the Ryder file and check out the few remaining shops in Town he had yet to investigate that stocked dolls as part of their merchandise and might or might not have sold two red-haired ones in the past fortnight.

None of them had.

The following morning found the two men packed, settled in Royce's carriage, and on their way to Kent—first to check out a half-dozen shops in that shire, then to proceed on to Medford Manor.

The final lap of the journey was silent, as Royce contemplated his unsuccessful attempts to learn who'd sold the killer those dolls, much less the identity of the man who'd bought them. He'd gotten nowhere fast. And his initial time had run out, as the Colby party was scheduled to begin tomorrow.

Unbidden, he found himself wondering how Lady Breanna had fared during his absence. Not bodily, for he felt confident she was safe—for the time being. Instinct told him her assailant had more emotional torment in store for her before he acted. But mentally—had her nerve held out? And physically—had her stamina held out?

He had a staunch feeling the answer to both questions was yes. Lady Breanna was a remarkably strong young woman.

He'd seen that strength mirrored in those carefully guarded jade-green eyes when she'd stood beside Damen and Anastasia last week, on the morning he'd left her estate, and officially asked him to take on her case. Quietly, graciously, she'd voiced her understanding that this meant she agreed to adhere to his tactics, that she'd follow the procedure he'd outlined for her between then and the day of the party. She'd concluded by expressing her appreciation for his time and effort, then wished him a joyous holiday and sent him on his way.

Royce had listened to her formal speech, watched her self-contained expression as she spoke. Once again, he'd been struck by the sure knowledge that there was far more to Breanna Colby than met the eye, far more that hovered beneath that exquisite, genteel veneer.

He was more determined than ever to help her.

Yet, so far, he'd accomplished next to nothing.

After first leaving Medford Manor for London— prior to his visit to Searby—he'd not only called on

numerous local shops in Town to ask about the dolls,
but he'd dropped in at Bow Street, spoken to Marks
about whatever information had been amassed on
Cunnings's murderer, his potential link to the Viscount Medford, and now his link to the threats being
sent to Lady Breanna.

As Royce suspected, Marks was more than willing
to turn over his file, which contained details on the
conversations he'd had with all those he'd questioned
about Cunnings—both then and now. The Bow Street
runner looked conscience-stricken and at the same
time relieved to learn that Lady Breanna had hired
Royce to follow up on the matter.

Royce understood both reactions.

Marks's relief was because he was being pressured
to devote all his energies toward solving the murders
of the local noblemen. And his attack of conscience
was because he'd been unable to help Lady Breanna,
unable to find out the name of the predator who was
stalking her.

How could Royce fault him, either for his priorities
or his regrets? He well understood that rueful expression on Marks's face. He had the uncomfortable feeling he'd be wearing a similar one himself when he
told Lady Breanna he'd uncovered nothing of impor-
tance as of yet. She seemed to have the same effect on
everyone, inspiring a surge of respect and a rush of
protectiveness that made people want to slay dragons
for her. And if that reaction was unusual for Marks, it
was unprecedented for Royce.

That fact notwithstanding, Royce had left Bow
Street armed with Marks's reports—reports that were
nothing more than routine chats with all Cunnings's
friends and colleagues. Fine. He'd pored over them

during his evenings at Searby, then kept them close by for reference. And now, after having spoken with shopkeepers throughout London, he and Hibbert had covered six or seven shops in Kent. Those visits had, as he'd suspected, yielded no information on the purchase of the dolls. Wherever the killer had bought them, it hadn't been in Town or in Kent.

The bastard was too clever for that.

"We'll be arriving at Medford Manor in about ten minutes," Hibbert announced, shooting Royce a sideways glance. "Would you care to discuss your somber mood?"

Royce shifted in his seat, crossed one long leg over the other. "The truth? I'm not looking forward to looking Damen in the eye and telling him I've got no news on who's trying to kill his wife."

"Did you think you *would* have news—after doing only a few days of preliminary digging?"

A scowl. "No. I didn't."

Hibbert arched a brow. "Are you sure it's Lord Sheldrake you're uncomfortable facing? Or is it Lady Breanna?"

Royce's scowl deepened. "I don't appreciate having my mind read, Hibbert. Not even by you. But if you must know, no, I don't like telling a twenty-one-year-old woman that a professional killer—one with a brilliant mind and a burning desire to terrorize and kill her—is closing in and I've done nothing to outmaneuver him or find out who he is." Staring broodingly at his portfolio, Royce added, "I've been unusually slow at turning up answers to young women's dilemmas these days."

Hibbert sniffed. "Ryder's daughter is like the proverbial needle in a haystack. We're not only searching for an eighteen-year-old girl who could be anywhere, we're searching for one whose father has never laid eyes on her. We have no description, no point at which to begin. The viscount hasn't so much as contacted Glynnis Martin since he impregnated her and discharged her nineteen years ago. He even destroyed the letter she sent him announcing their daughter's birth. Why, for all we know, Emma Martin doesn't even know her father's name, much less that he's alive and searching for her."

"That's irrelevant. It's *we* who are searching for *her*, not the other way around. *We* know *her* name and that her mother dropped out of sight immediately after having her."

"Glynnis Martin could have left England."

"With what money?"

"Fine. Then, she could have moved to another shire, changed her name."

"That shouldn't stop us from finding her—*or* her daughter."

"It won't stop us. But it might slow us down. Our men are exploring all the avenues you defined. We're waiting to hear back from them. We're also waiting for word on whatever death records they can get their hands on. Not that I hold out much hope. We have almost two decades and an entire country to cover, with only a name and a description of Glynnis Martin to go on. She's had eighteen years in which to die. So, for that matter, has her daughter."

"Damn." Royce pressed his fist into the seat cushion, leaving a deep imprint in the soft cloth. "I don't like being thwarted—not even for a few weeks. I don't intend to allow it. By New Year's Day we're going to have information leading us to Ryder's daughter."

"I see." Hibbert leaned back in his seat, eyeing his employer speculatively. "And Lady Breanna? Are your plans for our progress on her situation equally ambitious?"

"Yes." Royce's jaw set, his tone as unyielding as his claim. "We're going to find that bastard who's after her, Hibbert. We're going to find him soon."

"For Lord Sheldrake's sake," Hibbert supplied helpfully.

"Don't bait me. Yes, for Damen's sake. Also for his wife's sake, and Lady Breanna's sake. Hell, for *my* sake. I'm not going to lose. Not this time."

"*This* time?" A wry grin twisted Hibbert's lips. "As I recall, you haven't lost at *any* time."

"No," Royce concurred, staring out the window as the iron gates of Medford Manor sprang into view. "I haven't."

9

From the sitting-room window, Breanna watched Lord Royce's carriage round the drive, feeling a surprising sense of relief and an even more surprising sense of excitement at the realization that he was back.

But then, why should she be surprised at the relief that seeing him evoked? Royce Chadwick represented her only hope of finding and eliminating the assassin who was hell-bent on inflicting his vengeance on her and Stacie.

She'd been living a walking nightmare ever since that package had arrived, her entire body taut with fear every time she and Stacie left the house. Even with Damen perpetually by their sides, it was terrifying to know that somewhere—doubtless within scrutinizing distance—a brilliant marksman waited, gauging the right time to end their lives.

Yet he didn't strike—just as Lord Royce had predicted.

Damen's friend certainly knew what he was talking about.

True, his methods were risky, leaving both her and Stacie susceptible to attack. Still, the tactics he'd outlined were unarguably logical—the result of an astute mind that understood its adversary.

Perhaps that was the part she found exciting. Dangerous or not, Lord Royce's reasoning was fascinating, and listening to him detail his strategy had strengthened her conviction that he was the right person for the job. He possessed all the awareness and creativity Bow Street lacked—and the courage to see it all through.

She was curious to hear what he'd found out during his absence.

Letting the curtain fall back into place, she gathered up her skirts and made her way across the sitting room. She was halfway down the hall when Wells opened the front door, and Lord Royce and an elderly, silver-haired man walked in.

Damen's footsteps echoed from the second floor landing, and he strode down the stairs, reached the main level, and cut across Breanna's path, never even noticing her as he headed toward the doorway.

"Royce. Hibbert." He greeted both men tersely. "What did you find out?"

"We spoke to numerous shopkeepers," Hibbert began. "And Lord Royce paid a visit to Bow Street. After our initial inquiries—"

"Nothing," Royce interrupted with an adamant sweep of his arm. "We found out nothing." His chin came up and he met Damen's anguished gaze. "But we will." He handed Wells his overcoat with a nod of thanks. "Have there been further incidents?"

"No." It was Breanna who answered, walking forward to join the men. "It was just as you said. The three of us went about our business, Wells checked the mail every day, and—other than the responses to our party invitations that continued to pour in—we received nothing from that . . . that . . . man."

Royce turned toward her, his midnight blue eyes sweeping her briefly from head to toe, as if to assess her true state of mind. "Good," was all he said. Without averting his gaze, he gestured toward the older gentleman beside him. "My lady, this is Hibbert, my most trusted associate."

"Good afternoon, Mr. Hibbert," Breanna replied with a curtsy. "And since no one can tell my cousin and I apart, I'll spare Lord Royce the embarrassment by introducing myself. I'm—"

"Lady Breanna Colby," Royce finished for her. "I beg to differ with you. I have no trouble telling you apart."

There was something about his tone that made hot color tinge Breanna's cheeks. "My apologies. It seems I've underestimated you."

"It would seem so." A corner of Royce's mouth lifted. "However, it would also seem that I've embarrassed you. So I, too, must apologize. Your apology, by the way, is accepted."

Unexpected amusement danced in Breanna's eyes. "Then I'd be a boor not to accept yours—which is just what I suspect you were counting on me to say. You're quite a maneuverer, my lord. It's no wonder you're successful at getting what you want. Very well. Consider your apology accepted."

Royce continued to gaze steadily at her. "Thank you. You're very gracious."

Hibbert cleared his throat. "Lady Breanna," he said with a bow, his pale stare assessing her in one swift motion. "It's a pleasure."

"Thank you. And welcome to Medford Manor."
Catching her lip between her teeth, Breanna grew serious, mulling over Lord Royce's blunt announcement
that they'd learned nothing new. "So the dolls weren't
bought in London. I'm not surprised."

"Neither am I." Royce glanced curiously about.
"Where is the marchioness? I got the distinct impression your cousin never missed out on anything."

Breanna's forehead creased in concern. "She doesn't.
Unfortunately, she hasn't been sleeping well. She's upstairs, resting."

Royce frowned. "Is it anxiety that's keeping her
awake?"

"No, my lord." Anastasia descended the stairs,
shaking her head as she did. "It's not anxiety. It's
pregnancy." She smiled, an illuminating gesture that
drew attention away from her pallor, the dark circles
beneath her eyes. "In fact, I've thought of a new and
practical way to barricade our door to unwanted
guests. Line the entranceway with chamber pots.
They'll seal off the house, and I promise they won't go
to waste."

"A novel idea," Royce chuckled. "I'll give it
thought." He repeated his introductions, this time
presenting Anastasia to Hibbert.

The older man looked intently from Anastasia to
Breanna and back again. "Astonishing," he murmured, having properly acknowledged Damen's wife.
"And you're not twins?"

"We're not even sisters—at least not by blood,"
Anastasia explained. "Our fathers were twins. Our
mothers were sisters, and they, too, looked a great
deal alike. The resemblance between Breanna and me
is unusual, but not impossible. And as far as being

twins . . ." She tossed Breanna an affectionate smile. "In our hearts, we are."

"I see."

"When will your guests start to arrive?" Royce asked.

"Tomorrow morning." Breanna glanced at Wells, who nodded his agreement. "Anything you want to know about the guest list, see Wells. He arranged the entire party without mentioning a word to me."

"The decorating, the arrangements, all the finishing touches are Miss Breanna's gift," Wells refuted proudly. "She brings beauty to everything she touches."

"I'm not surprised." Royce's head came up, and he inspected the festive greenery more closely—the boughs of holly and sprigs of mistletoe that decorated the entranceway and halls, the freshly arranged vases of snowdrops and ivy that sat atop every table.

"Everything looks lovely," he murmured. "Warm, inviting, and incredibly beautiful." He meant it, too. Each carefully placed adornment, each colorful wreath emanated the elegant taste and grace that was Lady Breanna.

The notion of anything threatening such beauty was unthinkable.

Brow furrowed, Royce turned to Wells. "I'll need to see the guest list. I'm sure most of the names will be familiar to me. You've hired extra guards?"

"They're stationed all around the perimeter of the estate and near every door to the manor," Wells replied.

"Good. Then if it's all right with you, I'll have a word with the head guard—Mahoney, I believe it was—after I review the guest list. I want everything in place when the guests start to arrive. Most especially, I want the guards poised and ready tomorrow when darkness starts to fall. The big ball is tomorrow night. I don't want any surprises."

Damen shot him a worried look. "You think that's when the killer might strike?"

"I don't think he'll strike at all. What he might do is visit. If he does, I'll be prepared."

"I hope to God you know what you're doing, Royce."

Royce's gaze remained steady. "I do."

The sound of yet another approaching carriage split the quiet of night.

"I hope we haven't made the biggest mistake of our lives," Damen muttered, retying his cravat for the third time. "There are over a hundred people downstairs already. The entranceway doors are opening and closing ten times an hour. The French doors in the ballroom are all slightly ajar to let in some air."

"And there are dozens of guards marching around the estate with loaded pistols," Anastasia reminded him, walking over to fix the cravat Damen's valet had long since abandoned. "Damen, you have to stop worrying. We all agreed Royce's plan was the right one. Even Wells couldn't convince us there was another way. Because there isn't. The fact is, Breanna and I are at risk. We're going to be at risk until this killer is found and stopped. And it's up to us to do that." She smoothed her hand across her husband's jaw. "Besides, wasn't it you who sought out Royce Chadwick, brought him here to help?"

"Yes, God help me, it was."

"And we all agree he was the right person for the job—extreme methods or not." She grew thoughtful.

"Actually, I think it's uncanny the way he understands this killer's mind. If he's right—"

"It's if he's wrong that worries me." Damen threaded his fingers through his wife's hair, caressed her
cheeks with his thumbs. "It doesn't just worry me, it
scares me to death."

Anastasia's sharp jade eyes searched his face. "You
don't think he's wrong. You trust him. You'd never be
working with him if you didn't. What's more, *I* trust
him. So does Breanna. We all believe in his abilities."
She let her hand slip down her bodice, placed her
palm on her abdomen. "Believe me, I know what's at
stake. That's why we've got to go through with this."

Damen's eyes darkened. "Half of me keeps hoping
that madman has vanished," he muttered, laying his
palm over Stacie's. "We haven't received a single
communication from him in over a week."

"According to Royce, he was waiting to see if Breanna went through with the party. Well, by now, he's
seen guests flocking to Medford Manor. So he
knows—or believes—she's brushed off any worries
she might have had. He'll be reacting to that soon."

"And that's supposed to appease me?"

"No. It's supposed to make you realize that the
only way to catch this killer is to lure him out. This
unnatural calm is more frightening than anything
else. It's like knowing there's a terrible storm coming—one that's going to strike at any moment and destroy everyone you love. Only it hovers, gathers force,
and circles like some kind of predatory hawk." Anastasia shuddered. "This waiting, bracing for the as-
sault—it's unbearable."

Damen gathered her close, tucked her head beneath
his chin. "I know." His embrace tightened. "I'm not

leaving your side tonight. I don't care how you explain it. Tell everyone I'm insanely worried about your condition. Say whatever you want to. But don't expect to eat, talk, or dance unless it's with me."

His wife smiled against his waistcoat. "You've become very possessive, my lord. It's a good thing you're the best dancer and the most fascinating conversationalist in the room. Otherwise, I might be forced to protest."

Damen didn't smile back. "I love you," he said fiercely. "No one and nothing is going to hurt you."

Despite her independent nature, Stacie felt a surge of welcome relief, and she gave silent thanks to the heavens for giving her this wonderful man as her husband. "I love you, too," she breathed. "And I intend to keep myself and the babe perfectly safe. I promise." She leaned back, gazed up at him. "Let's try to enjoy ourselves. This *is* a celebration." Her lips twitched. "It's also the first opportunity I'll have to mingle with the businessmen I offended last summer when I asked them to finance my bank. I have quite a few fences to mend. Especially since most of those men are clients of yours."

"It's *they* who should be apologizing to *you*," Damen countered flatly. "Your idea was brilliant. Choosing to dismiss it simply because it was a woman who thought it up was their loss—and my gain. It gave me the opportunity to become your business partner. Our American bank is thriving. Believe me, sweetheart, if those men are feeling anything, it's jealousy and regret. And if any of them makes the slightest disparaging remark, they'll have me to answer to."

"My knight in shining armor," Stacie returned tenderly. "Thank you for always believing in me, and for rescuing me when I need it." A thoughtful expression flitted across her face. "That brings me to an interesting question. Damen, have you noticed any-thing . . . distinctive about the way Royce treats Breanna?"

"Distinctive?"

"Yes. Different from the way he treats the rest of us. Royce is a hard man, and a somewhat detached one. I suppose he has to be, given what he does. Yet with Breanna, he's gentler, more compassionate. It's not the words he uses with her, it's the tone. As if he's trying to cushion the ordeal she's going through. And the way he stares at her—like he's trying to absorb her, figure her out. I can't quite put my finger on it . . ." Stacie broke off, trying to find the right words to describe her perception.

"Are you suggesting Royce is interested in Breanna?" Damen asked with more than a trace of surprise.

Anastasia lifted one shoulder in an ambivalent shrug. "I don't think *interested* is the right choice of words. It's more like he's fascinated by her. Whether it's just a combination of attraction and protective-ness, or it's the prelude to something deeper—that I'm not sure. What's more, Breanna is drawn to him, too. I can sense it. She's thoroughly intrigued by him—on many levels. Not that she's said a word to me. She hasn't. Probably because she's still sorting out whatever it is she's feeling—if she's even aware of those feelings at all. Still, there's definitely something different about her since Royce's first visit. I can sense it."

Damen's brows lifted fractionally. "Royce is hardly the kind of man Breanna's used to. He's—"

"He's what—worldly? Experienced? A risk-taker?" Stacie's lips curved. "I know. Maybe that's just what Breanna finds intriguing." She dismissed the notion with a wave of her hand. "It's just a thought. A fascinating one to consider, though."

"In other words, you're going to be scrutinizing Breanna all night," Damen concluded dryly.

His wife's grin was impish. "She deserves to be scrutinized a bit. She certainly did the same to me when you and I first met and she was convinced we belonged together." A pointed look. "As it turned out, she was right. Then again, she and I usually are when it comes to seeing inside each other's hearts."

Damen rubbed one of his wife's auburn tresses between his fingers. "Indeed you are," he murmured, his features tightening with emotion. "And yes, Breanna was right about us. You're my life. Which is why I'm far more concerned about your safety—and Breanna's, for that matter—than I am about her romantic interests."

"All I meant was that maybe my instincts about her and Royce are also right and—"

"I know what you meant." Damen silenced her by pressing his forefinger to her lips. "And if you want to keep a close eye on your cousin all night and speculate about the prospect—however unlikely—of a future between her and Royce, feel free to do so. So long as while you're watching her, you stay close enough to my side for *me* to watch *you*. As I said, my main concern tonight is safety—yours and Breanna's."

Anastasia nodded. "I'll place *my* safety in *your* hands." Another faraway look. "I have a funny feeling I know whose hands Breanna's will be in."

*   *   *

Breanna studied her reflection in the looking glass, smoothing the satin trim adorning the bodice of her lilac silk ball gown, and checking for the third time to make sure her hair was in place.

It was.

Reflexively, her fingers brushed her cheeks and nape to make sure no strands had broken free of their upswept coronet atop her head. Finding no traitorous locks, she appraised the strand of pearls her lady's maid had woven through her tresses.

Her earrings and necklace were simple, gold with a dusting of amethysts in the center, left to her by her mother. She hoped the effect was enough, but she felt ridiculous doused in the amount of jewelry worn by most of her friends. So the earrings and necklace would have to do.

Her gaze shifted critically, starting at the crown of her head and descending to the tips of her slippered feet, only to retrace its path, hovering at her face and throat. Pale, unadorned, but adequate.

Why am I so preoccupied with my appearance tonight? she thought in disgust, twisting about and walking away from the looking glass. It wasn't as if she'd never attended a ball before. And this evening, for the first time, she didn't have her father to contend with.

Instead she had his hired killer.

Flinching, she walked about her bedchamber, running a fingertip over her porcelain figures and trying to calm her nerves.

Nothing was going to happen. Lord Royce had all but assured her of it. The assassin was not going to stroll into a ballroom and open fire.

Then why did she feel so ill at ease? So vulnerable?

She glanced about the bedchamber as she had a

dozen times since Jamie Knox had been murdered. She'd felt uneasy since that day, as if her domain had somehow been invaded. She couldn't shake the feeling that the killer had been here—at her home. She knew it was irrational, but she could actually feel his presence. He was watching her, waiting, coiled to strike.

But he *hadn't* been here. Not inside. Not in her house, and certainly not in her room.

She'd checked and rechecked, giving in to her inexplicable need to ensure her chambers hadn't been violated.

Everything was intact.

She'd inspected every personal item on her dressing table, every porcelain figure in her collection. Most especially her two favorites: the porcelain horse she'd had since childhood, and the porcelain statue of two little girls playing together among a field of flowers. *That* was her most cherished figure, because in it was wedged the precious silver coin her grandfather had given her.

Nothing had been touched; not the figures, not the coin—nothing.

And yet . . .

Breanna steeled herself, her gloved hands balling into fists as she drew slow, steadying breaths. This was ridiculous. She was letting her imagination run wild. And with no basis. There were guards posted all over the estate, manning each and every door. Further, the people gathered downstairs were her family and friends. And *she* was their hostess.

She had to gain control of herself. She'd survived on internal strength all her life. Now was no time to lose it.

Besides, Royce Chadwick would be there.

That thought crystallized out of nowhere, and Breanna was startled at how much comfort it brought her. Despite the limited amount of time he'd spent here, Lord Royce had come to represent strength, confidence and—no matter how risky his tactics—security.

It was more than the knowledge that he was good at his job. It was an instinctive awareness that somehow he would protect her. Protect her and at the same time make her part of that excitement he exuded—an excitement she never knew existed and wanted nothing more than to . . .

Breanna squelched that thought in the making, stunned at the direction her own reflections had taken. What in heaven's name was she thinking? Lord Royce was a professional, hired by Damen to do a job. He wasn't here to . . . to . . .

To what?

With a bemused shake of her head, Breanna turned her attention to her gloves, smoothing them more snugly up to her elbows. She was beginning to think too much like Stacie, she chastised herself. It was Stacie who possessed the romantic nature, not she.

Then again, it was Stacie who'd grown up seeing romantic love firsthand, having parents who adored each other—*truly* adored each other—with the kind of intensity she now shared with Damen.

Just thinking about Stacie and Damen—*and* the babe they'd now conceived—made Breanna's heart swell. If ever there was evidence of happily-ever-after, of two people who deserved joy and fulfillment, it was they.

If only they could keep the evils of the world at bay . . .

No, Breanna refuted silently. She was *not* going to revert back to that subject yet again. She was going to behave as tonight commanded she should—like a proper lady and hostess. It was time to stop procrastinating and get to that party.

Purposefully, she straightened her shoulders.

Then, without so much as another glance at her reflection, she marched out of her bedchamber and down the stairs to the ballroom.

10

"*M*iss Breanna." Wells greeted her at the foot of the steps, beaming with a paternal pride that was as intense as if she were his own child. "You look lovely."

"Thank you, Wells." Breanna squeezed his arm, grateful that a guard had been assigned to act as butler for the evening—not only because it meant added protection, but because it meant Wells could see the fruits of his labor by stationing himself at the ballroom door.

A cluster of chatting matrons breezed by, so engrossed in their gossip that they never noticed Breanna. They hovered at the ballroom doorway—all shimmering jewels and rustling silk—finishing their whispered conversation, then hastened in to rejoin the party.

A wave of familiar nervousness accosted Breanna in a rush, bringing with it the lingering remnants of a shy child who'd stayed in the background, let her bolder, more outspoken cousin lead the way.

"Wells," she murmured tentatively, rubbing her skirts between her fingers. "Would you do me the honor of escorting me in? You know how I hate making entrances."

Wells frowned, fully aware of Breanna's reticence—and its cause. "Your father's gone, Miss Breanna," he reminded her gently. "And, yes, I know you hate making entrances. You hate anything that makes you the center of attention. Well, tonight you *are* the center of attention—you and Miss Stacie. This party is in your honor. I refuse to pretend otherwise."

He cupped Breanna's elbow, guided her toward the ballroom. "In the eyes of the *ton*, I'm a butler. Which doesn't bother me a bit. I take great pride in my position. Besides, you and Miss Stacie view me as family, and that's all that matters. My point is, I won't escort you. That would cause those women who just passed by here to swoon, which would, in turn, detract from your entrance. What I *will* do is announce you—just as I announced Miss Stacie and Lord Sheldrake. How would that be?"

Breanna studied the throngs of people, the movement of light and color as laughing couples whirled about the dance floor, helped themselves to plates of food and glasses of punch. There were easily a hundred and fifty people already filling the room.

Her gut clenched.

"Please, Miss Breanna," Wells urged, resorting to the one tactic he knew would work. "Do it for me."

How could she not? Especially when he was looking at her like a proud father about to present his treasure to the world.

"All right, Wells," she managed. "Let's get this over with. Once everyone stops staring at me, I'll be fine."

"You're already fine," he countered. "You're far more than fine. In less than one minute, you'll be swamped by admirers, most of whom will be totally unworthy. I, myself, shall keep an eye on things, make sure you're not pestered by any one suitor for too long. Should you need further reinforcements, Miss Stacie and Lord Sheldrake are directly to your right, chatting with Lord and Lady Dutton and the Earl and Countess of Geldrick. Actually, they're not chatting. Both men are frantically trying to make amends to Miss Stacie for their stupidity in snubbing her business proposition last summer. And Miss Stacie is having fun watching them squirm. She's already done the same to the Duke of Maywood, the Marquess of Radebrook, and the Viscount Crompton."

Breanna couldn't help but laugh. "Thank you, Wells. For pointing out where I can find a safe haven and for giving me that status report."

"Your safe haven. I'm glad you brought that up." Wells's humor vanished, and his uneasy gaze traveled the room. "Lord Royce is near the French doors. So are two guards. The others are positioned everywhere on the estate. Given that a third nobleman was murdered in London last week, no one will question the added security. In fact, they'll be grateful for it. So relax and have fun. All will be well."

Soberly, Breanna nodded, sickened by the reminder of what was fast becoming an epidemic of killings. Three men had now died, and their wives had vanished. The whole situation was terrifying. Between that and the fear surrounding her own dilemma . . .

Her worried thoughts were interrupted by Wells trumpeting, "May I present this evening's other lovely honoree, Lady Breanna Colby. While I realize Lady Breanna is your hostess, I am temporarily relieving her of that role—long enough to ask you to join me in wishing her a very happy birthday."

Wells's utterly unconventional announcement yielded a round of laughter and a host of good-natured wishes. It also did wonders for easing Breanna's unsettled state—a state that had escalated from mere anxiety over a public appearance to blind fear over armed killers.

"You're incorrigible," she told Wells affectionately, grateful as always for his innate understanding of her. She knew he'd very intentionally made her entrance more relaxed and less ceremonious. And she loved him for it.

Drawing a slow breath, she walked into the room, greeting her guests as she did, finding that it was infinitely easier than expected to act the part of hostess. Many of her guests approached to thank her for considerately adding so many guards to the estate since, as expected, they were all terribly nervous about the string of murders taking place.

Breanna scarcely had time to answer before she was swept up into a whirl of activity, being claimed for a dance, then moving from one partner to another. She found herself wishing she could stop long enough to take a breath and exchange a word with Stacie.

Not that her cousin was any more idle than she. Dressed in an exquisite gown of bottle-green silk overlaid with French gauze, Stacie was holding her own kind of court. With Damen adhered firmly to her side, she was politely accepting the stammering apologies of a half dozen businessmen—apologies, Breanna suspected, that were motivated by equal doses of regret over their missed profit-making opportunities and worry over the glares they were receiving from Damen Lockewood, whose bank was at the heart of all their ventures.

As she circled the dance floor with the arrogant and handsome Lord Percy Gilbert, Breanna caught Stacie's eye, saw the amusement there, and nearly laughed aloud. Those poor men. They didn't stand a chance.

The strings fell silent, and Breanna was just about to excuse herself and head toward Stacie and Damen when she heard a soft, feminine voice ask, "Breanna, may I speak with you?"

She turned, surprised to see Lady Margaret Warner waiting impatiently beside her.

As the most sought-after young woman in the crowd, Margaret never approached anyone, certainly not at a ball. She waited for *them* to approach *her*. Ever coy, friendly but not eager, Margaret was always surrounded by far too many friends and admirers to break free and chat. True, she and Breanna had become friends over the past months, but doing needlepoint together and seeking her out at a ball were two different things entirely.

"Margaret." Breanna hid her surprise well. "Of course." She smiled at Lord Percy. "You'll excuse us?"

"Of course he will." There was that flirtatious charm Margaret exuded so well. She gazed intently at Gilbert, batted those long, irresistible lashes, and murmured, "His lordship understands that we ladies have things to discuss. You don't mind, do you?"

Gilbert bowed, an anticipatory gleam flashing in his eyes. "Of course not."

"I knew you'd understand." She touched his arm, ever so slightly. "Thank you."

With that, she led Breanna off, guiding her close to

the musicians so whatever they discussed would be drowned out once the dancing recommenced.

The next set began and Margaret came to a halt, pivoting about, the skirts of her blush-colored gown swirling about her ankles like a pastel cloud. "This ball is delightful," she told Breanna with an unexpectedly warm squeeze of her hands. "The whole party is a stunning success."

"I'm glad you're enjoying yourself." Breanna offered her new friend a genuine, if puzzled, smile. She waited, wondering what the real reason was behind Margaret's unprecedented behavior.

She didn't have long to wait.

"Tell me," Margaret whispered, leaning closer to Breanna as if to share a coveted secret. "I'm dying to know. How did you do it?"

"Do what?"

A puff of tinkling laughter. "You needn't be modest. Not with me. I'm duly impressed. So tell me, how did you convince him to come?"

"Convince *who* to come?" Breanna was beginning to feel like a total idiot.

The look Margaret gave her did nothing to erase that feeling. "*Who?*" she repeated incredulously. "Why, Royce Chadwick, of course. He's refused every invitation since returning from India. And last Season he made only three appearances, none of them for more than an hour. Yet you managed to lure him to your party. How did you do it?"

Breanna followed Margaret's line of vision, easily spotting Lord Royce conversing with a group of gentlemen. Then again, Lord Royce would be easy to spot anywhere, even in a large crowd such as this. His height and build, his powerful presence, those hard, dark, dangerously handsome good looks—especially clad in formal evening clothes—were enough to attract any woman's eye.

Clearly, they attracted *every* woman's eye. And Margaret Warner was no exception.

"I . . ." Breanna wet her lips with the tip of her tongue, desperately trying to think of a reply. She recalled Lord Royce mentioning that he rarely attended parties, but it never occurred to her that his appearance here would cause such an extreme reaction.

Then again, it should have occurred to her. Judging from the look on Margaret Warner's face, Royce Chadwick was not only *noticed* by every breathing unattached female in the *ton*, he was coveted by them, as well.

"Don't keep me in suspense," Margaret hissed. "Tell me. Have you known him long?"

"He's a friend of Damen's," Breanna finally replied, realizing that she couldn't stand there gaping and saying nothing forever. "I believe they're business associates." She prayed that wasn't a confidential tidbit she'd just revealed. But Lord help her, she had to say something.

"So you're not acquainted with him yourself." Margaret's face fell. "I was hoping you could put in a kind word . . . that is . . ."

Breanna understood precisely what Margaret was hoping. The question was, how did she respond?

She was mulling it over when Royce Chadwick looked up, staring directly toward the musicians and finding her with an ease that made her suspect he knew exactly where she was now, and probably where she'd been from the instant she entered the ballroom.

His midnight blue gaze locked with hers.

The impact was staggering, like a blow knocking the breath right from her lungs, and Breanna had to fight the urge to gasp in air. Instead, she merely stood there, unable to look away, watching as he made his way across the room, heading purposefully toward her.

"Breanna?" Margaret repeated, obviously unsettled by Breanna's silence, as well as by the fact that she had to humble herself in a fashion that was utterly foreign to her. "Have you met him or not?"

"Yes," Breanna heard herself say. "I've met him."

"Ah." Margaret released a heartfelt sigh. "Then Anastasia *has* introduced you. Good. Would you do me the same favor? I mean, I've actually been introduced—twice—and even shared a dance or two with him. But it can't hurt to refresh his memory. It would certainly ease my way—some idle chatter, a waltz, maybe even a moonlight stroll. After that, the rest should go smoothly."

Breanna scarcely heard what Margaret was saying. Because at that moment, the very man her friend was plotting to snare was reaching their sides.

"Good evening, Lady Breanna." Royce bowed, lifted her gloved hand to his lips. "Thank you for inviting me to this lovely party."

Breanna's heart began slamming against her ribs and, suddenly, she knew why she'd reacted so strongly.

This was a different Royce Chadwick, not the implacable man who hunted down criminals, understood their minds. This was an elegant, polished nobleman who blended in with the *ton*—polite, sociable, alarmingly charismatic. No—not just charismatic. Seductive. Desirable. Exciting in a way that had *nothing* to do with outwitting an enemy.

This man was more dangerous than the one she'd originally met.

"I'm delighted to have you, my lord," she managed, then felt hot color rush to her cheeks at the implication of her own words. She found herself praying it was only her heightened senses that were causing her to view her comment in such a lascivious fashion.

If Lord Royce perceived anything out of the ordinary, he didn't show it. "I'm delighted to be here."

Thank heavens. He'd missed it.

"You're flushed," he added with offhanded ease. "May I get you some punch?"

He hadn't missed it. Or if he'd missed the indecent connotation of her words, he certainly hadn't missed her flustered reaction to them.

Once again, Breanna summoned her now-faltering inner reserve. "Yes. Thank you. I do feel warm. I suppose it's all the excitement." From the corner of her eye, she spied Margaret, inching purposefully closer. "Lord Royce, are you acquainted with Lady Margaret Warner? If not, let me introduce you."

Royce's smile was the essence of gentility. "Lady Margaret and I have met. How are you, my lady?" he inquired.

"Very well, thank you, my lord. And, yes, I do recall our introduction. It was last year, during my first Season." Margaret lowered her lashes and moistened her lips—ever so scarcely—prompting Breanna to wish she could master the fine art of flirting as well as her friend.

"Will you excuse us?" Lord Royce was asking Margaret, simultaneously gripping Breanna's elbow. "Our hostess deserves something cool to drink."

"Of course." Whatever disappointment Margaret was feeling she kept carefully in check.

Royce led Breanna across the room and over to the punch bowl. "Here." He offered her a glass. "This will help."

Help what? Breanna wanted to ask. Her hand trembling, she accepted the glass, drinking down the entire goblet in an attempt to cool her throat and calm her nerves.

"More?" Royce asked.

It was only fruit juice, flavored with a little Madeira, a bit of champagne, and an insignificant amount of brandy, Breanna reminded herself. She nodded, swallowing the second glass almost as quickly as she had the first, then reaching eagerly for a third.

She was three-quarters of the way through with that glass when Royce murmured, "I think you should take a few breaths before going for a fourth."

He sounded amused.

Breanna glanced up at him.

He *looked* amused.

"I suppose so." Breanna wondered what his amusement was based on: was it her nerves, her excessive thirst, or that stupid remark she'd made about having him?

She'd have to find out in order to make the appropriate amends.

"My lord," she began, grateful that the area they were standing in was unoccupied. The last thing she wanted was to make a fool of herself in front of all her guests. And as it was, she could already feel the warming effects of the punch drifting through her, making her question whether she'd underestimated the amount of liquor that was mixed in with the fruit.

"Royce," he amended.

Breanna's head snapped up. "Pardon me?"

"My name. My *given* name. It's Royce. Not my lord. Nor Lord Royce. Just Royce."

She studied his face: the bold features and hard, square jaw, the thick raven-black hair and broad forehead over the twin black slashes of brows and midnight blue eyes. And the decisive mouth that was used to issuing orders—and having them obeyed.

Her gaze lingered there, studying the subtle curve of his lips.

She wondered what it would be like to kiss him.

God help her, she was foxed.

She was also still staring.

"My name," he repeated, those incredible lips moving ever so slightly, his deep baritone huskier than it had been before. "It's Royce."

She tore her gaze from his mouth, met his hooded stare. "It wouldn't be proper for me to address you that way."

He leaned negligently against the wall, regarding her with a kind of lazy curiosity. "Why not?"

"We scarcely know each other."

"Anastasia calls me by my given name. And she knows me precisely the same amount of time as you do."

That comparison elicited a fond smile. "That's Stacie. She's far more unconventional than I."

"I think you're more unconventional than you realize—more unconventional than that conventional veneer of yours allows."

Breanna's eyes widened, and she gaped at him silently.

"Ah, a waltz," Royce commented as the strings began to play. He straightened, took her near-empty glass, and set it down on a tray. "May I have the honor of sharing it with you? Once you've recovered from your shock, that is." He extended his hand, his gaze darkening, looking directly into hers. "By the way, I don't blame all these men for fighting over you. You're breathtaking."

Instinctively, Breanna placed her fingers in his. "Yes," she managed, first answering his request for a dance. "And thank you."

"Splendid. And you're welcome." He guided her onto the dance floor, his fingers burning through the fine material of her glove—and her gown—as he led her into the waltz.

For the first time Breanna understood why some people considered this dance to be scandalous. Then again, most people hadn't drunk three glasses of Regent's punch on an empty stomach before attempting it. Still, it was unlike any dance she'd shared with any man this evening. The steps, the motions, even the proximity—those were all the same. And yet . . .

"So far, so good," Royce murmured.

Breanna blinked, finding it suddenly difficult to focus on his face. "What's so far, so good?"

A corner of his mouth lifted. "Your party. The fact that there haven't been any unwelcome guests all day, nor thus far tonight."

"Oh." She nodded, wishing the punch had done more to eliminate the knot of dread this topic incited.

Royce seemed to sense her distress, because he frowned. "I'm sorry. I didn't mean to bring up this subject. You've been living with it too much as it is."

"That's your job. Besides, it's not something I can forget."

"Maybe you should—at least for a while." Abruptly, Royce halted, capturing Breanna's elbow and drawing her off the dance floor.

She blinked, wishing she weren't so dizzy and puzzling over how two and a half glasses of punch could wreak so much havoc. "I felt fine before," she announced.

"It takes time for the spirits to hit." Royce guided her forward, and she felt a blast of cold air strike her face and arms. Abruptly, she realized they were standing just outside the French doors. "Come with me," he urged. He led her onto the balcony, nodding as they passed the guards. "Lady Breanna and I are going to get some air," he said quietly. "We won't go far. And I have my pistol."

"Fine, my lord. We're here," replied one guard, a big, burly fellow whose size alone was intimidating.

"Where are we going?" Breanna asked, stumbling a bit and wrapping her arms about herself as her teeth began to chatter. "It's cold."

"I know. The cold air is good for you." Even as he spoke, Royce was shrugging out of his coat. He wrapped it around her, covering her bare arms and enveloping her in a layer of woolen warmth. "Better?"

"Yes." She felt odd, like she was floating, gloriously numb to the anguish of the past weeks. "I think I'll drink more often," she announced.

Royce chuckled, snaked an arm about her waist as she teetered on her feet. "I wouldn't suggest it. You don't hold your spirits too well."

"I guess not. A bit of fruit punch and look what happens to me."

"Fruit punch?" Royce echoed dryly. "There are several bottles each of Madeira and champagne in Regent's punch, not to mention a pint of rum, and a quart of brandy. No wonder you're foxed." He scanned the area, led her over to a small rock garden that was lined with shrubs—enough to ensure privacy but not isolation—and came complete with a small, outdoor bench. "Sit."

"All right." Breanna sank down, leaning her head back and staring up at the sky. "The stars are waltzing."

"Really? Who's leading?"

She didn't smile. "You're mocking me. I'm not too foxed to realize that. I suppose I can't blame you."

"I'm not mocking you." He stood beside the bench, hands clasped behind him as he stared off into the darkness. "I'm teasing you. I want you to smile."

"I do smile."

"Not often enough."

She twisted around to look up at him. "And how would you know that?"

"The same way I know you're less conventional than you think. And the same way I know you need relief from the worry you've been carrying around."

"Oh." Breanna's heart gave another of those little skips, and she wondered if Royce realized how excruciatingly charismatic he was, how powerful an effect he had on women.

"Royce?" she tried, finding it wasn't so hard to say his name after all.

"Hmm?" His smile told her he approved.

"Margaret wants you." She blurted it out without preliminaries or warning—even to herself. "She asked me to put in a good word for her." Pausing, Breanna's brow furrowed in thought. "I should do that."

Another chuckle, this one husky. "Should you?"

"Yes. And quickly. Because Margaret has a great

deal of competition. Apparently, dozens—scores of women—want you." Even as she spoke, Breanna wondered who in God's name was saying those things.

"Are you one of them?"

Royce's question, uttered with a fierce but quiet intensity, penetrated her clouded mind, made it swim even more. Her head dropped back against the benchtop, and she stared blindly into the night, struggling to regain her senses. "Your eyes are that color," she noted in a whisper. "That same midnight blue. Almost black. Ebony with a sharp tinge of color—color that makes them all the more riveting. It's hard to look away from eyes like that."

"Breanna." He was standing in front of her. He caught her arms, drew her to her feet, and tilted up her chin with his forefinger. "Answer my question."

She wet her lips, felt the coat he'd enveloped her in slip from her shoulders, topple to the bench.

Odd, but she was no longer cold.

"It's not fair of you to ask me that," she murmured. "Not when I'm foxed."

"You'd never answer me if you weren't."

She couldn't deny the truth of that. "You're right." Stunned, she watched her own gloved fingers reach up, trace the hard curve of his jaw. "I wouldn't answer it. I also wouldn't do this." Her fingertips brushed his lips as she'd longed to do before, felt their warmth even through her glove. "Let me ask you the same question, my lord."

"Royce," he corrected her, his voice even huskier than it had been before. "And go ahead."

"Royce. Do you want me?"

Sparks glittered in his midnight eyes. "Yes, I want you. You have no idea how badly. More than I realized. Much more than I should." He turned his lips into her palm. "Does that answer your question?"

Mutely, she nodded.

He kissed the pulse at her wrist. "Then answer mine."

Breanna felt a rush of warmth that had nothing to do with the punch. "Yes, I want you," she admitted, intentionally giving him the exact words he'd given her. "You have no idea how badly. More than I realized. Much more than I should."

She saw the triumph flash across his face an instant before he gripped her arms, drew her to him.

"Good," he said fiercely.

He paused only to lift each of his hands to his mouth, yank off his gloves with his teeth, and toss them to the ground—all the while staring at her, devouring her with his gaze.

Then, he crushed his mouth to hers.

If the impact of his gaze was stunning, the impact of his kiss was fatal.

Breanna gasped, clutching at his waistcoat as Royce's lips ravaged hers, possessing her in a series of deep, drugging kisses she felt to the depths of her soul. Their mouths fused, parted, fused again, and this time his tongue penetrated her, awakening her to an intimacy she'd never imagined. She followed his lead, opened her mouth to his, shiveringly accepting his tongue's caresses, then eagerly returning them in a way only the blissful effects of alcohol would allow.

Royce growled deep in his chest, and his arms closed around her with staggering force, pulling her flush against him. He kissed her again, more deeply still, cupping her head in his hands and angling his mouth to allow his tongue deeper penetration.

"Put your arms around me." He breathed his command into her lips, kissing her senseless while she complied.

Realizing she'd been clenching at his waistcoat to keep from collapsing, Breanna unknotted her fists, glided her palms up the hard planes of his chest, feeling his muscles contract beneath the fine material of his shirt. His shoulders flexed beneath her fingertips, and she stroked his neck lightly with her forefinger, lingering there to feel the warmth of his skin.

Royce must have sensed her need, or perhaps even shared it. Another harsh sound vibrated in his chest, and he dragged his mouth from hers long enough to capture her hands in his, yank off her gloves in a few quick tugs. "Now," he muttered, flinging them aside and bringing her arms back around his neck. "Touch me. Let me feel your hands on my skin."

Longing welled up inside her, and she gave in to it, brushing her fingers against Royce's neck, then letting her palms discover the corded muscles and smooth flesh.

A jolt of reaction shot through him, and his eyes darkened to near black. "God," he rasped, stunned disbelief registering on his face. "My God." He bent to take her mouth again, his arms contracting like bow strings, bringing her up and into him. The thin silk of Breanna's gown did nothing to hide the hardening contours of his body, but rather than freezing with horror and shame, she felt herself melt, soften as if to fit more snugly against him.

The world was spinning out of control, and Breanna never wanted it to stop. She explored his throat, slipped her fingers beneath his cravat to feel the heat of his flesh, then glided them through his hair, savored the silky texture. Her own hair had come undone, she realized absently, sighing with pleasure as Royce's hands captured the toppling auburn waves, savored their texture before tangling in them, lifting them away so he could stroke the nape of her neck, the exposed skin of her back and shoulders. God, these sensations were too exciting to withstand—yet unthinkable to abandon.

She pressed closer.

"Breanna."

Something inside him seemed to snap. He cupped her bottom, crushed her lower body to his as he ravaged her mouth, his tongue rubbing against hers until she thought she would die. Her breasts were tingling with sensation, her entire body heavy with longing, liquid heat pulsing through her with each plunge of his tongue, each nudge of his hips.

Almost violently, Royce tore himself away, biting off a curse as he lowered her feet to the ground, steadied her against the bench—an arm's length away.

Gasping in air, they stared at each other.

"Are you all right?" Royce demanded, his fingers digging into her arms.

Reflexively, Breanna nodded, inclining her head in dazed noncomprehension. She was still awash with sensation, her mind and body reeling with discovery, her mouth clamoring for his.

"Royce?" She said his name in question, in bewilderment. When he didn't answer, she blinked to clear her head, to make out the expression on his face.

His handsome features were taut, strained, a muscle working furiously at his jaw. His midnight eyes were blazing with sparks, and his forehead was dotted with sweat, despite the evening's chill. His teeth were clenched, his breath coming in hard rasps, sending erratic puffs of vapor into the night sky. He looked livid—no, not livid, tormented, as if he were fighting some harsh internal battle.

An internal battle over her.

Another long minute passed, and the cold began sinking back into Breanna's bones, causing her teeth to chatter.

Royce swore again, snapped into action. He bent, scooped his coat off the bench and wrapped it around her, rubbing her arms to warm them. "I'm sorry," he said hoarsely. "I don't know what came over me. I know that's no excuse, but it's the only one I've got." His hands glided up to cup her face, and he inspected her closely, frowning as he surveyed her disheveled tresses. "How do we fix your hair?"

Automatically, Breanna's hands came up, discovering the extent of the damage. "I can manage." At his dubious expression, she forced a weak smile. "I've had practice."

That made his eyes narrow. "Have you now?"

She realized instantly how he'd perceived her remark. "Not *that* kind of practice." She swallowed. "My father insisted on my looking immaculate at all times. That wasn't easy to manage, especially when I was a child. I learned how to readjust my hair in record time. Watch." She stepped back, smoothing loose waves of hair back up, twisting and braiding them until they'd reformed their original sleek coronet.

"I'm impressed." Royce was studying her from beneath hooded lids.

"Now all I need are these." Breanna stooped, picked up her gloves, and gracefully tugged them on. "There. As good as new."

"Just like before," he said in an odd tone.

"No," she replied quietly, meeting his probing stare. "Not just like before."

Silence.

Breanna gazed up at him, taking in the warring emotions crossing his face as he struggled with whatever internal demons were plaguing him. She wouldn't ask him what they were—that wasn't her right. She, better than anyone, knew the need to keep one's thoughts, one's conflicts, even one's memories private.

Memories like the ones they'd just made.

Dimly, she wondered why she didn't feel the shame she knew she should. She had, after all, behaved like a total wanton. Yet she felt more alive, more exhilarated, than she'd ever felt in her life. Was that because the full extent of what she'd done hadn't had time to sink in yet, or was it because what she'd done had felt so incredibly right?

So magnificently, incredibly right.

"Stop looking at me like that," Royce commanded roughly. "Or you'll be back in my arms before you've caught your breath."

"What makes you think I don't want that?"

She heard him inhale sharply. "Breanna, you're playing with fire." A weighted pause. "We both are."

"Fire." Her gaze remained steady on his. "Yes, that's what it felt like."

"I *don't* want you to get burned."

"All right," she whispered. "Just singed then."

"Damn." He gripped her waist, pulled her closer and took her mouth in one long, blazing kiss. "You should be slapping me," he muttered, his thumbs just grazing the underside of her breasts. "Pulling away, calling me a bastard, and slapping me."

"Is that what I should be doing?" She shivered, totally focused on the tantalizing motion of his fingertips.

"Yes." The kiss deepened, his tongue moving slowly, seductively against hers. "You should." His thumbs shifted, brushed her hardened nipples once, then stroked them in slow, teasing circles.

"Oh, God." Breanna's knees were shaking, pinpoints of almost unendurable sensation shooting from her breasts to her loins. She shrugged Royce's coat off her shoulders, let it drop, then stepped closer, wrapped her arms around his neck.

Royce shuddered, his entire body going rigid as he shaped and caressed her breasts. Each caress grew hotter, more urgent, more intimate.

His trembling hands reached for the top of her bodice.

"Breanna." He lifted his head slightly, his eyes molten with desire. "If I touch you, I'll take you. Right here. Right now. On this bench. With the entire *ton* carousing just inside those walls." His hands made the return journey to her waist. "I've got to stop."

"I know." Her eyes slid shut, a shivering sigh escaping her. "I know."

Royce caught her chin between his fingers, and her lashes lifted to see him studying her face for a long, searching moment. "Are you going to remember this later?" he demanded. "When the Regent's punch has worn off?"

A soft smile touched Breanna's lips. "I'll remember it," she assured him. "And the punch wore off long ago."

11

❦

Stacie glanced over at the French doors for the tenth time in the last half hour, nearly sagging with relief when she saw her cousin stroll in on Lord Royce's arm.

Finally. Breanna was back. Back and safe.

Thank God. No one had hurt her.

Then again, her protector had been by her side.

Besieged by a rush of curiosity, Stacie met Breanna's eyes, spied a definite sparkle that hadn't been there before, and had to fight the urge to rush over and ask what had happened during that stroll in the glittering winter moonlight.

Winter. And Breanna had stayed outside for thirty minutes without her mantle.

Interesting. She didn't look at all cold.

"Stacie?" Damen's voice was tender, but his grip, tightening ever so fractionally about her waist, was telling her in no uncertain terms that she'd better stay put.

Damn, the man knew her so well.

"Yes?" She gave him a sweet, innocent look, turning her attention back to the small group surrounding them—a group that had, in the short minutes while her mind had wandered, expanded from Lord and Lady Dutton and the Earl and Countess of Geldrick to include the Viscount Crompton and Lord Arthur Landow.

"The viscount was just commenting on how radiant you look," Damen prompted.

Anastasia felt a twinge of guilt when she saw the concern furrowing Lord Crompton's brow—and Lord Landow's, for that matter. Like Dutton and Geldrick, both these men had strong monetary ties to the House of Lockewood and both were uneasy about offending Damen. True, they'd rejected her request for financial backing last summer—as had every other businessman she'd approached. Still, that did nothing to shed doubt on their integrity, only on their open-mindedness. Like all Damen's clients, these were honorable men—the viscount a retired military general who'd served in the Napoleonic Wars, and Lord Landow a wealthy manufacturer whose products were sold both here and abroad.

By nature, Stacie wasn't cruel. Needling these men for missing out on a superb business opportunity was one thing. Forcing them to humble themselves, as they had been doing since the party began, was quite another. Enough was enough. The last thing she wanted was to add insult to injury by making Lord Crompton think he was being snubbed.

"Forgive me, my lord," she told him, relieved to see the intense consternation on his face ease a bit. "I appreciate your gracious compliment." Her mind raced, and she quickly came up with the ideal explanation for her rudeness *and* for Damen's constant presence at her side—a reason they'd like far better than their current belief: namely, that he was looming over them to retaliate, to make them squirm for offending his wife.

Sometimes the truth came in handy. Now was one of those times.

She shot Lord Crompton a grateful look. "Your kind words couldn't have come at a better time—especially when I know I look anything but radiant. I haven't slept in weeks, nor have I kept down a meal. That's actually why I missed hearing what you said. I was feeling light-headed."

Crompton now looked concerned. "Have you seen a physician?"

"Every day on the ship home," she replied with a smile. "Much to his dismay." She inclined her head, turned her smile up at Damen, whose twinkle told her he knew exactly what she was doing—and that he approved. "My illness is for the most wonderful of reasons. Damen and I are expecting a child."

"That's splendid." The viscount relaxed, raised his glass. "Congratulations to you both."

"Yes, congratulations," Landow echoed, as pleased by the congeniality of her tone as he was by her news. "What a delightful announcement." His good wishes—and his gaze—were clearly directed at Damen.

"I agree," Damen responded, drawing Stacie closer to his side. "I'm elated."

"He's also exceedingly anxious and protective," Stacie confided, tossing a you-understand glance at Lady Geldrick, in the hopes of eliciting the countess's support. It was well known that she and the earl were very much in love, and that she had gifted her husband with their second son just five months ago.

"That poor doctor couldn't wait to see the last of us," Stacie added, still speaking to Lady Geldrick. "Damen paid him three visits a day to verify that the symptoms I was experiencing were normal. And, as you can see, he refuses to budge from my side."

"Well, of course he does." It was Lord Geldrick who chimed in first, nodding vigorously and giving Damen a look of genuine sympathy. "It's your first child. I don't blame you a bit for your concern, Sheldrake."

"You shouldn't," his wife teased, her eyes twinkling. "You acted the same way when I was with child—especially the first time." She leaned forward, touched Stacie's arm. "Best wishes to you both. And don't worry about feeling ill. The sensation will pass in a few months. After that, you'll be hungry enough to eat three banquets a day."

"I'm relieved to hear that." As she said it, Stacie realized it was true. She also realized how good it felt to speak with another woman about her condition—something she hadn't yet done. In fact, she'd been so worried over the killer stalking her and Breanna that she hadn't stopped to give much thought to the more normal concerns surrounding pregnancy.

As if on cue, a wave of light-headedness accosted her, made her teeter on her feet.

"Stacie?" Damen felt the motion, whipped about to face her. "What's wrong?" Lines of worry tightened his face. "You're white as a sheet."

"I'm fine—really." She blinked to clear her head. "Just a bit dizzy."

"We're sitting down." He was already guiding her away from the group. "If you'll all excuse us."

"Certainly," Lord Crompton said, backing away to let them pass. "Tend to your wife, Sheldrake."

Damen intended to do just that. He drew Stacie over to an airy corner of the room, then eased her into a chair. Turning toward the hallway, he signaled Wells with his eyes.

The butler was beside them in an instant.

"Miss Stacie? Are you ill?" he demanded.

"No, Wells, just dizzy." Stacie wished the room would right itself.

"You've eaten almost as little as Miss Breanna did today," Wells admonished with a frown. "And *you're* eating for two. I'll bring you a plate of food."

"Good idea," Damen answered for her. "And something cool to drink. *Not* laden with spirits."

"Of course not, my lord." Wells sniffed. "I wouldn't think of it."

"Of course you wouldn't. Forgive me, Wells." Damen raked a hand through his hair. "I guess I'm more unnerved than I realized."

"I understand. No apology is necessary."

"Would you both stop staring at me as if I'm on the verge of death?" Stacie demanded, looking from one man to the other. "The guests will start thinking I have some rare disease."

"I'll be very discreet," Wells assured her. He glanced about the room, took in the merrymaking. "Believe me, no one has even noticed us. They haven't any idea what we're talking about."

Even as he spoke, Lady Dutton was passing the news of Stacie's pregnancy on to the Marchioness of Radebrook.

By the time Wells arrived back from the refreshment table, there wasn't a guest in the room who didn't know that the Marquess and Marchioness of Sheldrake's first child was on its way.

"I'm so glad we're being discreet," Stacie said in amusement, after the twelfth person had congratulated her. "Wells, you should know by now there's no keeping a secret in the *ton*."

"Maybe it's better this way," Damen muttered purposefully to his wife, simultaneously smiling his thanks at the retreating Duke of Maywood, who'd come over to offer his best wishes. "At least the guests are keeping you so busy you can't dash off to interrogate Breanna. That *was* where you were headed when you nearly collapsed at my feet, wasn't it?"

"Yes." Anastasia knew better than to insult her husband by lying. "Or rather, I was *considering* inching my way over to Breanna." Her curious gaze returned to where her cousin was still chatting with Royce. Breanna was obviously unaware that Stacie was feeling light-headed, or that the room was abuzz with news of her near-swoon. In fact, Breanna was unaware that anything out of the ordinary had taken place. Odd, considering how attuned to each other she and Stacie were. It would take a major distraction to preoccupy Breanna to the point where she wouldn't sense that an event involving Stacie had taken place.

Evidently, Royce Chadwick was such a distraction.

"Damen, surely you noticed—"

"I noticed." Damen followed his wife's stare. "But I think you're reading far too much into it. Royce is keeping an eye on Breanna—a practical idea under the circumstances. He knows I'm attached to your side for the night. You need no further protection. Breanna, on the other hand, is alone. So, he's serving as her sentry."

"Indeed," Wells agreed with a sniff. "There could be no other explanation for it."

"A sentry." Stacie rolled her eyes at the two men. "I see. And as her *sentry*, Royce took her for a half-hour walk on a night that's so cold no one else would dare venture out and he'd therefore be assured of complete privacy."

"No," Damen countered. "Knowing Royce, he probably took her for a walk to try to keep her mind off her anxiety. Breanna's coping with an enormous emotional burden. Not only is she grappling with her own fears, she's terrified for you and the babe."

"That's true." A pained expression crossed Wells's lined face. "Miss Breanna feels responsible—unfounded though her guilt might be—for jeopardizing you all. She feels that if she'd never taken that shot—"

"I'd be dead right now," Stacie stated flatly. "Breanna saved my life. I've told her over and over again that she's not responsible for the threats of a madman. But she won't be appeased until he's found and stopped. Nevertheless..." Stacie broke off, still studying Breanna pensively. "None of this has any bearing on what's happening here tonight. After all, worry wouldn't bring a glow to Breanna's cheeks, nor would her overly acute sense of responsibility cause tendrils of her hair to topple."

Wells frowned, puzzled. He polished his spectacles, then shoved them back on, peering worriedly toward Breanna. "Miss Breanna's hair looks fine to me."

"*Fine?* Wells, you know Breanna. Her hair is never fine. It's perfect. Except now. Even from this distance, I can distinctly see a few curls sagging at her nape." Stacie arched a brow, first at Wells, then at Damen. "What shall we attribute it to?" She paused for effect, then snapped her fingers in mock deduction. "I know—the wind!"

Damen's lips twitched, as much at Wells's vigilant glower as at Stacie's observation. "You made your point. Fine, maybe there is something going on between those two. But whatever it is, you're not going to find out about it until you've eaten and drunk every drop of that." He gestured toward her plate and glass.

"Whatever you say, my lord." She gave him a beatific smile and returned to her refreshment. "Stop glaring, Wells," she berated gently, sipping at her punch. "Breanna's a grown woman. She's entitled to share a chaste embrace with an enigmatic man—especially when that man is one we've entrusted to safeguard her life. Besides, aren't you the one who wanted Breanna to find someone special?"

"I didn't have a reckless womanizer in mind."

"If Royce is a womanizer, he's abandoned that trait tonight." Stacie took a small bite of her lemon tart. "He hasn't so much as danced with another woman. Only Breanna. As for reckless . . ." Another bite. "I wouldn't describe personal, full-time guard service as reckless behavior, would you?" She shot Wells a look. "I know you worry about Breanna. But give Royce a chance. He might surprise you." With that, she polished off her tart, dabbing at her mouth with a napkin.

"Ah, word about your condition just reached Breanna," Damen noted, watching Lady Dutton insert her plump figure between Breanna and Royce, then begin chatting excitedly. "Let's see, Breanna now knows you're with child, which she already knew, and she's about to find out that you're dizzy."

As if on cue, Breanna's head came up, and she whipped about to face Stacie.

Her cousin gestured to her that she was fine, that she was eating, and that Breanna could safely go about her business.

Visibly relieved, Breanna concurred, turning back to Lady Dutton—*and* deliberately ignoring the questioning look that flitted across Stacie's face as she glanced meaningfully from Breanna to Royce and back again.

"I'll have to get my answers later," Stacie concluded with a sigh. "Breanna's too private to confide in me during the ball." Shelving her curiosity, Stacie watched Lady Dutton move on to the next group to share her news. "I'm so glad we're providing the evening entertainment," she muttered. "My pregnancy is the topic of conversation among our guests."

"That's not necessarily bad," Damen replied, cradling her gloved hand between his. "At least they're discussing something other than the murders Bow Street is investigating. *That* topic has dominated the party thus far, and dampened the mood of the ball. Good news must feel like a welcome balm to everyone."

"The situation is terrifying," Stacie murmured, placing her empty glass and plate on the tray of a passing footman. "This is the third murder in a fortnight. Certainly Bow Street can't still suspect the men's wives. Three wives—three *young* wives scarcely older than I am—capable of murdering their husbands? I doubt that's possible."

"Yet all three women have disappeared," Wells reminded her.

"Maybe they were kidnapped," Stacie suggested.

"Possibly." Damen pursed his lips thoughtfully. "Then again, if they were kidnapped, where are the ransom notes? And who would the kidnapper expect to extort money from if the husbands in question are all dead?"

The assassin brushed by in time to hear Sheldrake's last comment, and a hint of a smile touched his lips at the knowledge that he was responsible for Sheldrake's bafflement and for the fear pervading the *ton*.

Good, he thought, heading down the hall, away from the ball and toward the servants' quarters. The marquess was as baffled as the detectives, and *he* was an exceedingly intelligent man, far smarter than the Bow Street runners. So, if he couldn't figure out the mystery of those noblemen's deaths, neither would they.

Then again, Sheldrake wouldn't be contemplating the London murders for long. The deaths of three strangers would soon pale in comparison to his own loss. In a matter of days, maybe weeks, the poor man would have his own, very personal, grief to deal with.

Pity Sheldrake had to be involved. Ah well. He'd married the chit *and* made things worse by falling in love with her and now filling her with his child. He'd have to suffer the consequences. He'd have to nurse a broken heart and reacquaint himself with the life of a bachelor.

Because Anastasia Lockewood would die. The babe she was carrying would die.

And then that bitch of a cousin of hers would die.

The assassin paused when he reached the flight of stairs at the darkened rear of the house. It was deserted.

Excellent.

He took the steps purposefully, but not so as to

call attention to himself—just in case anyone was watching.

He rounded the second-floor landing, and headed directly for Lady Breanna's bedchamber, still thinking about the snatches of conversation he'd overheard between Sheldrake and his wife.

It wasn't a shock that, with this third murder, the *ton*—and Bow Street itself—would begin to doubt the merit of their original theory that the wives of the murdered noblemen were responsible. The killings were adding up. Only a dolt would believe that these women had *all* killed their husbands. Instead, Bow Street would doubtless assume that the three women were being held for ransom.

Which was another reason he'd abandoned his plan to use Knox's death to his advantage—a decision he'd made even before discovering the victim had only sons. Knox was a working-class fellow, a security guard with a modest income. If a woman in his family were to suddenly disappear like the noblemen's young wives, it would contradict the notion that ransom was involved. Not to mention, Knox's murder had taken place too close to Medford Manor. And if his death were linked with the others, someone might get suspicious and tie the crimes to the threats Lady Breanna had received.

Someone like Royce Chadwick.

The assassin felt a warning tremor ripple through him.

Seeing Chadwick here had been an unexpected surprise—and not a welcome one. The man was clever— far brighter than everyone at Bow Street. He was also a rebel, certainly not the type to attend holiday gatherings. So why was he here?

At first, he'd attributed Chadwick's attendance to his friendship with Sheldrake, not to mention the fact that he was still poking around the *ton* to see if he could uncover information on Ryder's bastard daughter. Observations of Chadwick throughout the day seemed to support that theory. Sticking close by him during the day's events—the morning ride, the mid-day meal, the afternoon card games—and listening closely to what he discussed had yielded no cause for alarm. Chadwick's topics of conversation were predictable: business ventures, the likely contenders at Newmarket this spring, the trip he'd taken to India. Interdispersed with the discussions were frank inquiries of the men he had yet to formally question—inquiries about whether or not they knew anyone who'd employed a chamber maid matching Ryder's paramour's description.

It seemed Chadwick's intentions were innocuous, at least so far as *he* was concerned.

But tonight, watching the way he hovered around Breanna Colby . . .

Could Chadwick be here for another reason?

Could he be here to keep an eye out for him—the killer threatening Anastasia and Breanna's lives?

No, he silently concluded, reaching Lady Breanna's room. Royce Chadwick hunted down missing people; he didn't investigate murders. Besides, after seeing the heated way he stared at Lady Breanna at tonight's ball, it was obvious that if Chadwick had any other motive for being here, it was to get Lady Breanna into his bed.

As for the lady in question, she seemed interested enough. Maybe that explained her damnably good spirits.

The familiar anger knotted his gut.

He loathed her for her laughter, for her vitality, for her well-being. He loathed her for still being alive.

But that wouldn't last long.

He would kill her now if his hatred had its way. Fortunately, his brilliant mind and iron discipline kept him in check. The stage hadn't been properly set. Unfinished business remained—namely, Anastasia Lockewood. More important, Breanna hadn't suffered nearly enough. Not *nearly* enough. Tonight had demonstrated that. She was so infernally happy—greeting her guests, drinking her punch, strolling outside with Chadwick.

All that gaiety would vanish the instant she walked into her room tonight.

With that, he focused on the business at hand.

Pausing outside her bedchamber door, he scanned the hallway. Deserted. The guests were at the ball. Ladies Breanna and Anastasia were otherwise occupied. The guards were safeguarding the estate from intruders.

But he had no need to intrude.

On that ironic thought, he turned the door handle and crossed the threshold. Shutting the door behind him, he reached swiftly into his pocket to extract his little surprises.

The room carried her scent—sweet, floral—the lingering fragrance of her customary perfume.

He could picture her, cheeks flushed with excitement as she'd readied herself for her ball. Lighthearted, enthused.

She'd be neither when she went to bed tonight.

If she went to bed. She wouldn't be able to sleep. She'd feel violated, numb with shock, quaking with terror.

The image was exhilarating.

He crossed over to her nightstand, having decided it was the best place to leave his tokens. Not as intimate as the dressing table, perhaps, but far closer to the bed, and more visible from the doorway. Illuminated by a single lamp, his gifts would render their full impact the moment she walked in. They would make her feel all the more vulnerable—draped across her nightstand, just brushing her bedcovers.

With a bitter smile, he went to work, arranging the reminders just so.

Five minutes later, he let himself out of Lady Breanna's bedchamber and retraced his steps to the ball.

He was just about to enter the ballroom when he heard the argument.

Not an argument exactly, but a heated debate. Quiet but intense. Fervent enough to capture one's attention—if one was listening. And he was listening, especially given the repeated use of the name "Lord Royce."

The dispute was taking place in the front hallway. And the men involved were Wells, the efficient Colby butler, and Hibbert, Royce Chadwick's trusted manservant.

Whatever this discussion pertained to, it was worth eavesdropping.

He meandered toward the entranceway, threading his way through the tangle of guests moving in the opposite direction. Alone, he hovered near the staircase, an inconspicuous guest enjoying a bit of solitary time at a crowded party. Then, in one thoroughly unobtrusive motion, he slipped into an alcove behind the staircase. He pressed close to the wall so as to see but not be seen.

"I run this household," Wells was stating flatly. "When a message arrives, *I* deliver it."

"And *I* work for Lord Royce," Hibbert retaliated icily. "When a message arrives addressed to him, *I* deliver it."

"Deliver it, or read it?"

"Both."

The two servants glowered silently at each other, each standing his ground, yet each managing to retain the requisite amount of composure.

"I'll take full responsibility for my actions," Hibbert pronounced with arrogant certainty. "I—and *only* I—know this is what my employer expects of me. If you're so disturbed by my conduct, I suggest you go and summon him. But in the meantime, I intend to see that letter."

"As you wish." Wells's jaw was clenched so tight it looked as if it might snap. He slapped the missive into Hibbert's hand and walked around him. "I'll summon Lord Royce at once."

"Fine." A rustle of paper as Hibbert slit open the letter. "I respect your principles. I'm equally principled—and equally loyal to my employer. As you'll soon find out."

"We shall see." Wells marched by, heading directly to the ballroom, presumably weaving his way over to the French doors.

Two or three minutes passed.

Abruptly, Royce Chadwick emerged, preceding Wells, and crossing directly over to where Hibbert stood, openly reading the contents of the letter.

"What is it?" he asked his manservant quietly.

"One of your avenues paid off." Hibbert turned to face his employer, his tone no lower than normal.

Clearly, whatever was in that missive was not of a confidential nature.

"Which one? The list of noblemen I gave you to follow up on, or the list of wealthy matrons who help out abandoned women?"

"The latter. It's Lady Barton, the seventy-year-old matron you suggested contacting in Berkshire. She's been abroad, and only just returned. One of our men spoke with her. She remembers Glynnis Martin, went on and on about how pretty she was, how desolate she was left alone with her babe. It seems Lady Barton sent her to an elderly dowager's home—a Dowager Duchess . . ." Hibbert glanced at the message, "of Pearson."

"And the babe?"

"She went with her mother. Glynnis was hired as a paid companion. As far as Lady Barton knows, she and her daughter are still living at Pearson Manor in Berkshire."

"Excellent." Chadwick was triumphant. "This party will be over tomorrow night. I'll ride to the duchess's home straight from here. With any luck, I'll have news of Ryder's daughter for him by the first of the year."

"Fine work, my lord."

"Thanks to Lady Barton." Chadwick clapped Hibbert on the shoulder. "Come. This calls for a drink."

"In the ballroom?"

"Of course. Where else?" Chadwick paused to glance at Wells, who was looming behind them like a vigilant sentry, far enough away to ensure their privacy, but nearby enough to assert his position in the household—and to clearly demonstrate his disapproval over Hibbert's behavior.

"It's all right, Wells," Chadwick assured him. "I appreciate your diligence, but Hibbert was following my orders. He's instructed to read my mail. He also knew I was expecting this letter. So you can relax."

Wells nodded, although his back remained stiff. "As you wish, my lord."

"Would you care to join Hibbert and me for a drink?"

The butler cleared his throat. "No, thank you." He slanted a purposeful look at Hibbert. "I wouldn't feel right."

Chadwick shrugged. "Suit yourself." He gestured toward the ballroom. "Let's go, Hibbert."

Hastily, Wells interceded, taking an inadvertent step to block Hibbert's way. "My lord," he addressed Chadwick respectfully. "It really isn't appropriate—"

"I realize that." Chadwick was already in motion, his heels echoing as he bypassed Wells and headed toward the party. "But as you've probably heard about me, I rarely give a damn what's appropriate and what's not. I'm going into the ballroom for a drink. And Hibbert is joining me." He paused, angled about to face Wells. "My invitation still stands. You can make it a threesome."

"I think not, my lord."

"Fine. Until later then." Chadwick continued on his way.

Hibbert gave a dry chuckle as he followed behind his employer, ignoring Wells's censuring glare. "I don't expect the guests to be any more pleased than Wells is."

"Probably not. They'll probably be outraged. But they won't be surprised."

"And our hosts?"

Chadwick paused again, this time mere yards away from the stairway alcove. "Damen's known me for years. He won't even flinch. As for Anastasia, she might just applaud. And Breanna . . ." A poignant pause as Chadwick contemplated the woman he'd been squiring about all evening. "Breanna will be as gracious as she always is—no matter how taken aback she might be. And behind that proper veneer, she'll be smiling."

Maybe, the assassin acknowledged silently from his hiding place. *But she won't be smiling for long.*

12

$\mathcal{B}$reanna climbed the stairs, feeling equal measures of exhaustion and exhilaration.

The remaining hours of the ball had passed by in a haze. Through most of that time, she'd longed for nothing but the solace of her room. She needed to ponder exactly what had happened between her and Royce tonight and, more importantly, exactly what it meant.

She might be inexperienced, but she wasn't naive. Nor was she stupid. What she and Royce had shared had, by absolute standards, amounted to no more than a very heated kiss, something Royce might indulge in with countless women. But she *didn't* indulge in it with countless men. She'd never even yearned for that intimate a contact, never imagined herself capable of it.

Not until tonight.

So while Royce might have already dismissed the encounter, summed it up as the result of one slightly tipsy woman falling prey to his charms, she couldn't be so blasé.

She'd realized from the start that she was drawn to him, that he affected her in a way no man ever had. That in itself had been an intriguing discovery. But out there tonight, clasped in his arms, she hadn't even known herself. She'd been alive, uninhibited, hungry for more. What's more, now that reason had resumed, she still couldn't seem to summon one iota of remorse or shame.

Confusion, on the other hand—*that* she was feeling in abundance.

Understanding Royce's feelings, his motives, was imperative.

But more imperative was understanding her own.

She gazed longingly down the hall at Damen and Stacie's room, wishing Stacie was still awake to talk, that her curiosity had won out over her fatigue. Normally, it would have. But pregnancy was taking its toll and, after a long night of merrymaking, she'd been exhausted. Despite her protests, Damen had taken her up to bed several hours ago.

Even through drooping eyelids, she'd cast one questioning look after another at Breanna, obviously dying to interrogate her about what had happened.

That Stacie knew something had happened wasn't an issue. Awareness had been written all over her face—at least enough so that Breanna could see it.

What was Stacie thinking? How would she interpret Royce's behavior, and his reaction to Breanna's? How would she explain Breanna's uncharacteristic actions? What advice would she offer?

Breanna would have to wait to find out.

Glancing at the clock on the mantel in the hall, she sighed. It was almost 4 A.M. The last of the guests had retired over an hour ago, followed shortly thereafter by Wells. She'd feigned going to bed just so he would do the same. The poor man was spent and, knowing him, he intended to be at his post by eight o'clock in the morning—just in case he was needed. Royce and Hibbert had gone up at about the same time, deep in discussion over the letter they'd received earlier.

It was just as well. Breanna wasn't sure how to act around Royce after that ardent embrace they'd shared, and she was almost relieved when his attention was diverted by news of Lord Ryder's daughter.

She had to smile, recalling the *ton*'s reaction when Royce had strolled into the ballroom, Hibbert at his side. Dozens of flies could have found homes in the gaping mouths throughout the room. Even Lady Dutton had stopped gossiping for a full minute, a rarity indeed. Breanna had caught Stacie's eye, seen the twinkle there. And, beside her, Damen, his lips quirking as if to say: that's Royce for you.

As for Royce, he was clearly aware of the stir he was causing. It was obvious from the arrogance of his stance. Equally clear from that stance was the fact that he didn't give a damn *who* his actions offended.

Good for you, Breanna had found herself thinking. She could only hope that Hibbert's boldness would rub off on Wells. If anyone deserved to be treated like an equal, to *demand* such equality, it was Wells, who was more a father figure than a butler.

In any case, Royce had paused only to find her with his gaze, ensure she was all right. Then, he and Hibbert had launched into a discussion of Lord Ryder and locating his daughter. Between that conversation and the various colleagues who waylaid Royce for other reasons—having not seen him since his return from India—*and* the five or six women who inserted themselves in his path, insisting on saying hello, Royce was monopolized for the rest of the ball.

On the other hand, there were at least a half-dozen times when Breanna had felt his compelling stare find her, penetrate her with its intensity . . .

By three o'clock the house had fallen quiet, hushed but for the remaining footmen who were scurrying about, cleaning up and readying the manor for the new day.

Left alone, Breanna had wandered down the hall to the sitting room, curling up on the settee and savoring the darkness, just thinking over the turbulent events of the past fortnight. All that had happened, all that was still happening—the threatening package, Stacie's pregnancy, the murders plaguing Bow Street and paralyzing the *ton*, and now Royce Chadwick in all his complexity—was enough to make her head spin.

Having resolved nothing, she'd gone up to bed.

She reached the door to her room just as the clock chimed four. Everyone was asleep. Even her lady's maid, who had been instructed to retire early, given how late the ball was expected to run.

The manor was silent.

All the guests would sleep until noon, she reflected, turning the door handle. All but Stacie. Thankfully, Stacie would be up and about by ten. Sooner, if her lurching stomach demanded the chamber pot. Then they could talk.

Contenting herself with that fact, Breanna eased open the door, and shut it softly behind her. As always, she'd left the lamp on her nightstand turned down low, offering her more than enough light to guide her way. She moved directly toward it, intending to turn it up higher while she undressed.

She took one step and froze.

A white chemise lay draped across the nightstand, its lacy edge just touching the bed. A dark splotch of color stained its center, and an unfamiliar object sat alongside it.

Dread curling inside her like dark tendrils of smoke, Breanna walked over, cautiously placing one foot in front of the other as she approached the nightstand.

Her hand was shaking as she turned up the lamp.

Light flooded the nightstand, and Breanna let out a low cry, her hands flying reflexively to her mouth as if to stifle the sound.

The chemise was hers. The dark splotch marring the garment was red. Bright, vivid red.

Blood red.

Her horrified gaze shifted, took in the other object atop the nightstand.

It was a figure, a porcelain figure. At least it had been, before it was defaced. She bent over to examine it more closely, unable to bring herself to touch it. The figure wasn't one of hers. She'd never seen it before. It depicted two women standing on an elaborate pedestal base.

Red smears had been painted on both women's bodices near their hearts, and expressions of torment had been etched onto their faces.

Violently etched.

She sank onto the bed, her knees shaking too badly to support her. He'd been here. *Here.* In her room, going through her dresser. He'd taken her undergarment, tampered with it in a vile, sick manner. And the statue. Obviously meant to symbolize her and Stacie. Shot, bleeding.

Dying.

Oh God.

Breanna fought the urge to scream, to race down the hall and awaken Stacie and Damen. There was nothing they could do. Not tonight. Whoever this madman was, he was long gone. He'd taken advantage of the chaos generated by the party and found a way to slip into the manor.

How had he known which room was hers?

She knew the answer to that even as she asked herself the question.

He'd been watching the house. For weeks, probably. And now he'd gotten inside. Inside and upstairs. To her room.

She couldn't stay here another minute.

Jumping to her feet, Breanna nearly ripped the door off its hinges, then bolted out. Wild-eyed, she surveyed the empty hallway, reminding herself again and again that there was no one here. Not now.

Another quick glance toward Stacie's room.

And another dismissal of the notion to awaken her.

Tomorrow morning was more than enough time for Stacie to hear about this. Nothing could be gained by alerting her now—nothing except a selfishly attained peace of mind for Breanna. And that she wouldn't allow. Her peace of mind wouldn't begin to offset Stacie's distress. She'd have to face this soon enough anyway. She needed her sleep. So did the babe. It wasn't as if she was in any immediate danger. For tonight, she was safe. Damen was with her, their door was bolted, and no one could get in. Even if someone was still lurking in the house. Which, given the intelligence of the assassin, who knew the number of guards lying in wait for him, was doubtful.

No, awakening Stacie was out of the question.

So until morning, this problem belonged to Breanna. She'd never felt more alone in her life.

Wells. Maybe she'd awaken Wells.

Who would do—what? Comfort her, just as Stacie would. But nothing more. He'd have no better idea than she how to handle this intrusion. And he was nearly as exhausted as Stacie.

Which left no one to turn to.

No one except Royce.

His name sprang to mind, eliciting a surge of relief so acute, Breanna sagged against the wall. Royce. He was here. He'd predicted this very thing might occur. He'd know what to do.

With that thought, she gathered up her skirts, nearly running down the hall, veering around the corner to the wing that housed his chambers. Unlike the other guests, Royce hadn't been assigned to the guest wing. He'd suggested Wells put him and Hibbert in the main section of the house, just in case events happened that warranted their attention—attention he'd want to provide without alerting the other guests.

Thank heavens he'd thought of that.

Reaching the door of his room, Breanna knocked. *Please*, she prayed. *Let him be in there. Let him be awake, or at least hear my knock and wake up. Please.*

As if in answer to her prayers, a muffled voice called out, "Yes?"

"Royce . . . it's Breanna." She wet her lips with the tip of her tongue, fighting for some measure of composure. "I need to see you. Now. It's urgent."

"I'll be right there." There was nothing muffled about his tone now. He sounded awake and completely alert.

Breanna heard rustling sounds, an indication that Royce was donning his clothes. Although, at the moment, she wouldn't care if he walked out in his nightshirt. As long as he walked out.

As if on cue, the bolt turned, and the door swung open.

Royce stared at her intensely, his dark hair tousled, his shirt half-buttoned, tucked haphazardly into his breeches. "What's wrong?" he demanded, his gaze tightening with concern as he took in her ashen expression and trembling hands.

"My room," she said, amazed that her voice could sound so calm when her insides were twisting. "He was there. Sometime tonight. While I was at the ball. He left me some . . . things. I couldn't bear touching them. I couldn't even bear staying in the room, knowing he'd been there. I didn't know what to do, who to tell. So I came here."

"You did the right thing." Royce retreated into his chamber, opened his nightstand, and yanked out a pistol. "Then Anastasia doesn't know?"

Mutely, Breanna shook her head. "I didn't want to frighten her. I came straight to you."

"Good." Royce returned to her side, silently assessing her emotional state. "Breanna, are you all right?"

"Yes. I'm fine."

Without thinking, he caught her shoulders, tugged her against him. "You don't have to be so bloody strong," he muttered, brushing his lips through her hair. "You're afraid. You have reason to be."

She swallowed, fighting the urge to sink into his strength, fighting the more unnerving urge to cry.

She'd been taught since childhood never to fall apart in front of others. And she never did.

Why then, did she long to now?

"He won't hurt you," Royce said in a low, hard tone. "I won't let him."

Those simple words meant more to her than she could possibly explain. "Thank you," she whispered.

Royce drew back, tilted up her chin so he could see her face. "Would you be able to go back to your room if I went with you? I need to see what he left. I also need to look over the room, just in case he left any clues. And you're the only one who can tell me if something looks different in any way—added, moved, or touched."

Slowly, Breanna sucked in her breath, then nodded. "Yes. If that's what I need to do, I can do it."

An odd emotion glinted in Royce's eyes—something akin to admiration and a touch of amazement. "Good. Let's go." He paused, his knuckles drifting lightly over her cheek. "I'll be right beside you. You won't be alone."

Another nod, this one shaky. "I'll remember that."

He led the way, his pistol clutched by his side, Breanna right behind him. She could feel her insides clench tighter and tighter as they neared her bedchamber. She slowed, longed to stop. But she refused to give in to the impulse. Royce was right. This inspection was essential.

As if reading her mind, Royce glanced behind him. Studying her face, he reached out to capture her hand, gently leading her the remaining steps to her room.

They stopped in the open doorway.

Breanna crossed the threshold, and prickles of fear shot up her spine. The room she'd always regarded as a sanctuary was now a place to fear. Numbly, she wondered if she'd ever feel safe within it again.

"They're on the nightstand," she told Royce, halting just inside. "Both of them."

He gripped her elbow, drew her into the room. "I'm here," he said softly.

"I know," she replied, understanding just what Royce's assurances were meant to convey, and why he was offering them. "And you need me to be here, too. I have to come in—*all* the way in—or I can't help you, and you can't do your job." She forced herself to move deeper into her chambers, walking toward her bed as if in a dream. "There." She pointed at the nightstand, her head swimming with reaction. "Those are the things he left me."

Royce went ahead, examining the chemise and porcelain figure in the glow of lamplight. His expression was intense, never changing as he inspected the tainted objects more closely. "This chemise—is it yours?"

"Yes. I recognize the buttons. It's mine."

A nod. "The color is only paint. Not blood."

"I realize that. And the women are only porcelain, not human. But the message is clear nonetheless."

Royce's mouth thinned into a grim line. "It certainly is." He straightened, scanning the rest of the quarters. "Was anything else disturbed?"

Breanna studied the room as closely as her dazed mind would allow. She slid open each bureau drawer, checked inside her wardrobe and nightstand, even scrutinized each and every one of her porcelain figures. "Nothing else was touched—nothing I can detect."

"And nothing's missing?"

"No." Breanna crossed over to her desk, picked up the sketch pad and flipped through it. None of the drawings of Stacie's house had been tainted, no pages torn away. Beside the pad, her pile of unrelated sketches was stacked neatly, just as it had been earlier.

She eased open the desk drawers. Each one was precisely as she'd left it, all her quills and pencils intact. "It looks as if he only took the chemise."

"What about the statue? Was it originally on your nightstand? Or did he remove it from the bureau or fireplace mantel in order to place it beside the chemise?"

"Neither. It isn't mine. I've never seen it before in my life."

That detail seemed to disturb Royce more than anything else. His dark brows drew together, and his eyes narrowed in troubled concentration.

"What is it?" Breanna asked. "Why does that upset you so much?"

Royce opened his mouth to reply, then hesitated, reluctance written all over his face.

"Please, Royce," she requested quietly. "Don't hide things from me. I don't want to be protected. I want to know. I *need* to know. Why are you bothered by the fact that that porcelain figure isn't mine?"

His sober gaze met hers. "Because the fact that he chose to bring such a statue here, to use it to make his point, is too perfect to be a coincidence. He obviously knew you collect porcelain figures."

"How would he know . . . ?" All the color drained from Breanna's face. "You think he was here before this? That he'd invaded my room before tonight?"

An unwilling nod. "My guess is, yes. It would explain the appearance of this statue. It would also explain how he found the time to deface your chemise. He wouldn't want to carry paint with him, nor would he want to linger an instant longer than necessary. So he didn't. He probably slipped into your room at an earlier date—most likely before the additional guards were assigned—took the chemise, and left. He did his handiwork on it at home, bought and defiled the statue, then placed both things on your nightstand tonight. He wouldn't need more than five minutes to accomplish that."

Breanna could feel her insides lurch, and for one horrible moment she was afraid she was going to be sick. "He *was* here," she whispered. Awareness dawned, crept through her like some odious insect. That feeling she'd had—that nagging perception that had plagued her all week—it hadn't been groundless.

It had been accurate.

"I sensed it." Her panicked gaze darted about the room. "Ever since the day Mr. Knox was killed. I thought I was overreacting. But I couldn't shake the uneasy feeling that came over me every time I was in my room. I tried to attribute it to nerves, but after what you just said . . ." She broke off, pressing her palms together as if the very action could hold her emotions in check. "I know he was here."

"The day Knox was killed?" Royce jumped on her words, contemplated them thoroughly before giving a hard nod. "That makes sense. A *lot* of sense. The killer could have slipped in here that afternoon, taken the chemise, and been in the process of leaving the grounds when Knox came upon him. It would explain why Knox got shot."

"But why did the killer come here?" Breanna felt cold, so very cold—a chill that radiated from the inside out. "Just to take something that belonged to me? Or did he come to shoot me and, when my being out strolling the grounds made that impossible, settled for stealing my chemise to torture me instead?"

"No." Royce refuted the latter. Walking over, he pressed her cold hands between his. "He had no intention of killing you. He came for the chemise. He also wanted to familiarize himself with you—your tastes, your weaknesses. He was searching for the best ways to terrorize you."

"He found them." Breanna curled her fingers in Royce's—and felt her core of inner strength waver. "I can't stay in this room tonight," she blurted, unable to keep the words from tumbling out. "I just can't."

"That's not an option." Royce saw the terror flash in her eyes, and he shook his head, negating her fear. "What I mean is, you're *not* staying here. Not only tonight, but any night. Not until we find this animal."

Breanna started, her insides lurching again. "You think he'll be back?"

"Eventually," Royce said honestly. "But not to kill you. He has more to accomplish first. He's not finished tormenting you. And we're not going to give him the opportunity to do that to the point where he's ready to move on to the next stage of his plan." The phrase *to kill Anastasia and you* hung between them, echoing as clearly as if Royce had spoken it aloud. "Breanna," he added fervently, his grip tightening as he watched the expression on her face. "We're going to hunt him down. *I'm* going to hunt him down. I promise you that."

"How?" Breanna heard herself ask.

"He bought that statue somewhere. Just like he bought those dolls somewhere. I'm going to find out where. I have contacts all over England. I'll send them to every shire, every bloody town if I have to. But I *will* find this killer. You've got to trust me."

A shaky nod. "I do."

"In the meantime," Royce continued, "if he does manage to get back inside the house, he won't find you in your chambers. I'm moving you into the room next to mine. Hibbert and I will take turns guarding your door. You'll never be unprotected."

"Stacie." Breanna's thoughts were racing. "What about Stacie? She's in danger, too."

"Anastasia is safe. Damen's with her. The assassin would never enter their room and take the chance of alerting her husband."

"But if he shot her before Damen awakened, or if he decided to shoot Damen, too . . ."

Again, Royce shook his head. "That's not his plan. He's only after you and Anastasia. To close in on her, knowing full well her husband would be at her side and would, therefore, have to be eliminated, would be unacceptable. This man only kills those he means to— unless an unexpected victim like Knox gets in his way. In that case, killing is unavoidable. But to plan his strategy—his *ultimate* strategy—knowing the stage wasn't set precisely as he wanted it to be; to burst in with the foreknowledge that someone other than his intended victim would be there? That would be amateurish.

"Besides which, he'd never shoot Anastasia from inside the manor. He knows he'd be caught—if not by Damen, then by someone else who heard the shot. He'd want you and Anastasia isolated, away from prying eyes and alert ears. Remember, demonstrating his cunning is as much a part of this bastard's thrill as demonstrating his skill. No. I'm convinced that if he went to your chambers again, it would either be to leave something else to terrorize you or, at the very worst, to watch you when you're unaware."

"To . . . watch . . . me?" Breanna managed. She shuddered. "You mean while I sleep?"

"Yes."

"I see." Breanna recognized she was on the verge of totally breaking down and, desperately, she struggled to bring herself under control. Royce was offering her an alternative, a means to remain safe. She wouldn't reward him by sobbing like a child.

That thought prompted another.

"You said you and Hibbert would alternate standing outside my door," she said, her voice stronger, steadier. "That won't be necessary. The killer won't find me if I'm in a different wing of the house. Besides, I refuse to impose on you. You weren't hired as guards."

Royce raised her chin with his forefinger, those midnight blue eyes delving deep inside her. "That's my choice to make. Not yours." He released her. "Now collect your nightclothes and whatever else you need. We're getting you out of this room."

13

Breanna's temporary quarters were bare, void of personal touches and bedding.

Royce took care of that problem quickly and efficiently, carrying in a few blankets and pillows from his chambers to her new one, then building a healthy fire to warm away the winter chill.

Breanna couldn't seem to stop shaking, no matter how high the flames were fanned. She hugged herself tightly, trying to conceal the severity of her tremors, clenching her teeth to disguise their chattering.

"That'll do for tonight," Royce announced a half hour later. He stepped back from the fireplace, setting down the iron poker. The room was still barren, unlived in. But, barren or not, it was far safer than Breanna's.

His gaze flickered to Breanna, then to the window. "It'll be light in a few hours. You'd better get some sleep."

Sleep?

That word brought Breanna's head up, and her

stomach twisted into knots as she realized the implications of Royce's suggestion.

He wanted her to lie down, to close her eyes, to rest.

And he intended to leave her alone so she could do that.

Impossible.

Before she could stop herself, she'd reached out, clutched Royce's sleeve with her fingers. "No."

He glanced down at her hand, his own expression unreadable. "No?"

"I can't sleep. Not yet. Not alone. No, that's not what I meant," she amended hastily, hot color flooding her cheeks.

She sucked in her breath, tried again. "What I meant is, could you stay awhile? Just to talk," she added in a rush. "It's just that . . . that is . . ." This was even harder than she'd expected. Turning to someone for help—someone other than Stacie or Wells—it didn't come easily to her. "I'm not quite ready to be alone with my thoughts," she admitted at last. "Not after tonight's incident."

Royce smiled faintly, plucked her fingers from his sleeve, and brought her palm to his lips. "Was that really so difficult?" he murmured.

"Yes."

His smile faded, and his gaze intensified. Tersely, he nodded, as if in understanding. "I suppose it was." He guided her over to a chair, eased her into it. Then, he gathered up the blankets, spread them out over her, one by one, until she was totally enveloped. "I'll stay. We'll talk. Under one condition. You curl up under those blankets. We've got to warm away that chill of yours. You're shaking like a leaf."

Breanna looked sheepish. "You noticed."

"Noticed?" He leaned over her, his hands gripping the chair arms on either side of her. "Your teeth were clenched so tightly, I was afraid your jaw would snap. And your fingers were biting so deeply into your gown sleeves, I was afraid the material would wear away. Does that answer your question?"

Her lips twitched. "I suppose it does."

Royce's knuckles caressed her cheek ever so slightly. "You're an astonishing woman, Lady Breanna Colby. Tell me, does that inner strength of yours never falter?"

Breanna swallowed. "I'm not certain how to answer that."

"That doesn't surprise me." Royce studied her intently. "You're not even aware of how extraordinary you are. Every woman I know would be close to hysteria by now—crying, clinging, fainting dead away. But not you. You do none of those things. No matter how terrified you are, how dire things get, you stay strong."

"That's not strength," Breanna replied honestly. "It's self-control. I was raised to always exhibit it. After all these years of reinforcement, I suppose it's part of me."

An odd look crossed Royce's face. "I understand that reality only too well." He straightened, turned his attention back to the fire.

He might have been referring to *her* reality, to his knowledge of her father's crimes.

Somehow Breanna sensed otherwise.

The reality he was referring to was his.

And the self-control was one he understood firsthand.

Watching the stiffness of his posture, Breanna once

again resisted the urge to pry. "I appreciate all you've done tonight, all you're still doing. I needed your assistance—badly. Regardless of how you perceive me, I'm not really all that strong. My blood ran cold when I saw that chemise."

Royce relaxed, lowered himself to the rug by the fire. He stretched out his long legs, propped himself up on one elbow. "You're every bit as strong as I believe. If you weren't frightened by what happened here tonight, you'd be a fool. Don't confuse intelligence with cowardice."

"All right. I won't." Breanna tucked the blankets beneath her chin. "How do you think he got in?"

"That's a good question." Royce frowned, the light of the flames reflecting off his face, illuminating the hard angles and accentuating his pensive expression. "He could have slipped past the guards by climbing into one of the arriving guest's carriages and riding all the way to the manor. If he was dressed in black, he could have scaled his way to the second floor after that without being seen. Or, he could have smuggled himself into one of the delivery vehicles and ridden to the rear of the house, then crept up the rear staircase while the ball was under way. No one would have noticed him. All the activity was taking place in the front sections of the manor. Or . . ." Royce broke off, midnight sparks glinting in his eyes.

"Or?" Breanna prompted.

He raised his gaze to meet hers. "Or he could have simply presented his invitation at the door and walked in."

Breanna stared, her eyes growing wide as saucers. "You're suggesting this killer might be one of my guests? Someone we knowingly invited to this party?"

"I'm not suggesting it. I'm simply not ruling it out. After all, what do we know about this person? Only that he's a master at his craft and that he has a twisted, albeit brilliant, mind. That description could apply to anyone, in any walk of life."

"Including the *ton*." Breanna gripped the blanket with icy fingers. "If he *is* one of our guests, then he's still in the manor. He's here right now, sleeping under my roof, planning to do Lord knows what."

"*If*," Royce emphasized. "It's a slim chance, not a likelihood. None of your guests is exactly a stranger. Most of them have done business with Colby and Sons for years, including a fair number who were close acquaintances of your grandfather. Not to mention that a good portion of them, *I'm* acquainted with—well enough to doubt they're killers."

"That doesn't eliminate the possibility that he's here. So how can we either dismiss or confirm the notion? Should we begin questioning everyone?"

"Definitely not." Royce shook his head. "If we do, and if it happens we're on the right track, we'll only incite the killer in ways we'd be best off not doing. My reputation is not exactly a secret. If the assassin realizes I'm involved, that I'm actively looking for him, it would push him in a dangerous direction. He needs to believe he's in control. Let's let him think that. We'll find out what we want to know—subtly. Very subtly."

Royce paused, his mind racing. "I'll do some nosing around tomorrow before the first guests begin to leave," he decided. "Better yet, I'll have Hibbert do it for me. He has a way of getting information out of people without their realizing they've revealed anything. I'll concentrate on finding out where that statue was purchased. And the dolls, too. The killer won't notice any of that. He's too busy planning the next step in his scheme to terrorize you." A muscle flexed in Royce's jaw. "I'm going to beat this bastard at his own game."

"You certainly understand his mind," Breanna noted quietly.

Something cold and bitter flashed in Royce's eyes. "I've known others like him," he responded. "Predatory geniuses obsessed with their own superiority. Some call themselves assassins. Some don't. And some don't kill—at least not in the bodily sense, nor in ways one could describe as criminal. But their minds are twisted and their means destructive as hell—at least to those who are unfortunate enough to be their victims."

Like you? Breanna almost blurted out.

She bit her lip to silence the question, although she knew in her heart the victim Royce was alluding to was himself. And not in a professional capacity. Whoever had hurt him wasn't among the military personnel he'd dealt with. It was someone else—someone closer to him. She, better than anyone, recognized the signs.

So where did that leave her? True, she didn't want to pry. But, given her own life, was it possible she could help?

"I don't know very much about you," she ventured, broaching the subject cautiously, giving Royce as much or as little room as he chose to take. "I know only what Damen's told me."

"I'm not given to discussing myself," Royce returned bluntly. He angled his head to study Breanna's face. "Neither are you, I would imagine."

"You're right. I'm not." She rushed on without allowing herself time to reconsider and change her mind. "I'm also not given to extreme shows of affection. Tonight proved to be an exception—at least for me. Maybe it should be for you, as well. If not physically, then verbally."

A hint of a smile. "Maybe it should. All right, what would you like to know?"

"Only what you're comfortable discussing." Beneath the blankets, she drew up her legs, rested her chin atop her knees. "You said you spent Christmas with your brother and his family," she tried carefully. "Are you and he close?"

A shrug. "Not particularly. Edmund is a good man. His wife Jane is a decent woman. They're content in their roles as the Earl and Countess of Searby."

"Content. In other words, dull," Breanna surmised, her lips curving a bit. "Your brother sounds like most of the men I'm acquainted with. And now, having met you . . . I can't imagine you'd have much in common with him."

"I don't," Royce admitted. "But his sons are incredible—three bundles of energy. The hours with them are worth all the boredom. They're even worth spending a few days in that house. *On occasion*," he qualified. "Too often and I'm besieged by the ugliest damned memories . . ." Abruptly, he broke off.

Breanna recognized the bitterness in his voice, the pain and resentment in his eyes. She'd experienced those emotions all too often herself, incited by only one person.

That helped make her assessment of Royce easy.

It had to be his family. Not his brother, whom he talked about without anger. His parents. Most likely, his father—unless his mother was an unusually tyrannical woman. Yes, his father. That had to be who was behind Royce's bitterness. Breanna would be willing to bet on it.

"These memories—were they of your father?" she tried quietly.

"One and the same," was the sharp retort.

It was the only confirmation she needed.

"My guess is that he was much like mine," Breanna ventured. "Domineering and cruel. Edmund is one result of such a father. He must have turned out as I did: malleable, self-contained. And you? You're too dynamic for that. You veered off in the opposite direction. You're the rebel, the one whose will was strong enough to fight back."

Royce stared into the flames, and for a moment Breanna thought he didn't intend to reply.

She was on the verge of apologizing for overstepping her bounds when he said, "For the record, you're nothing like Edmund. Self-contained, maybe, but not malleable. And definitely not dull. As for me, I wasn't always as strong as you implied. I was once a frightened child. *Very* frightened. You see, my father's philosophy was to bludgeon us into what he called 'being men.' "

"He beat you."

"Oh, the beatings were the easy part. They were quick, they were predictable, and all they could hurt was my body. So I endured them. Edmund couldn't— not that I blame him. His passive nature was no match for my father's brutal resolve and vile temper. He crumpled by the time he was six, conformed to my father's wishes. That, combined with the fact that he was the heir apparent, freed him from my father's exercises in abuse. In my case, the exercises took a

new form—a series of challenges my father provided
for me to overcome."

"Challenges?" Breanna felt an unpleasant sense of
foreboding. "What kind of challenges?"

"The kind supposedly designed for me to prove
myself, but which, in fact, were designed to prove my
father's dominance and to destroy my will. When I
was five, I was ordered to ride a wild stallion who
had a history of throwing and trampling his owners.
My orders were never to fall. Each time I failed to stay
in the saddle, I was whipped. And each time I cried, I
was forced to endure an additional hour on the stallion's back.

"When I was six, I was locked in a cramped closet
and told to find my way out. If I dared fail or call out
for help, the next space I was locked in would be
more cramped, harder to escape. And when I was
seven, I was given books to read—in various lan-
guages—and told to memorize them. When reciting
them back, I was denied one meal for each mistake I
made. That usually meant going days without food.
Shall I continue?"

"No." Breanna shook her head, bile rising in her
throat. "How did you get through it?"

"By becoming resourceful, learning never to fail.
Every challenge my father hurled in my face, I mastered. Of course, that made him angrier. Which meant
his challenges grew harder and his punishments more
severe. He was determined to break me. It became his
obsession. He was brilliant, vicious, and relentless.
But, as you so astutely guessed, my will was stronger.
I withstood his brutality for twelve long years. Then, I
left for Eton. After that, I rarely came home. And once
my mother died, I stopped coming altogether."

"Your mother?" Breanna's head came up. "Didn't she intrude?"

"I wouldn't let her. Do you know what he would have done if his wife defied him? He would have brutalized her."

"But you were a little boy."

"I was a *resilient* little boy," Royce corrected. "She was a broken, defenseless woman. I did what I had to. If anything, it made me stronger."

"Stronger, perhaps," Breanna concurred softly. "But scarred. And I don't mean physically. Your wounds are entrenched—permanently. I know that firsthand."

"My wounds?" Royce shook his head. "I don't regard them as such. Probably because I don't regret what they made me. I suppose, in a way, my father did me a service."

Something about Royce's words touched something inside her. Perhaps it was the similarity of their upbringing, perhaps it was the conclusion he'd reached—one Breanna understood and shared with regard to herself. Perhaps it was respect for the man he'd become.

Or perhaps it just was.

On sheer impulse, Breanna squirmed out from beneath the blankets, lowered herself onto the rug beside him. "Now I understand what you meant by those who destroy without killing. I also see why you're determined to outwit your enemies, even if it means taking risks—maybe *especially* if it means taking risks. Your father provided a service, all right. But not for you. For the rest of us—the people you help." She reached out, trailed her fingertips across his jaw. "Thank you for confiding in me. You're a fascinating and complex man, Royce Chadwick."

The impact of her touch was jarring. Undercurrents of sensation radiated through them both, jolting them from candid revelations to naked awareness.

Abruptly, the mood in the room altered.

Royce went taut, his gaze finding hers, delving inside her in way that made her breath catch.

"I *am* a complex man," he said roughly. "I'm also a hard man. Despite how you perceive me, despite my concern for you *and* my attraction to you, I'm not given to tenderness or sentiment. They're not in my nature."

"But compassion is." Breanna's heartbeat had begun to accelerate.

"Compassion, yes. Compassion *and* passion." His reference was pointed, an intentional effort to assign a name to what he was feeling. Not for his sake. For hers.

He was trying to shock her into realizing they were alone in a bedchamber in the dead of night, where there was no one nearby to ensure they restrained themselves.

His efforts failed miserably.

"Passion—definitely. As I discovered earlier." Breanna had no idea where her bravado was coming from. She only knew it was there. She also had no idea what she was striving for by flagrantly baiting him as she was. She only knew that she had to see where it led.

Her thumb just grazed his lips.

"Breanna, stop." Abandoning all subtlety, Royce caught her wrist, tiny sparks flaring in his midnight gaze. "You're not foxed now. And you're playing a dangerous game."

"Yes, I recall. Fire, you said. And I said I wanted to get singed."

"And *I* said you were going to get burned."

She swallowed, wet her lips with the tip of her tongue. "Maybe it's time I learned to take some risks."

Royce's eyes narrowed on her face. "Not these kind. Not with me. I don't normally display the gallantry I did in that garden tonight."

"Of course not. That would be a show of sentiment—something you're not given to."

He was losing and he knew it. Breanna could actually see him weaken.

"Stop provoking me," he commanded. "Don't you understand what I'm trying to tell you?"

"What you mean is, trying to warn me about." Breanna eased closer, her heart slamming against her ribs. "Yes, I understand."

Royce sucked in his breath. He released her wrist, then rose to his knees, his fingers, of their own volition, gliding into the strands of her upswept hair. "This is a mistake."

"Is it?"

"Yes. You're unnerved by what happened tonight. You're feeling vulnerable."

"I'm feeling many things." Breanna tilted back her head, studied the hard angles of his face in the firelight. "But right now, vulnerable isn't one of them."

"Damn," Royce hissed. He leaned forward, sliding his palm around to cup the nape of her neck, and drew her closer, staring down at her with an expression that sent live flames licking through her. "This *is* a mistake. An unprincipled, reckless mistake."

Breanna gripped his shirt, raising up until their lips were inches apart. "I don't care."

With a harsh sound, Royce dragged her against him, crushing her mouth to his. There were no preliminaries this time. His lips devoured hers, parting them for the intimate invasion of his tongue. He delved deep, angling her head to give him greater access, taking her with heated, suggestive strokes of his tongue.

He twisted her around until he could lower her to the carpet. Then, he stretched out alongside her, half atop her as he continued his hot, drugging kisses. His tongue captured hers, caressed it in dizzying strokes, and his hand moved restlessly down to cover her breast.

Breanna was caught up in a vortex of physical awakening. When Royce's hand found her breast, she whimpered—a soft sound that Royce caught with his mouth. His thumb found and teased her nipple, circling it until it hardened and throbbed beneath his touch. She wound her arms around his neck, threaded her fingers through his hair. She was lost in sensation, in the sheer excitement of discovery.

Royce tore his mouth from hers, moved down her neck, her throat, searing her with each hungry caress. His lips closed around her nipple, tugged at it through the silk of her gown, and Breanna's eyes slid shut, her breath expelling in a rush. She clutched Royce's head, held him against her to prolong the pleasure. Shuddering at her touch, he stopped, but only long enough to reach behind her, undo the tiny row of buttons down her back.

He tugged down her bodice, his fingers automatically shifting to the ribbons of her chemise. "Tell me to stop," he ordered, his voice hoarse.

"No." Breanna shook her head from side to side, desperate to experience whatever magnificent sensations hovered just beyond her reach.

"Breanna."

Her lids snapped open, and she met Royce's molten gaze.

"Tell me to stop," he repeated, already tugging the first ribbon free.

"I won't," she said breathlessly. "I can't."

With a stifled oath, Royce dispensed with the final barrier that separated him from his goal. He parted the sides of her chemise, and an awed expression tightened his features before he lowered his head, captured her taut nipple between his lips. "You're so beautiful," he muttered thickly, cupping her other breast as he sampled its mate. "And your taste ... God, this is an even bigger mistake than I thought."

Breanna didn't answer. She couldn't. Everything inside her was concentrated on the sensations storming her body. Royce's mouth on her skin ... his hands ... his breath ... She wondered if pleasure this acute could be withstood.

Reflexively, she held him, wrapped her arms around his back. His shirt, which he'd haphazardly donned when her knock had awakened him, was half-free, only partially tucked into his breeches. She took advantage of that, slipping her hands beneath the shirt, gliding her palms along the warm, hard planes of his back.

Every muscle went rigid beneath her caresses.

"Breanna." He uttered her name in a hoarse rasp, his tongue lashing at her nipple even as his hands left her, moved to unbutton the front of his shirt.

Then, he was covering her, the hot, hair-roughened skin of his chest rubbing against her breasts.

This time, Breanna couldn't help but cry out. The sound was short-lived, because Royce was kissing her again. She opened her mouth eagerly to his, and he cradled her head in his hands, devouring her lips and shifting to increase the friction of his body against hers. Breanna savored every exquisite sensation, her nipples tightening painfully, liquid heat coursing through her.

"God, I want you," Royce muttered, burning a trail of kisses down her neck, nuzzling the valley between her breasts. "I want to bury myself so deep inside you that . . ." He stopped abruptly, as if the impact of his own words had suddenly registered. Forcing up his head, he stared down at her, his eyes burning with desire, his breathing harsh, uneven, tremors of reaction rippling through him.

Almost violently, he tore himself away, rolled to one side. "Dammit." He sat up, raked a hand through his hair. "Goddammit."

"Royce?" Breanna turned her head, stared at the rigid lines of his back.

In reply, he pivoted, his hot gaze raking her bare torso once before he pulled the sides of her chemise together, helped her sit up.

"I obviously do have the ability to be gallant twice in one night," he said, his voice still thick with desire. "Then again, that shouldn't surprise me. Not when it comes to you."

Breanna blinked, trying to still the swimming in her head. "I didn't want you to stop."

Royce's mouth thinned into a grim line. "I know you didn't. Not right now. Tomorrow would have been another story."

"Would it?"

"Yes." Royce buttoned his shirt in a few harsh motions. Then, he turned, yanked up Breanna's bodice and clasped her shoulders in his hands. "Breanna, you're beautiful. And I don't mean only physically, although Lord knows I can't keep my eyes, or my hands, off of you. You're beautiful to the core. You emanate something I can't begin to describe. But you need—you *deserve*—a hell of a lot more than a quick tumble on the floor. And you deserve it from someone who can offer it to you. Someone who has the depth of emotion to offer it to you."

"I see." With shaking hands, Breanna reached around to button the back of her gown. She was still too dazed to form a coherent thought. But she wasn't too dazed to recognize Royce's implications as untrue, even if he himself didn't realize it. "So, along with my life, you're now protecting my virtue."

A weighted pause. "I'm trying. Not very successfully, it seems." Royce shook his head in amazement. "I didn't count on this. I've never . . ." Unsteadily, his knuckles caressed her cheek. "It seems tonight was an exception for me, too. I *don't* lose control. Tonight, I did."

He rose to his feet, shoved his shirt into his breeches. "It's almost dawn. Try to sleep. I'll be right outside your door. We'll talk before breakfast. Then we'll tell Damen and Anastasia about the assassin's visit to your room." Extending his hand to her, he helped her up, then brought her fingers to his lips, his hard-edged demeanor softening a bit—whether at the mention of tonight's trauma or the memory of what had just happened between them, Breanna wasn't certain. "Will you be all right?" he murmured.

Breanna nodded. "I'll be fine." She studied his face, saw the intimate look in his eyes—a look he wasn't even aware of—and wondered if perhaps she didn't have her answer. "Good night, Royce."

A whisper of hesitation. "Good night." He turned, walked out of the room, glancing back at her briefly before shutting the door in his wake.

Breanna stared after him for a long time. She heard him drag a chair into the hall, place it against her door, and settle himself for the remainder of the night. Just knowing he was out there, safeguarding her against the madman who wanted her dead, brought her more than a small measure of relief.

Relief and a great deal more.

On that thought, Breanna gathered up the blankets, made herself a cozy bed by the fire, and snuggled into it.

Somehow this spot felt more comforting than the bed. Probably because she'd just shared it with Royce.

She had much to mull over. And, whether he knew it or not, so did Royce. She'd felt his reluctance when he'd dragged himself away from her. And she'd seen his ambivalence, his bewilderment, when he bid her good night.

They'd both encountered sides of themselves to-night that they hadn't known existed. What that meant, where it was leading, remained to be seen.

But one thing was certain. For a man obviously ex-perienced with women, Royce Chadwick was as con-fused as she.

Not so when it came to the assassin. There, Royce knew precisely what he aimed to do. He was hell-bent on capturing his adversary, determined to succeed.

Unfortunately, so was the assassin.

An icy chill shivered up Breanna's spine.

Lord only knew what tomorrow would bring.

14

"*I* can't believe I'm hearing this."

Damen stalked about the sitting room that adjoined his and Stacie's bedchamber, pausing beside the settee where his wife and Breanna sat. He slammed his fist against the ornately carved frame. "That madman invaded Breanna's bedroom while a ball was going on, and left those sick, mutilated . . ." He broke off.

"Yes." Royce leaned back against the tightly closed door, arms folded across his chest.

It was early—half past ten—and very few of the guests were awake. Still, Royce had chosen the privacy of Damen and Anastasia's quarters in which to have this talk.

"You must have been terrified," Stacie murmured, turning to study her cousin anxiously. "Why didn't you awaken me?"

"I considered it," Breanna confessed. "But there was nothing you could have done. Besides, you needed your rest. You were exhausted. And I knew you were safe. Damen was with you."

"I sat outside Breanna's door all night," Royce assured Stacie quietly. "Her *new* door," he amended. "I've moved her to the room next to mine. I don't want her in her usual bedchamber—not until the killer's caught."

Damen's mouth thinned into a grim line. "You're saying you expect him to be back."

"Maybe. *If* he ever left."

"You think he's hiding at the manor?" Stacie gasped.

"No. Either he slipped out the same way he slipped in, or he's here at your invitation."

A stunned silence filled the room.

"You believe he's one of our guests?" Damen demanded.

Royce shrugged. "What I believe isn't important. What I do, *is*. I have to investigate every possibility. It would be foolish to overlook anything, however remote." He picked up the disfigured statue he'd brought to show them, and turned it over in his hands. "Whoever and wherever he is, our killer's message is clear. But each time he delivers that message, he leaves clues along with it. The chemise is Breanna's. But this porcelain figure isn't. He bought it somewhere, just as he did those dolls. I intend to find out where. *Someone* will remember who bought these items."

"I assume you'll be leaving Medford Manor then," Anastasia concluded. "When, tonight? Or sooner, before the party ends?"

Royce scowled. "I'm not going anywhere until every guest is gone. After that—" He hesitated, visibly troubled. "I must go to Berkshire, check into the whereabouts of Ryder's daughter. I'm not happy about it, not in light of what's happened. But I have an obligation . . ." Unconsciously, his gaze flickered to Breanna.

"Royce, go to Berkshire," she said, her voice steady, rife with conviction. "If Lord Ryder's daughter is alive, he deserves to meet her. Family is a gift. If my grandfather taught Stacie and me anything, it's that. We'll be fine. Besides, you have to start somewhere checking into shops. Why not start in Berkshire? Maybe that monster bought the statue there."

Royce nodded, and Breanna could feel Stacie's scrutiny as she stared curiously from her cousin to Royce and back.

"All right," Royce conceded. "But I'm only covering the shires right around London. The rest I'll have my men take care of. I'll ride out to Pearson Manor tonight, get my answers on Glynnis Martin. Tomorrow at dawn I'll travel down to Ryder's home in Sussex. Along the way, I'll check out the shops. I'll be back here by tomorrow night, or the next morning at the latest. Also, I've decided that Hibbert will stay behind. I want him here, guarding your door. That will ease my mind considerably."

"Yours, maybe, but not Wells's." Breanna attempted a smile. "He and Hibbert are both rather territorial. It should be interesting to see them living under the same roof and sharing responsibilities."

"They'll work it out." Royce didn't smile. He set down the statue, turned to face the three of them. "Listen to me, all of you. I can't stress enough how important it is for you to act normally. What that means is, I want *no one* playing detective, interrogating our guests." He shot a meaningful look at Anastasia. "Leave the questioning to Hibbert and me. We have a whole day to probe. Don't impede us and endanger yourselves by doing anything stupid."

"Stacie?" Damen prodded, giving his wife's shoulder a gentle tap. "Do you understand what Royce just said?"

She rolled her eyes. "I'm neither deaf nor dense. I heard. And I'll do what Royce said."

"Breanna?" Royce pressed.

"I've already assured you, I won't interfere."

"Good. Then let's go downstairs. Your guests should be arising any time now. Damen, find a way to stay with Anastasia and Breanna. Use the excuse you conjured up last night—that you're a nervous father-to-be. No one will question it."

"And no one will try to kill either of the women if I'm there, since my presence isn't part of his plan," Damen finished for him.

"Exactly." Royce's nod was terse.

"Fine. Then it's needlepoint and tea for me." Damen placed a protective hand on each of the women's shoulders. "I'll leave the riding and shooting contests, and the gaming tables to you and Hibbert."

A fine layer of snow prohibited the men from holding their more ambitious races on horseback.

That suited the assassin just fine. It gave him a better opportunity to study Royce Chadwick.

Something wasn't right.

First of all, the man was too damned relaxed, something Chadwick never was. Which led him to believe it was all an act, being put on for someone's benefit. But whose? Lady Breanna's? And if so, why? Was it because he was trying to seduce her or because he was acting as her knight in shining armor? Did he know about what she'd found in her bed-chamber last night? Had she told him? If so, was he coming to her rescue, helping her find out who her tormenter was?

It was the only thing that made sense.

Added to that was the fact that Hibbert had made three appearances among the men today. That unto it-self wasn't unusual, given how unorthodox Chad-wick was about his manservant. Still, there was something about Hibbert's demeanor—a fine tension only the sharpest eye could discern—as if the elderly butler was delving for something.

Or someone.

Hibbert was subtle, nondescript. *He,* on the other hand, was more. He was brilliant. Nothing got by him. Certainly not the casual inspection of an elderly manservant.

Then there was Lady Breanna.

She hadn't slept a wink. The dark circles beneath her eyes told him that. Still, she was up and about, fresh and lovely in her yellow morning dress, her hair perfectly coiffed, as always, and her smile intact.

Inside, she had to be quaking.

But, dammit, he wanted to see her crack.

What was keeping her in check? Certainly not her own reserves. It had to be Chadwick.

Damn him to hell.

The assassin shoved his hands into his pockets, feeling that familiar rage boil up inside him. He'd been curtailing it for days now. But it was intensify-ing, refusing to be quieted. It spilled over, surged through his veins, pulsed through his blood. He gave in to it, savoring its fire, although outwardly he knew his veneer was intact. No one watching would know the fury lashing through him.

He had to act. To vent his rage before it consumed him.

It was a good idea anyway. He could use the physical exertion. It would keep him razor-sharp for when he eliminated the Colby women. He'd view his next victim as target practice. He'd arrange things perfectly. Everyone would make the obvious, terrifying assumption that this latest murder was tied to the three unresolved crimes that had preceded it. Except for Lady Breanna, who'd be gripped by the horrifying prospect that this new killing was unrelated to the others, that it was a brutal warning just for her.

No one would guess it was both.

As for the killer's identity, that would feed right into the *ton*'s natural inclination to believe there could never be a murderer among them. So deviant a mind must belong to a common criminal.

The stupid fools. There was nothing common about him.

A smile curved his lips as he visualized the pandemonium that would ensue. Both guests and hosts would be thrown into a panic. As a result, his remaining hours at Medford Manor would be thoroughly enjoyable.

Enjoyable but hectic. Too hectic to act.

He'd wait a day or two before absconding with the grieving young widow. Then, he'd ride to her home, grab her from there.

And have a lovely piece of merchandise to ship to Calais.

He glanced about, pleased to see that the gentlemen had split up, since riding conditions were not optimum. Some of them had remained outside to fish or shoot, some were heading inside to play whist. And some were going off by themselves, to enjoy a late breakfast or a strong brandy.

No one would remember who was where, and who was missing.

It was time to lure his target out to die.

Lord Richard Hart found the message in the pocket of his coat.

He had just left the manor, and was about to join a group of men who were fishing at the stream, when he discovered the folded slip of paper. Puzzled, he pulled it out, smoothed open what looked to be a sheet of feminine stationery. An anticipatory glint lit his eyes as he read the words, and the signature.

Ten minutes later, he was on horseback, galloping off to his destination.

He eased forward in his saddle, excitement rippling through him. He'd always been lucky with the ladies. Even now, at forty-five years of age, women were drawn to him. They were attracted to his still-firm physique, his natural charm, and, of course, his staggering fortune. He'd been approached by many women, with every offer from a swift, one-time liaison to a long-term mistress. He'd accepted more than his share. Rarely did the identities of those who approached him come as a surprise. He had a sixth sense for knowing when someone wanted him. But never in his wildest dreams had he guessed that Lady Breanna Colby was among them.

He smiled, urging his horse to pick up speed. According to her note, she wanted to meet him on the far western side of the estate, away from the guests and the construction, where she knew they could be utterly alone.

Her only stipulations were that he told no one he was coming and that he brought the note with him, so she could destroy it and eliminate any chance of discovery. Their tryst, she'd declared, had to remain a secret.

That was fine with him. The less people who knew, the less chance there was of his new wife finding out.

The notion of Lady Breanna wanting him, yearning for him, made his pulse race. True, this was one time he hadn't guessed, hadn't had an inkling of her desires.

But Breanna Colby was the ultimate lady, a woman who kept her feelings and her desires hidden.

The realization that he was to be the one to free them made his mouth water.

He glanced back at the manor, secure in the knowledge that his young, inexperienced wife was sitting among a cluster of women, chatting on some inane subject. Her youth and virginity, which a few short months ago had seemed so incredibly appealing, had quickly lost their luster. She was malleable enough, but passive, passionless. As a result, he was fast growing tired of having her in his bed.

Lady Breanna was different. Inexperienced, perhaps, but not passionless. After all, she was the mirror image of her cousin. And the heated expression on Sheldrake's face when he looked at his wife spoke volumes, proclaimed the exquisite Lady Anastasia to be all fire and initiative in bed.

So it would be the same with her cousin.

Lord Hart's smile broadened triumphantly as the

rows of hedges Breanna had described loomed into view. This must be where she was waiting. It was at the very edge of the estate, a few dozen feet from the road. The hedges were sheltered, private. Ideal.

He brought his mare to a halt, peering about in the hopes of spotting a glint of yellow. He well remembered the lemon-hued gown she'd been wearing at breakfast, and his loins tightened at the thought of removing it.

"Lady Breanna?" he called out. "I'm here, as you requested."

No reply.

Realizing she must be nervous, he yanked out the note she'd sent him, waved it in the air. "See? I've brought your message. No one knows my whereabouts. So there's no reason for self-restraint."

That yielded the desired results.

A glint of color flashed from the hedges.

But it wasn't yellow.

It was silver.

Hart scarcely had time to turn before the pistol fired. And he never realized he was going to die before the bullet found its mark.

Excellent, the assassin thought, watching Hart's body drop to the ground like a stone, the note fluttering to his side. A perfect shot. If any of the guards heard it, they would assume it was one of the gentlemen out gaming. Their job was to protect against intruders, not scrutinize those already present at Lady Breanna's invitation.

Still, he had to be prudent. He waited—just long enough to peer about and be sure no one was approaching. Satisfied that he was alone, he crossed over, sparing the body not even a glance as he leaned past it to scoop up the note.

Stuffing it into his pocket, he slipped into the hedges and made his way back to the manor.

It wasn't until late afternoon that the victim was missed.

His wife had assumed he was with the gentlemen, and each of the gentlemen had assumed he was with either one of their colleagues or one of their colleagues' wives.

But just after three o'clock, a group of men began looking for him. An afternoon thaw was allowing for a fox hunt and, fine sportsman that Hart was, they wanted him to join. Upon scanning the grounds, they noticed the mare wandering about. She was saddled, but minus a rider. The men were puzzled. As a result, Lord Percy Gilbert, who'd spied the mare first, rode her back to the stables to make an inquiry. He talked to a young stableboy, who readily told him that Lord Hart had taken her out hours ago.

A search got under way.

Forty-five minutes later, Lord Crompton spotted the body.

"Over there," he called, pointed toward the hedges.

The men hurried over, gathering around as the viscount squatted down, checked for a heartbeat, a whisper of breath, anything that indicated Hart might still be among them. But his body was cold and still, the smear of blood across his shirt telling them this was no riding accident.

"He's dead," Crompton declared grimly, rising to a standing position. "He was shot in the chest." Pale but composed, Crompton scanned the grounds, years in the military having accustomed him to staring death in the face. "The killer could have fired from there," he suggested, indicating the rows of hedges that offered a fine place from which an assailant could strike without being seen.

"Or he could have fired from the road." The Duke of Maywood gestured in that direction. "It's no more than twenty-five feet away, just past those trees. That makes a lot more sense to me. He could have hunched down by the roadside and waited for a victim to show up, to get close enough to be within firing range. But to sneak onto the estate? The killer would never have gotten past all those guards—and not only once, but twice—before he committed the murder and after."

"I agree," Lord Percy concurred, wiping sweat off his brow and glancing about apprehensively. "And if he did fire from the road, maybe he's not finished. He could be hiding nearby, waiting to shoot another one of us. Let's get back to the manor. We'll send the guards to collect Hart's body and take a look around."

Pandemonium did indeed ensue—as soon as the news reached the manor.

The men argued and muttered among themselves, the women wept and wrung their hands, and Lord Hart's young widow needed to be revived twice with smelling salts. It took the guards thirty minutes to get the full story from the men who'd discovered the body, and even longer to collect the body and search the area.

No assailant was discovered—not in the hedges, and not by the road.

The next hours passed in a frenzy, as the panicked noblemen battled each other to dispatch messages to

Bow Street, demanding that action be taken and offering huge sums of money for any runners willing to leave Bow Street and ride out to this shire or that in order to protect them and their families from harm.

Wells was equally frantic, trying to calm down their guests and simultaneously summon enough footmen to accommodate all the outgoing messages. Hibbert stood off to one side, keeping a clear view of both the hallway and the sitting room, unobtrusively studying the guests' individual reactions while awaiting a signal from Royce.

Inside the sitting room, Royce was watching Breanna from across the way, making sure Damen stood with her and Anastasia as they spoke to Mahoney, tried to learn all they could about what had happened.

She was shaken. Badly shaken. Especially after last night's violation—which none of the guests knew about. Ironically, if they did, they'd be relieved. Frantic to get away from here, but relieved. *If* they drew the same conclusion Breanna had drawn.

She believed that Hart's murderer was the assassin who was after her, not the criminal terrorizing Bow Street with his string of aristocratic killings. Royce believed she was right. Clearly, it was another message from that bastard, one that foreshadowed what he intended to be her fate. She was terrified, and with good cause. Worse, there wasn't a damned thing he could do about it.

Nothing except find the killer.

He stared over her head, gazing out the window and noting that the guards who'd been searching the grounds were returning to their posts. They'd done all they could. Their job was to keep other incidents from occurring.

And his job was to pick up where they left off.

He turned toward the hallway, signaled Hibbert with a look.

A short while later, the two men were scrutinizing the area near the hedges where Hart's body had been discovered.

"Are you concerned that the guests might see us, ask questions about our motives?" Hibbert asked.

"No." Royce shook his head. "At this point, anyone who knows me knows I'd be compelled to look around. That's my nature. It would be more out of character if I *didn't* do so." He paused, glanced at the row of hedges, then angled his head to gaze off toward the road. "I'm not convinced the killer shot Hart from outside the estate. He might have. But there's no real evidence that he did. He could just as easily have shot from those hedges."

"Agreed." Hibbert turned up his collar, and followed Royce's line of vision. "You're still contemplating the possibility that he's here. That he's one of Lady Breanna's guests."

"I can't eliminate it."

"No, you can't. But you can't prove it either. There's just as good a chance he's out there," Hibbert made a sweep with his arm, "watching Lady Breanna and lying in wait."

Royce scowled, unable to dispute Hibbert's reasoning. "He's smart as hell. He intentionally chose this spot to shoot Hart, so we'd find ourselves in precisely this dilemma. He's trying to make it look as if he's the murderer of those noblemen, rather than the killer after Breanna. Dammit!" Royce clenched his fists at his sides. "How can I leave her alone after this?"

"You don't have a choice. Every guest at the party

is aware of your plans to ride straight from here to Berkshire, to try to reunite Ryder and his daughter. If you alter those plans, there will be questions. Those questions could prove dangerous, especially if the killer *is* among the guests. Besides, from what you told me, Lady Breanna insisted you go. She wants you to bring Ryder and his daughter together." Hibbert studied Royce's expression. "I could go to Berkshire for you. It would be risky, but we could try to come up with some plausible excuse—"

"No." Royce shook his head. "You're right. I have to go. But Hibbert . . ." Royce fixed his friend with an unyielding look. "Don't leave Breanna's door tonight, not for an instant. Or tomorrow night, if I'm still not back. I don't think he'll guess she's changed bedchambers—I've asked Damen to make the room look lived in, to turn up the lamp in the evening and douse it at night, just in case that animal is watching. But if none of that works, if he should figure out that she's sleeping elsewhere and come looking for her, I want him to have to go through you."

A grim nod. "And so he shall."

The party ended early, an aura of morbidity settling over the manor as, one by one, the vehicles were brought around and the visitors took their leave.

Inside the sitting room, Royce hovered at the window, watching the activity taking place outside in the drive. Hibbert stood behind him, listening to the sounds of muffled voices and slamming doors that indicated the guests' departures.

Both men were waiting for Wells to come in and report that the party was officially at an end.

At last, the butler walked in, wearily proclaiming that the final carriage had driven away.

"Thank you, Wells." Royce was already in motion, crossing over to leave the room. "Where's Lady Breanna?"

"In the library, my lord," the butler supplied. "Just as you asked. With Miss Stacie and Lord Sheldrake."

"Good." Royce veered off down the hallway. "I want you and Hibbert in there, too."

Five minutes later, they were all assembled.

Breanna shut the novel she'd been pretending to read, and met Royce's hard stare.

"Everyone's gone," he said, addressing all the room's occupants, but looking directly at Breanna. "From this moment until whenever we find the killer, there are to be no more callers. None. Not even on New Year's Day."

"Callers?" Damen interrupted, bolting to his feet. "I want to take my wife and Breanna and get as far away from here as possible. My God, Royce, this assassin not only invaded Breanna's room, he shot and killed another man right under our noses. I won't just sit here and wait for him to do the same to Stacie and our unborn child."

"Those are your emotions talking, not reason," Royce observed quietly. "You know as well as I do that running would be a mistake. It would turn the women into moving targets. This man is a professional. He's hell-bent on killing Anastasia and Breanna. He'd follow them to the ends of the earth. They'd never be safe. They'd forever be looking over their shoulders. And one day—he'd be standing there. Is that what you want for your wife? For your child?"

Slowly, Damen sank back down into his chair. "No."

"Then listen to me," Royce urged. "Fleeing is not the answer. The answer is to eliminate this bastard permanently. Which I intend to do. The women must stay put. I know it's frustrating. But it's the safest way—the only way."

"I see your point," Damen murmured reluctantly.

"Good. As I said, from now on, no callers are to be admitted. To keep speculation from forming, keep tongues wagging. Make it public that Anastasia is still feeling ill, that's she's far too weak to entertain guests—and that her condition has worsened since Lord Hart was killed on her estate. Breanna, as expected, will be attending to her, as will you. Until Anastasia's health improves, no callers will be received."

Anastasia forced a smile, however strained. "This pregnancy of mine is becoming more than a blessing. It's becoming quite useful in manipulating people to suit our purposes."

Royce didn't smile back. "We'll use whatever we have, do whatever it takes. I want to rob the killer of every opportunity he might seize to get through those gates." He rubbed his palms together. "Which reminds me, the construction is set to resume after New Year's Day. That will have to be delayed. Blame the cold weather."

"Consider it done," Damen agreed at once.

"I'm leaving for Berkshire within the hour," Royce continued. "The sooner I dispose of the Ryder matter, the sooner I'll be back. I'd rather stay. But if I do, and if the killer discovers my change of plans, he'll start drawing his own conclusions. If he should figure out I'm hunting him down, he might lash out." A harsh edge laced Royce's tone. "That would be fine, if I were the one he was lashing out at. It would be more than fine. I'd welcome the chance to meet him head-on. But it's not me he'd vent his rage at."

"It's me," Breanna said quietly.

"Yes." Royce's gaze held hers. "He'd find another way to terrorize you. Right now he's appeased. He thinks he's winning. I'd rather he keep thinking that, until I get back. Then, we'll show him otherwise. But not until then."

"The *ton* thinks Hart's shooter was the killer Bow Street is looking for," Damen muttered.

"Our assassin wanted them to think that. He's shrewd as hell. This way, he terrified Breanna without arousing a shred of suspicion. Hopefully, his victory today will ensure us a short lull as he waits to assess Breanna's reaction. She's got to keep him wondering."

"How do I do that?" Breanna asked.

Royce's stare delved deep inside her. "Stay in the manor. Don't even let him see you, much less gauge how you're holding up. It will buy us time." A pause. "May I see you alone before I leave?"

"Of course." Breanna rose, smoothing the folds of her gown as she did. "We can talk in the green salon."

"I don't think it would be proper to—" Wells began.

"Oh, dear." At that exact moment, Anastasia jerked upright, looking like a rabbit about to bolt. "My stomach is beginning to lurch. It's my own fault. I haven't eaten since breakfast, and when I'm empty, I . . ." She clamped her lips together, as if stifling a wave of nausea.

Wells was already in motion. "I'll bring you some food. I'll be back in a minute."

He was gone in a heartbeat.

"Well done," Damen commended drily. "You accomplished just what you wanted to."

"I did, didn't I?" Stacie returned with a self-satisfied nod. She shot Royce a beatific smile. "You see? I told you my pregnancy was becoming useful. Now go. Before Wells comes to his senses and figures out what I've done—and why. And he *will* figure it out. He always does, as Breanna will attest."

A hint of amusement lurked in Royce's eyes. "I'm sure. Thank you for your warning, and your clever diversion."

He guided Breanna into the hallway, led her across to the green salon, and closed the door with a firm click.

All humor vanished, leaving only the raw emotions of fear, gloom—and something quite the opposite of both.

"Breanna," Royce said quietly, leaning back against the door and studying her beautiful, composed features. "I know you're terrified. But I promise you, this won't last much longer. I'll find him. You have my word."

Breanna drew a shaky breath. "I can cope with the terror. But this is the second man who's died because of me. *That* I can't endure."

"Sweetheart." Unaware he'd even uttered the endearment, Royce walked over, framed her face between his palms. "*You* didn't kill them. *He* did."

"I know. But his hatred for me prompted him to do so. That makes me responsible, even if indirectly."

Royce felt his insides tug—with compassion, with understanding, with something more.

Gently, he drew her against him, pressed her cheek

to his coat. There was something about this woman, a beauty that was unique by its very design, its very extent, that made him wonder if perhaps he did have a heart after all.

"Hibbert has instructions to watch you like a hawk. You'll never be alone. No one except he, Wells—and, of course, Damen, Anastasia, and I—know you've changed rooms. Oh, and your lady's maid. I told her your chambers were being redecorated. I showed her your temporary quarters, and instructed her to tell no one of their location."

That brought Breanna's head up. "What possible reason could you give her for making that request?"

"Discretion." A corner of Royce's mouth lifted. "I told her you'd chosen that particular room because you wanted to be near me."

Breanna stared at him for a moment, a pink tinge spreading up from her neck to her throat. Then, she began to laugh. "You're the most outrageous man I've ever met."

"I know." His thumbs caressed her cheekbones. "And you're the most extraordinary woman *I've* ever met." He lowered his head, brushed her lips with his—and broached a subject he'd vowed to himself to avoid. "I'm sorry if my actions last night hurt you. I didn't mean for that to happen."

"Which part are you sorry for?" Breanna murmured, making no attempt to pull away from his embrace. "Are you sorry for what we did? Or for the way you behaved afterward?"

"That depends on when you ask me."

Breanna lay her palm against his jaw. "I'm asking you now."

"Now?" Royce savored the pleasure of her touch,

fought the urge to drag her against him. "Right now, my conscience is warring with my instincts. My conscience is sorry I let things go so far. And my instincts are sorry I stopped when I did, that I didn't make you mine as I've wanted to do from the moment we met."

A teasing smile. "I prefer your instincts to your conscience."

"So do I." He kissed her again, a slow, dizzying exploration of her mouth. "We'll talk about this when I return. In the meantime, be careful. Stay inside. I'll be back by the morning after next, at the latest."

Slowly, Breanna nodded, her fists clenching in the folds of his coat. "I will. But Royce?"

"Hmm?"

"Hurry."

15

$\mathcal{H}$e lurked in the brush, waiting until Chadwick's carriage had pulled away.

It was no surprise that Hibbert wasn't in it. As he'd suspected, Chadwick had left his faithful manservant behind, no doubt instructing him to safeguard Lady Breanna's life.

How noble.

The rage he'd hoped to assuage boiled up inside him once again, stronger, more relentless, than it had been before he pulled the trigger, ending Hart's life.

And that rage was aggravated by Royce Chadwick.

The man was an unwelcome complication. He was too inferior to be a threat, but not too inferior to be a nuisance. He was delaying the inevitable, helping to ease Lady Breanna's terror.

He was involving himself in a war he'd never win.

Clearly, he thought himself clever—leaving Medford Manor as scheduled, heading off to Berkshire to try finding Ryder's daughter. He believed it would convince his adversary that he wasn't acting as Lady

Breanna's protector. But the fact that he'd left Hibbert behind said otherwise. It said that Chadwick was coming back.

So the fool hoped to match wits with him.

He was doomed to failure.

It was time to demonstrate that fact.

His mind racing, he massaged his hand, which throbbed beneath his glove after all the hours spent outdoors in the cold. The pain was worsening. He needed to warm it away, to soak his hand beneath some hot compresses in order to ease the knuckle that supported his wooden replica of a finger.

Not yet. Not until he resolved this issue.

But how?

In a flash of insight, he had his answer. Not just any answer, but a brilliant one—one worthy of great genius—its ramifications as exhilarating as its goal.

What a splendid way of putting Chadwick in his place, and furthering his own ends in the process. It would send Chadwick a message and, at the same time, divert the fellow's energies elsewhere—probably straight to Bow Street. Of course, that would mean a greater risk of discovery. Then again, greater risk meant greater excitement. No battle was worth pursuing if the opponent was totally unworthy or the odds of losing nil. By giving Chadwick this demonstration, leading him to a whole different set of answers, it would even the score.

It would also enhance the next shipment by one.

And why not deliver that shipment himself?

Instantly, rage was transformed to anticipation, the thrill of battle mingling with another, equally enticing thrill.

Maurelle. *She* could ease the demons raging inside

him, make him forget ~~the~~ agonizing pain in his hand.

And he could bring her the excitement she craved, satisfy her in ways no other man ever could.

Why hadn't he thought of this before? It was just what they both needed—a profitable cargo and each other.

Not wasting a minute, he crept back to his phaeton, slapped the reins, and rode off.

He was careful to keep a mile span between his carriage and Chadwick's. He knew where he was headed—to Ascot, where, if his exceptional memory served him correctly, Pearson Manor was situated. He didn't recall the precise location, but he'd attended a ball or two there when the dowager's husband was still alive. If need be, he'd stop at some local pub where the ale was cheap, and the patrons poor enough, greedy enough, to sell him a bit of harmless information, such as directions—for the right price, of course—after which they'd forget his visit *and* him. Either way, he'd find the dowager's home.

The easier method, of course, would be to keep Chadwick in sight, let him lead the way.

But Chadwick's instincts were too good.

And it wouldn't do for him to know he was being followed.

An ironic smile lifted his lips. Interesting. The pursuer being pursued. More than interesting. Ingenious.

The elderly, white-haired Dowager Duchess of Pearson listened attentively as Royce presented his facts. Her thin hands folded in her lap, her pale blue eyes unreadable, she sat, straight-backed, in the library chair, waiting until the entire story had been told.

Then, she sighed, her already-lined face creasing further with uncertainty.

"I've protected Glynnis for eighteen years now," she murmured, her tone weary with age and pain. "There's a part of me that would like to keep on doing so. I'd like to send you away, to tell you to advise Lord Ryder that he's lost any right to speak with the mother of his child, much less the child herself. But Glynnis is a grown woman, and a mother. In addition, my own circumstances have changed drastically in the last few months. So I'll let her decide for herself what she wants to do."

Tactfully, Royce refrained from prying, although he did wonder what circumstances the dowager was referring to. "You'll let me speak with her?"

"Yes. I will." Her posture stiffened and her pale eyes narrowed on Royce's face. "But let me warn you, Lord Chadwick. Glynnis's feelings for your client have long since changed from love to resentment, maybe even to hatred. I wouldn't expect a warm reception."

Royce had to admire the woman's loyalty. Moreover, he had to agree with her assessment of Ryder's actions. He'd been a selfish, arrogant fool. The difference was that *now* he knew it. Age had granted him its unique wisdom, opening corridors of his mind that had, at one time, been shut. And one thing that wisdom had afforded him was the realization that blood ties did matter, and that human emotions transcended the bounds of class or monetary status.

In short, he was sorry. Deeply sorry. And while it was much too late to make amends with Glynnis, perhaps it wasn't too late to form a bond, however tenuous, with his daughter.

"I appreciate your honesty, Your Grace," Royce said respectfully. "I have no illusions, nor false hope. I want only a chance to speak with Miss Martin, to explain to her where things stand."

"So be it." The dowager summoned her butler, who came directly to the library.

"Yes, madam?"

"Please ask Glynnis to join me."

"Of course." The butler withdrew, looking not the least bit surprised by the request.

"Glynnis has been my companion since she came to live here," Lady Pearson explained to Royce. "She reads to me, walks with me in the garden and, as of late, keeps me company when I'm confined to my quarters—which is more often than not. It's rare that she's not by my side."

Royce leaned forward on the settee, studied the emotion on the dowager's face. "You care a great deal for Miss Martin."

"She's like a daughter to me," was the shaky reply. "If this were a year ago I would have refused to let you see her. But now . . . I'm in failing health, Lord Royce. According to my physician, I haven't much time. I also have limited funds to bequeath to Glynnis. My poor late husband made some bad investments before he died and what little he left me went to running the estate. So, if there's a future for Glynnis—a good future—somewhere else, I won't stand in the way of her pursuing it. *If* it's what she wants."

A knock interrupted them.

"Come in."

"You sent for me, Your Grace?" Glynnis caught sight of Royce, and halted, looking hesitantly at her employer. "I'm sorry. I didn't know you had company."

"Come in, Glynnis." The dowager beckoned to her. "I'd like you to meet Lord Royce Chadwick. The matter that brings him to Pearson Manor concerns you."

A startled blink. "Very well." Glynnis Martin entered the library, approaching the settee with a shy yet curious demeanor. "My lord." She dropped a curtsy.

Having risen to his feet, Royce bowed. "Miss Martin. A pleasure." He straightened, eyeing her closely and seeing a woman who had once undoubtedly been quite lovely, with thick pale hair and wide gray eyes. But time and experience had taken their toll, and she now looked worn, resigned, her luster faded, her beauty diminished into plainness.

"What can I do for you, sir?" she inquired politely.

For an instant, Royce considered asking to speak with Glynnis alone, then abandoned the notion. To begin with, the dowager would never agree. Further, he sensed the elderly matron might turn out to be an ally, rather than an obstacle.

"Please, sit down," he began, gesturing toward the chair beside the dowager's. "As it happens, I've been searching for you for weeks now. Actually, for you and your daughter."

In the process of settling herself, Glynnis went rigid. "Emma? Why would you be searching for her?"

"On behalf of my client," Royce said gently. "Emma's father."

Shutters descended over Glynnis's eyes. "What do you know of Emma's father?"

Royce lowered himself back to the settee, speaking as frankly and objectively as he could. "I know who he is—the Viscount Ryder. I know you were employed in his home when Emma was conceived. I know he treated you abysmally when you told him you were with child. I know he abandoned you, and ignored your message informing him of Emma's birth." A weighty pause. "And I know that he's aging now, and deeply remorseful for what he's done. He realizes he can never make up for his callousness and negligence. But he wants to try—if not with you, then with Emma."

"Just like that." Glynnis Martin gave an incredulous shake of her head. "He seduced me, threw me out when I conceived his child, and denied that child's existence for eighteen years. And now he's remorseful. Tell me, my lord, how am I supposed to react? With compassion?"

"I'd be lying if I said yes to that," Royce stated bluntly. "Were I in your shoes, I'd probably hate the man. But your scars aren't really the issue here."

She looked taken aback, both by Royce's unexpected support of her plight and by his equally unexpected bluntness. "I see." She cleared her throat, her defensiveness visibly abating. "If my scars aren't the issue, then what is?"

"Emma is." Royce didn't diverge from his straightforward approach. "Look, Miss Martin. Despite all the insults we hurl at him, Lord Ryder *is* Emma's father. And—if it makes any difference at all—I can honestly say his regret at having rejected her, and you, is very real and very acute. He realizes he was a stupid, selfish fool. He also realizes he can't undo what's been done. But he's old, he's alone, and he's aware that his life is drawing to an end. He'd like to meet his child, to try to afford her—and himself—the chance to form some kind of relationship, however tenuous, before he dies. He'd also like to leave her his title, his estate, and his fortune—which is considerable."

Glynnis emitted a soft gasp. "I—I'm stunned. I had no idea." She pursed her lips, recovered herself. "But Emma is not for sale, my lord."

"I never assumed she was," Royce responded, unsurprised by Glynnis's reaction. She was clearly a proud woman, and a protective, devoted mother. All of which he admired—and planned to use, not only to his client's advantage but, whether Glynnis Martin knew it or not, to hers and her daughter's.

"I assure you," Royce continued, his tone and gaze unwavering, "that Lord Ryder has no desire to purchase your daughter. He's not luring her with the promise of money. He's simply offering her all that's his to give." A profound pause. "I'm a very good judge of character, Miss Martin, especially when it comes to my clients. The viscount has no ulterior motives, nor is he stupid enough to believe he can buy Emma's loyalties. He just wants to give her her birthright—and perhaps afford himself a measure of peace, a sense of having left something behind that's real and lasting. Surely you can understand that?"

Glynnis averted her gaze, indecision warring on her face.

"I believe that if you give this some thought . . ." Royce pressed.

"I'm not sure I want to."

"Why?" Royce inquired gently. "Because you might find yourself softening?"

"Glynnis," the dowager interrupted, reaching out to take the younger woman's hand in hers. "Listen to me. You're angry. You have reason to be. I share your anger and hurt, as I have from the day you told me what the viscount had done. But I'm a great deal older than you. And I have a perspective you have yet to acquire. Age changes people. They suddenly see things clearly that, in the past, they were blind to. I think that's what's happening here."

"You expect me to forgive him?" Glynnis asked her employer in amazement.

"Of course not. I expect you to think of Emma. Don't let your bitterness, however justified, cheat her out of what's rightfully hers. You'll regret it."

"What's rightfully hers," Glynnis repeated bleakly. "The viscount's money."

"There's a lot more involved here than money," Royce put in.

"Such as what? A title? Status?"

"You're missing my point. Greed is clearly not in your nature, so I'd be a fool to use it as an incentive to sway you into accepting Lord Ryder's request. I'm urging you to do so for a number of reasons: to give Emma a sense of heritage—something meeting her father would permit; to give her the formal acknowledgment she has been denied all these years; to ensure her future, so she's never out in the cold, alone and abandoned, the way you were." Royce paused, glancing down at the carpet before lifting his gaze to meet Glynnis's. "And last—despite what you've claimed, despite what we've *both* claimed—to offer a shred of charity to a lonely old man. Pain and resentment aside, she is his daughter, Miss Martin."

Her expression softened, and Royce watched her innate decency prevail over her bitterness. "Yes, my lord. I know she is."

"Discuss it with Emma," he suggested. "She's young, but she's hardly a child. I think she deserves the right to know her father has asked to see her, don't you?"

Wearily, she nodded. "Considering how often she's asked me questions about him—yes. She does."

Satisfied with the results of this first meeting, Royce made to rise. "I'll go then, give you a chance to talk with her. I'm staying at a local inn, so I can return—"

"Wait." Glynnis came to her feet in a flourish. "I appreciate how considerate you're being. But I know my daughter. The instant I tell her about this, she'll want to talk with you. So, if you don't mind waiting, I'll get Emma now. Just give me a few minutes alone with her. Then, I'll bring her to you. I'd be grateful if you'd explain the situation to her exactly as you did to me. Would that be too inconvenient, my lord?"

"No, of course not."

In truth, Royce couldn't be more pleased. If he could eliminate a night of waiting, that might enable him to cut his trip by a full day.

And get him back to Medford Manor by tomorrow night.

"Thank you," Glynnis was saying. "I'll get Emma." She turned to the dowager, frowned as she noticed the trembling of her hands. "Your Grace? Perhaps you should retire now. You're exhausted."

The elderly woman nodded, even that gesture appearing to tire her. "If Lord Royce doesn't mind waiting alone, I think I will."

"Please, go up with Miss Martin," Royce said, assessing the situation quickly, and stepping forward to kiss the dowager's quivering hand. "I apologize for tiring you."

"Don't apologize," she said, her fingers tightening briefly in Royce's. She raised her eyes to his, and he saw the shimmer of tears glistening there. "You've brought me just what I needed. Now I can leave this world in peace. Thank you, sir." With that, she accepted Glynnis's arm, leaning heavily against her as she came slowly to her feet. Pausing, she gestured weakly toward the sideboard. "Help yourself to a brandy. It will warm away the winter chill."

"I will. Thank you." Royce watched the two women walk away—Glynnis supporting the dowager's frail, aged frame—and he felt strangely moved by what had just taken place.

He blinked, stunned by his own reaction.

When had he started succumbing to sentiment?

He didn't need to explore that question to know its answer.

Breanna.

The thought of her brought his mind back to returning to Medford Manor by tomorrow night.

Swiftly, his mind raced, laying out plans. He'd reason with Emma now. Hopefully, if she was as curious about her father as Glynnis had implied, she'd agree to ride to Sussex and meet with him late tomorrow morning. That would give Royce the early morning hours to check out the Berkshire shops, and the remainder of the afternoon—after leaving Ryder's home—to cover the shops in Sussex. From there, he'd ride on to Surrey, chat with the shopkeepers before closing, then ride directly to Kent before nightfall.

To Kent—and to Breanna.

Royce gritted his teeth, acknowledging to himself that he had a lot to ponder with regard to Breanna Colby. Tonight, he promised himself. When he was alone in his room at the inn. There, he'd devote serious thought to what in the hell was happening between them, where this fixation was leading.

And what in God's name he was feeling.

It was half past ten o'clock that night when Stacie shut the door to Breanna's temporary quarters, leaned back against it as if to bar her cousin from leaving, and announced, "All right, Breanna. That does it. I'm not waiting another instant. We've made up the room. We've brought in your sketches, your needlepoint, and all your favorite porcelain figures. It's as much home as it's going to be. Now talk to me."

Breanna turned, placing her final statue—the horse she'd had since childhood—on the fireplace mantel. She raised her brows quizzically. "You know as much as I do. Damen is turning up the lamp in my chambers, then coming here to escort you to bed. Hibbert is sitting right outside this door, planning to guard it for the night. Wells is standing at his post like a stubborn sentry who refuses to rest. You and I are both expected to get some sleep, after which—"

"That's not what I'm talking about and you know it." Stacie folded her arms across her breasts, giving her cousin a pointed look. "I've waited since the ball. And I'm not budging until you tell me what's going on between you and Royce Chadwick."

A flush stained Breanna's cheeks. "Oh . . . that."

"Yes. That." Stacie inclined her head. "It's even more serious than I thought. I can tell just by looking at you."

Sighing, Breanna perched at the edge of her bed. "I don't know how serious it is. I only know that I feel as if I'm being tossed about in a windstorm and I can't seem to break free or catch my breath. What's more, I'm not sure that I even want to."

"That sounds suspiciously like love."

Silence.

Stacie came to sit beside Breanna, taking her hand in hers. "Are you in love with Royce?"

Breanna gave a helpless shrug. "I've known him less than a fortnight."

"That doesn't answer my question."

"I know." Breanna stared down at their joined hands. "I think about him constantly. When he's in the room, I can scarcely look away. When we talk, it's as if we understand each other completely, despite the fact that we're so very different in so many ways. And when we touch . . ." A pause, as Breanna struggled to give voice to such intimate feelings. "When we touch, I lose myself entirely. I ache. I burn. I want things I never even imagined wanting. No, not wanting— needing. It's as if there's a whole different me inside, a person I don't even recognize but one Royce seems to know. Does that make any sense?"

"Oh, yes." Stacie exhaled sharply. "A lot of sense." She tucked an unruly strand of hair off her face. "You're in love with him, Breanna. The question is, what are you going to do about it?"

A thoughtful pause. "I have no answer for you. Because I'm not sure how Royce feels about me."

"Find out," Stacie advised. "Better still, help *him* find out. I think you'll both be pleased with the results."

"We're in the midst of hunting down a killer. Surely I should wait—"

"No, you shouldn't." Stacie gave an adamant shake of her head. "Love doesn't wait. Not even for danger

to subside. Aren't you the one who taught me that not
too many months ago?"

A flicker of memory danced in Breanna's eyes. "It
appears my own advice is coming back to haunt me."

Stacie's grin was smug. "Yes. Pity, isn't it?"

At that same moment, Royce was hovering just inside the entranceway at Pearson Manor, patiently answering the last of the two dozen questions Emma
had fired at him since agreeing to meet her father the
next day.

She was a delightful young woman. Much, Royce
suspected, as her mother had been in her youth. She
was charming, inquisitive, and lacking in artifice—her
golden hair unbound, her gray eyes keen and intelligent. She'd been without a father her whole life. At
last she was being offered an alternative. And she was
eager to explore it, if somewhat cautiously, for all the
right reasons.

"Will he expect me to move in right away?" she
asked Royce, concern lining her face. "Because I can't
make that commitment. It depends upon my mother's plans, the dowager's health and, truthfully, how
well the viscount . . . my father," she corrected herself,
"and I get on together."

"Lord Ryder has no expectations, Emma," Royce
replied in total candor. "He'll be elated that I found
you, and that you agreed to see him. After that . . . I'm
sure he has his hopes, but they're not demands."

"He has no right to demand anything," Glynnis put
in quietly.

"You're right." Royce met her gaze, seeing the kind
of bleakness that resulted from having her youth
stripped away, along with whatever hopes and

dreams she'd possessed. Now those dreams belonged to her daughter, and it was clear that, while the dowager might think of Ryder's offer as a future for Glynnis, Glynnis regarded it only as a future for her daughter.

For her, there was only the present—or whatever was left of it when the dowager passed away.

"Mother, will you ride to Sussex with Lord Royce and me?" Emma was inquiring, trying to include her mother in this all-important step.

Royce knew the answer to that before Glynnis spoke it.

"No, Emma. I won't. I can't. Her Grace needs me."

Emma studied her mother speculatively. "That's not the only reason, is it?"

Glynnis drew a slow breath. "It's a very important reason, but, no, it's not the only one. This is one journey I can't take with you. It's one you *must* take in order to move ahead with your life. But, in my case, it would be like slipping backwards, into a past I've finally managed to put behind me. As I said, you have to go. But I can't."

Understanding flitted across Emma's face, and she hesitated, torn between loyalty to her mother and desire to complete a circle that, for her, had never been closed.

"Don't even consider changing your mind." Glynnis obliterated her daughter's dilemma in one fell swoop. She went to Emma, placed a gentle hand on her shoulder. "You must meet him, form your own opinion. He's your father. He's looked high and low for you. You'd never forgive yourself if you refused." Glynnis paused, weighing her next words carefully. "I'll never stop being your mother, Emma, no matter where either of us goes. But I've made my choices. It's now time for you to make yours. Do you understand what I'm saying?"

A solemn nod.

"Good. Then go upstairs and pack. It will be day before you know it."

Emma squeezed her mother's hand. "Thank you." She turned to Royce. "And thank you, my lord."

"You're welcome, Emma." Royce opened the front door, having tactfully retreated to it during the private moment between mother and daughter. "I'll see you tomorrow at ten." His gaze flickered to Glynnis. "Good night, Miss Martin."

She managed a small, if weary, smile. "Good night, my lord. I appreciate your searching so hard for Emma, and for offering her a chance to meet her father."

Royce should have felt satisfied as he descended the front steps of Pearson Manor.

But he didn't.

Instead, he felt uneasy.

He paused at the foot of the drive, glancing behind him and watching the lights go out, one by one, as the footmen readied the house for slumber.

Emma was excited about her upcoming adventure. Glynnis was resigned, if not thrilled, by the unexpected opportunity that had presented itself to her daughter.

The situation was as positive as it could be, given Ryder's deplorable conduct eighteen years ago. As a result, Royce's assignment with the viscount was nearing an end—a successful end. Which was just what he'd hoped for.

So what the hell was bothering him?

Puzzled, he walked toward his phaeton, trying to analyze the unsettled feeling he had deep in his gut. On the verge of climbing into the driver's seat, he paused, turning once again to study the manor, intent on determining the reason for his restlessness.

Everything looked calm, the household settled in for the night.

He pivoted slowly, peering across the grounds, scrutinizing the shadows of trees, the thin layer of fog that was unfolding to hide the moon from view.

All was still.

Still frowning, Royce swung into his seat, unable to explain or shake free of his uneasiness.

Maybe it wasn't Ryder's case at all. Maybe it was worry over Breanna that was plaguing him.

Accepting that as a very real prospect, Royce slapped the reins, guided his carriage onto the road. Anything was possible, he mused, especially when it came to Breanna. It went without question that he wouldn't feel totally at ease until he was back at Medford Manor, overseeing her safety himself.

And catching the bastard who was after her.

He had a feeling sleep wouldn't be forthcoming— not for hours, if at all.

He steered his phaeton toward the village inn.

He waited until the last distant echo of hoofbeats had faded, and the road leading to Pearson Manor was silent.

Chadwick was gone.

The fool should have listened to his instincts, checked out the grounds to see who was lurking about. Not that it would have mattered. He wouldn't have found him.

Well, it was a moot point now. Chadwick had left. Only until morning, judging from the snippets of conversation he'd overheard when the front door opened. Tomorrow morning, he'd be back to take the girl to her father.

Or so he thought.

Slipping his gloved hand into his pocket, the assassin closed his four good fingers around the pistol. His other arm tightened around the horse blanket he carried—one that would serve two purposes tonight.

He'd have to strike swiftly, abandon some of his finesse in lieu of speed and skill. Ah, well. One had to be adaptable, especially when one's attack was spontaneous, one's tactical planning limited to a few brief minutes.

His timetable was excitingly tight—and not only in terms of his invasion of Pearson Manor.

After leaving here, he had to ride to London, make last-minute arrangements with his crew, then rush off to collect the final piece of his cargo.

He also had a package to send off to Medford Manor, the contents of which would ensure Lady Breanna's terror remained at a peak during his two-day absence.

All of this had to be done by daybreak, when his ship would be sailing for Calais.

An almost insurmountable challenge.

One he'd relish—and master.

Soundlessly, he moved toward the manor.

Glynnis Martin stood by the window, listening to her daughter shove a few final items into her bag, then snap it shut, having readied herself for the trip.

Emma was going to her father.

The thought felt more strange than it did upsetting. Perhaps that was because so many years had passed, taking much of the hurt and anger with it. Or perhaps it was because whatever fervent emotion she'd once possessed had long since drained away, given freely and lovingly to her daughter and the dowager.

Eighteen years had passed. Emma had grown to be a secure and level-headed young woman. The dowager had grown to be a trusted mentor and to depend upon Glynnis for friendship, for companionship, for strength.

But now, Her Grace's life was ending.

Emma's, on the other hand, was beginning.

And she?

Most of the time, the only thing she felt was tired. So many years had passed, taking with them her vitality and her hope, leaving behind only a sort of passive acceptance and prayer that Emma's life would be better.

Maybe that prayer was about to be answered.

Emma was young. She could find the energy and the will to forgive—both of which Glynnis lacked. As for the viscount, he'd be captivated by his daughter. Now that he'd taken this important step, decided to acknowledge Emma as his own, Glynnis was certain of that. He wasn't an evil man, only a weak one. And once he met Emma, saw his own charm, sharp mind, and melting smile reflected in her—he couldn't help but love her.

And he could offer her so much that Glynnis couldn't.

Perhaps she'd grown too soft-hearted. Or perhaps she'd just grown weary of battling an emptiness that had lapsed into futility.

"Mother?" Emma came up behind her. "Are you sure you're not upset that I'm going?"

"No, Emma. I'm not upset. In fact, I'm glad—for many reasons." She sighed, wondering how to explain to her daughter that she lacked what was needed to propel Emma into adulthood, that she hadn't the enthusiasm, the means, or even the energy to do so. "I'm tired, Emma," she began, starting to turn. "Sometimes I find myself wishing I could just close my eyes and . . ." She broke off, her words dying on her lips as she spied the intruder.

"And what—sleep?" the man in black inquired. He flourished his pistol, crammed the blanket against its muzzle. "I'm delighted to oblige."

The shot was muffled by the thick wool.

But the result was no less effective.

Glynnis Martin slumped to the floor.

The assassin was beside Emma before she could scream.

Dropping the blanket, he grasped the barrel of his pistol, brought the butt down against the side of her head. Dispassionately, he noted the shocked look in her eyes go dazed, then fade into nothingness.

She sagged forward, unconscious.

He glanced down at her, frowning a bit as he studied the lump already forming on the side of her head. He hated damaging the merchandise. Still, youth was an astounding thing. She'd heal by the time it mattered.

Resuming his work, he leaned over, dragging the blanket over Emma's head and pulling it down around her until she was fully covered. He'd tie her up later, when he was a safe distance away—long before she awakened.

Sidestepping Glynnis's body, he swung Emma over his shoulder, making his way from the room and reversing the path he'd carefully taken to get to her—down the shortest corridor of the servants' quarters and out the rear door of the manor.

Royce Chadwick would be so disappointed, he mused ten minutes later, tossing Emma's unconscious form into his carriage, and climbing in beside her.

As for the Viscount Ryder, he'd be positively despondent.

Unfortunately, there would be no one to carry on his title and his name.

Both would simply have to die when he did.

16

Royce stalked across the small room at the local inn, pouring himself a brandy and tossing it off in an effort to relax.

It wasn't like him to be so unnerved, he thought, unbuttoning his shirt and flexing his back muscles. But he felt unusually on edge, as if he were needed.

Could Breanna be in trouble?

No. He dismissed the notion, not out of fear, but out of pragmatism. Hibbert would never let anyone get to her. Besides, this assassin they were dealing with wasn't interested in storming Medford Manor, alerting the entire staff to his presence. He was interested in isolating Breanna, making her beg for her life before ending it. And that was only after terrorizing her and murdering Anastasia.

The prospect made his blood run cold.

Worry. Fear. Protectiveness.

He was even more personally involved in this case than he'd allowed himself to fathom.

And it wasn't because of his friendship with Damen.

It was because of his feelings for Breanna.

Feelings. That in itself was uncharted territory. The only feelings he'd known until now had been uncomplicated ones—determination, anger, compassion, lust. Those he could deal with; those he understood. Anything more, he'd never received nor learned how to give.

And this preoccupation, this desire to protect, this bloody sense of being off-balance—not only had he never experienced these sentiments, he'd never believed himself capable of them.

Obviously, he was wrong. Whatever emotional deficiencies he thought he suffered from as a result of his upbringing were not entirely irreparable.

But, whatever sentiments he could cultivate, were they enough?

Slowly, Royce sank down onto the edge of the bed, somehow aware that he'd gotten to the heart of his misgivings, his reticence to care for Breanna.

She was all he'd told her she was—beautiful to the core. Yet all that beauty had gone unnurtured for twenty-one years. She'd spent her entire life deprived of the very caring she so naturally offered others. True, she had Anastasia, and a houseful of servants who adored her. But she deserved more. She deserved a man who cherished her as Damen did Anastasia. She deserved a man who recognized her for the exquisite and rare flower that she was, and offered her all that was necessary to make her bloom.

And he? Here he was, slamming into her world like a thunderstorm, taking advantage of her fear and vulnerability, causing her—unconsciously or not—to depend on him. And then, disregarding her innocence, intentionally coaxing forth her natural sensuality, seducing her with words, acting as if he had the right to be that man.

He'd known he wanted her, probably from the first instant he set eyes on her. But what had happened between them last night—whether or not it was the result of the raw emotions generated by the assassin's visit—had been dumbfounding. He'd never experienced anything like it. He was no stranger to passion or its nuances; he'd explored them with more than his share of women.

But last night he'd been drowning. Holding Breanna in his arms, feeling her skin against his, he'd damned near lost control, torn off the rest of their clothes and buried himself inside her. And judging from the look in her eyes, the flush on her cheeks—she would have let him.

God help him, what was he doing? What was he thinking? He had no right to toy with her this way, not unless he was willing, able, to give her everything she needed.

They were so very unalike.

Except for the ways in which they were the same.

And even in their differences, she seemed to see inside him, understand him with a clarity that was startling.

He'd confided things to her he'd never spoken of before. His childhood was a distant memory, a painful precursor to the man he was today. His father was dead. And whatever hold he'd had over Royce had died long before that.

The hold, yes. But the residual pain?

Scars, Breanna had said. Well, maybe she was right. Maybe he hadn't escaped without some of those, even if he was stronger for it, more sure of who he was.

He was hard, detached. He'd told that to Breanna last night. And it was true. Too true, perhaps.

The problem was, he wasn't detached when it came to her. With her, he was in over his head.

Why and to what extent—those were the questions that needed answering.

Was he in over his head because he'd never met a woman as incredibly beautiful, both inside and out, as Breanna—a woman who was so strong and at the same time so delicate; whose depth of passion even she had yet to fathom, much less explore? A woman he wanted almost beyond bearing, certainly beyond resisting? A woman he wanted to protect and devour all at once?

Or, as he was beginning to suspect, was the reason he was in over his head something far deeper?

He'd best find some resolution—soon. Because if he wasn't the right man for Breanna, if he wasn't capable of being all she needed, he had to get away from her—fast. If last night was any example of what happened when they were together, he couldn't rely upon his self-restraint. Despite his best intentions, despite his supposed iron will, all she'd done was look at him, touch him, and every shred of reason had vanished.

He shouldn't go back to Medford Manor at all, certainly not to sleep in the bedchamber right next to Breanna's.

But that insight wasn't going to stop him.

He wasn't leaving until he found that son of a bitch who wanted her dead.

Morning brought with it a blistering headache from too much brandy, and little in the way of resolution.

Still, Royce was dressed and out early, riding to several local villages in the hopes of finding either the shopkeeper who'd sold the dolls or the one who'd sold the statue. Berkshire was a strong possibility—close enough to be accessible to Kent, near enough to London to be bustling, filled with enough shops for the assassin to find an unobtrusive one in which to make his purchases.

The dolls continued to be a lost cause. They were too common, several similar ones having been sold in each of the five shops Royce visited.

The porcelain figure yielded far better results.

It happened in the third shop Royce strolled into. The store, which sold various novelties and trinkets for women and their dressing tables, was tucked away in a village halfway between Ascot and Reading. Sure enough, Royce spotted a row of small porcelain figures near the back of the store.

He summoned the shopkeeper, an amiable enough fellow named Barker, and questioned him about the specific statue he was hunting for.

Halfway through the description, Barker's entire demeanor changed, and he became wary, shifting uneasily from one foot to the other. "I might have seen the statue you're talking about. Why are you asking?"

"Why are *you* unnerved by my asking?" Royce challenged, realizing the man knew something and using the most aggressive tactics possible to scare the information out of him. "Is there some reason you don't want to discuss that particular statue—some reason that might get you into trouble?"

"Yes. No. Not in the way you mean." The man blanched, taking in Royce's powerful build and gauging the distance between him and the door.

"I wouldn't bolt. It's a bad idea." Royce tapped his pocket, made it clear he was armed. "If you'd prefer we could continue this conversation at Bow Street." It was a bluff, but he suspected it would yield the desired results—*if* Barker's fear was the honest kind.

It was.

"Are you a constable or something?" Barker asked hopefully, visibly heartened by the mention of Bow Street.

"Or something." Royce's stare bored through him. The man wasn't a criminal. But he *was* scared. The question was, why? Had he been threatened by whomever bought that statue?

"You're not under suspicion," he continued, offering just enough information to assure Barker's cooperation. "Quite the opposite. It's possible you could help me find someone who's, shall we say, shady. What can you tell me?"

By now, Barker looked more than convinced. "I know the porcelain figure you mean. There's actually a whole group of them similar to the one you described. They're all of two women who look like sisters doing different things together—gardening, sewing, picking flowers. The entire set was on display and for sale. But not in my shop, in my cousin's. His store is in Canterbury."

"You said the figures *were* in your cousin's shop," Royce repeated, furious with himself for missing the obvious. The arrogant son of a bitch bought the statue in Kent. Right out from under their noses. He'd assumed they'd never check the local shops, since they'd already checked there once, for the dolls.

He'd been right. They hadn't.

"So your cousin sold the statues," Royce probed,

determined to get some facts, however limited. "I'll need the name and address of his shop. How recent were the purchases made? How many of the porcelain figures sold? Will he have a record of the sales?"

The shopkeeper waved away Royce's questions. "I can give you Henry's address. But it won't help. He doesn't have any record of the sales. Normally, he would. He keeps fine records. But the statue you're asking about, along with the other half-dozen from that collection, was stolen."

"Stolen?"

"Yes. That's why I got nervous when you asked about the statue. I thought you might be a friend of the thief's."

"Hardly." Royce's mind was racing. "When were the statues taken?"

A thoughtful look. "About ten days ago, I'd say. Henry went home, locked up as usual first. When he opened up the next morning, the statues were gone. Whoever stole them went to a lot of trouble. Cut a pane of glass from the door and let himself in. Perfectly neat pane, too. You'd think he'd smash the glass, climb in and grab all he could, then run before he got caught. No. This thief, whoever he is, cut a square just small enough to fit his hand through. He took nothing but the statues—not even the money Henry keeps in the front drawer." A shrug. "Makes no sense to me. Not to the local constables either. They've been at Henry's shop already. They found nothing."

It makes perfect sense to me, Royce thought silently. *This bastard needs to be superior at everything he does.*

Aloud all he said was, "Thank you for your help, Mr. Barker. I'll still need your cousin's name and the address of his shop, just so I can talk to him and have a look around."

"Sure." The shopkeeper scribbled down the information. "You never said who you were," he commented, eyeing Royce curiously as he handed over the slip of paper.

"An investigator," Royce replied tersely. "And if I find out anything about your cousin's property, I'll let you know. I'll also let Bow Street know how cooperative you were."

The man stood up a little straighter. "Happy to oblige, sir. I hope you catch the man."

Royce's jaw clenched. "Don't worry. I intend to."

Royce's day went from bad to worse.

He arrived at Pearson Manor on schedule, only to see the scarlet coats of two Bow Street runners in the entranceway. The men's backs were to him as they spoke with the dowager's butler. They were nodding, scribbling notes in a pad as the butler mopped at his brow with a handkerchief.

An ominous knot coiled in Royce's gut.

"What's wrong?" he demanded, taking the front steps two at a time.

The men turned. Royce recognized Marks right away, as well as Carson, a younger lad who'd been with Bow Street a little more than a year.

"Chadwick. I'm glad you're here," Marks greeted him tersely. "We sent a messenger to the inn to find you, but you'd already left. I understand you were scheduled to take Emma Martin to the Viscount Ryder's home today."

"That's right."

Marks glanced swiftly at the butler, who looked as

if he were about to swoon. "You can go now. I'll send for you if I need you."

"Thank you, sir." The man practically bolted.

"Marks, what the hell is going on here?" Royce repeated.

"Emma Martin is gone."

"Gone? Are you saying she's run off?"

"I'm saying she's gone. I don't know under what circumstances. She's gone, and her mother is dead. Shot to death in her daughter's room. Sometime last night, it looks like. No one here saw or heard anything. Except, I suspect, the girl. And she's missing."

Royce tasted bile. "What about the dowager?"

"She wasn't hurt—at least not by the shooter. But the news of Glynnis Martin's death was too much for her. Her Grace died a half hour ago."

"Dammit," Royce muttered, his hands balling into fists at his sides. "Goddammit."

Marks scratched his head, studying Royce's reaction. "As you know, Berkshire's not exactly our territory. But when we heard who Emma Martin really was, where you were taking her today—"

"It occurred to you that this murder might be tied to the others you're investigating. The ones involving the London noblemen."

"Exactly."

"Except why would the killer shoot Ryder's mistress?" Carson interjected to ask. "That doesn't fit into his pattern. Why kill the woman?"

"Damned if I know." Marks's answer was candid, his shrug as uncertain as his words. "None of us has any idea what's inciting this lunatic. He's killed four men and kidnapped their wives. Maybe Ryder's next on his list and he came here looking for him. News is all over Town about Chadwick figuring out who the viscount's daughter is. Maybe the killer thought Ryder would come here to claim her, rather than the other way around."

"You're thinking that when the killer broke in, he went straight to Emma's room to find Ryder. And that Glynnis Martin was there and saw him, so he shot her." Carson nodded. "Makes sense."

"It doesn't explain Emma's disappearance," Royce pointed out, although he was already forming his own theory—and it bore no similarity to anything Marks was going to come up with.

"She is Ryder's blood relation," Marks tried. "A mistress isn't bound by blood or marriage. A daughter is. Maybe he grabbed her for ransom."

"But who'd pay that ransom if Ryder was dead?" Royce countered. "For that matter, who's paying the ransom for the other women who were kidnapped? Their husbands' beneficiaries?"

Marks shrugged again. "I don't know any more than you do, my lord. We haven't seen a single ransom note yet—not in any of the four cases."

"Four?" The number finally sank in, and Royce's head came up. "Why are you including Hart in your count? He was killed at Medford Manor, which is in Kent, not London. And his wife wasn't touched."

"Lord Hart was shot in Kent, but his home's in London," Marks corrected. "Everything else about the crime fit the pattern exactly. The target was a nobleman; the method, a gunshot to the chest. As for Lady Hart . . ." A slight hesitation, and Marks exchanged glances with Carson. "This isn't public knowledge yet, Chadwick. We're trying to keep it quiet as long as possible, to avoid mass hysteria. But under the circumstances, you should know. At the same time we got word about what happened here, we got word that Hart's widow disappeared from her London Town house last night. Both crimes happened sometime between eleven P.M. and dawn."

Royce sucked in his breath. "The kidnapper got past Hart's guards?"

"Yes. Just as he did here. Just as he always does. It's like he's a mind-reader or a genius of some kind. He times it perfectly, so he gets by the guards and goes unseen by the staff."

A genius of some kind. Gets by the guards. Goes unseen by the staff. The same method—a gunshot to the chest.

Realization exploded inside Royce's skull.

Of course. It all tied together. It didn't explain the kidnappings, but it sure as hell explained the murders, and the precision with which all the crimes were committed.

He'd assumed Marks and Carson were exploring the wrong path. They weren't. What they were doing, was exploring only *one* of the right paths.

He knew the other.

Royce's brain began pounding with details, one after the other, as pieces of the puzzle fell into place. The murders—when they'd begun happening, the deliberation with which they were committed—it all fit. All but the missing women. That motive was yet to be revealed. But the rest?

The rest spoke volumes.

All the killings, with the exception of Glynnis Martin, were target practice for the killer.

Because that killer and the assassin tormenting Breanna were one and the same man.

The bastard was toying with the authorities while he honed his skill for the ultimate prize.

And that prize was Breanna.

As for Glynnis Martin's death, that had been retaliation, a taunting reminder of who was the master.

That reminder was aimed, not at Breanna, but at him.

Obviously, the assassin had guessed what he was about. Having overheard what Royce intended him to overhear—that he was riding to Pearson Manor to bring Emma Martin to her father—the killer had somehow deduced the rest: that Royce would be returning to Medford Manor, that he'd taken on the role of Breanna's protector.

He knew. The son of a bitch knew everything.

And he was warning Royce to stay the hell out of this—or else.

"Chadwick?" Marks pressed, his eyes narrowed on Royce's face. "Have you come up with something we missed?"

Royce schooled his features, resisted the urge to blurt out his suspicions. To do so would be a mistake. Bow Street couldn't help Breanna any more now than they could before. They needed proof. He had none to offer. All he had was gut instinct. And, however certain that instinct was, it still wasn't proof.

Plus, there was another reason for his silence.

He wanted to get that son of a bitch himself.

"Chadwick, what's on your mind?" Marks demanded.

"I was thinking of Ryder," Royce replied, turning their attentions toward a different concern. "If he is this killer's next intended victim, he'd better be warned."

Marks nodded. "We'll ride straight to Sussex from here."

"Ryder's expecting Emma, not you," Royce said grimly. "I sent him a missive late last night, explaining that I'd found her and that I'd be bringing her to his estate this afternoon. Now, instead of meeting his daughter, he'll be confronted with news of her kidnapping. Not to mention the remorse he'll feel over Glynnis's murder."

"We'll handle Ryder." Marks shot Royce a pointed look. "Leave him and his safety to us. That's our job. Yours was finding the girl—which you did."

"Only to lose her again—and this time not to the safe haven provided by her mother." Royce frowned. "I'll leave Ryder to you. But as for Emma, I'm starting a new search. I intend to find her. That's what I'm being paid to do."

"*After* we find the killer."

"Agreed. The killer comes first." Royce chose his words with care, deliberately avoiding a blatant refusal to leave the detective work to them. Not because he agreed with Marks's assessment. Nor because he intended to stay out of Bow Street's way. But because he knew in his gut that the assassin wasn't after Ryder.

No, the son of a bitch had made his point, right here at Pearson Manor today. Now, Royce would be willing to bet that he'd be returning to circle his true quarry like the vicious predator he was.

Royce's gut clenched tighter.

Let Bow Street guard Ryder.

He was speeding back to Breanna as fast as his phaeton could travel.

17

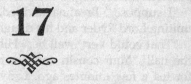

*B*reanna had been on edge all day.

She'd tried doing her needlepoint, then abandoned it after pricking herself three times. She'd then turned to her sketches, but couldn't seem to get the colors right. Finally, she picked up the novel she'd been reading, and found herself staring blankly at the words.

The tension was beginning to get to her.

She tossed down the book, smoothing her hair and glancing at the clock.

Just after four—ten minutes later than the last time she'd checked.

Sighing, she left the bedchamber for the third time since lunch.

Hibbert jumped up from his chair the instant she emerged. "My lady?"

"I'm fine, Hibbert," she assured him, touched by the concern she heard in his voice. "Losing my mind, but fine." She rubbed the folds of her gown between her fingers. "You haven't received word from Royce, have you?"

The barest hint of a smile touched Hibbert's carefully schooled features. "No. Nor do I expect to. He'll finish his business and ride back here as quickly as possible. If not tonight, then tomorrow."

"I suppose." Breanna nodded. "He's probably reuniting Lord Ryder and his daughter as we speak."

"That could very well be." Hibbert gestured down the hall. "Your cousin and her husband went down for tea a few minutes ago. Lady Sheldrake said you should feel free to join them."

"Thank you. I will." Breanna paused. "And so will you."

"Pardon me?"

"Oh, come now, Hibbert." This time it was Breanna who smiled. "Certainly a man irreverent enough to join his employer for a drink in the middle of a ballroom isn't shocked by the notion of joining my family for tea."

"Good point, my lady." One brow rose fractionally. "I am rather thirsty."

"Besides, Wells will be there. The two of you can resume glaring at each other like two male cats fighting for their territory. That should please you."

Hibbert actually chuckled. "A rousing activity, I agree. Very well, you've convinced me. Tea it is."

They were halfway down the stairs when the knock resounded at the front door.

At his post, Wells stiffened. He threw a quick glance at the sitting room, then turned to fix his stare on Breanna, noting that Hibbert was one step behind her.

"I'm armed, Wells," Hibbert said quietly, reaching for his pocket. "Go ahead and open it."

With a terse nod, Wells yanked open the door.

Mahoney stood there, a parcel in his hands.

"This was just delivered to the front gate," he said without preliminaries. "It's for Lady Breanna. The messenger had no idea who sent it. It was left on his employer's doorstep, along with a ten pound note."

"Like the last time." Breanna felt everything inside her go cold. Outwardly, she remained calm, continuing to descend the steps. She put one foot in front of the other, watching Wells and Mahoney stare up at her, seeing Stacie and Damen walk out of the sitting room and into the hall, where they, too, turned anxious gazes to her.

The scene unfolded as if it were a dream.

More aptly, a nightmare.

"You don't have to open it, Miss Breanna," Wells interceded, planting himself between her and Mahoney as if to stave off the inevitable.

"That's true," Mahoney concurred. "I can just toss it out."

"No," Hibbert refuted. "You can't. We have to know what's in there." He made his way to the doorway, leaned around Wells, and took the box from Mahoney. "Thank you. We'll deal with this from here."

Mahoney shot Wells a quizzical look, waiting for official instructions.

This time there was no argument. Wells nodded. "Hibbert's right. We'll deal the matter. You can go, Mahoney. Thank you for bringing the package to us."

He shut the door behind Mahoney's retreating figure, his face ashen as he stared at the box in Hibbert's hands.

"I'll open it, Hibbert." Breanna took the package, which was about the length and width of a portfolio, though twice the thickness, and fairly light of weight.

"Are you sure, my lady?"

"Yes. I'm sure. It's addressed to me." A slight tremor rippled through Breanna's fingers as she tugged off the paper and string, pulled off the lid.

Inside was a smaller box, cushioned by what appeared to be just a rumpled sheet of paper.

It wasn't.

Setting the box on a table, Breanna smoothed out the folds of the rumpled page, and realized it had come from a sketch book.

Her sketch book.

She recognized at once what *had* been her drawing—an expanse of snow-covered ground, flakes falling everywhere, Medford Manor in the background.

Two women had been added to the picture.

Both had green eyes and auburn hair. Both stood, side by side, pain etched on their faces.

Both had blood trickling from the bodices of their yellow gowns to form crimson puddles on the snow beneath them.

"Oh, God," Breanna whispered.

"That's supposed to be us." Anastasia had come to stand beside her cousin, and her voice was choked with horror.

"It's my sketch." Breanna wet her lips, struggled for composure. "At least it was. I drew everything in this picture except the women. And the blood." She swallowed. "It was in my room, in a pile of unrelated drawings. That's why I didn't notice it was missing."

"He must have taken it when he broke in," Hibbert concluded. He took the sketch, frowned at the detail. "These gowns are identical to the one you were wearing yesterday," he told Breanna. "The lemon color, the lace around the sleeves—he had to have seen it. He was either a guest at the party or nearby enough to study you at close range."

"I'll open the smaller box," Wells announced firmly. "Miss Breanna's been through enough."

He walked to the table, removed the inner box and raised the lid.

A puzzled expression crossed his face. "A blanket?" he muttered, reaching inside and lifting out what appeared to be a child's quilt.

"There's something wrapped inside the blanket," Hibbert informed him. He went over, carefully unfolding the layers until he revealed a miniature wicker basket, within which lay a tiny doll—an infant doll—its head smothered by the quilt, its eyes tightly closed.

Pinned to the basket was a note that read: *Lady Anastasia's babe will never see the light of day. Mother and child will die. You, my dear, will watch. Then I'll have the pleasure of watching you die. It's almost time, Lady Breanna. Your bullet awaits.*

From behind her, Breanna heard Stacie's harsh gasp of distress.

She turned, automatically striving to comfort her. "Stacie." She gripped her hands, feeling ill at the sight of her normally dauntless cousin literally quaking with fear. Stacie had gone sheet-white, and was staring at the note with a wild-eyed expression, her control on the verge of snapping.

"I'm all right," Stacie managed, squeezing Breanna's hands in return, before gratefully leaning back into her husband's comforting embrace.

"He's not going to get near you," Damen said fiercely.

"I know." Stacie blinked back tears. "And when it's

only me he threatens, I can handle it. But our child . . ." Her voice quavered.

"We knew the threats would continue," Hibbert said in a quiet, calming tone. "And that's all these are—threats. He's heightening your fear. But he's no closer to touching either of you than he was before. Try to remember that."

"Damen, I'm not feeling very well." Stacie lay an unsteady palm on her stomach. "I'm going to lie down."

"I'll go with you." Damen shot Wells a we'll-talk-about-this-later look.

Stacie paused to glance anxiously at Breanna. "Will you be all right?"

"Of course." Breanna wondered where that composed voice was coming from. "Take Stacie to your room," she instructed Damen.

Watching the two of them climb the staircase, seeing Stacie unconsciously caress her abdomen as if to protect her unborn child, Breanna couldn't help but feel a surge of guilt. Logically, she knew the emotion was irrational. She'd shot that assassin to save Stacie's life. Still, it was because of her that Stacie and the babe were in danger.

And she felt helpless to eliminate it.

Her gaze flickered over the basket and the sketch, and she shuddered, turning away.

"Come, my lady," Hibbert urged, walking over to take her arm. "Let's have that tea we discussed. Wells," he added, without a trace of the usual goading. "Join us."

"Certainly." Wells took Breanna's other arm, and the two men escorted her into the sitting room.

They'd barely poured the tea when a frantic banging began at the entranceway door.

"Now what?" Wells sprang up, rushed to his post.

Breanna clenched her hands in her lap, almost afraid to wonder who it was.

She heard the door swing open.

"Lord Royce." Wells sounded as relieved as he did surprised. "You're back early. Thank heavens."

"Is Breanna all right?" Royce's voice was closer, his heels echoing as he strode down the hall. "Where is she?"

"In the sitting room. And she's . . ."

Royce was through the sitting-room door before Wells could finish. His gaze found her immediately, and Breanna was stunned at the intensity of her relief. *Thank God*, she found herself thinking fervently. *Thank God he's back.*

"Has he been here?" Royce demanded, looking from Breanna's haunted expression to Hibbert's strained one.

"He sent another package," Hibbert replied. "It arrived a few minutes ago."

"But he himself didn't show up, strike directly in any way?"

Hibbert inclined his head in question. "No. What's happened, my lord?"

"A lot." Without elaborating, Royce went directly to Breanna, sat down beside her. He took her hands in his, frowning at how icy cold her skin was. "Breanna?"

She met his gaze, determined to stay strong. She wouldn't fling herself into his arms as she longed to do. Nor would she give voice to the wealth of emotion churning inside her—the numbing terror, the crippling worry, the weak-kneed relief.

The surge of love.

"His gift was even more unnerving than the last,"

she said with as much dignity as she could muster. "But I'm fine."

Royce's stare delved deep, and she had the uncomfortable feeling he could see clear down to her heart.

"Come here," he ordered softly. Without a word, he drew her against him, pressing her cheek to his coat and rubbing her back in slow, soothing strokes. "Still determined to take on the world alone, I see."

Breanna said nothing. But she couldn't resist the need to lean on him. She sank into his strength, her hands balling into fists as she fought the urge to do something she rarely did—not even when her father beat her.

She fought the urge to break down and sob.

If Royce sensed her turmoil, he said nothing. He merely held her, met Hibbert's gaze over the top of her head. "Tell me about the package."

Hibbert complied, describing the entire event from the moment Mahoney knocked on the door.

Royce scowled, rubbing his chin over the smooth crown of Breanna's hair. "Listen to me," he told her quietly. "He's aiming for your vulnerabilities. He knows how much you care for Anastasia. That's why he sent the message about her babe. He wants you to feel twice the terror you would if it were only your own life at stake."

"Then it worked, because I do." She drew back, gazed up at Royce. "What if we can't find him? What if he never gives himself away?"

"We will. And so will he." Royce gripped her shoulders very gently. "He's figured out I'm involved. And he's not happy about it. He's taking action to stop me. That means taking risks. Which makes it more likely he'll give himself away."

She blinked. "How do you know all that?"

Royce hesitated, and Breanna could see him trying to assess her state of mind.

"Tell me," she commanded. "What's happened? Why did you come rushing back the way you did?"

"I was afraid he'd get here first. And I'm unsure of his state of mind right now. Although my guess is, he's gloating."

"Get here? What makes you think he left?"

"Because he was in Berkshire and in London. He followed me to Pearson Manor. And after I left there last night, he killed Glynnis Martin and kidnapped Emma."

For a minute, Breanna wondered if she'd heard right. "What?" She forced the room to right itself. "You'd better explain."

Royce did, beginning with his interviews with the dowager and Glynnis and Emma Martin, moving to Emma's decision to go to her father, and then touching on the uneasiness that had besieged him upon leaving the manor that night. He culminated with what had happened this morning, when Bow Street gave him the shocking news of Glynnis's murder and Emma's disappearance.

"I don't understand," Breanna replied, attempting to sort out all Royce had just said. "Why would you assume the assassin did this? It sounds more like the work of that killer Bow Street's looking for."

"It is. They're one and the same."

"Yes," Hibbert murmured behind her. "It would seem they are." He rose, pacing about for a minute before turning to face Royce thoughtfully. "All the noblemen died the same way?"

"Yes. A bullet to the heart."

"Just like the dolls, the chemise, and now the sketch," Hibbert responded. "The blood on all of them is painted in the chest area." He pursed his lips. "You think the murders were all part of a game?"

"More like target practice. Except Glynnis. That was a message to me."

"He wants you to stay away."

"Exactly."

Breanna stared from one man to the other. "He killed people as *practice?*"

Royce didn't insult her by softening the truth. "Yes."

"You didn't tell your theory to Bow Street, I presume," Hibbert said, more a statement of fact than a question.

"No. I have no proof."

One of Hibbert's brows rose. "Not to mention that you want to catch this blackguard yourself."

"Not to mention that," Royce concurred, a cold light glittering in his eyes. "There's a missing piece, though."

"The kidnappings."

"Right. That's the other thing Marks told me. The news hadn't gotten out yet, but apparently Hart's wife was kidnapped last night, too. So now all the victims have missing wives."

"Except Ryder, who has a missing daughter." Pensively, Hibbert stroked his chin. "Ransom makes no sense. Who would pay it?"

"That's what I want *you* to tell *me*. Check out all the victims. Find out everything you can: who'd inherit if their wives were gone, who drew up their wills, who had a grudge against them—anything that might give us some answers. This assassin doesn't do anything at random. Everything is planned with the utmost precision. He specifically chose his victims, just as he chose to kidnap their wives. There's got to be a reason why. Which means there's a common thread among the victims, besides the fact that they were all of noble birth."

"Glynnis Martin wasn't of noble birth. But then, I notice you've omitted her from your reasoning."

"Bow Street thinks the killer came looking for Ryder and killed Glynnis when she spotted him."

"And you think he killed Glynnis to warn you away from Lady Breanna."

"I know he did."

"I agree. What's more, he probably took her daughter to best you."

"Or to divert me from Breanna."

"Yes—or that." Hibbert pondered his impending task. "I'll begin looking for the common link among the victims. All but Glynnis Martin. I'll assume his motive there was to get at you."

"A wise assumption." Royce looked about restlessly, spied Wells hovering in the doorway, his expression stricken. "Wells, I'll need to see the sketch. And the basket." He hesitated, turned to Breanna. "Do you want to go upstairs and lie down? You don't have to go through this again."

"No." Breanna gave a hard shake of her head. She might be dazed, overwhelmed by all she had to process, but about this point she was adamant. "I want to stay here. I need to help resolve my own fate, as well as Stacie's and her babe's."

"All right." With a flicker of understanding, Royce signaled to Wells to get the package, then waited while he complied.

"The killer had to have been here," Royce murmured, after carefully studying each item. "Not just outside the gate, or on the grounds, or even stealing in and out of Breanna's room. He had to have been in the manor for a substantial period of time. Enough time to see Breanna up close, memorize the details of what she was wearing. He also had to have been at the party to hear news of Anastasia's announcement. It's too soon for outsiders to know about her pregnancy. The party just ended last evening. The package was left on the messenger's doorstep before daybreak. And the killer spent the night rushing from Berkshire to London. So he didn't stop to eavesdrop on street corners."

"Not to mention that he had to have been here if he followed you to Pearson Manor," Breanna added. "How else would he have known you'd located Emma Martin, and that you intended to ride out to see her? You got that message during the ball. Only those present knew about it."

"True."

"So where do we begin looking?" Breanna demanded. "Do we go back to our plan to interrogate the guests?"

"*We* don't do anything," Royce replied pointedly. "Hibbert and I do. We didn't have much of a chance to question anybody before Hart was killed. We'll have to rectify that. Before that, we'll eliminate any other possibilities, however small: workmen who still have access to the grounds, drivers who delivered provisions for the party, even Mahoney's guards. Anyone who could gain entry to the estate."

"You don't really think any of those people is the killer, do you?"

"No. I think the killer is on your guest list." Royce scanned the note. "This was penned by an educated man. It's well-written, polished. I don't know too many workmen with the kind of privileged lives that would afford them a formal education. That, combined with the effortless way he got into your room and onto the grounds to kill Hart, his knowledge of what went on at the party—I'd say it looks more and more likely that the killer was one of the guests. Still, I don't want to overlook anything."

Breanna sank back against the settee, bile rising in her throat. "The very thought of him chatting with my family, laughing with us, eating with us, maybe even dancing with—"

"Breanna, stop." Royce pressed a silencing forefinger to her lips. "There's no point in speculating. It saps strength and wastes time. The important thing is that we find him." He rose, gave the box back to Hibbert. "Find out all you can about the victims," he instructed. "Wells, before Hibbert leaves, give him a list of everyone, from delivery boys to final members of the construction crew, who had access to the grounds this week. Also, tell Mahoney I want to see him. I plan to interview each of his men separately."

Hibbert nodded. "You'll guard Lady Breanna's door tonight, I presume?"

"Oh, yes." Royce's jaw tightened fractionally. "I'll be there. I intend to use those hours to pore over the guest list and do some thinking. Between what you find out for me tomorrow and what I figure out on my own, I intend to come up with some answers."

18

The brothel was posh, significantly more elegant than the dingy one outside Paris where she'd worked as a girl.

Then again, she'd been a child then, grateful for a place to sleep and a few francs in her pocket. She'd have done anything to keep from starving, even work in the Maison Fleur, offering her body to any soldier who could pay for it.

She'd come a long way since those dark days at Maison Fleur, when Napoleon's rise to power was at its peak. She'd clawed her way out of poverty, demonstrated herself to be a shrewd businesswoman. She'd taken a new name, bestowed it upon Le Joyau, the luxurious establishment of which she was now the proud proprietor.

She hadn't expected to see Ansel again.

Their affair had ended long before the war. They came not only from different countries, but from different worlds. It was one thing when he'd been merely a patron. In bed, they'd been equals. He'd paid handsomely for her time; she'd provided the extravagant levels of sexual gratification he craved. But when feelings had intruded, complicating the relationship and transforming it from lust into passion into something even more—something strong enough to compel him to keep her in his life—everything had changed.

Suddenly they were no longer equals. Suddenly, he was demanding that she become an aristocrat's mistress—a role she found far more demeaning than that of whore. Being someone's "kept woman" would strip her of her independence, a condition she couldn't abide. After all, she was as proud and vital as he, his match in every way.

Which was what he found so fascinating about her.

She'd never said good-bye. It would have been too overwhelming. He would have been infuriated. His rages were difficult enough to control, although she knew just how to do so. In her own way, her fires burned as fiercely as his. But he would have misconstrued anything she said, taken it as rejection—and *that* would have pushed him too far. No, it was better to simply drop out of sight, allow him to conjure up whatever excuse his brilliant, arrogant mind chose to.

His finding her again, particularly now, had been a spectacular surprise. Because now her circumstances were different. Now, she could meet him on her own terms. She was financially independent, mistress of her fate, in the prime of life and in extraordinarily high demand.

Not only was their reunion exhilarating, but its timing was *bonne chance*.

Or, if not luck, an unexpected but welcome series of circumstances.

Either way, he was back in her life—a life that was already thriving and now promised to soar.

Draped across the sheets of the lush, oversized bed, Maurelle sighed, stretching her arms overhead and feeling that bone-weary contentment only Ansel could ensure.

Beside her, he exhaled sharply, releasing whatever lingering fragments of tension still plagued him.

"Better?" she murmured, tipping up her chin to study him.

He smiled, a rare gesture that reached up to his enigmatic eyes. "Much. Finally."

She laughed, rubbing her thigh against his. "It did take more vigor than usual to quiet your rage. You've been in my bed for hours."

"And I'll be here hours more." He pulled her over him, his anger transformed once again into that bottomless lust that made their reunions so frenzied and so satisfying.

He drove into her with a violence she found thrilling, and her eyes slid shut, her body tightening as if to meet his violence with her own. He groaned, impaling her again, battering her with the force of his thrusts.

This climax was even more shattering than the last.

Afterward, she leaned up on her elbow, her hair a dark curtain sweeping his chest. "You really are edgy," she murmured, when she was able to catch her breath. "Usually your job drains you. Not so this time. To whom do I owe my good fortune—or need I ask?"

He regarded her from beneath hooded lids. "I won't rest until she's dead. The torture is taking longer than expected. She's acquired a knight. He has to be diverted—or eliminated."

"I see." Maurelle nodded, leaned up to nibble on his chin. "So that explains the rapid delivery of this shipment—and the fact that you came with it?"

"Partly. The rest is simply because I missed you." His good hand reached up, fingers combing her hair off her face. "It's been too long. And I don't intend to let you slip away again."

Maurelle smiled, shifting to bring him more fully inside her. "I'm not going anywhere." Seeing the familiar scowl, she added, "I told you why I left last time, darling. I felt unworthy. Things are different now. I won't be disappearing."

"Soon I'll be here to stay," he told her, the scowl fading as quickly as it had come. "We'll spend the winters where it's warm. And summers we'll spend anywhere you want—Paris, the Far East—anywhere."

She trailed her finger down his chest. "Will I be enough excitement for you, I wonder."

"I could ask you the same."

"Oh, yes, quite enough." A melting smile. "We're well-matched, you and I. In business and in bed." Thoughtfully, she contemplated his promise for the future. "Until the day comes when you're here for good, I'll have to settle for these visits. How long can you stay in Paris this time?"

His hand stilled its motion. "Only a day. I must complete things." A flicker of interest crossed his face. "It should be fascinating to see what Lady Breanna's protector has done during my absence. If he's half as clever as I suspect, he's probably looming over the desk of that Bow Street runner Marks, telling him the killer who shot Glynnis Martin is the same one who's hunting down Breanna Colby."

Maurelle started. "If that's true, won't Bow Street be closer to finding you?"

"Not at all. Linking the two killers tells them nothing. Chadwick has to uncover my flawless plan—and my equally flawless aim. My guess is, he'll figure out the latter—eventually. He won't deduce the former."

"In other words—?"

"In other words, you're quite safe, my love. Chadwick will make the connection between the precise method I used to murder those noblemen and the one I intend to use on Lady Breanna. My gifts alone should have shown him that. As to who I am, why I chose those particular men and, most particularly, my relationship with you, that he'll never piece together. But, if he should, I'll either have finished my business in England and be here with you permanently, or he'll be silenced, permanently. Either way, raising the stakes has made this a much more exciting chase. Don't you think?"

"It certainly sounds that way." She inclined her head, more curious than worried. She knew Ansel and he was too brilliant to leave any stone unturned—most particularly any stones that might endanger her. "What about Bow Street?"

"Bow Street?" A scornful laugh. "They're less of a threat than Chadwick. By the time they've absorbed all the information his lordship provides, decide what to do with it, you and I will be sailing the world."

"Mmm. That sounds heavenly." She gave him a quizzical look. "Chadwick—is that the name of Lady Breanna's knight?"

"Indeed it is. Lord Royce Chadwick. Eminent locator of missing people." The hard edge had crept back into his voice.

"Really." Maurelle kept her tone light. "Then I have more than Lady Breanna to thank for your fervor. It seems I have Lord Royce Chadwick to thank, too."

A brooding stare. "Excitement comes with its price, Maurelle. So if you're probing to find out if my earlier rage extended to Chadwick, I'll save you the trouble. The answer is yes. The man might represent a challenge, but he's also an unwelcome intrusion. I look forward to either besting him or killing him—whichever comes first."

Sensing it was time to change the subject, Maurelle settled herself closer. She could still feel the undercurrents of violence rippling through him, and she draped herself over him, cloaking him like a comforting blanket. "Obviously, some of that rage and excitement are still lingering. Give me an hour to regain my strength. Then, I'll burn away the rest."

He didn't answer. He just lay silently beneath her, savoring her softness and continuing to twine his fingers in her hair.

The clock ticked on, and he felt her breathing even into slumber.

It was times like this when he realized just how much he needed her. He rarely let himself ponder that fact. It only served to remind him that she was his weakness—his *only* weakness. But he knew in his gut that's precisely what she was. What's more, she knew it, too.

She was far too smart to betray him.

However, she was also far too smart not to perceive—and to use—her power over him.

And oh what power it was.

He'd been vibrating with fury when he arrived in Paris. He'd been that way from the moment he saw

Chadwick's carriage leave Medford Manor—without Hibbert in it. Did they take him for a fool? They now knew otherwise. He'd beaten them at their own game.

Winning hadn't helped. He'd still felt that burning emotion churning in his stomach, pounding through his veins. Neither the murder at Pearson Manor nor the kidnapping of Emma Martin and Lady Hart had appeased it. He'd sailed from London immediately and, upon reaching Calais, he'd ridden for Paris like a wildman, his two pieces of cargo in tow.

It was only now, after hours in Maurelle's bed, that he felt the anger recede, the tension seeping from his body like the blood would soon seep from Lady Breanna's.

No one, nothing, did that for him but Maurelle.

He could hardly wait to have her forever.

Idly, he wondered how long it would take Chadwick to figure out the identical methods he'd used to kill all his victims. Probably not long. The bullet wounds were in the exact same spot on each body. One bullet. One clean shot, directly to the heart.

He never needed more than that.

Chadwick would become a permanent fixture at Bow Street, urging them to listen to his theory. They wouldn't, of course, not right away. Breanna Colby's hardships were not their problem, nor was the death of Glynnis Martin who, in their estimation, was nothing more than a servant. Their attention would be focused on investigating Hart's missing wife, tying together the four murders that mattered.

Pleading his case would keep Chadwick busy.

He'd have to stay in London, a substantial distance from Medford Manor.

Leaving only Hibbert to contend with.

The thought brought a tight smile to his lips. The old man didn't stand a chance of stopping him. Neither did that aged butler Wells. The same for Sheldrake. The marquess was a gifted banker, but an inept opponent.

Within the week, Sheldrake's wife and unborn child would be dead.

And then . . . Lady Breanna.

Ah, that reminded him. He had a purchase to make while he was in Paris. Maurelle would do the honors. After which, the gift would accompany him back to England.

Where it would be delivered to Breanna Colby's door.

Something was nagging at Royce.

Sitting outside Breanna's door, he shifted his weight, stretched his legs out in front of him and re-settled himself in the chair. Intently, he stared at his journal, poring over the details about the killer he'd listed.

Some of those notes applied to the assassin who'd killed four noblemen. Some applied to the assassin who intended to kill Breanna.

Being that those men were one and the same, there had to be a link.

But what?

He was convinced the killer had been a guest at Breanna's party.

That certainty had come after repeatedly reviewing the names of the workmen and delivery companies that Wells had provided, then speaking with Mahoney and each of the guards—and eliminating them all as suspects.

So the guest list was the key.

Royce scanned it again, wishing some name would jump out at him as the logical choice.

It didn't.

He leaned his head back against the wall, temporarily abandoning his notes to contemplate what he knew about the assassin.

He was educated. He was well-bred, a member of either the gentry or the *ton*.

Which meant that financial status factored heavily into his life. And *that* meant that, if his own financial status were threatened, and he could somehow gain access to all the victims' funds, it might provide a motive for murder.

That avenue, Royce had already explored. Farfetched or not, he'd pursued it throughout a good portion of the evening. He realized the question of access to the victims' funds would have to wait until Hibbert returned with whatever information he uncovered. But, in the interim, Royce had set out to learn who might be experiencing financial trouble.

He hadn't far to go for his answers. No one knew more about the status of people's finances than Damen. Not only was he at the heart of England's banking community, virtually every one of the guests had funds at the House of Lockewood.

Damen had spent two full hours reviewing all the names on the guest list. He'd compared them with his personal sources as well as his banking records.

Not one of the partygoers fit the bill.

Not that Royce was surprised. Instinct told him that greed had little to do with this. This was showmanship in its truest form. A show of power, superiority, and control, coupled with the vindictiveness and rage of a twisted mind.

He knew the type well. He'd dealt with it many times, and could spot it in a heartbeat.

But it had never been this brilliantly concealed.

Which brought him back to his notes.

He leaned over the page, staring at the words he'd jotted down.

A man paid to kill. Yet one who was willing, no *eager*, to kill for reasons other than money, at least in the case of Breanna.

If the assassin's nature was as Royce suspected, it wasn't money that drove him. It was power. Which explained why he'd killed four other victims to taunt Breanna and hone his skills for her demise. But the *particular* victims he'd chosen—now that was another matter.

Why had he selected those specific noblemen? What the hell did they have in common?

Royce's eyes narrowed on the page. He had the distinct feeling he was overlooking something that was staring him right in the face.

Dammit.

He was just about to start poring over the facts anew when Breanna's door opened a crack. "Royce?"

He pivoted in his chair. Breanna hovered in the doorway, looking a trifle uncertain. She was still fully dressed despite the fact that it was nearly 3 A.M.

"I thought you were asleep." Royce frowned, rising to his feet and taking an inadvertent step toward her. "Is something wrong?"

"No, nothing's wrong." She wet her lips with the tip of her tongue, then blurted out, "You told me to ask for help when I need it, not to take on the world alone. I'm having trouble settling down. My mind is racing. I'd like someone to talk to." A dignified pause. "If you don't mind."

He rubbed the back of his neck, reminding himself that this was the second night he hadn't slept, that his reserves and his self-restraint were severely worn. He had long hours of work ahead of him, and being alone with her was a terrible idea, especially in light of the fact that he was still grappling with his raw, unresolved feelings for her.

He was about to say no, to point out all the reasons why he couldn't do as she asked. Then, he met her gaze, saw how much this expression of need had cost her. To turn her away would be like a harsh slap in the face.

To her, and perhaps to himself.

"I don't mind," he replied, gathering up his notes and stepping into the room. "I'm hitting my head against a brick wall right now anyway."

Breanna nodded, smoothing her hair in that proper way she had—a way that belied the astonishing sensuality he knew hovered just beyond reach.

Beyond everyone's reach but his.

He squelched that particular line of thought, determined to give her whatever comfort she sought.

"I built up the fire," she told him, shutting the door and rubbing her arms for warmth. She crossed over, indicating the two armchairs she'd pulled over to the hearth. "Is this all right?"

"Perfect." Royce waited politely until she was seated, then followed suit. "The fire feels wonderful," he murmured, realizing even as he said it that it was true. "Just what I needed."

A flash of guilt flickered across her face. "You're

cold and you're exhausted. You haven't slept in days. I feel terrible—and responsible."

"You're not responsible; the killer is. And you've tried sending me away three times already. It's not going to work. I'm not leaving you alone. So let's drop that particular subject."

"Very well." Her back was rigid, her palms pressed tightly together as she stared into the flames.

Clearly, she was distraught, whether or not she chose to admit it.

"Breanna . . ." Royce leaned forward, gently touched her arm. "I'm on the verge of figuring out something important. I'm just not certain what it is— yet. But I will be. Hibbert will be back tomorrow, and between the two of us . . ."

To his surprise, Breanna rose abruptly, shaking her head and waving away his explanation. "That's not it. That's not what I wanted to discuss." She whirled about to face him, her fingers knotting in her gown as she spoke, her chin coming up in a purposeful gesture that seemed to contradict her nervousness.

"The next few days are going to be an emotional nightmare," she proclaimed, her words frank and deliberate. "I don't want to have this discussion then, not when the assassin is closing in and you might misinterpret my feelings to be something less than they are, or worse, to try unduly to protect those feelings *and* me. I want to have this conversation now, when I'm still strong and in control and you realize I mean what I'm saying, and that you also realize I won't fall apart from the conversation's outcome."

She gave Royce no chance to respond.

"Having said that, I have to add I'm a novice at this," she confessed, never averting her gaze, although twin spots of red stained her cheeks. "But then, so are you—not at the physical aspect, since I know you're quite seasoned at that. I'm referring to the emotional aspect. That part's as new to you as it is to me. Well, neither of us has much experience at speaking our hearts. And since one of us has to have the courage to go first, and since your scars are apparently more extensive than mine, I decided that someone should be me."

This time she did pause, but only to draw a slow, unsteady breath. "I'm falling in love with you, Royce. And whether you laugh in my face or bolt from the room, I have to tell you so. What's more, I believe you have feelings for me, too—deeper feelings than you choose to. If I'm right, tell me so. Then, take whatever time you need to decide what you want to do about it. If I'm wrong, or if what you're feeling is simply lust and not love, just say so. I've endured a great deal in my life. I won't shatter. But having lived amid secrets, I know I'd much rather face the truth than cling to a lie. So tell me what you're thinking, and what you're feeling. Not about the assassin. About me."

She broke off, watching his reaction, a flushed but expectant look on her face.

Royce just stared, wondering if he'd ever been rendered so off-balance. This was Breanna, casting aside propriety and self-restraint, not in the throes of passion, but to speak her mind. She was relaying her feelings with all the dignity she possessed and a directness that came with great effort.

His first coherent thought was how incredibly proud of her he was. What she'd just done had taken an amazing measure of courage—a measure of courage he was a stranger to.

Ironic, he was reckless, daring, downright formidable when it came to his enemies. He was also the consummate risk-taker. Yet, when it came down to it, she was far braver than he.

His second thought wasn't a thought at all. It was a surge of feeling so strong it nearly felled him—as did the realization that accompanied it.

She might be falling in love with him, but his fall was already complete.

All that was left was to acknowledge it, to her and to himself.

Slowly, he rose, watching the firelight turn her hair to an auburn blaze as he reached out, framed her face between his palms. "You've given me candor. Let me give you the same in return." His voice sounded hoarse to his own ears. "I thought about you every minute I was away. I told myself I wouldn't hurt you, that if I couldn't be everything you needed, I'd walk away. But I won't. I can't. Because, whether or not I believed myself capable, whether I can give you every fragment of emotion you deserve, whether it happened so fast I never saw it coming, I love you. I love you in a way I never imagined, much less experienced." His thumbs caressed her cheeks. "Does that answer your question?"

"One of them, yes." Breanna gave a shaky nod. "The next question is harder. What do you want to do about it?"

"What do I want to do about it?" Royce's reply emerged with a will all its own, having formed somewhere inside him that required no conscious awareness. Yet even as he spoke the words, he knew they were true. "I want to protect your life with my own. I want to immerse myself in your beauty every moment for the rest of our days. I want to drag you off to the nearest church and make you my wife."

Two tears slid down Breanna's cheeks. "I didn't expect . . ." She brought herself under control. "I didn't expect an answer. Not right away. I told you to think about it."

"I don't need to. My answer won't change." He captured her tears with his thumbs. "Don't cry. Just consider my proposal. I know I'm not the staid, conventional man you expected to marry. But—"

"I don't need to consider it. I accept." Breanna stood on tiptoe, brushed his lips with hers. "I love you. I want nothing more than to marry you. As for the last . . ." Her eyes sparkled through her tears. "Since I met you I discovered something about myself. I loathe convention. It bores me to death."

"Does it?" Royce was still reeling with the impact of what had happened, all he'd just discovered about himself. Feeling almost giddy, he caressed Breanna's nape, continuing to let his impulses guide him. "May I test that claim in a way I've wanted to since the first instant I laid eyes on you?"

"By all means."

His fingers glided into her hair, caressing the satiny crown before—in slow, exacting motions—he began tugging out the pins, tossing them randomly about until her auburn tresses tumbled free.

He threaded his fingers through them, draping them around her, then capturing her shoulders, pulling her to him. "Beautiful," he murmured. "Now come here."

She stepped closer, and his arms encircled her, brought her up against him. "No one's ever seen your hair this way—free, uninhibited—have they?"

Breanna's breathing was unsteady. "No. Not my hair, and not me."

"Good." He lowered his head, covered her mouth with his.

The kiss was slow and hot and deep, and Breanna's soft sound of pleasure vibrated through them both. Royce gathered her more closely to him, savored her taste, the softness of her lips, the exquisite feel of her tongue as he possessed it with his own. She leaned into him, molding the contours of her body to his, wrapping her arms around his neck and wordlessly showing him how much she loved him.

Royce responded with a hard tremor, lifting her up and into him until there was nothing separating them but the impeding layers of their clothing.

The kiss went on and on, ending only to begin anew, generating fiery currents that flowed between them, intensified more and more with each passing second.

It was Breanna who eased away, leaning back a fraction, and staring up at him with jade eyes that were smoky with passion. "Royce?" His name was a wisp of sensation against his lips.

"Mmm?" He could barely speak.

"I really wanted to give you time to think about our future."

"I know. I didn't need it."

"That's not what I'm getting at." Her fingers trailed across his jaw, drifted down the side of his neck. "When I asked what you wanted to do about the fact that you love me, I meant it in the more immediate sense." A suggestive pause. "As in, what do you want to do about your feelings *now?*" Her lips traced the path her fingers had taken, feathering kisses along his heated skin. "Right now."

Royce's eyes slid shut, her vivid invitation making hot need explode in his loins. "Breanna . . ." His fingers tangled in her hair, intending to move her away from him but never quite doing so. "I promised myself I wouldn't—"

"Break that promise," she whispered.

All Royce's good intentions crumpled. "You want to know what I want to do about my feelings?" he rasped, his palm moving down to cup her breast, his thumb teasing her already hardened nipple. "I want to lay you down by the fire and bury myself inside you."

She shivered, stifling a cry as she shifted herself more fully into his hand. "Follow your instincts. They've always served you well." Blindly, she pushed open his coat, slid her palms up the front of his waistcoat.

"Breanna—"

"Don't be noble, not this time." She unfastened his buttons one by one—first his waistcoat, then his shirt. "It took all my courage to bare my heart to you. Please don't shield yours from me now." She slipped her fingers inside his shirt, caressed him tentatively. "Protect me when I need it. Not when I don't."

He felt her delicate touch on his skin, and the last of his resolve disintegrated into dust. "Sweetheart . . ." He forced out the words, determined to say them before it was too late. "This time I won't be able to stop."

Her smile was tremulous. "I'm glad."

"Are you?" It was a lost cause, and he knew it. He was already reaching around to dispense with the buttons of her gown, frantic to have her in his arms, under his body. "First, we should be talking about the future. What you need, what you deserve."

"We'll do that later. What I need now is you."

Something inside Royce snapped.

He swept Breanna up into his arms, placed her on the rug in front of the fire, and followed her down. His mouth devoured hers, leaving it only to blaze kisses down her throat and neck to the top of her bodice. His fingers finished their task, and he tugged down her gown, his mouth continuing its journey even as his fingers shifted to the ribbons of her chemise.

His lips surrounded her nipple, and he tugged at it, first through the barrier of her chemise and then beneath it. He lost himself in her flavor, his tongue lashing across one hardened peak and then the other, and he reveled in her cries of pleasure, the uninhibited motions of her body.

His hands were shaking as he dragged away her clothing, tearing the delicate material in his frantic haste to have her naked.

When he finished his task, he sat back on his heels and stared.

She was breathtaking, more beautiful than even his fantasies had evoked. There were no words profound enough to express his feelings, so he settled for making love to her with his eyes, drinking in the glow of her skin by firelight, the perfect curves and hollows that she'd offered only to him.

God, he was blessed.

"Royce?" She reached for him, not with uncertainty, but with eagerness. "Please—"

"Have you any idea how beautiful you are?" he choked out, letting his hands explore her, stroking upwards from her legs to her hips, then higher to cup her breasts, whispering over the tender points of her nipples. "Any idea?" He absorbed her quivering sigh, his hands retracing their journey, this time pausing to caress her thighs, to part them to his touch. "You humble me." He brushed the auburn cloud that beckoned him, first lightly, then more intimately, his fingers opening her, gliding inside to explore the velvety folds.

She was so perfect, Royce thought he'd die from it. He repeated the caress, and Breanna cried out, arching against his hand, her entire body responding to the new, unbearably erotic sensation.

Royce's fingers slid deeper, pushing into her gradually, his entire body pulsing with a need so acute, he actually wondered if he might spill himself before ever getting his breeches off.

Breanna provided that answer.

When she inadvertently tightened around him, warm and wet, tiny tremors shimmering through her, he regained control—only to feel it slipping away again.

Shoving himself to his feet, he tore off his clothes, scarcely giving her time to breathe before he covered her body with his. He moved against her, torturing himself with the motion, then kissing her fiercely as he repeated it.

Breanna undulated beneath him, rubbing her breasts against his chest, urging her lower body up to his, and wrapping her arms around his back.

"Don't." He shuddered. "God, Breanna, don't."

"Why?" she whispered breathlessly. "It feels so good."

He tore his mouth away, stared down at her through a red haze of passion. "Because I want you too much. I'm not going to be able to hold back." Another shudder. "I already can't hold back."

"I don't want you to." She caressed his spine, traced the taut muscles of his back. "Please, no holding back."

"I'll hurt you."

"No you won't." She arched restlessly beneath him. "Tell me what to do."

"Just . . . yes . . ." he grated out, as her thighs parted beneath him. He nudged them farther apart, settling himself in the cradle between them, his rigid shaft finding the heated entrance to her body.

"Like this?" she whispered, raising her knees to hug his flanks.

"God . . . yes." He was already crowding into her, his hips moving reflexively, blatantly ignoring the dictates of his mind, which warned him how small she was, how delicate and tight. As if to further test him, Breanna melted around him, hot and clinging, stretching to take him deeper, her soft moans of pleasure obliterating any hope his mind had of regaining control. "Sweetheart . . ."

"Make love to me," she breathed, her hands gliding down to the base of his spine, as if that motion alone would be enough.

It was.

Cupping her bottom, Royce pushed into her, reached the barrier of her innocence, then thrust beyond it. He sank into her, sweat drenching his body as he buried himself inside her the way he'd burned to do from the start.

Breanna tensed, instinctively biting back her cry of pain—which gave Royce the strength he needed to wait.

"Don't," he said fiercely, raising his head to look deeply into her eyes. "Don't hide what you're feeling—not your pleasure or your pain. No holding back." Deliberately, he repeated the same phrase she'd spoken to him.

Slowly, she nodded, her body relaxing even as she did. "It doesn't hurt anymore," she murmured, wonder in her eyes. "It feels so . . . oh . . ." She cried out, this time with pleasure, as Royce drew back slightly, then pressed forward, sinking deeply into her.

"So incredible?" he finished for her.

"Yes. Incredible." She urged his mouth back to hers. "Don't stop."

"I couldn't if my life depended on it." He kissed her hungrily, beginning an exquisite motion of plunge and retreat that made the world spin away in a torrent of sensation.

Instinctively, Breanna understood the rhythm, and her hips lifted, undulating to meet each one of his quickening downward strokes.

A roaring commenced in Royce's head, a passion he'd never known mingling with a love he'd never imagined, his every nerve ending attuned to Breanna, and to the engulfing culmination that hovered just beyond their reach.

"Royce . . ." She was frantic now, her inner muscles taut, slick with need, her nails scoring his back as she struggled for that elusive peak she couldn't yet fathom but was desperate to capture.

Beyond conscious thought, Royce simply reacted, hooking his elbows beneath her knees and pulling her legs up higher around him, opening her fully to his possession.

He penetrated her with one deep, inexorable stroke, then another—this time caressing her inside and out, only to do it again and again and again.

Breanna plunged over the edge.

She arched wildly, a dazed, stunned look widening her eyes as she reached the pinnacle of sensation, and fell.

Royce covered her mouth with his, swallowing her sharp cry of pleasure and shuddering as her hard spasms gripped him, spiraling out from deep inside her—quickening in pace, intensifying in strength—clenching his engorged shaft until he could take no more.

He climaxed violently, his own release slamming through him with the force of a blow. Biting back a shout, he gave in to the wildness, his hips moving convulsively as he poured himself into her, each burst of completion more powerful than the last.

The moment seemed to go on forever, tiny aftershocks of Breanna's climax rippling over him, triggering yet another burst of wetness as the last of his seed emptied into her.

Then . . . peace.

Royce collapsed on top of her, his head dropping into the crook of her neck, his body blanketing hers. The room was silent, but for the crackling of the fire and the harsh, rasping sounds of their breaths.

Sanity returned in increments and, slowly, Royce became aware of his surroundings. Beneath him, Breanna sighed, her legs unclenching and sliding down to sink into the rug, her arms going lax around him. Her breathing was still ragged and, abruptly, he realized she was trembling.

"Breanna?" He tried, unsuccessfully, to lift his head, and settled for murmuring in her ear instead. "Sweetheart?"

"Mmm," was the muffled reply.

"You're shaking."

"And you're astonishing."

He smiled at the dreamy quality to her voice. "That compliment belongs to you. I think I'm half-dead."

"No, you're not." Her fingers trailed lightly down his back. "I can vouch for that."

He kissed her neck. "Am I crushing you?"

"Only in the most wonderful way."

Forcing himself to move, Royce rolled to one side, taking Breanna with him and keeping their bodies tightly joined. Then, he groped around until he found the blanket he'd seen lying near the armchair, pulling it over them until they were securely covered. "How's that?"

"Ummm," she responded, snuggling closer and rubbing her thigh over his with that innate sensuality he found so unbearably arousing. "That's perfect."

He cupped her face between his palms, studied her intently. "Does it hurt?"

She shook her head, sending masses of her newly freed hair tumbling about. "Not even a bit. It feels," she wriggled slightly, taking him deeper into her, "more right than I can say."

Royce felt his body leap in response—an astounding fact considering that minutes ago he thought himself incapable of moving, much less making love.

More astounding was the emotion that accompanied it.

"Breanna," he said, determination lacing his words. "I meant what I said earlier. We need to talk. To make plans. The minute I eliminate that bastard who's after you, I'm dragging you off and putting a wedding ring on your hand."

She traced his lips with her fingertips. "You'll get no

argument from me." A pause. "Although I really meant it when I said I didn't expect you to decide our future right away. Love is one thing, marriage quite another. You're a very independent man, Royce. I don't want you to feel as if you're sacrificing that independence."

"If you're telling me not to need you, don't bother. It's too late." Royce kissed her fingertips. "I don't feel less independent. I feel lucky." A heartbeat of a pause. "And I want to give you everything you deserve."

"Including a depth of emotion you're still not sure you're capable of," she replied astutely. "Well, you might not be sure, but I am. And I happen to be a very wise woman."

Royce chuckled, tangling his hands in her glorious auburn hair and kissing her tenderly. "Yes, you are."

She wrapped her arms about his neck. "I love you," she whispered.

Royce's eyes darkened with emotion. "I didn't realize what I was missing. Now I do." His palm slid around to caress her nape. "You're the most beautiful, courageous—"

"Surprising?" Breanna added with a shaky laugh. "I've never been so forward in all my life. I still can't believe I just seduced you."

One dark brow rose. "Is that what happened? Funny, I recall it being very mutual."

"But I initiated it. I think there was a part of me that knew it would happen the minute I stepped into the hallway." She gave a dazed shake of her head. "My heart was pounding when I walked out there. Because I was determined to tell you that I love you. I'm sure you've guessed I'm rarely so audacious. In fact, I can only think of one other time I shocked myself as thoroughly as I did tonight."

"When was that?"

"When I held my father at gunpoint."

Royce propped himself on one elbow, feeling more intrigued than stunned. "Was that when he was going after Anastasia?"

A nod. "He planned on selling her. He meant to ship her off to some animal named Rouge, who sold women as prostitutes. And he was going to beat me until I told him her whereabouts. I couldn't allow any of that. Something inside me just snapped." She inclined her head, gazing thoughtfully up at Royce. "I often relive that moment. And I wonder what I would have done if he'd disregarded my threats and continued advancing toward me. Would I have pulled the trigger? I honestly don't think I could have—not then. Maybe because he's my father, and maybe because I hadn't yet actually heard him hire an assassin to do away with Stacie. If I already had, or if I'd seen Father either hurt Stacie or shove her onto that ship bound for Calais, my anger might have won out over my reticence. I don't know."

She inhaled shakily. "But with the assassin, it's different. He's a cold-blooded killer who's made it flagrantly clear he intends to murder Stacie and her unborn child. In his case. . . . Royce, I think I could shoot to kill."

In response, Royce's jaw clenched. "I know you could," he replied, that fierce mixture of pride and protectiveness welling up inside him. "But you wouldn't be able to do it fast enough. I'd beat you to it. Because I'm the one who's going to kill that bastard."

A tiny shiver went through Breanna, as if some premonition told her that's precisely how it would happen.

Blindly, as if to ward off the ugliness of their discussion, she reached up, twined her arms around Royce's neck. "No more." She tugged his mouth down to hers, obliterating all talk of the assassin by rekindling the beauty they'd just shared. "No more talk about him tonight." She pressed closer, shifting her hips ever so slightly, drawing Royce into her melting warmth. "Tonight is ours," she whispered. "I want nothing else to intrude."

Royce responded with an overwhelming urgency, his body hardening to rigid fullness, swelling to fill hers. "It won't," he murmured, rolling her to her back, pressing deep inside her. "Not tonight. Not ever."

19

"*Y*ou're saying there's no connection among the victims, at least not financially," Royce stated, taking a healthy swallow of brandy and leaning against the sitting-room mantel, regarding Hibbert, who'd just returned from his investigative excursion.

"None." Hibbert settled himself in a chair, and glanced through his notes. "Except that they all lived in London and were all affluent."

"What about their wills?"

"Four separate solicitors drew them up. I spoke with all of them. They had nothing substantial to offer in the way of information. As for the beneficiaries, none were common among the victims. Each of the wives stood to inherit first. But, in the event the wives died before they did, each gentleman made different provisions. In two of the cases, the estates were bequeathed to grown daughters by a previous marriage, in one case to a grown nephew. In the case of Lord Hart, it was left to a son he'd sired with one of his mistresses."

Royce frowned. "Nothing to the children they shared with their current wives?"

"There were no children with their current wives. That was the only other link I found among the four noblemen. Their wives were significantly younger than they, and had been married a relatively short period of time—three years or less. My guess is that's what led Bow Street to suspect the women were involved. They had huge fortunes to gain and long years in which to enjoy them."

"Have any of the beneficiaries pressed to collect their money?"

"No." Hibbert shook his head. "They're all wealthy in their own right, other than Hart's illegitimate son, who ran off years ago and took to the sea. The other three are waiting patiently. They're more interested in finding out who killed the victims and kidnapped their wives than in claiming an inheritance."

His frown deepening, Royce stared off into space. "So the men all had young wives—wives who disappeared, taken by a kidnapper who's made no attempt to get at their husbands' money." He took another swallow of brandy. "Which brings us to the question, if the killer isn't holding these women for ransom, what did he do with them? Murder them? If so, why haven't the bodies turned up? If not, what would he want with them?"

Abruptly, Royce broke off, his own words finding their mark.

Realization struck hard, and the missing piece fell into place.

"Dammit," Royce bit out, slamming his goblet to the sideboard. "It's been right in front of me all this time and I never saw it." He turned, his hard stare finding Hibbert. "We've been assuming the men were his intended victims. They weren't. They were merely sport—as I said, a sick game of target practice to ready him for Breanna. It's their wives who were his true marks. *They* were the ones he wanted. And, as you discovered, they're the ones with something in common—their youth, their childless state."

Hibbert gave him a puzzled look. "You've lost me."

"Something Breanna said last night just sank in." Royce began prowling about, his forehead creased in thought as he polished his theory. "Or rather, two things she said in the same breath. She referred to overhearing her father arrange for the assassin to kill Anastasia, and she referred to having to bear the knowledge that he intended to sell her cousin as a prostitute."

"We knew both those facts."

"Yes, but we didn't look for the common link between them. We never directly tied the assassin to Medford's selling of women. But there is a tie, a strong one—Cunnings."

Hibbert's head came up, his eyes narrowed as he caught his employer's implication. "It was Cunnings who Medford paid to hire the assassin. So we know Cunnings and the killer were well-acquainted. We also know that Cunnings was aware of Medford's business of selling women. Which means he could very well have mentioned that fact to his colleague."

"Cunnings was more than *aware* of what Medford was doing," Royce corrected. "From what I remember of the Bow Street report, he was right in the thick of things. While he went about hiring the assassin, he was also trying to provide a substitute for Anastasia— another nobly-bred young woman to send to Paris.

That way, Anastasia would be eliminated, and George Colby would still get paid by his French buyer. Cunnings knew he'd be handsomely rewarded for managing both."

"A fact he could have boasted to the killer," Hibbert murmured.

"Right. After all, he was taking on a daunting task. Highborn ladies don't vanish as easily as workhouse women do. They're missed—*if* there's someone alive to miss them."

"You think the assassin picked up where my father left off?"

Both men started, jerking about to see Breanna standing in the doorway, her face drawn, her eyes filled with pain. "You think he sold those four women?"

"I think it's a strong possibility." Royce walked over, took her hands in his.

"But why? We've determined he doesn't need the money . . . Don't answer that," she amended, with a shiver of disgust. "The challenge. Winning. God, this is sickening."

"But it makes sense," Hibbert said quietly, glancing at his notes. "As you pointed out, none of the wives had yet borne children—which probably means they were fresher, more youthful-looking, and therefore more desirable to whomever purchased them. None of them had relatives, other than parents who lived far away and represented no threat to the assailant."

"All but Emma Martin." Royce raked a hand through his hair, another glimmer of insight taking shape. "That miserable bastard not only bested me by killing Glynnis and stealing her daughter, he furthered his own sick scheme in the process."

"Emma must have been among his latest shipment." Hibbert nodded. "I agree. Which brings to mind another fact. All the women lived in London, which made them easily transportable to the Continent. All except Emma. My guess is she was dragged there by the killer, who then sent her off along with Lady Hart."

"Sent off to whom?" Breanna asked. "Has that Rouge person my father dealt with resurfaced? Or is there someone else buying these women?"

"I don't know. But since Emma and Lady Hart were kidnapped two days ago, the shipment that included them had to have left between then and now. We'd better act fast." Royce was already in motion, crossing the threshold into the hallway. "Wells," he called, summoning the butler. "Where's Damen?"

"He's upstairs with Miss Stacie," Wells reported. "I didn't alert them to the fact that Hibbert had returned. It's after eleven o'clock and Miss Stacie is exhausted. I assumed we could disturb them if it became necessary."

"It just became necessary," Royce informed him. "Get Damen. Tell him to come down here, and to bring every bit of information he accumulated on that M. Rouge who was buying Medford's cargo."

Wells blinked. "Is Rouge the killer?"

"No. But he might know him." Royce turned back to Hibbert. "One of us has to ride to London. I want to check the manifest of every ship that has sailed in the past few days. Perhaps something will strike us as suspicious. Or maybe someone at the docks will even remember Emma Martin or Lady Hart, if we describe them."

"Pardon me, Lord Royce, but I have a suggestion."

Wells had paused on his way to the stairs. "Neither you nor Hibbert has slept in days. What's more, the docks will be practically deserted until daybreak, with no one either knowledgeable enough or sober enough to talk to. My advice is to go to bed directly after your meeting with Lord Sheldrake. That applies to Hibbert, as well. I'll stand guard outside Lady Breanna's room tonight. After a decent night's rest, you can ride to London."

"Thank you, Wells, but I . . ." Royce broke off, realizing how absurd it would sound for him to say he trusted no one other than himself when it came to Breanna's safety.

A look of gentle understanding touched Wells's features. "I've protected her for twenty-one years, sir. I'm certain I can continue to do so—during those rare times when I'm needed."

"You'll always be needed, Wells," Breanna said softly. She gazed reassuringly at Royce. "I'm in excellent hands. Do as Wells suggested and get some rest."

Royce nodded. "All right—*after* I've spoken with Damen."

"I'll get him at once." Wells hurried up the stairs.

"Breanna," Royce said, turning his attention back to her. "I know Bow Street questioned your father thoroughly when they brought him in. Did he tell them anything specific about this French contact of his, this Rouge?"

"No." Breanna shook her head adamantly. "Just as Father never met the assassin, he never met Rouge. Their only contact was by post. Rouge was very careful to keep it that way. Evidently, he's the one who originally sought my father out, not the other way around. The way Father described it, Rouge sent him a letter, said he had a proposition he thought could benefit them both. He was aware of my father's financial woes. He was also aware of the fact that my father would go to any lengths to resolve those woes. Father responded at once, and their alliance began."

"You're sure your father was telling the truth, that he wasn't concealing anything?"

Breanna sighed. "My father is a coward, Royce. If there were any chance of lessening his own punishment by blaming someone else, he would jump at the opportunity. So, yes, I'm sure he was telling the truth."

"Then there's no point in my wasting time at Newgate. As for Rouge's knowledge of your father's desperation and lack of ethics, he could have picked that up anywhere—at a club, a tavern, right here in England, or in Paris from a chatty English visitor. There were certainly enough people who knew Medford's ways." Royce pursed his lips, thinking. "Let me hear what Damen knows. Then, I'll get some of my less reputable contacts involved."

"Less reputable contacts—you mean, criminals?"

Breanna sounded more intrigued than shocked, reminding Royce yet again that she was far stronger than her delicacy suggested.

A corner of his mouth lifted. "Yes, but not hardened killers. Just seedy types who have more wits and brains than scruples. They get me information, I pay them well."

"Snitches, you mean."

"Yes."

"That makes sense. After all, finding unscrupulous people is what you do."

"Indeed it is. And one thing I've learned is that

there's no one better equipped at ferreting out a criminal than another criminal."

"Which is certainly what we're dealing with here," Breanna replied bitterly. "Whether it's Rouge or someone else, we're dealing with an animal, someone who buys women."

At that moment, Damen strode down the stairs, his mouth drawn in a grim line. In his hand was a letter.

"Wells stayed upstairs," he announced. "I want him guarding our bedroom door. Normally, Stacie would have beaten me down the stairs to take part in this conversation. But she's asleep—the first real rest she's gotten in days. She never heard Wells knock, and she didn't budge when I left the room. I've never seen her sleep so deeply. Frankly, I'm worried sick about her."

"She's under a lot of strain, Damen," Breanna said, trying to soothe him—and herself. "This pregnancy was difficult to begin with. And now, fearing for her babe, her strength is depleted. As soon as we stop this assassin . . . as soon as we . . ." Her voice quavered, and she broke off, averting her gaze.

"Breanna, I'm sorry," Damen responded at once. "This has been hell for you. I didn't mean to be insensitive."

"You weren't." Swiftly, Breanna composed herself. "I'm as worried about Stacie as you are. But I truly believe Royce will catch this monster."

"I intend to. Is that all the material you have on Rouge?" Royce interrupted, pointing to the letter Damen held.

"Yes." Damen handed the correspondence to Royce. "It's an explanation from Dornier, the manager of my Paris branch. As you know, Rouge and Medford used the House of Lockewood—both the London and Paris branches—as hubs through which to send messages. Cunnings was their intermediary. When I attempted to check out Rouge, I contacted Dornier for my initial answers. That's his reply you're holding. Go ahead and read it."

He waited while Royce complied.

"According to Dornier, Rouge himself never made an appearance at the bank," Royce muttered as he skimmed the letter. "Everything was forwarded to an address in Paris ... 4 Rue La Fayette. Rouge was never seen by anyone—not even the messenger, who was instructed to slide the letters under the door and leave."

"Exactly. That's as far as my investigation got. I advised Dornier to hire someone to follow the messenger the next time he arrived for Rouge's mail. But next time never occurred. Medford was caught, and Rouge simply dropped out of sight."

"Seemingly."

Damen's brows drew together. "Seemingly? Does that mean you suspect he's still involved in all this?"

"Someone is." Swiftly, Royce recounted his latest suspicions to Damen, explaining what he'd pieced together about the assassin and his overseas dealings.

"But we have no idea if the person receiving these women is Rouge," Damen noted when he'd finished. "Or even if he's receiving them in France."

"No, we don't." Royce rubbed his chin thoughtfully, altering the subject slightly. "Let's talk about the night Cunnings was killed. Do you recall what Bow Street found on his desk when they discovered his body?"

"Of course. Stacks of files detailing our bank's clients—including their personal histories. That came as no surprise. He was looking for a substitute to send Rouge in place of my wife."

"Now let's talk about what Bow Street *didn't* find. Isn't it likely that Cunnings was making notes on what he read in those files? That he was jotting down enough pertinent details to allow him to make the proper selection?"

Damen exhaled sharply. "You think the assassin took those notes when he killed him?"

"If Cunnings had boasted about how difficult his challenge was, how certain he was that he could master it by finding the ideal candidate for Rouge? Absolutely."

"Let's assume you're right. In that case, the assassin either has a different buyer or he and Rouge are contacting each other directly. Because John Cunnings is dead, and no one else in my bank is a criminal."

"I agree." Royce turned to Hibbert. "Get the right men out there to dig up what we need. I want details on anyone even remotely suspected of buying or selling women."

Hibbert nodded. "Should they focus primarily on England and France?"

"My instincts say yes. In any case, no farther than the Continent. The assassin would want immediate results. His nature wouldn't permit him to wait months while his cargo sailed to the Far East or to India. But give me until morning. Once I visit the docks, I'll know exactly where we should focus our efforts. Someone's going to tell me what ships sailed and where they went these past two days. Then, I'm going to pore over those manifests. And with any luck, I'll find something that will help narrow down our search."

* * *

Royce left at daybreak.

Breanna heard him go, and she wanted more than anything to rush into the hall and see him off. But Wells was at his post outside her door, and he wouldn't think too kindly of a public display. Especially since he didn't even know of her wedding plans.

So she settled for listening to Royce's deep baritone, quietly conferring with Wells, thanking him for watching over Breanna and assuring him he'd return as soon as he could.

The morning hours were intolerable.

Not only was the knot of tension in her stomach coiling tighter with each passing moment—almost as if she sensed the assassin was closing in—but Breanna felt as if she would burst if she didn't share her secret with Stacie.

She was pacing in the hallway when her cousin wandered downstairs for breakfast, and Breanna pounced on her, dragged her into the sitting room.

"Breanna, what is it?" Stacie demanded, blinking at her cousin's uncharacteristic impatience. "Has something happened? Damen told me what Royce figured out last night. He also said Royce was riding to the docks first thing today. Have you heard from him?"

"Not yet. He's still in London." Breanna shut the door, leaned back against it. "Stacie—"

"I can't believe I slept through all the excitement. I suppose I just—"

"Stacie!" Breanna broke in, unable to wait another instant. "There's something I want to tell you. Something that has nothing to do with the assassin. But I'm going to explode if I wait any longer."

Stacie's entire demeanor changed, and a spark of anticipation lit her eyes. "This is about Royce."

"Yes." Breanna watched her cousin's expression. "I told him I love him." A pause. "Are you shocked? Because, if so, here's something even more shocking. He loves me, too."

Joy erupted on Stacie's face, and she rushed over, hugged her cousin fiercely. "Shocked? Why would I be shocked? I knew it! I knew it the first time I saw you two together."

"I appreciate your faith," Breanna laughed. "Did you happen to hear what I said about who initiated these declarations? *I* did. I called Royce into my bed-chamber and announced that I love him."

Stacie drew back, approval shining in her eyes. "Good for you. If you're waiting for me to be astounded, don't. I know all about that inner resolve of yours. You're as strong and determined as I am. It was only a matter of finding the right man to bring out those qualities."

Breanna smiled. "I've found him. And, Stacie, he's asked me to marry him."

"You said yes, of course."

"I did." Breanna lowered her voice to a conspiratorial whisper. "And then I seduced him."

This time Stacie's jaw dropped. Recovering herself, she began to laugh. "Now I *am* impressed. Although having seen the way Royce looks at you, I doubt you had to work very hard."

"True enough." A becoming flush stained Breanna's cheeks. "Stacie, I know how frightening everything in our lives seems right now, how terrified we are for the future of your babe. I have no right to feel these bouts of joy—but I do. In fact, I cling to them. It's as if they're all I have to keep from going mad."

"Listen to me." Stacie gripped her cousin's hands

tightly. "Don't you dare apologize for the joy you feel. Being in love with Damen was the only thing that kept me sane when your father was hunting me down. Happiness is something to seize, to revel in. And that's precisely what we're going to do. You and I are going to use these endless hours of confinement to plan your wedding. Just think how elated Grandfather would be."

"You're right. He would." Breanna swallowed past the lump in her throat. "You'll be my bridal attendant, of course."

"Naturally." Stacie grinned. "And I promise not to carry a chamber pot down the aisle with me."

They'd just started making plans when the sitting-room door nearly burst from its hinges, and Damen and Wells exploded into the room.

"Hibbert was right. They're in here," Wells said, sagging with relief.

"Why did you leave the room without me?" Damen demanded, glaring at his wife. "I thought you were still abed."

Stacie sighed. "Damen, you finally fell asleep. It was half after nine. I couldn't bear to awaken you. So I came downstairs for some breakfast." She exchanged glances with Breanna, and grinned. "Which I still haven't eaten, by the way."

Now Wells looked totally stricken. "You haven't? I'll bring you something at once."

"Wells, wait." Breanna rose, going over to him and laying her hand gently on his forearm. "Forgive me for detaining Stacie. But I had a very good reason." She paused, searching for the right words. "You and I have a very special bond, my dear friend. You've protected me from my father my whole life, even those

years when Stacie was in America. You've been my
friend, my rescuer and, in all ways that matter, my
family. So I have a request to make. Actually two requests. Royce has asked me to marry him. It would
mean a great deal to me if you'd give us your blessing. Also, I'd be honored if you'd walk me down the
aisle, give me away to the man I love."

Moisture actually glinted in Wells's eyes, and he
swallowed twice before replying. "I'm not surprised
by the announcement. But I am overwhelmed by the
requests." He covered her hand with his. "Lord Royce
is a fine man. He loves you deeply. Your grandfather
would be overjoyed. And so am I. So, yes you have
my blessing. And just as I stood in for your grandfather once, gave Miss Stacie to Lord Sheldrake, I'd be
elated to do the same for you and Lord Royce."

"Thank you." Breanna rose up on tiptoe, kissed
Wells's cheek, then turned to accept Damen's congrat-
ulatory hug. "Now," she informed the two men, "you
may feed my poor starving cousin."

They all laughed, and the very sound of it felt wonderful after the strain of the past few weeks.

It also made them crave normalcy even more.

Normalcy was not yet to be.

They were all enjoying their late breakfast when
Hibbert walked into the dining room, a sober expression on his face.

"Hibbert, what is it?" Breanna was on her feet. "Is it
Royce?"

"No, my lady. He has yet to return from London."
Hibbert flourished a small box. "This was just delivered to the front gates. Mahoney brought it up."

"Oh, no."

"Actually, I'm not surprised to see it. I'm more surprised it's taken so long to arrive. Considering the killer's desire to intensify your terror, I would have thought he'd be increasing the frequency of his reminders by now." Hibbert paused, giving Breanna a measured look. "Do you want to open it, or shall I?"

"I'll do it." Breanna walked over, saw the familiar penning of her name on the box. This parcel was smaller than the last, about the size of one of her porcelain figures.

Taking a few deep, calming breaths, she tore it open.

Inside was a bottle of perfume—a pear-shaped bottle, its glass facets carved atop a gilded mount, its design intricate.

Its color blood red.

The note lay beneath it.

Death's sweet scent is upon you, Lady Breanna. Retreat is impossible. So is rescue. Tell your warrior his efforts are in vain. Urge him to give up the battle or his blood will spill, too. Either way, you and Lady Anastasia are doomed. Your walls cannot protect you any longer. I've toyed with you, let you believe you were safe. That's over. Precious hours remain until I strike. Your blood is my vengeance.

20

❦

Breanna pressed her lips together to still their trembling. "This note not only threatens me and Stacie, it threatens Royce, as well."

"Good," Hibbert stated with some satisfaction. "That means Lord Royce has unnerved him."

She started. "Is that what it means?"

"Of course." Despite his show of nonchalance, Hibbert was rereading the note, clearly bothered by its contents.

Before Breanna could question him further, he'd turned his attention to the bottle. Pensively, he studied it, then opened its elegant gilded stopper to waft the fragrance under his nose. "An interesting scent. Jasmine and rose, I should say. Which probably means it was produced in Grasse. And the glass bottle—Louis XIV–style—definitely French."

Breanna stared. "How do you know so much about perfume?"

Hibbert gave her one of his hints of a smile. "About five years ago, Lord Royce had a client who was an apothecary. The gentleman had invented a promising recipe for a new fragrance. Before he could produce and sell it, a competitor of his stole it and ran off. The thief changed his name and was halfway through Italy before we caught up with him. In the interim, we had no way of knowing whether or not he'd already reproduced the fragrance and was selling it. As it turned out, he wasn't. He was looking for an isolated spot where he'd never be found before starting his business.

"To get to the point, our client gave Lord Royce and me quite an education before he sent us off. We learned what type of bottles were manufactured where, what ingredients originated in individual provinces, even the names of specific jewelers in France, Germany, and Austria who were famous for setting precious stones on the more ornate bottles." Hibbert ended his explanation, glancing back at the bottle in his hands. "The gilding here is sophisticated, as is the design of the base. I'll wait for Lord Royce to confirm it, but I'm fairly certain this bottle was crafted by one of three jewelers in Paris."

"So we know the killer favors French perfume," Damen stated flatly.

"The question is, does he also favor working with French business associates?"

"Are you implying the perfume was some kind of payment from his contact?" Breanna demanded.

"More like some kind of purchase." Hibbert returned the bottle to its box. "I doubt whoever bought those women would take the time to forward a bottle of perfume as a token of thanks. And if he did, he'd send gentleman's cologne, not women's perfume." A thoughtful pause. "After Lord Royce returns, I think I'll take a quick jaunt down to Dover. I want to see if I can find out anything about the passengers who arrived from Calais this morning. Dover is a quieter port than London—far too risky to use when one is shipping questionable cargo but ideal if one is crossing the Channel, on a return trip to England alone."

Breanna drew a slow breath. "You think the killer actually went to Paris and bought the perfume himself?"

"It would certainly explain why we haven't heard from him these past few days. Perhaps he arranged a business meeting with his associate. He could have traveled from London with his cargo, delivered it in person, met with his contact, bought the perfume, then left Calais and sailed for Dover."

"And now he's back. Ready to carry out the final stages of his plan."

"In his mind, yes."

"He's implying he can get to Stacie and Breanna whether they're inside the manor or not," Damen said quietly, skimming the note. "Is that true?"

Hibbert met his gaze head-on. "I don't know, Lord Sheldrake."

"But you think it might be." Damen got his answer in the silence that ensued. "Dammit, Hibbert. You and Royce said they'd be safe if they didn't venture out."

"And they were. *Then*. He wasn't ready to kill yet. He wanted only to taunt Lady Breanna, to draw out her torture. Which he's obviously still doing. But the tone of this note is more ominous than the others. He went out of his way to address exactly what you just mentioned—the safety of your wife and Lady Breanna if they stay indoors. He's announcing that he's stripping away that safety. Also, he's now specifying a matter of hours before he acts, rather than alluding to some imminent but vaguely in the future time frame. He's running out of patience. And eventually . . ." Hibbert drew a slow breath. "The problem is, I don't know when eventually will be."

Royce was on edge when he returned to Kent.

He'd interrogated enough people to find out that no one had seen any suspicious cargo being loaded at London's docks over the past several days. He'd also seen enough manifests to know that ten ships had left port that were large enough to hide the kind of cargo he was looking for—namely, at least two unconscious women. Maybe more. He had no way of knowing whether the killer had shipped the five women en masse or separately.

All the merchant ships that fit the bill were headed for distant ports, with brief stops on the Continent. Every one of them had captains of impeccable standing, who always verified the contents of their cargo, and whose honor and decency would never permit them to carry women in their holds.

Which left the smaller packet ships.

The manifests here were sketchier, so it was quite possible that someone using a phony name had arranged to ship illegal cargo by listing that freight as sacks of wheat, coal, or something equally innocuous. Or, perhaps the killer worked with a crew of his own choosing—a crew he paid to do his bidding. In which case, the entire manifest could have been falsified.

There was no way of telling.

Not unless Royce awaited those ships' return. And some of them were not scheduled to sail back into London for months.

Breanna didn't have months.

Besides, every instinct in Royce's body was scream-ing that the cargo he was searching for had been shipped to Calais. It made absolute sense. Calais was nearby. It promised immediate results for the assassin. Most of all, it gave him the ultimate satisfaction—an-other demonstration of his superiority. In short, John Cunnings had failed. George Colby had failed. *He*, on the other hand, would not.

Fine. So Calais was the likely destination. But to whom was the cargo being delivered? To Rouge? Or had Rouge been replaced by someone else? And how did Royce get to that someone?

Before leaving the docks, he interviewed a line of crane operators and porters. Some knew the crewmen who worked on those smaller ships. A few knew the captains.

But it was one wiry old fisherman who supplied Royce with the morning's most significant tidbit of in-formation.

The old fellow recalled a packet ship that had sailed two days ago, just after sunrise. The reason he re-membered it was that none of his longshoremen friends—the ones who usually worked the early shift—were there to attend it. Which was odd, almost like none of them knew it was scheduled to sail. Curi-ous, he'd watched the crew hoist a few bags on board, then untie and cast off, as if they were in a great hurry to get going.

Unfortunately, he didn't know any of the crew members personally, other than by face, so he couldn't tell Royce much about them. And he knew nothing about the ship's destination or when it was scheduled to return.

However, he did recall one thing, and that was the ship's name. It was called the *Triumph*.

Royce acted on that immediately. He issued strict instructions—along with a twenty-pound note—to one of the wharf rats he gave occasional work to, ordering him to advise Royce the instant the *Triumph* sailed back into port.

It might be nothing more than a coincidence. On the other hand, it might lead to the kidnapped women.

The problem was, it wouldn't lead to the assassin— not fast enough to stop him.

Time was running out.

By the time Royce reached Medford Manor, he'd made a decision. Someone had to go to Calais. Armed with a description of the missing women, this someone had to be subtle enough and shrewd enough to ask the right questions, investigate this matter from the receiving end in the hopes of finding the buyer, which, in turn, could lead to the assassin.

Unfortunately, that someone couldn't be him.

Because the hunt would take several days at least, especially since it meant following leads from the port of Calais to wherever those women had been taken. And he wouldn't, couldn't, leave Breanna for that amount of time.

Hibbert, however, could.

Royce drew his carriage up to Medford's iron gates.

Rather than just waving him on, Mahoney approached the carriage, simultaneously gesturing for his men to begin opening the gates.

"There was another delivery late this morning," he told Royce. "I left it with Hibbert. I thought you should know."

Nodding tersely, Royce waited only until Mahoney

had backed away. Then, he slapped the reins and sent his carriage racing down the drive.

He mounted the front steps two at a time.

"I'm glad you're back," Wells greeted Royce, flinging open the door at once.

"Mahoney told me about the package," Royce replied, his gaze darting about, searching for Breanna. "Is everyone all right?"

"Yes, my lord." Wells didn't pretend to misunderstand. "Lady Breanna and Lady Anastasia are in the library playing cards with Hibbert and Lord Sheldrake. I felt more comfortable guarding the door. But now that you're back . . ." He made a sweep with his arm. "I'll join you."

Royce strode down the hall, veered sharply into the library, Wells only three paces behind him.

Breanna looked up, and Royce nearly sagged with relief at the sight of her, unharmed, outwardly composed as she played her game of whist.

"Did you learn anything?" she asked softly, laying down her cards.

"Nothing concrete. I'd rather discuss the package first."

"As would I." Hibbert rose, abandoning the game to cross over, hand Royce the box they'd received hours ago. "I'd like your opinion."

Royce read the note through twice, his frown deepening as he did. Then, he turned to the bottle, looking it over quickly before opening the stopper, sniffing the fragrance. Replacing the stopper, he studied the bottle more closely.

"This will narrow down the search," he muttered. "The women are not only in France, they're in Paris. Or not far from it."

"So you agree that's where you'll find the jeweler who designed this bottle."

"No. That's where *you'll* find the jeweler who designed this bottle." Royce's stare bore into Hibbert's. "I need you to do this for me. I'm not leaving—not now. The situation here is far more immediate, and more dangerous, than the one at the receiving end."

Damen jumped to his feet before Hibbert could reply. "You're saying he's about to—"

"Damen, stay calm," Royce interrupted quietly. "I don't think it's a matter of hours, although he wants us to believe it is. But I do think he's losing patience."

"Then what's stopping him from shooting?"

"I am." Royce lowered his head, reread the note. "Not actively, but by what I represent—the ultimate contradiction. On the one hand, my involvement is plaguing the hell out of him. He wants me to get scared, back away. On the other hand, he wants me to figure out what he's about, and to confront him. That way, he gets to enjoy the challenge—and to win. Without that, I'm just another obstacle to eliminate, which would be a great disappointment. So he'll wait a bit longer, see what I do."

Royce looked up, his mind racing. "In the meantime, he has no idea we've linked him to Medford's selling of women. If he sees me leave the country, he'll assume I succumbed to his threats. He'll feel momentary triumph, then great disappointment. That will lead to restlessness and then rage. All his anger will focus on the one person he blames for everything: Breanna. *That's* when he'll act. *That's* when Anastasia's— and then Breanna's—lives will be at greatest risk." A pause. "And *that's* why I'm staying right here."

Anastasia took Damen's hand in hers, interlaced

their fingers. "That makes sense," she said, addressing Royce but speaking to her husband. "And it makes me feel much more secure."

Royce was studying the package wrapping. "This was dispatched from here in England?" he asked Hibbert.

"Yes." Clearly, Hibbert realized his employer was thinking along the exact same lines as he had. "And it's the first package Lady Breanna's received since the doll and the sketch came, two days ago."

"He went to Paris. He bought the perfume there."

"Yes, and now he's back in England." Hibbert rubbed his palms together, making swift plans. "I'd intended to wait for your return, after which I was going to ride down to Dover, glance over the manifests of this morning's arriving ships. I'll follow through on that. After which, I'll take the first packet to Calais, then ride on to Paris. I'll find out everything I can."

"I have a strategy to help you do that." Royce's gaze drifted back to Breanna. "Hibbert, go pack a bag," he instructed his friend. "Include some formal clothing. I'll explain the details later."

"Fine." Hibbert looked distinctly unsurprised by Royce's abrupt dismissal. Rather, he glanced about, leveling a pointed gaze, first at Wells, then at Anastasia and Damen, before delicately clearing his throat and heading for the door.

"A subtle hint," Stacie noted, coming to her feet. "I think my cousin and her *betrothed*," she emphasized the word, "would like a moment alone. Come, gentlemen," she told Damen and Wells. "You may both escort me to the sitting room. We have wedding plans to continue making." She paused as she walked by Royce, rose up to kiss his cheek. "You, my lord, are a very lucky man. You're also perfect for Breanna, just the man I prayed she'd find. I wish you every happiness." A tremor crept into Stacie's voice, the only indication of her persisting fear. "May your brilliant tactics prevail, so you can share a long and happy future."

"Thank you, Anastasia." Royce squeezed her shoulder gently. "And I agree—my luck is incredible. As for the future, it *will* be long and happy for us all. You have my word." He turned to Damen. "As do you."

Damen shook his friend's hand. "I echo Stacie's sentiments—with one additional comment. Perhaps now you'll begin to understand why I'm irrational when it comes to my wife."

A corner of Royce's mouth lifted. "I've already begun."

"My congratulations as well, sir," Wells said with an approving nod. "I was wrong about you. I should have listened to Miss Stacie's instincts. You're a fine man. I wish you and Miss Breanna great joy."

"Thank you." Royce was torn between gratitude and amusement.

He waited until the door had closed and he and Breanna were alone before asking, "What exactly was Wells wrong about?"

Breanna smiled as she walked toward him. "Oh, Wells thought you were a little too wild and daring to be suitable for me. I think he also feared you were a bit of a womanizer."

"Did he?" Royce reached for her, pulled her against him. "The wild and daring I can't argue with. As for being a womanizer . . ." He tilted up her chin with his forefinger. "The only woman I want is you." He lowered his head, covered her mouth with his. "I'm consumed with you, Breanna Colby," he murmured into her parted lips. "I think about you all day, burn for you all night. And I worry about you every minute I'm away."

"Then don't go." She twined her arms around his neck. "Guard me personally. Especially at night. The closer you are to me, the safer I feel."

A chuckle vibrated through him. "Is that so? Then we'll have to see how close I can get."

"Tonight?"

"Tonight," he promised.

"Perfect. Because I just remembered we have something to celebrate." Breanna brushed Royce's lips with hers. "Today is New Year's Day."

"That's right. It is." Royce's arms tightened around her, and he molded the contours of her body to his. "No wonder the docks were so quiet. I'd completely forgotten."

"So did I." She shivered, pressing closer. "But now that I've remembered, I must say I much prefer this method of celebrating to the line of gentlemen callers I originally intended to receive."

"I'm relieved. Otherwise, I'd be calling out a lot of men." He silenced her response with his mouth, kissing her until she was trembling in his arms. "I hope you got at least a little sleep last night. Because tonight you won't be shutting an eye. And it won't be fear keeping you awake. It will be me."

"How enticing." Breanna's eyes glowed. "I'll leave the door unlocked."

Ten minutes later, Hibbert packed his final article of clothing and snapped the bag shut.

"Do you think I should contact Girard as soon as I arrive in Paris?" he inquired.

"Definitely." Royce was perched at the edge of a chair, his posture rigid as he issued Hibbert's instructions. "You know how good Girard is. His instincts are exceptional."

"Almost as good as yours," Hibbert commented, a statement of fact rather than acclaim. "I agree. He's our most valuable contact in the area. Very well. I'll stop in and see him before I visit the jewelers. How much do you want him to know?"

"Whatever you can tell him in a half hour. Don't waste your time or his. He already knows about the assassin. I've asked him to do some checking, to see if he can find the physician who treated that wounded hand."

Hibbert pursed his lips. "I never thought of that. But it makes sense. He didn't dare have an English doctor look at his wound. It would be too risky."

"Not to mention that if the trigger finger's as damaged as I suspect—enough to make him drop out of sight for months and then compel him to return just to kill Breanna—he'd need a physician of extraordinary skill. An expert."

"Perhaps he first met his business contact while recuperating abroad," Hibbert suggested. "Whether by chance or intent."

"Most likely intent. Pose that notion to Girard. Then tell him, in addition to the doctor, to start digging for whoever's been buying the women, whether it's Rouge or someone else. In the meantime, you trace the perfume. Just let Girard know what you're doing so he can watch your back."

"You mean, Lord Hobson's back," Hibbert corrected dryly. He quirked a brow at his employer. "I think I'll enjoy playing the part of a nobleman."

"I'm sure you will." Royce rose, thinking through the final steps of his plan. "You know what to say in those letters?"

"Of course." Hibbert grasped his bag, swung it off the bed. "I'll take care of things at my end. You just keep everyone here safe." A penetrating look. "Including yourself."

"I intend to." Royce glanced restlessly toward the window. "He's out there, Hibbert. I can feel it. If only I could force him to confront *me*, to vent his rage at *me*, rather than Breanna."

Hibbert studied Royce for a long, thoughtful moment. "You've taught me well. So let me give you some of your own advice. A bit of apprehension is healthy. It's what keeps our wits sharp and our senses honed." A profound pause. "However, this is more than mere apprehension. It's fear. That's because the stakes are personal. Very personal. The life of the woman you love is at risk. So you're terrified—terrified and determined to protect her, even at the expense of your own life."

Royce's head came up. "And you take exception to that?"

"No. I admire it. But I'm not the issue here. The killer is. He'll use your vulnerability to his advantage. If he so much as senses the intensity of your feelings for Lady Breanna, it will make things worse for her. Don't let him know how much she means to you, my lord. Don't."

Hibbert's words echoed in Royce's head all evening. He knew his friend was right. The worst thing he could do was alert the killer to his feelings. Lord only knew what kind of leverage that would provide.

Which meant only one thing.

Royce had to keep his distance from Breanna. Not just when they ventured outside or stood near windows, in full view of the world, but inside, as well. The killer's latest message had made it clear he had access to the house—a taunt that might or might not be true. Consequently, Royce couldn't take chances. Moments such as the one he and Breanna had shared earlier had to cease.

Except in one place: her bedroom.

It was the only detail Royce was convinced the killer hadn't yet discovered—that Breanna was sleeping in different quarters. He, Damen, and Wells had been careful to continue making her room look lived in, especially at night. Obviously, they'd been successful. The assassin's actions, or lack thereof, told them that. If he'd been aware of the switch, his arrogance would have insisted he throw it in their faces. He'd either have invaded Breanna's new quarters or at least made some terrifying reference to doing so in his notes.

He hadn't.

Which meant he didn't know.

And *that* meant that Royce and Breanna still had the nights.

Starting with tonight.

Royce didn't even bother dragging a chair into the hallway when he positioned himself outside Breanna's door. He was far too restless, too fidgety, too rife with energy to sit still.

He was also frantic to hold Breanna in his arms.

He spent the first part of the night pacing outside her door. And the minute the house fell silent, he reached for the door handle, let himself in.

Breanna was sitting on the bed, sketching by the thin filaments of moonlight that drifted through the window. Other than that and the glow of a crackling fire, the room was unlit, cast in shadows.

For safety.

And for him.

She looked up when he entered, putting aside her sketchpad and rising to her feet. "I'm glad you're here."

Royce caught his breath. She was wearing only a thin nightrail and robe, both of a sheer ivory silk, the lacy edges of the robe barely touching, loosely tied.

She smiled, reaching up to tug the first pin out of her upswept hair. "I left this task for you," she added softly.

Restless energy exploded into raw hunger.

Royce turned the key in the lock with such force he wondered if he'd snapped it in two.

He hoped so. In that case, they could stay here, locked away together, forever.

He couldn't stop staring at her. Staunchly, he fought to control the tidal wave of desire that surged through him, all his earlier tension converging, crashing through his loins.

"Royce?" Breanna took a step toward him, opened her arms.

Restraint vanished.

Royce scarcely remembered closing the distance between them. All he knew was dragging Breanna against him, seizing her mouth with more urgency than he knew he possessed. He tugged the pins from her hair, gathering handfuls of it as he continued kissing her. Her robe dropped to the floor, her nightrail followed, and Royce savored the exquisite silkiness of her skin as he lifted her, placed her on the bed.

He felt her fingers on the buttons of his waistcoat, but he couldn't wait. Stepping away, he tore off his clothes, coming down over her the instant he was naked.

Breanna let out a soft moan of pleasure, rubbing her breasts against his powerful, hair-roughened chest. She clung to him, understanding and sharing his urgency, wanting to savor every moment, to savor him, yet frantic to feel him inside her.

"Later," he muttered, answering the conflicting emotions waging inside her. "We'll go slowly later. Now, I've got to have you." He was already wedging her thighs apart.

She felt him tense, as if remembering how new this was to her, and her breath caught as his fingers found her, slid inside to assure him of her readiness.

She was more than ready for him.

Royce shuddered heavily as he encountered her satiny wetness, stroked her softly.

Breanna seized his wrist, pushed his hand away. "Later," she whispered, echoing his sentiments.

Royce's gaze darkened to near black. His hands slipped under her, gripping her bottom and angling her to receive him, his rigid shaft probing the entrance to her body.

He entered her in one slow, inexorable thrust, pushing as deep as he could go.

Breanna cried out, arched to meet him, her entire body softening and opening to take him, to sheathe him inside her. She whimpered in protest when he left her, only to cry out again as he pushed forward, filled her even more fully than he had the first time.

"Does . . . it hurt?" Royce could barely speak.

She shook her head, her arms tightening around him. "Don't stop."

"Stop?" Royce was moving again, each lunge of his hips sending skyrockets of sensation shooting through her. "I'd die first."

There were no more words then, nothing but the harsh rasps of their breath, the frantic kisses and caresses, the broken sounds of need, the grating of the bedsprings beneath them as their motions became more frenzied, wilder, more abandoned. Royce lost himself inside her, and Breanna tossed her head on the pillow, the pleasure too acute to bear, the tension coiling tighter and tighter until she thought she'd die of it.

It peaked ... and unraveled in a rush, throbbing spasms of completion radiating out from inside her, clenching again and again, contracting frantically around his engorged length.

Royce gave a hoarse shout, throwing back his head and groping for the headboard. His fingers closed around the bedposts, his knuckles turning white as his own climax slammed through him. His hips moved convulsively, pushing him into her, heightening her contractions as he met each one with a scalding burst of heat.

Breanna bit her lip to keep from screaming. She could feel him spurting into her, sensations so erotic they retriggered her spasms, sent them spiraling even higher than before.

When it was over, they collapsed, neither capable of moving. Breanna sank into the bed, reveling in Royce's weight, the inadvertent shudders still racking his body, the final drops of his seed trickling into her.

"I love you," she whispered, pressing her lips to his shoulder.

He swallowed, an audible sound in the silence of

the room. "You have no idea," he answered hoarsely. "No idea." Reflexively, his arms closed around her, as if that act alone could keep her safe. "I'm going to spend a lifetime showing you." He raised his head, stared deeply into her eyes. "Beginning tonight."

Breanna smiled, smoothed damp strands of hair off his forehead. "You've made an extraordinary start."

He caught her hand, brought her palm to his lips. "That's all it was—a start." He rolled to one side, taking her with him. "I just want to hold you, feel you against me, for a minute."

"And then?"

"Then, I'm going to make love to you the way you deserve to be made love to, the way I still haven't mustered enough control to do."

A sated sigh. "I've no complaints."

His expression singed her. "You'll have even fewer by morning."

"I'm intrigued."

"Are you?" He bent to kiss her, cradling her head in his hands as he made love to her mouth. His lips moved slowly over hers, circling and tasting, nudging them apart for the intimate invasion of his tongue. He teased her with light, shivery strokes, awakening every surface of her mouth, his tongue gliding over hers in unhurried, lingering caresses, until her breath was coming faster and she was clinging to him, desperately trying to escalate the pace.

Clearly, the minute was up.

Still, Royce kept himself in check, although his body swelled inside hers, throbbed in a way that told her what this delay was costing him. But he didn't give in, waiting until she was frantic before letting the fire of their kisses take over.

Breanna's inner muscles softened and tightened around him, her body reflexively asking for more.

Maddeningly, Royce refused.

Rather than begin the rhythm she craved, he withdrew, separating their bodies and dragging his mouth away from hers.

"Royce . . ." She whimpered a protest, but he ignored it, his lips burning an open-mouthed trail down her neck, her throat. He kissed her shoulders, the spot where her heart was racing, then down to the upper swell of her breasts. He savored each curve, moved lower, letting his warm breath tease her nipples into aching points, then grazing them with fleeting brushes of his lips and tongue.

Breanna's nails were digging into his shoulders when Royce gave in. He slid one arm beneath her back, arched her up to his mouth and drew her taut nipple inside, tugging and releasing, tugging and releasing, then lashing across the hardened peak with his tongue. He didn't stop until she was twisting on the sheets, chanting his name in harsh, broken gasps, and even then only to shift to her other breast, lavish it with the same attention.

Drowning in sensation, Breanna cried out, her insides clenching with every pull of Royce's lips. The urgency was building again, that desperate need for release, and she caught his head between her hands, trying to tug him upward, to urge him over her. If he didn't cover her, fill her, she'd die.

He let her ease his head from her breasts, but ignored her unspoken plea. Following his own compulsion, he caught her wrists, held them away.

His mouth continued its path, down her waist, across the hollow of her abdomen to her thighs.

She had no time to think, or even to wonder.

Releasing her wrists, he draped her legs over his shoulders, bent his head, and sank his tongue into her.

Raw, unimaginable sensation jolted through Breanna, and she shoved a fist into her mouth, knowing there was no other way to silence her scream. She'd never imagined anything like this in her life. She was dying . . . dying.

Royce intensified the torture, making love to her with his lips and tongue, tasting her, savoring her flavor. His fingers glided high up inside her, moving seductively to heighten her pleasure. She tried to wrench away, to keep herself from flying apart, but he was relentless, unbearably precise, finding where she needed him most and deepening his caresses.

"Royce . . ." It was a primitive sound, one she didn't recognize, even though it came from her.

"Let it happen," he commanded in a voice thick with desire. "God, your taste. Let it happen."

It was already happening. Breanna couldn't stop it. It was a dark roaring wave that boiled up inside her, crashed down over her, drowning her in its wake. She sobbed aloud, giving in to its power, her entire body wrenching beneath the spasms.

She felt Royce's grip tighten as he heightened her pleasure, tasted every nuance of her climax. Then he was on her, in her, his own control shattering as he surged deep, spurting hotly into her, rasping her name with each pulsing burst of release.

This time recovery took longer. Breanna felt dazed, stunned by the magnitude of what had just happened, and by the intensity of her own body's response. *My God,* was all she kept thinking. *My God.*

Eventually, Royce raised up on his elbows, his breathing still unsteady as he gazed down into her face. "You're mine," he said fervently. "And I love you."

Tears shimmered in Breanna's eyes. "I never imagined it could be so . . . so . . ."

"Nor did I."

His implicit meaning made what they'd shared that much more profound.

"I wish we could hold back the morning," Breanna whispered, realizing how silly she sounded, how unlike herself, and yet unable to stem the words or stop herself from feeling them. She was no longer the woman she'd been a month ago. Now, she was a woman in love. And she was terrified that the faceless killer out there would shatter all the wonder she and Royce were only just discovering.

That . . . and worse.

Royce kissed her tenderly, his thumbs caressing her cheeks. "The morning is hours away."

"But it *will* come. And when it does—"

"When it does, we'll face it," Royce murmured. He rolled onto his back, taking Breanna with him and pressing her head to his chest. He sifted his fingers through her hair, staring quietly at the ceiling. "He's waiting for me to make some kind of move. And I will—as soon as I think of the best way to lure him out."

Breanna tensed, and she raised her head, her eyes wide with fear. "Lure him out? But, if you lure him out—"

"I'll kill him," Royce finished quietly.

"He's an expert marksman," Breanna returned in a small, shaky voice. "Killing is his craft, his passion." A hard swallow. "If anything happens to you . . . Royce, I'd rather take one of his bullets. It would destroy me far less."

"Stop it." Royce drew her mouth down to his, kissing her with a ferocity that strove to burn away all the frightening possibilities that lay ahead. "Nothing is going to happen to you. *Or* to me. I won't let it."

Breanna nodded, willing her surge of fear to subside. "I know you won't." She caressed his jaw, watching the unyielding look in his eyes and saying a silent prayer.

Let this nightmare be over, she prayed. *Let us all be spared. But if something has to go wrong, if someone has to die at that monster's hands, don't let it be Royce. Keep him safe. And please, please, protect Stacie and her babe. If it has to be someone, let it be me.*

Royce studied the play of emotions on her face, and his features hardened, as if he knew just what she was thinking. "Come here," he commanded, pulling her more fully atop him, draping her hair around them like a shimmering curtain. "You wanted to hold back the morning," he reminded her in a low, urgent tone, framing her face between his palms. "Well, so do I." His hips lifted, pushing his lower body upward until his rigid length surged fully inside her, possessed her. He withdrew, then repeated the motion, gritting his teeth and waiting only until her glazed eyes and soft moan told him he'd eclipsed her fears—for now. "And I know just the way to do that."

21

"*L*ord Hobson. I like that idea."

Philippe Girard chuckled, pouring two brandies and giving one to Hibbert before settling himself behind his desk. "Please. Have a seat." He waited until Hibbert had lowered himself into one of the plush mahogany armchairs that decorated Girard's elegant office. "Was this new identity your idea, or Chadwick's?"

"It was Lord Royce's." Hibbert sipped at his drink, an expression of wry amusement on his face. "But I've taken to it quite nicely."

"*Évidemment.* So I see." Another chuckle as Girard set down his goblet, leaned forward to study Hibbert intently. "You've been to the three jewelers?"

"Yes. Right after I left here this morning."

"Forgive me for not speaking with you at that time." Girard's smile vanished, and his dark brows drew together. "I had no idea you were here. My clerk is new, or he would have recognized your name. He certainly would have known Royce's. Either way, he would have interrupted my meeting. It won't happen again."

Hibbert waved away the apology. "Your clerk was just doing his job. He was most efficient. He took down my name, gave me an appointment for half after two, and saw me to the door. That gave me a chance to do my preliminary investigating."

"And you found the right jeweler?"

"In less than an hour. I followed my first instinct and went to Passeur on Avenue De Villiers. I was right."

Girard's lips twitched. "You're becoming as arrogant as Chadwick. And as shrewd. Passeur does indeed craft elaborate bottles for the most discerning customers." He rubbed a palm over his clean-shaven jaw. "Now what?"

"As I suspected, the bottle is exclusive to Passeur. It's also quite expensive. Only five customers have purchased it—quite regularly, in fact. As luck would have it, all five live here in Paris."

"You have all their names, of course."

"Actually, they have mine—or rather Lord Hobson's." Hibbert enjoyed the perplexed look that crossed Girard's chiseled features. "Another of Lord Royce's fine ideas—one that was acceptable to Monsieur Passeur. As anticipated, the jeweler is an ethical man who refused to divulge the names of his customers. Lord Royce's plan spared him the necessity of doing so."

"I'm intrigued. Please, go on."

Hibbert complied. "Through Passeur, I sent off five urgent messages, one to each customer. I told them I was in a delicate predicament. I'd spent one unforgettable night with a beautiful woman whose name I neglected to take, but whose scent I could never forget. I confessed that I'd traced the perfume in the hopes of renewing our acquaintance during my brief trip to Paris—no matter what the price. I closed by asking if they might know this woman and, if so, could I prevail upon them to urge her to contact me—immediately, as I'll only be in Paris for a day or two. And I provided my name and the name of the inn where I'm staying."

This time Girard threw back his head and laughed. "In other words, you appealed to the passion so typical of the French."

"Yes. And the greed so typical of criminals." Hibbert gave an offhanded shrug. "I expect I'll hear from several very irate husbands."

"I'm sure you will."

"When I find the source of this bottle, it's possible I'll need your help. Depending upon who that source is, of course."

"Consider it done." Girard polished off his brandy, and eyed the empty glass speculatively. "You're hoping this will lead to whoever is buying the women who have been kidnapped."

"Exactly."

A terse nod. "Then I suspect I'll be hearing from you. In the meantime, I have your descriptions of the women in question. I'll see what I can find out. Oh, and I should be hearing back any day now on my inquiries regarding the physician Chadwick's looking for."

"Good. Because it's possible the killer first met his business associate en route to or from that physician."

"That makes sense." Girard organized his notes. "With any luck, all these pieces will be found while you're in Paris, and you and I will be able to assemble them." Girard shot Hibbert a curious look. "This isn't

Chadwick's usual type of case. Nor is he going about
it in his usual detached manner. Is that because Sheldrake's a friend of his? Or is it more?"

Hibbert's expression never changed. "Lord Royce
and the marquess have known each other since their
days at Oxford."

"*Oui.* And Lord Royce and Lady Breanna have
known each other less than a month. Yet I get the distinct feeling Chadwick's determination has a lot more
to do with her than with Sheldrake."

Another bland look, although Hibbert knew his
employer wouldn't object to Girard knowing the
truth. Still, baiting him was far more enjoyable. "I'll
let Lord Royce answer that question himself, when
you see him."

"Ah, and will my answer be in the form of an invitation, perhaps?"

"It might be." Hibbert rose, gathering up his things.
"*If* you help solve this case."

Girard stood, a broad smile on his face. "You drive
a hard bargain—*Lord Hobson.* However, being that I
wouldn't want to miss out on what I'm fast coming to
believe will be Royce's wedding day, I'll see what I
can do." Abruptly, all levity vanished. "Good luck
with your search, Hibbert. But be careful. You don't
know what you're dealing with—yet. When you do,
come to me."

Hibbert's nod was equally solemn. "I will."

By late afternoon, three replies, one incensed husband, and one round woman well past middle years
with an eager gleam in her eye had arrived at Hibbert's inn.

The woman was both hopeful and persuasive. She

spent twenty minutes assuring Lord Hobson they'd
spent a torrid night together—one she'd be thrilled to
repeat, with or without payment.

Hibbert sent her home to her husband.

The second arrival—an incensed man who introduced himself as Monsieur Blanc and then called Hibbert every French obscenity he was able to recognize,
and a few he couldn't—swore that his wife was faithful and that if Lord Hobson ever contacted her again,
he would shoot him.

Hibbert sent him home to his wife.

He then ordered a brandy, collected his three written messages, and took them upstairs to his room.

He tore open the first message.

It was written by an insolent butler, who informed
Lord Hobson that the Duc had received his note, but
had elected not to reply for personal reasons. He
added that it would be highly indiscreet for Lord
Hobson to press the matter, as it would offend the
Duc, his wife, and his mistress, for whom the perfume
was purchased.

Hibbert contemplated the butler's meaning for only
a minute before putting aside the reply. It didn't warrant further attention. His instincts told him it rang
true. Besides, the specifics would be easy enough to
check out.

He turned his attention to the other two replies.

One was from a Mademoiselle Chenille, who regularly purchased the perfume for her grandmother,
most recently as a Christmas gift. She expressed regret
at not being able to provide Lord Hobson with the answers he sought, and wished him the best of luck. She
added that she was leaving Paris the day after tomorrow, first to visit her grandmother in the hospital,

then to return to the convent at which she'd soon be taking her vows to God. But if Lord Hobson had any further questions, he was free to contact her there. She closed her letter by blessing him, and providing him with the name and address of her religious order.

Hibbert winced, and refolded the note. It was replies such as these that made one feel guilty about using deception as a means to get at the truth. Then again, it was decent young women like Mademoiselle Chenille whom he and Lord Royce were trying to protect through their actions. So in the end, it was worth it.

He would, of course, verify the story—if it came to that. But he had little doubt she was telling the truth.

Which brought him to the last reply.

This note was penned in a flowery, feminine hand, and Hibbert's discomfort vanished, his instincts roaring to life when a hint of the fragrance he was searching for drifted to his nostrils.

The recipient had taken the time to dab her letter with a provocative touch of the perfume he'd mentioned. That meant she was interested.

The question was, was he?

Slipping his finger under the flap, Hibbert opened the letter, and read:

Lord Hobson, I'm fascinated by your letter. We should meet. I'll be at the front steps of Notre-Dame at seven o'clock, wearing your perfume.—Maurelle Le Joyau.

Maurelle Le Joyau.

Hibbert reread the name and the note, then glanced at his timepiece. Half after five. That gave him enough time to catch Girard before he left the office, find out more about the lady in question.

After which, he'd be on his way to the cathedral.

* * *

Maurelle Le Joyau was an extraordinarily beautiful woman—every bit as beautiful as she'd been described.

Her thick black hair was swept off her face, emphasizing her fragile, fine-boned features and wide, dark eyes. Her costly silk gown and fur-lined pelisse cloak were the height of fashion, and her diminutive height and build made her look like a china doll swathed in expensive material. She looked young, vulnerable— the kind of woman a man would want to protect and, at the same time, to possess.

Hibbert studied her impassively as he approached the front steps of Notre-Dame, thinking that all the information he'd been given didn't do her justice. She was breathtaking. Without a doubt, she could pass for a woman a decade younger than her thirty-two years. She had an untouched quality to her beauty that was unmistakable.

Except that she happened to be the owner of a very elite, very expensive Paris brothel.

"Lord Hobson?" She gave him a dazzling smile, inclining her head just so as she stepped toward him.

Hibbert played his part, scrutinizing her with an element of longing, and an equal amount of regret. "Miss Le Joyau?"

"Yes."

He bowed, brought her gloved fingers to his lips. The perfume—he could smell it even in the crisp evening air. "I'm as disappointed as I am entranced," he confessed. "I wish I could say we've met. But as we both know, we haven't." A charming smile. "Although, to be honest, I wish it was you I was searching for. The young woman I recall was wearing your exact scent. Still, she doesn't come close to matching you in beauty."

Maurelle flushed accordingly, although Hibbert
was aware that her show of maidenly shyness was
just that: show. Indeed, at the same time that she attempted to preoccupy him with her allure, she was
assessing him with a shrewd but subtle thoroughness
the average man would never have perceived.

Hibbert perceived it.

"*Merci.* What a lovely compliment," she murmured,
her English punctuated with a soft French accent.
"However, now that we meet face to face, I have to
sadly agree you're a stranger to me, as well. Still, perhaps I can help in your search." She tucked a tendril
of hair off her face. "You're English. Yet your message
said you met this woman in Paris. May I ask when?"

Interesting that she didn't ask *where*, Hibbert noted.

His brows raised in a semi-hopeful gesture. "Why?
Do you know another woman who wears that scent?"

"Possibly. But I don't know *you* well enough to
say."

"Ah, you're being cautious." Hibbert nodded his
understanding. "I don't blame you. One can't be certain whom one is speaking with these days. Well, I
assure you, I'm an honorable man. Lonely, but honorable. What would you like to know? My name is Albert Hobson. I live in Surrey, but I also have estates in
Yorkshire, Dorset, and Devon. I'm a man of considerable means, and can provide handsomely for the
young woman in question. As for when I met this
mystery lady, it was last summer. I was in Paris on
business."

"I see. She must have thoroughly impressed you,
to still be in your thoughts six months later. Yet you
didn't get her name."

"Unfortunately not." Hibbert gave a discreet cough.

"I'm not sure how to say this delicately, but it was an arranged evening. I'd had a fair amount to drink when the liaison began. I can describe her to you, if that would help."

Maurelle lowered her lashes. "You're very frank."

"Have I offended you?"

Her lashes lifted. "No. I prefer candor to evasiveness." Another pause. "I'd like to hear more about you, and about this woman you're seeking."

"Indeed. I'll tell you anything about myself you wish to know." Hibbert shivered a bit, turned up the collar of his coat, and glanced about. "It's cold. Can I take you somewhere warm where we can talk?"

She rubbed her gloved palms together, still inspecting him closely—his expensive clothing, his cultured demeanor. "*Oui,* my lord," she said at length. "I believe you can. You can take me to my establishment. There, we'll continue our chat."

Le Joyau looked more like an opulent manor than a brothel.

The entire dwelling was furnished in rich blue velvet and carved mahogany, its drawing rooms warm and cozy, each with a cheery fire burning and adorned with plush sofas and drapes of gold brocade.

Maurelle escorted Hibbert into one of the rooms, after giving their coats to a sophisticated young woman at the door, who greeted mademoiselle and her guest politely, then went off to get them some refreshment.

Hibbert warmed his hands by the fire, thinking it was no wonder affluent men came here. With very little effort, they could pretend they were calling on a virtuous lady, rather than buying a prostitute for the night.

"My lord? Won't you have a seat?"

He turned, his smile back in place, and noted that Maurelle had situated herself in the center of the sofa. Even now, in her establishment as she called it, she looked anything but what she was. Straight-backed, her skirts draped formally around her, she looked like a young woman awaiting her beau, her hands folded primly in her lap, her expression warm but not seductive.

"Thank you." Hibbert crossed over, sat down on the sofa—a respectable distance away.

"I should begin by asking if you're shocked by where I've taken you." Maurelle beckoned to the woman who'd greeted them at the door, gesturing for her to leave the two goblets of brandy and plate of cakes on the table beside her. At the same time, she never averted her gaze from Hibbert. "I should, but I won't. You see, my lord, I'm as straightforward as you are. And I think we understand each other well enough to continue this discussion without the annoyance caused by silly displays of ignorance. It only wastes time—time you could be spending with the right woman."

"I agree."

"Besides," Maurelle added, handing him a goblet. "Since the perfume you used to trace me is fairly exclusive, I suspect you've been here before, probably while I was away. *Quel dommage.* Had I been at home, I would have personally seen to your satisfaction. But since I wasn't, I'm glad one of my ladies was able to give you such a memorable night. Even if you were too deep in your cups to remember her name or where you could find her."

"Indeed." Hibbert waited until Maurelle had lifted

up her own goblet. "Shall we toast, then? To renewed acquaintances and new friendships."

Maurelle raised her glass, and the two of them drank.

"Now," Hibbert continued, his lips curving. "What else can I tell you about myself? My age? My success rate at White's or at Newmarket? Or would this character reference suffice?" He reached into his pocket, pulled out a thick wad of pound notes.

Her eyes gleamed. "That's an excellent start, monsieur. Why don't you describe this young woman to me."

Hibbert stared broodingly into his drink. He had to begin as generally as possible. After that . . . well, if things went well, after that he'd make the challenge more interesting. "She had a beautiful smile. Her hair was pale—blond or light brown. Her eyes were light, too—gray, maybe blue. Mostly what I recall was her scent. That and . . . her considerable other charms."

"I see. That's all you remember?"

"I'm afraid so."

"Hmm." Maurelle's lovely brow furrowed as if she were baffled, but Hibbert could see that her mind was completely unclouded—and racing. Clearly, she was pleased with what she'd heard, since his recollection was vague enough to fit a half-dozen women, any of whom she could douse in perfume and send to him—in exchange for a small fortune. "And for how long would you require her—one night? Two?"

That was his cue. It was time.

With a sorrowful smile, Hibbert said, "I would require her for much longer than that. However, given the type of woman we're referring to, one night will be fine."

"I don't understand," Maurelle returned with a genuinely perplexed look. "I thought you wanted . . . ?"

"What I *want*, and what's available to me are two different things." Hibbert tossed off his brandy, glad he'd had the presence of mind to fill his stomach with a large meal before leaving his inn—just in case he needed to lessen the effects of any liquor he'd consume.

Heavily, he set down his glass, taking in her uncertain expression, and attempting to explain. "I'm a realistic man, Miss Le Joyau. Candid, as you yourself said. I know my attributes . . . and my limitations. I'm well past fifty. I'm not displeasing to the eye. But I'm hardly able to capture the fancy of a beautiful, well-bred young lady. I can pay for a roomful of women. But the one I truly want can't be found at a brothel, no matter how elegant."

The tiniest flicker in Maurelle's eyes was his only indication that what he'd said had struck a chord.

Calmly, she reached for a piece of cake, nibbling at it as she asked, "And what type of woman is that?"

He waved away her question. "Please, my dear. You're not required to listen to my fantasies." He peeled off several hundred-pound notes, pressed them into Maurelle's hand. "Where shall I await my liaison?"

"*S'il vous plaît*—in a minute." Maurelle set the bills aside, her fingers closing around his. "My job is to see that you're happy. If there's something more you need, just ask for it."

He quirked a brow. "Forgive me, but what I need is not something you can provide."

"Let me be the judge of that."

"Very well." Hibbert averted his gaze, staring off toward the fire. "It's quite simple. I'd like a companion. Not just for a day, or a week. For an extended period of time, maybe even for the rest of my life."

"But you object to paying for her," Maurelle guessed softly. "You want her to fall in love with you."

A dubious laugh. "That's a delightful notion. But I'm not impractical enough to expect it. No, I don't object to paying. Love isn't the issue."

"Then what is?"

"Breeding. Breeding and chastity."

Silence.

"I see our discussion has reached an end," Hibbert said, glancing over to give Maurelle a rueful smile. "I didn't mean to offend you. But you did ask. Now perhaps you'll understand why I didn't want to pursue the subject."

"I'm not offended." Maurelle caressed his fingers. "Just so I understand, monsieur, you're saying you'd prefer to buy one of my ladies for an indefinite period of time—if she's well-bred and untouched?"

"*Nobly* bred and untouched," Hibbert corrected. "Any companion I acquired would have to be of the same class as I am. And, at the same time, young and beautiful." The warmth left his face. "I hope you're not toying with me, Miss Le Joyau. I might be lonely, but I'm not stupid."

"I'm not toying with you, my lord."

"Then why are we pursuing this discussion?"

"Because I might be able to supply you with precisely the companion you want." Maurelle withdrew her hand, suddenly all business. "For the right price, that is."

"Do we understand each other?" Hibbert asked bluntly. "I'm referring to a noblewoman. A young lady born of the peerage. And a virgin. Someone who's never lain with a man before."

"I know what a noblewoman is, my lord. Just as I know the definition of a virgin."

"And why would I find either, much less both, in a brothel?"

"Because the young woman I'm thinking of just arrived, this week in fact. She has yet to entertain her first client." Maurelle leaned forward, obviously sensing a windfall. "I would give you a guarantee, of course. I have my reputation to consider."

Hibbert remained dubious. "Suppose I accept your guarantee. You've assured me of her innocence. What about her roots?"

The barest of pauses, as Maurelle adjusted her story ever so slightly. "She's English, like yourself. Her late father was a viscount. He died, leaving his family destitute. Until recently, she lived with her mother. Unfortunately, her mother died, too. The girl came to Paris, penniless and alone. I took her in."

He permitted himself to appear hopeful—wary, but hopeful. "What does she look like?"

"As luck would have it, she's just what you're seeking. She's lovely. Like the woman you came in search of, she, too, has pale hair and eyes. She's just eighteen. I was going to put her to work tonight, but . . ." Maurelle bit her lip thoughtfully. "I could change my mind—*if* I were properly persuaded."

"You said she was alone." Eagerness laced Hibbert's tone. "That means she has no ties. Could this arrangement be permanent?"

"As permanent as you wish."

"Let me meet her."

Maurelle hesitated, well aware she now had the upper hand. "We haven't agreed upon a price."

"If she's all you say, you may name your price. I'll give you every pound in my pocket, and a signed note for the rest. I'll have my banker authorize the remaining funds the instant I return home. But first—I must meet her."

Maurelle squeezed his hand, her own eyes glowing with the triumph of victory. "*Naturellement.* I'll bring her to you. You won't be disappointed."

"I'm sure I won't be."

Hibbert remained in his seat, glad for his own ability to remain unreadable. He felt a surge of relief, supplanted only by his deep-seated anger and disgust. He knew only too well who Maurelle would be bringing out to meet him. He also had an excellent idea of the state she'd be in. It was up to him to disregard that state, to keep her in the dark long enough to get her out that door with him—for her own sake.

After which, he'd tell her the truth, reassure her fears, and elicit her help.

And somehow convince her to be strong for a little while longer.

"Here we are, my lord." Maurelle guided a lovely young woman into the room—a woman whose description perfectly matched the one Lord Royce had provided of Emma Martin. Her ashen complexion and terrified expression told Hibbert she'd been warned not to do anything to discourage her potential buyer—probably at the risk of physical harm, or worse.

"This is Emma," Maurelle supplied. "Emma, please greet Lord Hobson."

"Hello, Emma," Hibbert said gently, coming to his feet.

"Sir." Emma gave a brief curtsy, her eyes downcast.

"She's a little shy," Maurelle explained. "Under the circumstances, I'm sure you can understand why."

"Indeed I can." Hibbert forced himself to go through the motions. He clasped his hands behind his back, walking around Emma and inspecting her as one would a prize thoroughbred. His smile widened with each passing minute, although it sickened him to see the way she was trembling.

"You're a very charming young lady," he complimented. He raised her chin with his forefinger. "I hear you're English."

Her lips quivered.

"I won't hurt you," he said quietly. "You've nothing to fear."

A lone tear slid down her cheek.

Enough was enough. Hibbert could take no more.

His gaze lifted to Maurelle, and he gave an emphatic nod. "Pack her things."

*W*hy didn't he *do* something?

Breanna's insides clenched, an overwhelming sense of desperation claiming her.

She hovered near her bedchamber window, peeked out from behind the drape, and scanned the darkening skies.

He was lurking out there somewhere.

But where?

It had been two days since he'd sent that perfume. His note had said precious hours remained until he struck.

So where was he?

Had he guessed what Hibbert was about, where he was going and why?

No. If that were the case, he'd have reacted.

Was he watching them, peering through windows and gauging their fear, waiting for it to peak before he acted?

Was *that* the cause of his utter silence? Was he doing it intentionally to heighten her agony? Or was he plotting something horrifying, anticipating the exact moment in which to strike?

And if he did strike, what form would it take? Was he going to send them another of his threatening gifts, or had the time come when he meant to step out of the shadows, make an attempt on Stacie's life?

Dear God, she was losing her mind.

Dragging in a breath, Breanna pressed her palms together, determined to bring herself under control before she went down to dinner. She couldn't let Stacie see her like this. Her poor cousin was frightened enough as it was, more so since that last note had arrived. For the past two days, she hadn't had a minute's reprieve, not an instant to lose herself in something other than the danger to her life. Now Damen *never* left her side, not even allowing her to make solitary trips from their bedchamber to the sitting room or to walk down and visit Breanna in her chambers. He guarded her round the clock and, during the scant hours when he slept, he arranged for Wells to take over. The butler was as steadfast as Damen, appending himself to Stacie like a shadow and escorting her about.

Breanna didn't blame them. She was as worried as they.

And still the nagging thought persisted: What if the killer found another way? What if he got to Stacie despite all their precautions? What if . . . ?

No. Breanna gave an adamant shake of her head. She wouldn't let her thoughts wander in that direction. If she did, she'd break down entirely.

She moved about the room, watching the early evening moonlight wash the furniture, and wondering how a winter night could look so lovely and, at the same time, feel so terrifying.

As if in search of something to combat the fear, to reinforce all the joy and hope in her life, she paused by the bed. Lovingly, she ran her fingers down the post and over the bedcovers, eliciting the familiar surge of warmth that accompanied her memories of the hours she spent in Royce's arms.

Their lovemaking had gotten more frantic each passing hour over the last two nights, as they both wordlessly sought the wonder and peace that only their joining could bring. Afterwards, they'd lie in each other's arms, talk until dawn—about anything and everything but what they feared most. Instead, they shared pieces of their pasts, learning more about each other and planning a future Breanna only prayed would happen.

Unfortunately, morning always came.

With the daylight hours, everything altered drastically. Even though Royce guarded her closely, he stayed at arm's length, appearing more like her sentry than her future husband. The two of them never touched, never even sat close together. Not because of protocol. Because of the assassin. If he could see into the manor, he could see them. And Royce was adamant that he not know what they meant to each other.

Breanna complied without question, although her reasons for doing so were different than Royce's. *He* was protecting *her*. *She* was protecting *him*.

The tension at Medford was becoming unbearable.

Royce spent long, concentrated hours reviewing the guest list, then comparing his updated facts to the reports that arrived daily from his contacts, after which he'd amend the list accordingly. Some of the guests' names were struck, others were labelled with a question mark as Royce went through the laborious process of verifying and eliminating in order to determine the assassin's identity.

The rest of the household was beginning to crumple.

Stacie had dark circles beneath her eyes, and Damen looked like death. Wells was haggard from lack of rest. Even Mahoney and his guards were testy, beginning to wonder if the intruder they were being paid to stop would ever come out of hiding so he could be captured.

The overall effect was maddening.

Each day the assassin didn't strike heightened everyone's sense of terror. Each of them silently wondered where he was, what he was thinking, what he was planning.

At the same time, they dreaded their answers.

Breanna prayed Hibbert would return soon, bearing *something* that would lead them in the right direction.

Most of all, she prayed Royce would get the killer before the killer got to him.

Sighing, she crossed the bedchamber, seeking her greatest tangible source of comfort.

Her porcelain figure.

Not just any figure, but her most prized one—the statue of the two girls picking flowers.

The one that held her silver coin.

Breanna lifted the statue and touched the coin, reliving the moments when her grandfather had gifted it to her, and its mate, the gold coin, to Stacie.

He'd wanted so much for them. He'd wanted their future.

Dear God, how she wanted to give that to him.

"Breanna?" Royce hovered in the doorway, his tone

gentle. "It's almost time for dinner. I'll walk you downstairs." A pause. "Are you all right?"

"Of course." She forced a smile to her lips before turning to face him. "I was just thinking."

He didn't look one bit fooled by her pretense. He walked deeper into the room, then spied what she was holding. "We have a few minutes. Would you like to tell me whatever it is you're conveying to your statues?"

"Not all my statues," she corrected softly. "Just one in particular."

"Ah." He walked over, studied the porcelain girls amid the flower bed. "Does that figure have special meaning?"

"Yes. Very special." This time her smile was genuine. "Do you remember the coins I told you about? The ones Grandfather gave Stacie and me when we were six?"

He nodded. "Silver for you, gold for Anastasia."

"With Medford Manor engraved on both, so we'd someday find our way back home forever—obstacles or not. It was Grandfather's way of reminding us what was important. And that something is family." She worked the coin free. "I keep it here, in this statue. The girls remind me of Stacie and me." She held out her hand. "Would you like to see it?"

"I'd be honored." Royce took the coin, turned it over in his palm. "It's the perfect symbol for you and Anastasia. Your grandfather was a very wise man."

"Wise and loving. I always wished he'd been my father instead of my grandfather." She swallowed, stared down at the floor. "I never want to disappoint him. In a way, I feel that by endangering Stacie and me—and most especially his future great-grandchild—I have."

"That's ridiculous." Royce glanced about the shadowy room, then over at the window. Convinced it was dark enough so they couldn't be seen, he reached for her, took her in his arms. "Your grandfather could be nothing but proud. You're a remarkable woman."

"Extraordinarily special," Breanna murmured, ribbons of memory drifting through her mind. "That's how Grandfather always referred to Stacie and me."

"I couldn't agree more."

Breanna gazed up at Royce, her smile returning as she recalled the other pivotal event that had occurred on the day her grandfather gifted them with their coins.

"I can't attest to how special we were, but we were certainly resourceful," she confided. "Do you know what we'd done just minutes before Grandfather gave us the coins? We'd made a pact. We vowed that whenever one of us got into trouble—the kind of trouble that would go away by our switching places—we'd do so."

Royce chuckled. "And did you ever carry out that pact?"

"Oh, several times." Breanna's eyes twinkled. "Beginning that very night. It was Grandfather's birthday. We'd sneaked outside to play. My dress was covered with mud. My father would have beaten me senseless. Stacie was wearing the identical frock. She played me to perfection."

"And you? Did you pretend to be her?"

"Yes. I loved every minute of it. It was the first time I ever spoke my mind without fear of punishment." Breanna laughed softly. "And that wasn't the only time we switched places. We did it again this past summer— every day for weeks. It was during the time when

Damen and Stacie were falling in love. My father wanted it to be me Damen was courting. And so it was."

Now Royce was grinning. "It was really Anastasia?"

"Absolutely." An exaggerated sigh. "Keeping my cousin's hair intact was the hardest part. Stacie can't go five minutes without sending, first strands, then tresses, toppling down. She's hopeless. Still, to be with Damen, she managed."

"I'm sure she did. I wish I'd been here to see it." Abruptly, Royce's amusement vanished. "I wish I'd been here to see everything. I'd have broken your father's jaw for ever laying a hand on you. And I'd have put a bullet through that son of a bitch he hired to kill Anastasia." Royce's gaze hardened. "I'll get my chance yet."

Fear knotted Breanna's stomach—the same fear that paralyzed her every time he made that claim. Reflexively, her fingers gripped his coat. "I saw several reports arrive for you today," she said, reverting back to the topic they tried so hard to avoid. "Did your contacts provide any answers?"

Royce's arms dropped to his sides, and he raked a frustrated hand through his hair. "Yes and no. This process is so damned tedious. Remember, there were two hundred fifty people at your party, two hundred forty-nine of whom are innocent. I've eliminated over half that number."

"All from the information your snitches provided?"

"That and my own knowledge of the guests." Royce rubbed his palms together, explaining the basis for his reasoning. "For example, one hundred four of the party goers were women. That leaves one hundred forty-six. Of those, over half have the wrong build— they're either short, brawny, or just plain fat. That brings us down to sixty-three. Here's where the reports come in. From what I'm reading, a good percentage of the men have alibis, either for the times when one of the murders occurred or for the night last summer when Anastasia was almost shot. Every few hours more information arrives, and I update my facts. Right now, I've narrowed the search down to thirty-four."

"You're amazing." Breanna shook her head in wonder. "Is this the kind of work you did in the military?"

"Yes. Whitehall relied upon what they called my deductive skills. During the war with Napoleon, I went back and forth from London to the Continent, depending on where I was most needed. The War Department knew I was good at reasoning out the enemy's strategy. I'd compile all the facts, consider the personalities involved, and make a prediction as to their intentions. My projections were usually right."

"That doesn't surprise me. You're brilliant." Breanna inclined her head quizzically. "What happened when the war ended? How did you decide to keep doing this?"

"Fate decided for me. Near the end of my service, I was approached by a general I'd worked with during my months in France. As a commander, he was admirable. I had great respect for him. As a man, he was inflexible and overbearing. When he sought my help, he was worried sick about his son, a junior officer who'd disappeared during battle and whose body was never recovered. I went about trying to find the boy. I analyzed the circumstances, talked to his associates, and figured out what I'd suspected from the start: that the general's son was a deserter. Not because he wasn't loyal to England, but because he didn't have the strength to stand up to his father."

"His father wanted him to follow in his footsteps, to pursue a career in the military," Breanna guessed.

"Right. And he had no stomach for it."

"I don't need to ask why you felt committed to the situation."

"No, you don't. The similarity to my own upbringing was definitely there—*with* some important differences. The general wasn't cruel, whereas my father was. This man truly loved his son. By the time he came to me, he would have willingly accepted his son's decision, just so he could have him home, alive and well. That worked in my favor. When I tracked down the boy, he was frequenting a seedy brothel on the outskirts of Paris. He refused to go home, said it would kill his father to hear he'd deserted his country. So, we reached an agreement. We never revealed what had really happened. Instead, our story was that he'd been captured by the French, but had escaped and was trying to make his way back to England when I found him. This spared his father embarrassment and him imprisonment. In return, I insisted he announce to his father that he didn't want to stay in the army, and then resign his commission."

"Did your plan work?"

"Beautifully. Everyone was happy."

"Including you." Breanna caressed his jaw. "You're a fraud, my love. You claim to be hard and removed, but I know it made you feel wonderful to give that boy something you never had." Her gaze was rife with compassion. "I'd have felt the same way."

"Yes, you would have." Royce kissed her fingertips. "In any case, word of mouth took over after that."

A smile. "In other words, the general raved to everyone about your brilliant rescue of his son, and suddenly scores of influential people had someone they needed you to find."

"Scores?" Royce chuckled. "That's a bit of an exaggeration. But, yes, it happened something like that."

A sudden thought struck Breanna. "You've never failed, have you?"

"Never."

"No wonder you were so determined to fight your feelings for me. Love is a daunting challenge, especially for a man who believes he has no depth of emotion—a man who never fails. Success would be far from guaranteed. That's unnerving, and risky."

Royce's knuckles caressed her cheek. "It was worth the risk."

"The risk is over," she murmured. "You've triumphed yet again."

"This time it was pure luck." His jaw tightened. "With my next challenge, it won't be."

Breanna knew just what path his thoughts had taken.

"Royce—"

"I'm not going to do anything stupid," he assured her, his tone as rigid as his jaw. "But I'm also not going to lose. Not this time. The stakes are too high. I'm going to figure out who he is. And then I'm going to kill him."

An urgent knock at the door brought their conversation to an abrupt halt.

"Lord Royce?"

Breanna blanched. "It's Wells. He sounds upset."

She was across the room before Royce, yanking open the door. "Wells? It's not Stacie, is it?"

The butler shook his head, far too preoccupied to worry about the impropriety of Breanna being alone in her room with Royce. "Miss Stacie is fine. Another box just arrived. It's downstairs."

Royce took Breanna's arm. "Let's go."

The box was small, the size of a book, and addressed, as always, to Breanna.

Stacie and Damen were waiting in the hallway, and the five of them crowded into the sitting room, where Royce pulled the drapes closed before nodding for Breanna to unwrap the package.

She did so in a sort of numbed state, peeling back the paper to lift out a porcelain figure. It depicted the same two women as the previous statue, only this time they were sitting side-by-side on a sofa. Across their laps was a pale blue quilt, and their hands were poised, preparing to sew on some lacy trim.

Crimson paint had been slashed across the quilt and the lace, staining both a sickly shade of red.

More blood.

This time the blood led to the women's hands.

Instantly, Breanna saw why.

Their right hands had been mutilated, the index finger of each broken off, saturated with red paint.

A note lay beside the statue, penned in the same bold, defined hand as always.

I can feel your terror. It makes my vengeance complete. I'm here, Lady Breanna. My pistol is aimed at your cousin's heart. Sheldrake can't save her. Nor can Chadwick save you. His reconnaissance is inferior. There's no time. A bullet takes only seconds.

Succumb to your fate. The battle is lost.

My finger . . . your life.

23

*H*ibbert waited until he'd ushered Emma into his room at the inn.

Then, he told her everything.

For a long moment afterward, she stared at him in disbelief. Then, she broke down, harsh sobs racking her body as she absorbed the realization that her nightmare was at an end. She wrapped her arms around herself, tears coursing down her cheeks as she wept.

"Come. Sit down." Hibbert led her to a chair, handing her his handkerchief and laying a reassuring hand on her shoulder. "Can I get you anything?"

She shook her head, battling for her sobs to subside. "Forgive me," she choked out. "I just never thought . . . She said you were buying me. She warned me that if I breathed a word of the truth, she'd find me and—"

"You don't need to explain, and certainly not to apologize. I'm just grateful I got here in time. Lord Royce was distraught when he went to fetch you at Pearson Manor and learned what had happened."

She gulped. "That monster—he killed my mother."

"Who?" Hibbert couldn't help himself, not when it came to this. "Who killed your mother, Emma? Did you see him?"

"Yes." An unsteady nod. "I saw him. I'm the only one who did. The other women—the ones who were locked in that room with me, whose husbands were killed—they never saw his face. But I did."

"Those other women, they're all at Le Joyau?"

Another nod. "We weren't all shipped at the same time, but, yes, we were all there. *They* still are."

"Locked in a room together?"

"Yes. They're not with Maurelle's women. That's because they're for sale. Not for a night—forever. Like I was. Maurelle said I'd bring the highest price because I was so young and because I was untouched. But she was expecting a fortune for them, too. They're noblewomen and not much older than I am." Emma buried her face in her hands. "She's selling them like chattel."

"We'll get them out." Hibbert squatted down beside the chair. "Emma, I know you're still in shock. But I need your help. That man who shot your mother has killed many times. He's threatening to kill again. We've got to stop him. So, please, tell me everything you remember about him, everything you can."

"I only saw him for a minute," she said, raising her head, a haunted look on her face. "But I'll never forget his eyes. They were like chips of ice. Empty and unfeeling."

"What did he look like? Describe him."

A horrified shudder. "He was tall. And very fit. Not stout or pudgy like most men his age. More like you, only not thin—muscular. I could feel his strength when he dragged me around." She squeezed her eyes shut. "I don't remember anything else. Except that his hair was dark, and graying at the temples. He was wearing all black." She drew a quivering breath. "He shot Mama through a blanket. Then he hit me. The next thing I knew, I was in a canvas bag in the cargo hold of a ship. I was unloaded in Calais, then taken here by carriage. He let me out a few times, but I was blindfolded. So I never actually saw him again."

"What about his voice—can you describe it?"

Another tremor ran through her. "Cold. Clipped. I'd recognize it if I heard it again. I think we all would."

All. That brought Hibbert back to the matter at hand. He needed to get those other woman out of that brothel.

And he needed to get Maurelle under lock and key.

"Did he deliver you to Le Joyau personally?"

"Yes. The women who work there said he and Maurelle were friends."

"Friends?"

"More than friends."

"I see. And did they refer to him by name?"

"No. Even Maurelle never said his name. She just called him 'my noble assassin.' She seemed to find that amusing."

"Did she?" Hibbert replied thoughtfully. That told him a great deal about Maurelle. It told him she was aware of how her lover was providing her with saleable noblewomen.

Maurelle Le Joyau was a bitch, and even harder than he'd realized.

It was time to consider his options. The sooner he acted, the better. Maurelle needed to be stopped before she could sell any of the other women. She also needed to be escorted to England, where Royce could pry information out of her—information that would lead him right to the "noble assassin."

On the other hand, none of this could be done hastily. Hibbert knew better. He couldn't risk alerting Maurelle before he'd freed those women. It was too dangerous. If she had any idea what he was planning, she'd either move the women, or silence them. The timing had to be right. He needed the element of surprise.

And he needed help.

He glanced at Emma, saw her teeth chattering, tears still flowing down her cheeks, and he knew she couldn't be left alone. Not only for compassionate reasons, but for practical ones. He couldn't be sure she was coherent enough to understand that she wasn't to leave this room under any circumstances.

He'd summon Girard.

Quickly, he went to the nightstand, picked up the paper and quill.

He only prayed he was in.

Girard arrived at Hibbert's room at the inn just before midnight.

His eyes widened when he saw Emma, curled up asleep on the bed, two blankets wrapped around her to calm the chills that had racked her body for nearly an hour.

"*Mon Dieu*," he muttered, rubbing a palm across his jaw. "No wonder your message was so urgent." His eyes narrowed as he studied Emma, noting her age, build, and features. "My guess is that this is the girl Royce was searching for—the daughter of Lord Ryder."

"Yes." Hibbert spoke quietly, although Emma showed no signs of stirring. Having endured a week of hell, she'd fallen dead asleep, and was totally unaware of Girard's arrival. "I found her in Maurelle Le Joyau's brothel," Hibbert continued. "She's on the verge of emotional collapse. That's why I couldn't leave her here alone."

"Has she spoken to you?"

A terse nod. "All the kidnapped women are at Le Joyau. I'll give you the details. After that, I'll need that help you offered."

"Consider it done."

It was nearly 4 A.M. when Emma stirred.

She pushed herself up on one elbow, and for a brief instant, she looked like the innocent young woman she'd been a week ago, before the assassin destroyed her life.

Then reality intruded, and she went rigid, her eyes snapping open to survey her surroundings.

Relief flooded her face when she saw Hibbert sitting in the chair by the desk.

"It wasn't a dream. You really did take me away from there. Thank God." Her gaze flitted to Girard, who sat on another chair, this one blocking the door against intruders.

She struggled to a sitting position, her brows drawing together in concern.

"It's all right Emma," Hibbert assured her. "This is Monsieur Girard. He's a friend of Lord Royce's. He lives here in Paris. He's come to help us."

Emma relaxed. "You're French?"

"*Mais oui.*" His smile was gentle. "And you're a very strong young woman. You've endured a great deal. But it's over now. Hibbert and I will see to it."

She managed a small smile. "Thank you."

Hibbert stood, fetched a tray from the nightstand, and offered it to her. "I had some tea sent up. It's probably cooled off a bit, but I think you should drink it. There are rolls, too. I want you to eat. You've got to regain your strength."

Emma's lashes lowered as she contemplated the tray on her lap. When they lifted again, there were tears in her eyes. "I hope my father turns out to be as fine a gentleman as you are."

Hibbert felt an uncustomary surge of sentiment. "Your father is very fortunate to be getting you as a daughter. And, yes, he's a decent man. I think you'll like him. I know he'll be very relieved to learn you're all right."

A spark of curiosity lit her eyes. "You know the Viscount Ryder?"

"I assist Lord Royce with his work. So, yes, I'm acquainted with the viscount."

"Will you tell me about him? Later, when all this is over and the other women are also safe?"

Hibbert and Girard exchanged glances. It was no surprise that Emma Martin needed something to cling to. Nor was it a surprise that her thoughts had turned to her sire. He might be a stranger to her, but he was all she had left. What *was* surprising was that, after all she'd been through, she was caring enough to postpone her own needs and think of others.

Lord Ryder was luckier than he knew.

"There's no need to wait until after the rescue," Hibbert replied. "It's not even dawn. Once Girard and

I have worked out a plan, I'd be pleased to tell you whatever I know about the viscount."

Some color was beginning to return to her cheeks. "I'm grateful." She poured herself some tea, took a sip. "What can I tell you that would help?"

"Three things," Girard responded, rising to his feet and pacing about. "First, when is the best time to break into Le Joyau? Should we wait until evening when the women are . . ." He broke off, gave an awkward cough.

"It's all right, Mr. Girard," Emma assured him with a quiet dignity that tugged at the heartstrings. "Thanks to Mr. Hibbert, I was spared being defiled. Nonetheless, I lost my innocence at that brothel. Beforehand, actually—when that animal shot my mother. Yes, the best time to break into Le Joyau is when Maurelle's women are working. Not before midnight, because most of them are still doing their more formal entertaining in one of the parlors. But afterwards, when they've retired to the bedchambers to earn their pay." She pursed her lips thoughtfully. "Sometime between one and three A.M. That way, you'll avoid those patrons who choose to depart early," contempt laced her tone, "to return home to their wives."

Girard nodded, averting his gaze out of some instinctive respect for this decent young woman. "Can you think what the best way would be for us to get in?"

She gave a bitter laugh. "I don't need to think. I *know* the best way for you to get in. It's the same way I dreamed about escaping through every moment of the day I spent in that particular room." She shuddered, took another long sip of tea. "There's a window in back, on the ground floor. It leads to an empty storage room. That's the room where the killer first brought me. Later, Maurelle dragged me down the hall and put me in with the other women she means to sell."

"How many rooms did you pass along the way?"

Emma frowned, trying to recall. "Not many. It was very quiet in that area of the house. Maurelle wanted it that way. She had to be sure that, if any of the women cried out, nothing could be overheard by her patrons."

Girard's disgust was evident. "I understand. Tell me, Miss Martin, did you happen to notice if the window in that storage room was locked?"

"As I said, I planned my escape at least two dozen times. So, yes, I studied the window, and its lock. It's actually a latch. Not a very strong one. A man could definitely break it. Also, the window is hidden by some ivy. That makes it hard to find." She set aside the tray. "When do you plan to break in?"

Surprise darted across Girard's handsome features. "Why?"

"Because I want to be there. I can show you where the window is, and where the women are being kept. I can also help keep your presence a secret. When you first burst in, those women are going to be terrified. Someone is bound to scream. But if I go in before you, explain what's about to happen, they'll be prepared."

Girard's jaw dropped. "You would do that? You'd go back there, after all you've been through?"

"For this? Yes." She gazed from Girard to Hibbert. "When shall we go?"

"Tonight." Hibbert's mind was already racing. "It must be tonight. The sooner we grab Maurelle, the sooner she'll lead us to the assassin. Time is running out."

348   Andrea Kane

"That leads me to the third question," Girard continued, nodding his agreement. "Miss Martin, where are Maurelle's chambers?"

"They're in a separate section of the house. But you won't find her there. She doesn't retire until daylight, after all the night's payments have been collected. She reads all night in the front parlor—the one I met Mr. Hibbert in. The only exceptions are when she's away, and when her noble assassin visits. But he's not at Le Joyau now. So she'll be in the salon, not her chambers."

"I'll get the women," Girard told Hibbert quietly. "I'm sure you want the pleasure of seizing Mademoiselle Le Joyau."

A terse nod. "She'll be accompanying me back to England," Hibbert informed him. "You keep the women here in Paris. Find a safe place for them. Until the killer is caught, it's not safe for them to go home. We can't run the risk of him finding out they've escaped. That includes you, Emma."

Her shrug was sad. "That's fine. I'm not sure I'm ready to go home and face a future without my mother."

"I'll make the arrangements," Girard agreed. His gaze drifted to Emma, and there was an intensity in his eyes that was palpable. "You'll be cared for and safe."

"I appreciate that."

"Emma, one more question," Hibbert concluded. "You said the assassin is gone. Do you remember when he left, and how long he stayed at Le Joyau on his last visit?"

She squeezed her eyes shut. "One day spilled into the next. I didn't see him leave. It must have been several days ago. As for how long he stayed, I overheard Maurelle's women whispering about how she was closeted in her chambers for a whole day with him. Oh—I also heard some gossip about him coming back next week, after he finalized some urgent business."

"Urgent business," Hibbert repeated grimly. "I can guess what that is. And we must prevent it from happening."

The next porcelain figure arrived at Medford the following night, just after sunset.

It, too, was part of the set of statues that had been stolen from the Canterbury shop—the set depicting two identical women. This time, the women were posed arranging white flowers in a vase. A quiet, tranquil scene.

Except that the flowers had been stained with red paint, as had the women's gowns over their hearts.

The same monstrous touch as last time had been added.

The women's right hands had been stained red, and their right forefingers had been hacked off.

The accompanying note read: *Flowers for Lady Anastasia's grave. Even flanked by Sheldrake and Wells, she'll die. Like an arrow to its target, my bullet will bypass their ranks and find her heart. One bullet. Then one for you. Severed finger, severed lives.*

The household was still reeling from that delivery, when the next one arrived the following afternoon. It was another statue, similar in design, identical in disfigurement, and with a similarly ominous note.

Royce was becoming more and more troubled by the pattern.

His instincts told him that the assassin planned a

steady stream of these deliveries until all the statues had reached their mark.

After which, he planned to strike.

If that shopkeeper Barker was correct, there were seven statues in all. Which meant only three were still remaining to be delivered.

Time was running out.

So was Royce's patience.

He'd narrowed things down as best he could. There were twenty-five names remaining on his list. Caution decreed he wait until he'd cut that number in half before confronting the suspects.

But caution had never been his strength. He was a risk-taker by nature. He pushed the boundaries and then some. That was how he'd survived as a child, and that was how he achieved his success as an adult.

In this case, however, the risk was acute. By aggressively pursuing the killer, he'd be making himself a walking target. And by doing so without having a damned good idea who the killer was, he'd be relinquishing the upper hand, leaving his own back exposed to attack.

Jeopardizing his life.

Before now, he'd have met that challenge head-on.

But now, there was Breanna—Breanna and their future together.

How could he put that future on the line?

He couldn't.

Except that, fairly soon, he'd have to. There would be no other option. Because if it came down to a choice between Breanna's life and his, there was no choice to make. He'd die before letting that bastard hurt her.

So, if the stream of statues finished arriving at Medford before he finished conducting his investigation, he'd be forced to take action.

By stepping into the middle of things, he'd disrupt the assassin's plan, break his building momentum. Not only that, he'd also divert the assassin's attention from the women to him, acting as a decoy of sorts. He'd venture out to the front gates, announce to Mahoney that he'd narrowed down the list of suspects to three, all of whom he was on his way to confront. On that unnerving note, he'd ride off like the wind. And, like a vicious dog who'd been thrown a piece of meat, the killer would veer off after him, ready to attack his more immediate and dangerous enemy.

The killer's identity would still be unknown.

But he'd be called off Anastasia and Breanna, focused on stopping the man who was threatening to best him.

And when the moment of truth arrived, when the son of a bitch emerged to silence and outwit him, Royce would have his chance to obliterate him.

One chance.

It was a risk. A big one.

The question was, who could shoot first?

Given equal odds, Royce's answer would have been different. But the odds weren't equal. Not when he had no idea who the enemy was. The full advantage lay with the killer.

If there was just a little more time. If Royce could pare down the list to, say, five or six, strengthen his position.

Then he could make his move.

A confident move.

With vehement determination, he returned to his analysis.

Another tortuous day passed.

The next afternoon arrived, menacing skies and icy temperatures matching the somber mood that permeated the house.

Breanna moved about the sitting room, fluffing some cushions, brushing some invisible dust off the wood, and trying to calm her nerves.

She couldn't bear the tension any longer.

She glanced over at Royce, who sat on the settee, his head bent over his work, and watched him slash another three names off the guest list.

She was going to go mad.

Wandering over to the window, she perched at the corner of the ledge, peering around the curtain and surveying the frosty grounds.

A moving object caught her eye, and she squinted, focusing on it and waiting until she could make out who it was.

It was Mahoney, approaching the house at a brisk pace.

Dear God, could it be *another* package?

Breanna held her breath, waiting to see if he clutched a parcel in his hands.

He didn't.

Instead, he had a letter. That meant that another of Royce's contacts had come through, providing an additional bit of information.

She stole another cautious peek at Royce. He looked haggard, his handsome face lined with strain. She couldn't remember the last full hour's sleep he'd had. He was obsessed with his pursuit, relentless in his investigation.

He was also only human.

And Breanna wanted desperately to help him.

She was the only one who could. Hibbert was away. Stacie was the assassin's immediate target. Damen and Wells had to stick to Stacie like glue—just in case—and the guards had to stay, armed and ready, at their posts.

She *had* to do something.

Scrutinizing Royce, Breanna knew this was her chance—maybe her only chance. He was engrossed in a report, not concentrating on her. Besides, it would never occur to him that she'd do anything impulsive. As a rule, impulsiveness was not in her nature.

He was about to learn that every rule had its exceptions.

Slowly, Breanna eased toward the sitting-room doorway. She and Royce were virtually alone in this part of the house; she knew that. The servants were scattered about, in the kitchen or upstairs, performing their duties. Stacie was napping. Wells had gone up an hour ago, to relieve Damen so he could shut his eyes for an hour. No guests were expected, nor would Mahoney allow them through the gates, so it didn't matter that the entranceway was temporarily unattended.

It was now or never.

She slipped into the hallway, hurrying to the front door and opening it before Mahoney could knock.

The head guard looked startled. "Lady Breanna?" he guessed, taking in her neatly coiffed hair. "Why are you attending the door?"

"It's all right, Mr. Mahoney," she assured him.

"Everyone is taking a much-needed nap. I don't want to disturb them." She indicated the letter. "Is that for Lord Royce? I'll see that he gets it the minute he awakens."

"Yes, it is. But . . ." Mahoney frowned, as if uncertain what to do. He peered into the deserted hallway, then glanced swiftly back over his shoulder, scanning the grounds in uncomfortable scrutiny. Clearly, he was worried about leaving his post for so long.

In the end, he decided it was best to get back to the gates and do what he'd been hired to do, rather than to stand here and argue with her ladyship.

He placed the note in her hand. "Here. Now please—go inside."

"I will." With a grateful smile, Breanna complied, shutting the door and leaning back against it.

She tore open the envelope.

The information was terse, but pivotal.

Apparently, Royce had contacted some of his more technically knowledgable men, instructing them to uncover any gunsmith who had the ability to construct a sophisticated and unusual weapon—one designed for a four-fingered man. This reply, from someone named Rogers who was clearly an intelligent, reliable source, stated that he'd found such a gunsmith, although he no longer worked as such—at least not formally. His name was Wilkens, and his shop had been in London. But he'd shut the shop down hastily after finding out that Bow Street was on their way to ascertain whether or not he was supplying weapons to criminals. Now officially retired, he'd just spent several months abroad, and had returned to settle down at his home in Maidstone. An address was provided.

Maidstone? That was only an hour's ride from here.

Breanna put down the letter on an end table and scooted across to collect her mantle. Finally, she could do something to help Royce. She'd go and speak with this Wilkens, find out if he was the one who'd crafted the assassin's pistol. She'd do it subtly, of course, ask him questions without alerting him to her intentions. Now that she considered it, she'd probably get farther than Royce would, anyway. The gunsmith, unlawful or not, would be more apt to let down his guard with a wide-eyed young woman than a formidable-looking man.

She reached for the door handle, and hesitated.

The assassin was out there. What if he saw her?

Of course he'd see her—if he hadn't done so already. Her job was to use that fact to her advantage. She knew he wasn't ready to kill her yet. Not with Stacie still alive. So she'd have to do something to satisfy him that she was going somewhere imperative, and for some plausible reason.

She'd better make this convincing—for all their sakes.

On that thought, she left the house, shut the door quietly behind her.

She held her breath the entire time she waited for the phaeton to be brought around. It was eerie standing outside in the open, knowing she was being watched, praying she'd accurately assessed the killer's intentions.

Her heartbeat accelerated, and she tensed, half-expecting a shot to ring out, to cut her down where she stood. At the same time, she listened for noises sounding behind her—noises that would indicate

Royce had discovered her absence and come storming from the house to drag her back inside.

She prayed that wouldn't happen. Because if the assassin saw Royce rush to her rescue, exhibiting the emotion she knew he would, Lord knew how he'd react. He might just decide to further torture her by killing the man she loved—the very thing she'd been trying to prevent.

Never had a phaeton taken so long to arrive.

Finally, it did—without incident.

She thanked the footman, climbed into the seat, then took up the reins and led the horses toward the front gates.

Whatever she said had to be believable—not only to Mr. Mahoney, but to the killer.

One thing she'd learned from surviving two decades with her father, dodging his anger and avoiding being beaten, was that the most convincing lies, the ones you desperately needed to work, were the ones that stuck closest to the truth. The further from the truth you strayed, the more nervous you became and the more likely you were to slip up.

So be it.

She braced herself as she neared the gates, slowing down as Mahoney stepped in her path, holding up his palm and barring her exit.

He approached the phaeton, a stunned expression on his face. "My lady, what in heaven's name . . ." He broke off, inclining his head and staring at her, obviously trying to ascertain if she'd lost her mind—the only logical explanation he could come up with for her to attempt this insane antic.

"I'm not mad, Mr. Mahoney," she supplied, making no attempt to hide her apprehension. Not only was it genuine, it was necessary that she convey it to the assassin. Her gaze darted about, in a very real attempt to ensure her safety and, at the same time, to let the assassin see her sense of urgency. "I must ride out," she announced to Mahoney. "That last correspondence you delivered said there was a second letter—an important one—that should have been delivered along with it. I've got to go after that messenger, catch him right away."

Mahoney's stunned expression didn't change. "With all due respect, my lady, you're hardly the one who should be going after—"

"Mr. Mahoney—please!" Breanna interrupted, her voice and hands shaking. "I realize I should be in the house. But I don't want to take the time to awaken the men. By then, the messenger will be gone. And I certainly can't send Stacie—the initial threats are on her life. It's got to be me." She tightened her grip on the reins. "We're wasting time arguing. If you let me go now, I'll be back in minutes. The longer we wait, the longer it will take to return."

"My men will go." Mahoney turned, raising his arm to issue the order.

"No!" Breanna reached forward, grabbed his sleeve. "That would mean fewer guards to protect Stacie. And if anything happened to her . . ." She sucked in her breath, assuming a tone she rarely used. "Mr. Mahoney, I don't want to put it this way, but I am mistress of this house. If I have to, I'll order you to let me pass. Now, open those gates, before the messenger rides all the way back to London."

Mahoney hesitated another moment. Then, he complied, waving his arm and ordering the guards to open the gates. "I'll give you a half hour," he informed her. "Then, I'm alerting Lord Royce."

She didn't pause to argue. She simply nodded, then slapped her reins and led the horses on.

She sped down the road, then veered west toward Maidstone.

The assassin watched her go with some interest and an unforeseen tinge of respect.

He hadn't expected her to be so brazen. Nor so clever. She'd correctly assessed his determination to adhere to the order in which he meant to carry out his plan. In an odd way, she was baiting him. Well, he wouldn't let her win by giving in to the temptation to shoot her down now, when she was alone and unguarded. Her cousin had to die first—first, and right in front of Lady Breanna's horrified eyes.

He'd made that clear. Nonetheless, she was taking a risk, lest he change his mind.

And all to go after a messenger, to get her hands on that second letter.

Then again, if the information in the letter was *that* important, it would warrant such prompt attention, risk or not. Her reason was sound.

It was also a lie.

From the thick branches of the tree he'd just scaled, he could see her phaeton, heading southwest.

London was northwest.

And, based upon the fact that she'd just intercepted one of Chadwick's messages—a message that probably provided answers to a piece of the puzzle he'd fully expected a worthy opponent like Chadwick to investigate—he had a fairly good idea where she was riding.

And to whom.

Pity. He'd hoped Wilkens could have remained a mystery for a while longer—long enough to speed this process to its natural conclusion while sparing the poor fellow's life. Now, it would set things back a few hours, not to mention forcing him to find another gunsmith, one with as great a flair for the creative as Wilkens had.

It couldn't be helped. Lady Breanna was too fetching, Wilkens too susceptible to beauty, too easily duped, to be relied upon to keep his mouth shut.

Swinging lightly to the ground, the assassin eased through the trees, making his way to the road, then the hidden brush beyond, where his own carriage was concealed.

A sudden, pleasurable thought struck, made his eyes glitter with anticipation.

He knew a back route to Maidstone. He'd beat Lady Breanna there by twenty minutes, take care of his task, and get back to Medford Manor ahead of her—*and* Chadwick, who'd undoubtedly go rushing after her the minute that guard gave him the news of her departure. As for the guards, they'd be frantically searching for her ladyship, cursing themselves for ever allowing her to go.

Leaving the manor vulnerable to attack.

24

"*Y*ou let her do *what?*"

Royce nearly struck Mahoney, visibly controlling himself as the head guard delivered word of Breanna's departure.

Mahoney mopped his brow. "I had no choice, sir. She ordered me—"

"I don't care if she held you at gunpoint." Royce drew a slow breath, biting back his anger in lieu of reason. "Where did she go?"

"After the messenger."

"*What* messenger?"

"The one who sent you that last piece of correspondence, the one I brought to the door right before Lady Breanna left." Mahoney swallowed. "She took it from me herself, said she'd give it to you when you woke up."

"She didn't. And I wasn't sleeping." Royce scanned the hallway, and spied the letter on the end table. He snatched it up, read through it quickly. "This says nothing about another message. It says . . ." He came to the word Maidstone, and his jaw snapped shut. "God, no."

He nearly knocked Mahoney down in his haste to leave. "Go inside. Tell Lord Sheldrake that I think Breanna's ridden to Maidstone. Post a few guards outside Anastasia's chambers. Then get the rest of the guards to begin a search, just in case I'm wrong and Breanna's gone elsewhere. We've got to find her."

The cottage was quiet.

Breanna brought her phaeton to a halt, taking a minute to compose herself and review her story before approaching Mr. Wilkens.

She had to seem pathetic, to weep real tears as she told him her fabricated story of the tragic accident that had claimed her father's trigger finger. She'd scatter in as many facts as possible, confess that her father had been involved with unsavory types. She'd say that out of desperation, she'd used those contacts, taken unorthodox steps to find out who the most qualified gunsmith was to craft a new pistol for her father, who was confined to Newgate, and desperate to escape.

An ironic smile touched her lips. Who'd ever have thought her father's unscrupulous dealings would serve her so well?

She climbed down, gathered up her skirts, and marched to the door.

Her first knock went unanswered.

So did the repeated ones that followed.

Oh, God, he has to be home, she thought fervently. *He has to be.*

Resorting to something she never would have considered, Breanna turned the door handle and entered.

The door swung open.

"Mr. Wilkens?" she called.

No response.

Breanna stepped into the small, cluttered house, praying the gunsmith was either asleep or hard of hearing. Just so long as he was home. She made her way down the hall, calling out his name as she did. She paused at each room, stepping inside and checking to see if he was there.

The door to the sitting room was shut.

"Mr. Wilkens?" she tried hopefully, twisting the handle and giving it a push.

The door wasn't locked. But it wouldn't budge.

Frowning, Breanna shoved at the wood, only to be met with the same resistance. Finally, she threw her weight against it, jarring the door until it shifted enough to let her squeeze through.

A blast of cold air accosted her from the open window in the far corner of the room.

She shivered, drew her mantle more tightly around herself as she stepped inside.

A scream froze in her throat.

Wilkens's body lay on the floor, a stream of blood trickling from his chest, pooling on the floor beneath him.

He was dead.

"Dear God," she whispered, pressing her fist to her mouth. "Oh, dear God." She backed away, unable to stop staring at the man's lifeless form as she inched toward the hall.

Powerful hands grabbed her from behind.

This time her scream broke free, and she began struggling violently against whoever held her captive.

"Breanna, it's me." Royce swung her around, seized

her shoulders in his hands. His eyes were nearly black with anger, his features taut with worry. "Are you all right?"

"Royce." She sagged toward him, happier to see him than she'd ever been to see anyone in her life.

"Reckless little fool," he muttered, dragging her against him and holding her with arms that shook. "You scared the hell out of me."

She gripped the lapels of Royce's coat. "He's dead," she managed, gesturing toward the sitting room. "Shot like the others."

Keeping one arm snaked tightly around Breanna's waist, Royce leaned past her, peered inside. Frowning, he released Breanna long enough to check Wilkens, verify he was dead.

"That son of a bitch beat us here," he pronounced, rising to his feet, noting the open window. "And not by much. Wilkens couldn't have been shot more than a half hour ago, judging from the body. Somehow that bastard knew where you were headed. He used the window to escape."

Breanna was trying to steady her breathing, to clear her head. "How could he know my destination? He didn't read Rogers's letter. It was sealed when Mahoney delivered it. He must have seen through my story about pursuing the messenger." Her voice quavered. "It's my fault this man is dead."

"No." Royce drew her against him, stroked her hair. "Wilkens was doomed the minute Rogers's note was delivered to Medford. Had I received it first, I would have done precisely what you did—ridden to Maidstone to question Wilkens. The assassin is smart. He knew I was checking into the gunsmith who crafted his pistol. He'd have seen where I was headed, and

put two and two together. He'd have dashed on
ahead of me, killed Wilkens before I had the chance to
talk to him. Just as he did with you. The only difference is, *I* would have been the one in danger. Which is
how it should have been."

Royce buried his lips in her hair. "Dammit, Breanna, don't do that to me ever again. I was terrified." He
paused, realized she was trembling. "Let's go home.
Anastasia is probably frantic by now."

That had the desired effect.

"Stacie knows where I've gone?" Breanna asked,
worry supplanting shock.

"By now, yes. I told Mahoney. The whole household is probably in turmoil. And the guards must be
scouring Kent looking for you."

Breanna's grip on his coat tightened. "If so, they
won't be guarding Stacie."

"Yes they will." Royce eased her worry, his knuckles gently stroking her cheek. "Damen and Wells are
with her. They're both armed. I had Mahoney post
guards outside her room, as well. No one will get by
them."

"We've got to go." Breanna was already heading for
the door.

Royce escorted her to the phaeton, stopping only to
harness his mount to the front, alongside the horse
who'd guided her here. "I rode here on horseback. It's
the only way I could gain the time I needed. We'll ride
back together. I'll hail a local constable along the way,
tell him about Wilkens's body."

Breanna nodded mutely, sitting in a numbed state
as Royce turned the phaeton around, headed for
home.

An icy premonition began forming deep in her gut.

It spread, crawling up her spine, intensifying as their carriage neared Medford Manor.

She'd known that premonition before. It had struck last August, an instant before the assassin stepped out of the shadows, took a shot at Stacie.

He was closing in, nearing the moment when he'd complete his unfinished execution.

Abruptly, Breanna seized Royce's arm. "Royce, I've got to get home. Now."

Royce studied her terrified expression, instantly slapping the reins to comply. "What is it?"

"It's the killer. He's getting close to Stacie."

Lady Anastasia would wait.

The assassin's lips curled in a mocking smile as he peered around the corner of the hall, watched the two guards standing rigidly in front of the marchioness's door.

Putting them there had no doubt been Chadwick's doing. He was making sure Lady Anastasia stayed safe while he dashed off after her cousin. Well, Chadwick needn't have worried. It wasn't time for her ladyship to die—not yet. Not without her wretched cousin there to watch the life drain out of her. That would defeat his whole purpose, take the satisfaction out of his revenge.

No, this visit would serve a different purpose. This visit would be to deliver his ultimate gift to Lady Breanna.

Getting inside the manor had been pathetically easy.

The guards were dashing about like frantic mice, leaving gaping holes in security.

He'd made his way across the grounds, then

slipped inside via the servants' quarters. He'd waited in the shadows, assessing the area to ensure it was clear. Not surprisingly, it had been. Lady Breanna's loyal staff was undoubtedly combing the house, room by room, looking for a sign of where their mistress had gone.

He'd scaled the stairs, then hovered in the alcove off the landing before easing his way down the hall to scrutinize Lord and Lady Sheldrake's chambers.

Scornfully, he turned away, wondering if the guards actually thought him stupid enough, amateur enough, to lunge for the door with them standing outside it. Perhaps they were novices. He was not.

He moved furtively toward Lady Breanna's chambers.

Noiselessly, he twisted the door handle and walked in.

It took him ten seconds to realize something wasn't right. The room looked far more barren than before, a sense of abandonment hovering in the air.

He scanned the room swiftly, realizing at once that the porcelain figures were gone, as were the other personal touches.

Lady Breanna had been moved elsewhere.

Rage boiled up inside him.

The little bitch had changed rooms, and she'd done so successfully, without alerting him. She'd obviously staged her regular evening routine so he'd think all was as usual.

She'd pay for this victory. Pay dearly.

Where were her new chambers?

He didn't have to rack his brain for an answer.

Chadwick. He'd moved her closer to his room, put her somewhere he could keep an eye on her.

A triumphant glint flashed in his eyes.

Their little deception had just ended. Now, it was his turn to gloat.

Breanna burst into the house.

She gathered up her skirts, dashing up the stairs and down the hall to Stacie's room.

The two guards looked startled by the commotion. But, seeing who was causing it, they relaxed, very relieved to see Lady Breanna home, unhurt.

"Is my cousin all right?" she demanded.

"Yes, ma'am," one guard replied. "We've been posted outside her room for over two hours now."

"And no one's tried to get in?"

He gave an adamant shake of his head. "No one."

At that instant, the door was flung open, and Stacie bypassed Damen and Wells, stepping into the hallway and giving Breanna a fierce hug. "I heard your voice. Thank God, you're all right."

Breanna nearly wept with relief. "My sentiments exactly. I had the most awful feeling. I thought that . . ." She broke off, drew a steadying breath. "It doesn't matter. What matters is that you're safe."

"*I'm* safe?" Stacie asked in amazement. "*You're* the one who went out in the open, left Medford Manor to ride to Maidstone. Why? Who was in Maidstone?"

Before Breanna could reply, Royce came up behind her. "I'll answer your questions, Anastasia," he said quietly. "I think Breanna needs to lie down."

Even as he spoke, Breanna realized her knees were shaking. She felt weak and wobbly, the aftermath of discovering a murdered man's body, then fearing for her cousin's life, more severe than she'd realized.

"I . . . Yes, I think I should lie down—for a few minutes," she added, seeing the concern on Stacie's face. "I'm fine. Just spent."

Royce gestured to one of the guards. "Walk Lady Breanna down to her room. Stay outside the door until I get there."

"Of course, m'lord."

Breanna shot Royce a grateful look, then turned, headed toward her new chambers, the guard by her side. All she needed was a few minutes to herself—time to lie down, put a cool compress on her pounding head. Then she'd be fine, ready to go back and discuss where things stood now that the gunsmith was unable to tell them anything.

She nodded politely at the guard, opened the door to her room, and shut it behind her. She was relieved to know he was out there. Still, she loathed this need for confinement. She couldn't wait for the day she could come and go again as she pleased.

If that day ever came.

Unbidden, the image of Wilkens's lifeless body flashed in her mind, and she fought back the sickness that rose in her throat.

How many more people would die before this nightmare ended? How much longer would this assassin's rampage continue?

Distraught, she crossed over, turned up the lamp on her nightstand to offset the effects of the intensifying dusk.

A horrified scream lodged in her throat, and for a moment, she actually stopped breathing.

In the center of the bed lay a white glove. The glove had been impaled by a sword, which was now imbedded deeply in the mattress. It had been driven all the way through the glove's index finger. Three-quarters of that finger had been sliced off. Red paint was splattered everywhere, staining the bedcovers and trickling onto the carpet. On either side of the glove sat a statue—both from the same set as the previous statues. Once again, the women had been disfigured, their right index fingers lopped off, their right hands and the front of their gowns covered with bright crimson stains.

On the pillow, lay a note. It read:

Your strategy was a mistake. You changed quarters to outsmart me. Instead, you enraged me. I'm an expert tracker. And you're a fool. Your evasive tactics have now guaranteed Lady Anastasia a more agonizing death. Listen to her screams, as her life drains away. Your cousin's time is up. Her blood is on your hands. My satisfaction will come when I see yours flow. The invasion is about to commence.

Die, Lady Breanna.

For a long moment, Breanna just stood there, paralyzed, besieged by a sort of white shock. She stared at the note, the glove, the crimson splotches that looked so much like blood.

Hysteria bubbled up inside her.

Then, the dam burst, and she shattered.

Letting out a low cry of pain, she covered her face with her hands, tears coursing down her cheeks. Her entire body shook with the impact of her sobs, everything converging in an unendurable knot of anguish that tore her entire soul apart.

She couldn't take anymore.

She sank down on her knees on the rug, fear and agony converging, slashing through her in clawing talons. Her sobs tore at her, emerging in low, wrenching gasps as she rocked back and forth, emotionally surrendering to that which she could no longer fight.

As if from far away, she heard the door open.

"Breanna, my God, what is it?" Royce crossed over, then stopped. A muffled oath escaped him as he saw what had occurred.

He lowered himself to his knees, enfolded Breanna in his arms. "Shh," he murmured, cradling her to him, feeling her tears drench his shirt. "I'm here, sweetheart. I'm here."

"I'm s-sorry," she sobbed. "I j-just can't be strong anymore."

"You don't have to be." Royce's grip tightened, and he squeezed his eyes shut, aching for what this was doing to her. This incredibly strong, resilient woman, this woman he loved to the core of his being, had been pushed beyond human limits.

At that moment, Royce loathed the assassin with a murderous hatred so powerful, he could have torn him apart limb from limb, killed him with his bare hands.

"I'm weaker than you b-believed me to be," Breanna whispered, in a broken voice that tore at Royce's heart. "I-I didn't mean to disappoint you."

"You didn't disappoint me," he returned fiercely. "You're every bit as strong as I believed. And as brave. Everyone has a breaking point, Breanna. Everyone. Most would have reached theirs long ago." Royce's furious gaze raked the bed, darkening as it settled on the mutilated glove. "There's no one alive who wouldn't crumple after walking in and seeing that."

Breanna nodded, her sobs beginning to lessen from the sound of Royce's soothing voice, the feel of his arms around her. "I was right about his being in the house," she managed, her muscles relaxing as Royce stroked her back in slow, soothing circles. "Seeing the guards must have stopped him from going after Stacie. Instead, he went to leave me those . . ." a shudder, "things. And he found out I'd changed rooms."

"The guards weren't his only deterrent. You kept him from going after Anastasia."

She leaned back, gave him a teary, quizzical look. "I?"

"Yes. Your not being here." Royce brushed his lips across her cheeks, taking her tears with him. God, how he wanted to comfort her, give her his strength. "Remember, the bastard wants you present when he takes aim at Anastasia. He knew you were in Maidstone. So shooting your cousin was out. That wasn't the reason for his breaking in here today."

"Leaving me his most hideous gift was."

"Yes." Wisely, Royce omitted telling her his theory about the statues, that he believed the assassin was delivering the remaining three figures, then striking.

Two of those remaining figures were now sitting on Breanna's bed.

Which left one.

"Royce . . ." Breanna pressed her wet face against his shoulder. "I can't stay in this room another night. I don't know where to go, what to do."

"Stay with me." He rose, gently easing her to her feet. "Not just tonight, but every night until this ordeal is over. I don't give a damn what protocol dictates. You're sleeping in my bed, by my side. What's more, not only will Wells agree, he'll hand-pick the guards who stand outside our door. But sweetheart," he added, trying to give her a measure of peace. "I don't think he means to break into your room again. This was his final appearance."

Rather than relieved, Breanna looked more unnerved, fear darkening her eyes. "That's what terrifies me. It's like this was a culmination of sorts. And, if so, he's about to shoot Stacie."

"To *try* to shoot her," Royce corrected. "He won't succeed." He walked over to the bed, picked up the note, and reread it carefully. "Something about these notes keeps nagging at me," he muttered. "I'm going to line up the whole lot of them and read them together." He turned his attention back to Breanna. "*After* we get you settled." He went back, tilted up her chin. "Better?" he asked softly.

A slow nod. "I've never lost control so totally," she murmured self-consciously, her hand fluttering over her hair. "You must have thought I'd gone insane when you walked in and saw me on the floor, weeping like that."

"Stop it." Royce caught her hand, tugged it away from her hair, and brought her palm to his lips. "I thought we'd broken down that ludicrous wall of self-restraint by now."

Her lashes lowered. "We have."

"Breanna, do you trust me?"

Her head shot up. "You know I do—with my life."

"Then trust me with your vulnerabilities, as well. I promise, I'll protect them."

Breanna's eyes misted. "You're such a wonderful man," she whispered.

"I'm a man in love." Royce kissed her tenderly. "And, by the way," he added with a twinkle. "You *have* lost control so totally. You do so every night in my arms."

She flushed, his teasing comment having the desired effect, melting away a bit of the past hour's horror. "You're right."

"And have you ever regretted it?"

"Never."

"Then don't regret this either." He enfolded her against him for one brief, intense moment. "I'll never let anyone hurt you," he said in a raw voice. "Not physically or emotionally. You have my word." He released her, guided her toward the door. "Now, let's get you out of here."

Outside, the assassin watched the room go dark.

Chadwick was taking her out of there, hiding her elsewhere.

It didn't matter.

There was no need to invade her bedchamber again.

He'd selected a different battlefield for her death.

25

$Royce$ made Breanna drink an entire glass of Madeira, then ordered dinner for two to be served in his chambers.

Instructing two guards to remain outside his door, he left Breanna only long enough to tell Anastasia, Damen, and Wells what had happened, as well as what provisions he'd made.

He'd dealt with their distress as expediently as possible, answered their questions with terse directness. Then, he informed them they'd discuss this tomorrow, after Breanna had gotten some sleep.

"Royce, is she all right?" Anastasia had asked anxiously.

"She's badly shaken. But you know how bloody strong she is." Royce had frowned. "How strong she *insists* on being. I'd let you see her, but I want you to stay put. I'm going to go over those letters the killer sent. Maybe there's something there that will point me in the right direction. We'll discuss it at breakfast."

With that, he'd left them. Wells, as he'd suspected,

was more relieved than shocked to learn where Breanna would be sleeping. The safety of his beloved charges was more important than his adherence to protocol. After quietly thanking Royce for caring for Miss Breanna, he'd summoned two footmen, ordered them to clean up the violated bedchamber immediately; removing all traces of the break-in, but saving the defaced items for Lord Royce's later inspection.

Royce had returned to his room, expecting to find Breanna huddled by the fire. Instead, she was sitting at the desk, scrutinizing the assassin's notes.

She looked up when he entered, her composure fully restored, her brows knit speculatively. "I was paralyzed when I first read tonight's message," she murmured. "But now that I examine it with a clear head, one of the killer's phrases triggered a memory—a memory of something Mr. Cunnings said to my father at their meeting in the tavern."

"The meeting you eavesdropped on."

"Yes. The one at which they made arrangements for the assassin to execute Stacie."

"Go on," Royce urged.

"I remember Father asking about the assassin's credentials, and Mr. Cunnings assuring him there was no one better at tracking people down and killing them—no matter where they were hiding. Cunnings's exact words were that the assassin was an expert tracker and an even better shot."

" 'An expert tracker'—the very words the assassin uses here." Royce walked over, reexamined the notes with that in mind. "Interesting. And maybe not as straightforward as I originally thought."

"What do you mean?"

"I realized from the start that every one of these

messages sounded like a battle call. But I just assumed it was this arrogant bastard's way of making
you feel like he was the hunter, and you the prey. But
looking at it in light of what Cunnings said—maybe
there's more to it than that."

Breanna twisted around to gaze up at him. "Like
what?"

Royce's eyes narrowed, a flash of insight illuminating their midnight blue color. "Maybe that's what's
been bothering me. These notes are all full of military
jargon: retreat, flank, reconnaissance, strategy; and
phrases like 'evasive tactics' and 'the invasion is
about to commence.' "

"True," Breanna concurred. "I wouldn't have recognized the ones you just mentioned, having never
served in the military, as you did. But even I know
that words like battle, warrior and ranks are combat
terms."

"So maybe we're overlooking the obvious," Royce
concluded. "Maybe this isn't just an arbitrary choice
of analogies. Maybe it's based on the killer's personal
experience."

Breanna rose slowly. "He had to get his training
somewhere. What better place than the army?"

Royce was already yanking out the guest list, grab-
bing a quill. "I'll make a list of these twenty-two remaining names. First thing tomorrow, my contacts
will check into every one of their backgrounds, see
who's served." He frowned. "Offhand, I see three or
four names this could apply to. Obviously, Crompton
was a general. He tells that to anyone who will listen.
Radebrook was an officer in the infantry. Landow
spent a few years in the horse artillery, if I'm not mis-
taken. The Duke of Maywood served, too—I believe

in the cavalry. His enlisting was a big scandal, since he was heir to his father's dukedom. He only served a few months before his father won out and he returned."

"When did all this happen?"

"Fifteen or more years ago. I was young, away at school. All I recall is the gossip surrounding the event. I have no idea how adept any of these men are at shooting, or if there are others on this list who are equally competent. I want every name looked into, every military man found. I want to know where they were stationed, what branch they served in, details of their service records. We'll line up the information, compare it to the traits I've established for this killer, and see if we come up with some plausible matches. Then, I'll pay visits to all those matches. I'll accuse each man of being a murderer, if need be, tell them I have evidence of their crimes, just to gauge their reactions. All of them will call me out. Only one will follow me back to kill me. I don't care how damned risky it is. Not anymore. It's the only way I'm going to get at the truth in time."

Breanna was about to protest, when a commotion from downstairs met their ears.

Voices. Slamming doors. Treading feet.

Breanna went sheet white.

Royce whipped out his pistol, moved slowly toward the hallway. "Stay put," he ordered Breanna. "Don't go near the door or the windows. I'll find out what this is about."

He was halfway to the door when the knock sounded. "Lord Royce?" one of the guards called. "Mr. Hibbert's back. He needs to see you immediately."

Royce and Breanna exchanged glances. "Tell Hibbert to come directly to my chambers," Royce instructed the guard.

"Yes, sir."

Three minutes later, Hibbert walked in, looking rumpled and tired, but rife with purpose. "I have some crucial information and even more crucial cargo . . ." He broke off, spying Breanna leaning against the desk. "My lady," he acknowledged. His forehead creased with worry as he saw the frightened state she was in. "What's happened?"

"A great deal," Royce answered for her. "But all that can wait. Something obviously took place in Paris. Were you able to learn who bought that perfume?"

"Bought not only the perfume, but the women, as well," Hibbert corrected.

Breanna gasped. "What?"

Hibbert swiftly relayed the details of what he'd discovered: Maurelle's identity, her relationship to the assassin, her part in the sale of the women. He told them about Emma, how he'd bought her from Maurelle, and how she'd assisted him and Girard in rescuing the others.

"Is she all right?" Breanna asked. "And the other kidnapped women—are they unharmed?"

"Other than being badly shaken, yes. Fortunately, we got there before any real damage had been done. The first thing I did was to grab Mademoiselle Le Joyau. Then, I questioned her employees, only to find out that none of them had any more information on the killer than Emma did. Their description of him matched hers, as did the fact that they knew him only as the noble assassin."

"My God," Breanna managed.

Hibbert rubbed his palms together. "I escorted Mademoiselle Le Joyau out of her establishment and into a carriage headed for Calais—at gunpoint. We boarded the first ship to Dover. As for the kidnapped women, Girard is keeping them in Paris until it's safe for them to return. And Maurelle Le Joyau," he concluded with a tight smile, "is downstairs in the servants' quarters, being looked after by three guards. I'll take you to her whenever you wish."

Royce rubbed the back of his neck pensively. "So the assassin's partner is a woman. Tell me about this Maurelle Le Joyau."

"Obviously, she's French. She's also exquisitely beautiful and equally cunning. She was more than charming to Lord Hobson. Especially when she saw how wealthy he was. To Hibbert..." A mocking smile. "She's refused to speak a word since we left Paris. Girard is running a check on her background and history to see what he can find out. He said he'll dispatch his findings posthaste. Oh, he also said to tell you that the physician who treated the assassin's finger was a doctor named Helmett. He's German-born, extremely wealthy and successful. He's a genius at reconstructing limbs. He's also on an extended holiday. But it seems no one knows where he's gone or when he'll be returning."

"Convenient. Hopefully, we won't need to hunt him down. Not with Mademoiselle Le Joyau at our disposal. She'll lead us to the killer more quickly than his physician." Royce's features tightened into fierce lines, his predatory stance making him look like a wolf about to close in on a sheep.

"Stay with Breanna," Royce instructed Hibbert. "Keep her in this room—with you by her side, and the guards outside the door. As for Mademoiselle Le Joyau, I want to see her. *Immédiatement.*"

Hibbert nodded. "I thought you might."

Royce took a step, then halted, as a troublesome prospect struck home. "Did you and Mademoiselle Le Joyau arrive in an open carriage?"

"No." Hibbert had obviously anticipated this question. "I hired a closed carriage. And when we neared Medford Manor, I insisted that Mademoiselle Le Joyau lie down beneath the opposite seat, covered by some blankets. She wasn't pleased. Nevertheless, my pistol ensured her cooperation. I smuggled her in the rear entrance, the blanket over her head. Believe me, my lord, no one saw her arrive."

"Excellent." Anticipation glinted in Royce's eyes. "That means her presence at Medford is our little secret. Fine work, Hibbert. That resolved, it's time for me to pay mademoiselle a little visit. Where in the servants' quarters can I find her?"

"In the vacant room next to Wells's quarters." An ironic lift of Hibbert's brows. "I hate to admit it, but Wells has proven himself to have stamina, a quick mind, and fine instincts. All of which," he added, with a quick sideways look at Breanna, "I will deny having said, should anyone feel compelled to tell him." A hint of a smile. "In any case, given Wells's abilities, I thought it best we restrict Mademoiselle Le Joyau to an area he can oversee—when he isn't guarding Lady Sheldrake's door."

"I agree." Royce paused only long enough to go to Breanna, frame her face between his palms. "Will you be all right?" he asked tenderly. "I won't be gone long."

"I'll be fine," she assured him, actually able to force

a smile, thanks to Hibbert's light banter. "Hibbert will take excellent care of me. And I'll fill him in on what happened here since he left. Now, go. I'm itching to hear what this Maurelle Le Joyau has to say. *If* she'll say anything, that is."

Royce's jaw clenched. "Oh, she'll say plenty—beginning with that bastard's name. Because if she doesn't..." He sucked in his breath. "Let's just say she won't like the consequences."

Royce stalked into the tiny room in the servants' wing firmly intending to intimidate Maurelle Le Joyau into telling him everything, even if he had to choke the information out of her.

Two things stopped him.

One, was his immediate assessment that this was no ordinary woman.

Despite her fragile appearance, Maurelle was impervious as steel, her chin held high, her dark eyes mocking him and any attempt he'd make to extract information from her. She wouldn't relent, his instincts proclaimed, not even if he thrashed her. Violence didn't frighten her. Knowing her relationship to the killer, she was probably accustomed to it—witnessing it and, quite possibly, enduring it. So, threats would be wasted.

And then, there was the second thing.

Royce had seen this woman before.

He wasn't quite sure where. But the instant he laid eyes on Maurelle Le Joyau, he was certain of it.

She didn't know him.

There wasn't a flicker of recognition on her face, not even before she had time to school her features. She simply sat at the edge of the chair, her hands folded primly in her lap, her taunting stare daring him to do his worst.

Instantly, Royce abandoned his plan to take the harshest, most direct avenue possible, to go in for the kill simply because they were running out of time.

A different approach was in order with this woman—one she wasn't used to. The direct approach. No tricks, no casually asked questions she was too smart to answer, and definitely no browbeating.

He'd learn far more about her this way.

And in the process, figure out where he'd met her.

"Hello, mademoiselle," he greeted, shutting the door behind him and leaning back against it. "My name is Royce Chadwick."

A glint of interest. "Ah, so you're the infamous Lord Chadwick." She inclined her head, appraising him thoughtfully. "You're not what I expected."

"Really?" Royce purposely abandoned his sentry-like stance, strolling over to pull up a chair directly across from her. "What did you expect?"

"An older man. One with more wrath and less charm."

Royce leaned back in his seat, crossed one long leg over the other. "How did you form this opinion? From what Hibbert told you?"

An arrogant smile, one that confirmed Royce's belief that she was far too shrewd to fall into a trap. "No. Mr. Hibbert and I didn't discuss you at all. *Au contraire*, my lord, you need no discussion. Your reputation precedes you. It travels all the way to the Continent—even to establishments like Le Joyau."

"I'm flattered." Royce tried to place her voice. He'd heard it before—briefly. But mostly what he recognized was her face. Where had he been when he'd seen it?

"Maurelle—may I call you Maurelle?" he inquired politely.

"*Mais oui.*" She gave a careless shrug. "Suit yourself. You're in charge here."

"As you were at Le Joyau."

"*Certainement.*"

Royce drummed his fingers lightly on his leg. "I don't enjoy playing cat and mouse, Maurelle. I suspect you don't either. So why don't I refrain from insulting you? I want the name of the noble assassin. And you're going to give it to me."

Maurelle didn't bat a lash. "You're insane if you believe that."

"Why?" Royce demanded. "Are we engaged in some sort of contest? A battle of wills? Are you determined to best me, just as your friend is?"

"You flatter yourself, my lord. You mean as little to me as you do to him. You're just an obstacle, nothing more. So, no, I'm not trying to best you. As for him—let's say our motives are quite different. He has his, and I mine."

"And what are yours?"

"To protect him. Which I will do, no matter what you do to me." Maurelle rose, shook out the folds of her gown, and braced herself before him, as if preparing for a vicious beating. "I'm sure you require proof. So go ahead. Do your worst. You'll find out I'm true to my word."

Royce feigned shock, letting his jaw drop a notch. "You'd endure physical abuse just to protect a lover?"

Anger flashed in her eyes. "He's not *just* a lover. In fact, the word 'just' never applies to him. He's not 'just' anything. He's extraordinary."

"You're in love with him."

A brittle stare. "Did you think women like me didn't fall in love? That because we've been with hundreds of men over the years that there could never be one that actually meant something? If so, you're a fool."

"I'm no fool, Maurelle." Royce stood, steadily meeting her gaze. "I was just making a statement, not a judgement. You're in love with this man."

"*Oui*—now more than ever."

Now more than ever? An interesting choice of phrases.

How long had these two known each other?

Royce pursued the question from a nonthreatening angle. "As for your bedding hundreds of men, I was under the impression that you're the proprietor of Le Joyau. Do you entertain customers, as well?"

"Only him. That part of my life is over."

Just the answer he wanted.

So, Maurelle Le Joyau had been a prostitute before graduating to her more lucrative role. Had it been at the establishment now known as Le Joyau, or had it been elsewhere? And when had she met the assassin—before or after she changed roles?

Royce had to tread carefully to get his answers.

"Tell me, Maurelle, how would your noble assassin feel if he knew you were once a common whore?"

A throaty laugh. "I assure you, I was never common—no matter how shabby my surroundings. I was always a treasure. A coveted treasure—worth everything a man had and more. There's no one like me. Not then, not now, not ever. No one understood that better than he."

She'd given Royce both his answers. Her days as a prostitute had been spent somewhere else. Somewhere shabby. And the assassin had already known her there.

"So he's familiar with who you are," Royce acknowledged, diverting her attention from the fact that she'd just supplied him with vital information. "What about you, Maurelle? Do you know what he does? How he gets you the women he delivers?"

That scornful look returned. "Ah, you're hoping to deliver a crushing blow. To shock me into revealing his name. Don't bother. Yes, Lord Chadwick, I know what he does. I know how he rids the women I sell of their family ties. And I know what he intends for your friend Lady Breanna. Death—one bullet to the heart." Her brows arched in sardonic question. "He's a superb marksman, wouldn't you say?"

Royce forced his features to remain impassive, fully aware she was trying to goad him into an emotional reaction. "Indeed he is. A filthy animal, but a superb marksman."

"Now you're trying to provoke me, monsieur. That won't work on me any more than it just did on you."

"I'm impressed. You're a formidable adversary." Royce studied her closely, focusing on her face. What was it about her? Her features, her mannerisms. The utter self-confidence of her stance.

No matter how shabby my surroundings . . . I was always a treasure. A coveted treasure . . .

Abruptly, an image flashed through Royce's mind—a younger, less sophisticated Maurelle, but Maurelle nonetheless.

The pieces slammed into place, the scene replaying from start to finish.

He had his answer.

It was time to do something with it.

Unaware of the direction Royce's thoughts had taken, Maurelle played right into his hands, assuming she was taunting him.

She stretched her arms high over her head, then covered her mouth to stifle a yawn. "If you're not going to beat or brutalize me in any way, I'd like to get some sleep." A mocking smile. "May we continue this interrogation tomorrow?"

Royce nearly laughed aloud. Maurelle was waiting for him to fly into a tirade. While, in truth, he was delighted to comply with her request. He was impatient to get out of that room, itching to put his new realization to work.

Still, he couldn't arouse her suspicions.

Feigning irritation, he gave a curt nod. "As you wish. But tomorrow begins quite early here. Don't expect to get much sleep."

Maurelle looked amused. "I can do with very little sleep, my lord. It's a necessary talent in my business. *Bonne nuit.*"

No, Maurelle, Royce countered silently, making his way from the servants' quarters. *Not bonne nuit.*

Fini.

His first stop was Damen and Anastasia's room.

There, he explained the situation in a few terse sentences, then requested Damen's help. Damen offered it instantly.

The message was written and, ten minutes later, was in the hands of a footman who was rushing it to Damen's swiftest courier. The attached note from Damen instructed his envoy to dispatch Royce's message to the Continent within the hour.

It would be in Paris by morning.

Satisfied that the wheels were in motion, Royce headed directly to his quarters, where Breanna and Hibbert were discussing the events of the past few days while eyeing the door, waiting for Royce to reappear.

They both jumped up when he walked in.

"Did Maurelle tell you anything?" Breanna burst out.

Triumph gleamed in Royce's eyes. "Far more than she realized."

"Then she gave you enough to figure out the killer's name?"

"Definitely not. Maurelle Le Joyau is as tough as they come. And smart. She'll die before exposing the killer. Especially since it's clear she's in love with him."

Breanna gave a bemused shake of her head, puzzled by the victorious expression on Royce's face. "What *did* she say?"

Swiftly, Royce relayed their conversation.

When he was finished, even Hibbert looked baffled. "I see where your questions were headed. You wanted to find out about her past, figure out where and when she and the assassin met. Hopefully, Girard will do that for us."

"Oh, he'll definitely do that for us. Very effectively, with the help of the note I just sent him."

"A note," Breanna repeated, sensing this piece of information was directly tied to whatever was making Royce feel so encouraged, "telling him what?"

"That I've encountered Mademoiselle Le Joyau before tonight. And that I remember exactly where and when that was."

Even Hibbert stared. "You've met?"

"Not officially, no. Which makes it all the better, as she has no memory of me, while I have an excellent memory of her. She was the main attraction in Paris some years ago—at least to a very confused young man who was reluctant to return with me to England and to his anxious father. I had to drag the boy out of that brothel, so taken was he with his paid companion's beauty and numerous charms. I never knew her name—we weren't exactly formally introduced. But I never forget a face. It's she, all right."

By now, Breanna had caught on. "You're talking about your first case—the one you told me about. That junior officer you found for his father the general. The man you located at a seedy brothel outside Paris."

"Maison Fleur," Royce supplied. "That was the name of the brothel. I don't know whether or not it's still standing. But when it was, Maurelle Le Joyau worked there. Their clientele were chiefly soldiers."

"Including the assassin," Breanna declared.

"Right." Royce rubbed his hands together. "Damen arranged for his fastest courier to get my message to Girard. We'll have Mademoiselle Le Joyau's complete history in a matter of days. In the meantime, tomorrow my men will start compiling information on all the men on the guest list who have military records—which will reveal exactly who was stationed near Paris, and when. Between that and what Girard tells us, we'll figure out the identity of our assassin."

"But will it be in time?" Breanna asked.

Royce shot her an uneasy look, trying to ascertain how much she'd deduced.

"Royce, I know you're trying to protect me." Softly, she answered his unspoken question. "But I'm not stupid. That animal is taunting us by delivering a stream of those porcelain figures—the ones stolen from the shop in Canterbury you told me about. If there really were only seven statues in all, then he's down to the last of them. And after that . . ." She shuddered. "After that, there will no longer be a reason for him to wait."

"We'll give him a reason." Royce went to her, seized her shoulders in a tender but determined grip. "Remember something, sweetheart. Now we have something he wants—a bargaining tool to dangle before him."

"Maurelle."

"Right. My guess is, he's as involved with Maurelle as she is with him. Which means he's vulnerable when it comes to her. And his vulnerability is our weapon."

"How can we inform him we have her if we don't know who he is?" Breanna asked.

"There are ways," Royce returned quietly, thinking he'd parade Maurelle Le Joyau across the front lawn at gunpoint, shouting out that she was his prisoner in order to get the assassin's attention, if need be. "Some of those ways are riskier than others. But let's not get ahead of ourselves. The last statue hasn't arrived yet. Until it does, we have time. Let's use that time. Maybe we'll have our answers by then."

"What are you planning?"

"I'm going to interrogate Maurelle Le Joyau. I'm bound to learn something, however small. Maybe I'll run Cunnings's name by her, or even your father's. She might know something about them."

"How?"

Royce cleared his throat. "Men are known to be less

guarded when they're in a woman's bed. They talk more openly. Maurelle knew about you—she taunted me with the fact that her assassin meant to kill you with one bullet. That means he said something, not only about his plans, but about his belief that you and I are involved. Why else would she expect me to react to your intended fate?"

"I see."

"I might learn enough to strike a few additional names from the guest list. At the same time, I'm going to send a deluge of letters out to my contacts—as many as I can write tonight and tomorrow. That will keep messengers rushing on and off the estate, which, in turn, will keep the assassin wondering what the hell is going on. It might also interfere with his ability to get close to the manor. I'm buying time, Breanna. Just a day or two. By then, I'll have what I need."

"Unless the last statue arrives first. In which case, our time has run out."

Royce's jaw clenched. "In which case, so has his."

26

The next day passed in a frenzy of activity and a knot of tension.

By nightfall, two dozen messages had gone out, five had arrived, and no packages had been delivered.

The distraction had done its job.

As for Maurelle, she was as unyielding as ever. She staunchly refused to discuss her lover, other than to hail him as a genius and declare her commitment to him.

Still, Royce chipped away at her reserve, finding out tidbits of information about their relationship—enough for him to realize this was a longstanding liaison, formed over many years, and that it centered around a sick preoccupation with each other that Maurelle viewed as love.

Love between a murderer and a heartless bitch who sold women.

The whole notion made Royce sick.

It was late at night when he finished interrogating Maurelle. After that, he began amassing the initial information that his contacts had provided. It was sketchy, but it did enable him to eliminate ten names, men who definitely hadn't served in the military.

That still left twelve.

He could hardly wait to get his hands on the thorough background checks of the possible suspects. With a modicum of luck, those reports would arrive at Medford Manor by late tomorrow.

It was half after three when he finally crawled into bed.

Breanna was awake, her nightrail tangled from tossing about, trying to sleep.

Royce reached for her, gathered her against him, and held her tightly.

"I wonder if I'll ever shut my eyes again," she whispered. "Or if he'll haunt me forever."

"He won't. It's almost over." Royce pressed his lips to her shining crown of hair, feeling that now-familiar surge of protectiveness and need. "And the instant it is, I'm dragging you off somewhere and marrying you."

She smiled against his chest. "You won't have to drag me. I'm as eager as you." She continued talking, desperate to forget the present, to cling to the hope of their future. "There's a little church about a mile from here. I used to walk there a lot when my father was away. Actually, I discovered it as a child, with Grandfather. He took me there for the first time when I was eight. My father and I were visiting Medford, and father had flown into one of his rages. I was desperate to get away from him. The church is so peaceful and lovely; it has a sort of quiet dignity about it that reminds me of Grandfather. It conjures up special memories of him for me. I'd love to get married there."

"Then we will." Royce tilted up her chin, brushed her lips with his. "We'll ride there the day this nightmare ends, speak to the vicar. I'll get a special license, if need be. We'll be married as soon as Wells and Anastasia are finished organizing the kind of wedding you deserve."

Breanna swallowed. "Do you think I'm foolish for wanting something traditional?"

"I never think you're foolish. I think you're beautiful. And I think you're entitled to the most perfect wedding day any bride ever dreamed of."

The raw emotions of the past few days converged, welled up inside her, and Breanna felt a sharp need to relieve them, to lose herself in a way only Royce could ensure. "Royce," she murmured, her voice unsteady. "Make love to me. Please."

She felt his sharp intake of breath, sensed her own urgency come alive in him. He unbuttoned her nightrail, pushed it down and off, and tossed it to the carpet. Then, he pulled her against him, kissing her fiercely as he rolled her beneath him.

"Forget everything," he muttered thickly. "Everything but how much I love you, and how right it feels when I'm inside you."

Breanna complied, wrapping her arms around him and opening her body to his.

The rest of the night was theirs.

The reports began arriving after lunch.

Four more names were eliminated by the time late afternoon tea had been served.

"That leaves eight," Royce announced, looking around the sitting room, where Breanna, Anastasia, and Damen were seated, with Hibbert manning the doorway. "All with lean bodies, graying temples, and around forty-five or fifty years of age."

Damen nodded, taking Stacie's hand in his. "Let's analyze each one of them, see if we can make an educated guess as to which one is the killer."

"No." Royce gave an adamant shake of his head. "I've purposely avoided doing that. Our views on all these men are subjective. Whoever this killer is, he's a master at deception. He's managed to fool us, and the rest of the *ton* for Lord knows how long. Let's get all the facts. *Then,* we'll analyze."

Restlessly, Damen nodded. "You're right. I'm just losing my mind."

"I have a feeling we're on the verge of something," Anastasia murmured. "I'm not sure why, but I do."

"So do I," Breanna concurred. "So it must be true."

Ten minutes later, Wells rushed into the sitting room, waving an envelope.

"Lord Royce," he said, proffering the letter. "This just arrived from the Continent. Lord Sheldrake's envoy delivered it. It's from your colleague, Mr. Girard."

"Good." Royce went taut, snatching the envelope and tearing it open.

His eyes widened as he read, first with surprise, then with realization. "Damn," he said, rising slowly with a sharp exhalation of breath. "This is unbelievable."

"What?" Damen bolted to his feet, too. "What did Girard find out about Maurelle Le Joyau?"

"Did he confirm that she worked in that brothel— Maison Fleur?" Anastasia questioned eagerly.

"Indeed he did." Royce skimmed the letter again, then lowered it to meet the five expectant stares glued to him. "She worked at Maison Fleur for over a decade, until about four years ago. She began her career there, as a young girl in her teens. She formed quite a reputation among Wellington's men. Over the next eleven years, she made a bloody fortune servicing them in bed. Enough to buy the townhouse that's now Le Joyau and redecorate it from top to bottom, turn it into a plush abode. She hired some girls who were almost as much in demand as she was, and opened the doors to Paris's most elegant brothel."

"And?" Breanna prompted, recognizing the look on Royce's face, impatient to hear the rest.

"And it's no wonder Girard was finding it so bloody hard to uncover anything about her past before my message arrived. Without knowing she worked at Maison Fleur, it was virtually impossible to dig up a single detail on her history. Maurelle covered her tracks like a seasoned criminal. It's as if she appeared out of nowhere four years ago." Royce paused, filled in the most essential piece. "Because at the same time that she acquired Le Joyau, she acquired the name she christened it with."

"Her real name isn't Maurelle Le Joyau?" Breanna demanded.

"No." Royce shook his head, his midnight gaze glittering with sparks. "Her real name is Maurelle Rouge."

A heartbeat of silence followed Royce's revelation.

Then, the impact sank in, and everyone began talking at once.

"Maurelle Rouge . . . M. Rouge," Breanna breathed. "My God, it was her all along."

"No wonder my men couldn't find George's Paris

contact," Damen realized grimly. "It never occurred to any of us *he* was a *she*."

"Right." Royce's lips thinned into a pensive line. "Apparently, Maurelle renounced the name Rouge when she left Maison Fleur. She only uses it for buying and selling women. The rest of the world knows her as Maurelle Le Joyau."

"Wait." Anastasia held up her palm. "If this is true, if Maurelle is Rouge, and if the assassin was intimately involved with her when she was using her real name, then his establishing a business relationship with her at this particular time makes sense. The night he shot John Cunnings, Cunnings was searching for a woman to ship to M. Rouge—even if he didn't know who M. Rouge was."

"But the assassin *did* know who she was," Breanna finished for her. "He would have recognized the name when he saw it. He would have seized Cunnings's notes. And he would have planned to pursue things with Maurelle when he got to the Continent."

Stacie frowned. "The only problem with that theory is that Royce believes the relationship between the killer and Maurelle is longstanding, not sporadic. So why would he need Cunnings's notes to figure out what she was up to? Why wouldn't she just have told him? She seems to be aware of all his sinister activities. Why wouldn't he know of hers?"

"Unless . . ." Royce pursed his lips thoughtfully. "Maurelle keeps making references to her feelings for the assassin being more powerful than they've been before. She emphasizes that she loves him now more than ever—almost as if she's had time apart from him to realize the depth of her feelings. Maybe, at some point, they severed ties. I don't know when, or for how long, but maybe they lost touch. Maybe he never knew her as Maurelle Le Joyau—until he found Cunnings's notes and went in search of M. Rouge. Maybe they only recently rediscovered each other."

"But if they're so deeply involved, what would make them sever ties?" Breanna wondered aloud. "Could he have frightened her off?"

"No." Royce shook his head. "Maurelle is as cold-blooded as they come. She doesn't frighten easily. If they ended things, even for a while, it wasn't because she was afraid of him. Maybe it was *he* who had his reasons. I don't know. But it certainly gives me another angle to pursue. I'll see what I can find out." A hard smile curved Royce's lips. "I have a great many more facts now, and some strong leads to pursue. Not only Maurelle's tie to the killer, but her tie to Viscount Medford. Maybe I can learn the fate of all those poor women she did sell."

Maurelle was thumbing through a novel when Royce walked in.

She glanced up indifferently, noting his arrival, then tucking her legs beneath her on the chair and resuming her reading.

Royce shut the door with a firm click. "Put down the book."

His icy tone gave her pause.

She arched a brow, surmising from the unyielding set of his jaw, the brutal determination in his eyes, that he was angrier than he had been previously, and more purposeful.

"Very well." She tossed aside the novel and eyed him expectantly.

"Sit up." Royce barked out the command.

She complied, uncurling her legs and lowering her feet to the floor, shaking out the folds of her gown as she did. "There. Is that to your satisfaction, monsieur?"

"Nothing about you is to my satisfaction," he returned, folding his arms across his chest. "But all that's about to change. We're about to have a very informative chat."

Her expression hardened. "You're wasting your time. I won't give you his name."

"Forget *his* name. Let's talk about *yours*—Mademoiselle Rouge."

A flicker of surprise, if not alarm. "*Bon.* Now I *am* impressed, my lord. I see how you earned your reputation."

"And I see how you earned yours—beginning fifteen years ago at Maison Fleur." Royce crossed over, dragged up a chair and sat directly across from her. "You met your lover then, when you were no more than a prostitute. You held his—and scores of other soldiers'—attention for years."

Silence, but the proud tilt of her chin told Royce he was right.

"Let's discuss a more recent matter, then," he suggested icily. "You were Viscount Medford's Paris contact. He sent you the women you sold."

Maurelle's sniff was haughty. "Medford was pathetic. So was his merchandise. They were nothing more than workhouse women—common and unrefined. Worse, they were drained of youth, beauty, and vitality. In short, they had nothing to offer. What affluent customer would pay to buy such refuse?"

"Clearly, you found buyers."

"A few. No one worth the trouble."

Royce clenched his teeth, fighting back the urge to shake Maurelle senseless and make her realize these were human beings they were discussing. He stifled the impulse. Losing control would only weaken his position. Besides, pleas for humanity could do nothing but fall on deaf ears when it came to this bitch.

"Would you like *their* names, monsieur?" Maurelle taunted, clearly perceiving at least some fraction of Royce's outrage. "Those I'd be happy to provide. And who knows? Maybe you could find the lowlifes I dealt with, rescue the pathetic wenches Medford provided from their lustful hands."

"You graduated beyond lowlifes," Royce shot back instead, his voice devoid of emotion. "As of your last correspondence with Medford, you'd stepped up to aristocratic buyers."

"I improved the caliber of my merchandise and my patrons. But no thanks to Medford. He sent me nothing. He's an insipid fool. He deserves to rot in Newgate."

"So you turned to your lover instead. He took over out of lust for you and the thrill of executing people. He's even rich enough to forego the money. Lucky you. He probably gave you every pence of the profits. Pity you two had lost touch, or he might have served as your business partner from the start. Then, you'd never have had to turn to a weakling like Medford."

With that, Royce arched a sardonic brow. "Obviously your charms aren't quite as acute as you believe. Your beloved assassin was able to stay away from them for years. What was the problem, Maurelle? Were you beneath him in station? Was that what made him leave you at Maison Fleur, cut you off?"

Anger flared in her eyes. "You're grasping at straws.

You're also insulting me. So rather than listen to your offensive words, I'll put an end to them. I'm the one who severed the relationship, not he. I was foolish. I didn't want to be a nobleman's property. I vanished. He found me. I won't make that mistake again. I believe that answers your question, *n'est ce pas?*"

Royce's eyes narrowed as he digested that tidbit of information. Purposefully keeping her from pondering how much she'd revealed, he segued back to the previous, and less inflammatory, subject. "How did you and Medford start working together?"

"*We* didn't start. *I* did. That fool never even met me, much less knew who I was. He knew only the name M. Rouge. Which was how I wanted it. As for why I approached him, it was a wise business decision. I had the money-making scheme. He had the connections and the desperate need for money."

"How did you find out about that?"

Maurelle's mocking smile returned. "Men are fools when in the throes of passion. My girls listened and often encouraged their patrons to talk. What they learned convinced me that Lord Medford was a fine candidate for what I had in mind. He knew influential people who could supply him with ships and cargo. He was deeply in debt and taking stupid chances to recoup his losses. I gave him an opportunity to do that. He jumped at it."

"And when you heard he got caught by Bow Street?"

She shrugged. "I'd already arranged for M. Rouge to drop out of sight. Lord Sheldrake was digging around, trying to find out who I was. Medford's going to Newgate only reinforced my decision. It was time for Rouge to go on holiday."

"But that's not what happened. Instead, your lover showed up and helped you resurrect the role, and the business of selling women. Only now the quality of women was elevated to a higher standard—and the means of acquiring them, murder."

"*Oui*. Exciting, wouldn't you say?"

"Depraved, I'd say."

A purposeful knock sounded at the door.

"Yes?" Royce called.

Hibbert stepped into the room. "The confirming documents you've been awaiting just arrived, my lord. I thought you'd want to know."

"I do." Royce was already heading for the door. He turned, shot Maurelle a glittering, triumphant look. "We'll continue this shortly, Mademoiselle Rouge."

Royce's lips curved as they rounded the corridor of the servants' quarters, strode toward the sitting room. "That bluff worked nicely. It's the first time I've seen Maurelle look worried since she arrived."

"I'm hoping it won't be a bluff, sir. If these reports tell us what we expect, we'll have our answer. Then we'll need Miss Le Joyau only to verify it." He frowned. "She won't do that willingly. We'll have to be very convincing."

"We will be." Royce bore down on the sitting room. "And she'll tell us exactly what we need to know. Her loyalty to her lover will ensure it."

The reports were comprehensive.

Eight of the remaining twelve men had served in the military. However, three of those had done so either during the wrong years or in the wrong places, and were stationed too far from Paris to be viable choices.

Which left five men who could be the assassin.

Damen stood beside Royce, poring over the five names as Wells and Hibbert stood on either side of the settee, flanking Anastasia and Breanna, who sat upon it, eagerly awaiting some answers.

"Maywood? He's afraid of his own shadow," Damen muttered. "His father browbeat him until the day he died. He balks at the slightest risk of losing money, much less lives. No. I don't see it. And Crompton's one hell of a shot, but he's also eccentric as hell. He talks so much about his days as a general, we can all recite them by memory. If he'd been involved with a woman like Maurelle, she'd have been the high point of his tales. A cold-blooded killer? I can't imagine it. Radebrook, I'm not sure of. He's quiet. He doesn't talk much about himself. It says here his aim is exceptional. Maybe—"

"He's married," Royce interrupted. "Happily married. And the father of three, two of whom are still young enough to live at home. That makes him the least likely candidate of the bunch. Our killer is a loner. He's not a family man. Nor is Maurelle the type to share. I'd strike Radebrook before I struck anyone else."

"Fine. That leaves Arthur Landow, who's uneasy about squashing a bug, and James Fairwood, who I didn't expect to be listed here. He always talks of himself as a naval officer."

"He was a naval officer." Royce was rereading the pages. "After Napoleon crushed our navy, he switched to the army. Apparently, he's an expert marksman."

Damen slammed his fist against the mantle. "So where do we go from here? How do we figure out which one it is?"

"We don't." Royce began organizing the reports into five separate, carefully-labelled folders. "We let Maurelle act as our bloodhound."

A startled look. "Royce, you've spent the past two days telling us how staunch Maurelle is when it comes to refusing to betray her lover. Do you honestly believe that by waving five files beneath her nose you're going to goad her into blurting out his name?"

"No." Royce carefully lay the most damning pages atop each report, before closing the files. "I believe that by leaving five files beneath her nose I'm going to goad her into acting to protect him."

Breanna's chin came up. "You're using her love for him to trap her into giving him away. You're going to leave her alone in the room with those files. Instinctively, she'll go over and read the report on her lover. She won't be able to help herself. She'll want to see what facts you've compiled, how close you are to finding the man she loves."

"Exactly." Royce shot Breanna an admiring look. "You've become quite the sleuth, my love."

"You've trained me well. Too well." Breanna rose, walked over to him. "Royce, it's a mistake. Not the idea, the execution. If you casually leave those files lying about in Maurelle's room, she'll know you're up to something. She won't go near the reports. And what will you do? Kneel outside her door all night, peeking through the keyhole, hoping she'll relent?"

Royce's brows rose in surprise. "You have another way?"

"Yes." Breanna nodded, lifting her chin in a gesture that was becoming more and more natural for her to make. "Let me go in there and get the results we need."

"No." Royce was already shaking his head. "Absolutely not. You're not going anywhere near that bitch."

Gently, Breanna lay her hand on his forearm. "We only have one chance. If she figures out we're uncertain, she'll never give anything away. I can throw her off-guard. You can't. Her defenses go up whenever you walk into that room. You're a man—and a brilliant one, at that. I'm a woman—a gentle, delicate, weak-minded woman." Breanna's lips twitched at her own description. "Maurelle will have no regard for me. She'll assume I'm faltering, on the verge of collapse. I'll use that to my advantage."

Anastasia had perked up and was nodding her agreement. "Breanna has a point. Maurelle is used to battling wits with men, not women. I doubt she believes any woman is as strong as she, much less a soft-spoken, composed woman such as Breanna. If anyone can prove Maurelle wrong, it's my cousin."

"Royce," Breanna pressed, her jade gaze holding his midnight one. "I'll get what we need."

Royce swallowed. "How?"

Her lips curved. "I'm a very good sketcher. And, as you just said, I've also become an excellent sleuth. Between the two—I have a plan."

Maurelle was moving restlessly about the room when the door opened.

She turned, eager to confront Lord Royce, to probe until she found out just what had incited that arrogant smirk he'd worn when he left her an hour ago.

Did he really have confirming documents, or had Hibbert been lying, trying to incite a reaction from her? The older man was an excellent actor. He'd fooled her once. He wouldn't fool her again.

She forced herself to look nonchalant, to watch casually as Lord Royce entered the room.

But it wasn't Lord Royce who stepped into the chambers.

It was a woman. A very pretty, very genteel woman, whose unusual coloring and haunted expression left little doubt as to her identity.

"*Bon.*" Maurelle folded her arms across her breasts, studying the woman she knew to be her lover's ultimate execution target. She was clutching some folders tightly to her body—folders she seemed unaware of holding.

Interesting.

"Lady Breanna Colby, *oui?*" Maurelle inquired.

"*Oui.*" Breanna halted to lean back into the hallway. She glanced about furtively, searching the area in a most thorough fashion. Then, she gestured to that wretched butler of hers, who magically appeared out of nowhere and proceeded to hover just outside the door. "Stand guard," she instructed him in a fierce whisper—one Maurelle managed to overhear. "Don't let Lord Royce know I'm in here. He thinks I'm behaving irrationally, letting my emotions rule my head. But he doesn't understand. I must try this my way. I must." She inhaled sharply. "Knock twice if you see him approaching."

Waiting only for her butler's assent, Lady Breanna shut the door and faced Maurelle.

"I had to see you," she announced in a small, shaky voice. "No matter what Lord Royce says, I refuse to believe any woman could remain immune to another woman's anguish. Not in this case. Not if she fully understood it."

Maurelle kept her features carefully schooled, although her gaze flickered to the folders clutched in Breanna's arms. What was in them? Was this some kind of ploy?

Doubtful. The insipid girl's state of mind was far too precarious for Chadwick to entrust her with his work. Still, those folders had to contain something. But what?

She had to find out—for *his* sake.

"Go ahead," she replied carefully. "I'm willing to listen."

Breanna swallowed, clearly fighting for control. "I won't denounce you for loving this man. I can only guess you've never seen the side of him I have. I've come here to share that side of him with you, in the hopes that you'll realize what he's capable of, and that you'll help me stop him." Tears glistened on her lashes. "I don't want to die, Maurelle. I'm twenty-one years old. My life is just beginning. Please, help me."

"What is it you intend to share with me that will plead your case—your words, your fears?"

"No. My proof." Breanna began crossing over toward the desk.

Halfway there, she paused, becoming aware of the five files she still gripped. With a shudder of revulsion, she tossed them down on the table alongside the wardrobe, keeping only some loose papers in her hand as she made her way to the desk.

"Proof?" Maurelle followed her automatically, her dark gaze focusing on the pages Breanna was spreading out on the desk top.

"Yes. His letters to me. The ones that describe what he intends to do to me, and to my cousin. My cousin is with child, Maurelle. And he knows it. He means to kill her unborn babe. He specifically says so."

"Does he?" Maurelle controlled her amusement, her glance shifting from the letters she already knew of to the files Breanna had abandoned near the wardrobe. "Those files—are they also proof?"

Breanna looked up, followed Maurelle's gaze, and shuddered again. "Those are what *Lord Royce* calls proof. They're facts, dates, and worst of all, drawings, for me to go over." Her voice trembled. "I can't do that. It's too painful. Especially seeing his face again. I realize Lord Royce has narrowed the search down to five men, and that I'm the only person who can identify the killer—other than Emma, who's too dazed to speak, much less confront the man who killed her mother."

"You've actually seen him?" Maurelle asked, keeping the fear out of her voice.

"Twice." Breanna lowered her lashes, her entire body trembling as she spoke. "The night I shot him, and several days ago, when I left the estate. The first time it was dark, so all I could make out was his build. But the other day, I saw his face, his features, the coldness in his eyes. I can't brave that again. I've described him to Lord Royce. I can't help it if my description could apply to any of those five noblemen. I just can't bear looking at him again."

"I find it odd that you'd need to," Maurelle said carefully. "If you really saw him in such great detail, why didn't you recognize him? Surely you've met him at one social gathering or another."

"Lord Royce said the same thing—a dozen times. But, as I told him, my father kept me isolated. I never attended a full London Season. So, I wasn't formally introduced to anyone. The gentlemen are all a jumble of faces."

"I see." Maurelle's mind was racing, trying to find a way to use that to her advantage.

Slowly, she began backing toward the wardrobe.

Lost in her own pain, Breanna buried her face in her hands, weeping softly as she spoke. "I'm begging you, Maurelle. Read these letters. Tell us his name. Don't make me go through any more than I already have. Please . . . spare me. Spare my cousin. And most of all, spare her unborn child, who's innocent and deserves a chance at life. Please."

Maurelle halted beside the files. "Read me the letters," she ordered. "Let me hear this firsthand. I can't believe the man I love would kill an unborn child."

Eagerly, Breanna complied, drying her eyes with a handkerchief, and composing herself enough to pick up the first note, read its contents aloud.

By the time she'd reached the final, dooming letter, Maurelle had completed her perusal, and her work—silently, rapidly, and as thoroughly as time would permit.

The information she had the chance to skim was equally damning to all five men. Any of them could be her noble assassin.

The drawings were another matter entirely.

Fear had prickled up her spine as she realized how accurate the visual depictions were, how easy it would be for Lady Breanna to identify her stalker by looking at his likeness.

Destroying the drawing was unthinkable. So was defacing it enough to disguise his features. Either of those steps would alert Chadwick to the fact that she'd tampered with the file, not to mention leading him to precisely the man she was determined to protect.

So how could she save him, buy him enough time to kill this interfering bitch and vanish?

There was only one way. It was risky, but it was a chance she had to take. After all, the chit had said she wouldn't know one man from the other.

In one swift motion, Maurelle had opened his file, plucked out his picture, and slipped it into the file behind it. Then, she'd stepped away from the reports.

Lady Breanna was reading the final phrase of the last letter. That alerted Maurelle to the fact that she hadn't time to get back over to the desk, where she was supposedly still standing, without calling attention to herself. Even an overwrought fool like Lady Breanna might become suspicious if she saw her enemy standing so close to a report that would condemn her lover. And the last thing Maurelle wanted was to arouse her ladyship's suspicions.

She acted on impulse.

Reaching for the wardrobe, she grabbed at the first item of clothing she could find. A night robe. Fine. She'd feign distress, make it look as if what she'd just heard had upset her so greatly, she couldn't stay still and bear it. She had to busy herself to keep from breaking down.

And what more logical outlet for her anguish than donning her nightclothes, retiring to bed to bury her pain?

Breanna was staring at the page in her hands, her breathing unsteady as she fought back tears. When she finally looked up, Maurelle was unbuttoning her gown in dazed, jerky motions, watching her with a shocked expression.

"Now do you understand?" Breanna beseeched her.

"*Oui.*" Maurelle kept her voice low, shaken. "How could I not?" She stepped out of her gown, untied the ribbons of her chemise. "I never imagined . . ." She finished undressing, then, with trembling hands, shrugged on the absurdly pristine night robe that had been left for her. "I don't know what to do," she confessed. "To betray him . . . It's not only love. I'm afraid."

"We'll protect you," Breanna assured her quickly. "We'll keep you safe until he's caught. Please, help me. If not for my sake, for the sake of Anastasia's babe."

That, ostensibly, clinched it.

Maurelle nodded, pain twisting her lovely features. "I will." She pressed her palms together, summoning up all her courage. "No unborn child should be killed without ever tasting life." A heartbeat of a pause. "His name is Arthur," she whispered, forcing out the words. "Arthur Landow."

She watched relief sweep Breanna's face.

Slowly, she counted to ten.

It was time for her seemingly virtuous move.

"Lord Royce will want your verification," she informed Breanna, dabbing at her eyes. "He's a man, and will never understand your qualms about viewing the drawings. But I'm a woman. I do. So, while I know you must confirm what I've told you, I don't think you should subject yourself to doing so—not alone." She crossed over, picked up Landow's file, holding it so Breanna could see his name penned in bold letters across the front. "Here. Do it now. With another woman beside you for comfort. Then, you'll never have to do it again." She tugged out the sketch she'd placed atop Landow's, flourished it before Breanna's horrified eyes. "Is this not he?"

Breanna stared at the drawing. Her gaze shifted to Maurelle's compassionate expression, and she shuddered, biting her lip to stifle a sob. "Yes. It's he." She turned away from the sketch. "Put it away. I never want to see him again."

"*Mais oui.* I understand." Maurelle hurried back to the stack of files, slipping her noble assassin's sketch back in its proper place before laying Landow's file atop it.

Maurelle picked up the entire stack of reports. "Why don't you give these to your butler right now? He can turn them straight over to Lord Royce, and you need never see Arthur's face again." A shaky pause. "Just as I won't."

Breanna stood, gathering up the letters and walking over to Maurelle. "Thank you, Maurelle," she said fervently, taking the files from her. "I know how difficult this was for you. But you did the right thing. Just as I knew you would." She opened the door, gestured for Wells to approach. "Take these," she directed him. "Give them to Lord Royce. Tell him I have his answers. I won't need to see these sketches again."

27

Everyone was gathered in the sitting room when Breanna and Wells walked in.

Breanna's ashen expression was no longer feigned, but very real.

"It's done," she stated simply, her voice more hollow than shaken. "We finally know who he is." Her gaze flickered from one beloved face to the next, finally settling on Royce. "Viscount Crompton," she supplied. "He's the assassin."

"You're certain." Royce's words were more statement than query.

"Yes." Breanna nodded, interlacing her fingers tightly in front of her. "Maurelle went first to his file. She looked at it twice, once before and once after she skimmed the others. Then, she removed my sketch of Crompton from his file and slipped it into Arthur Landow's. She brought Landow's file over to me, made sure I saw his name on it, and flourished the drawing of Crompton, admitting to me that Arthur Landow was indeed the man we sought. Once I acknowledged recognizing his face, she put the sketch back where it belonged and told me I need never look at it again." Breanna exhaled slowly. "It's Crompton."

Royce crossed over, enfolded Breanna in his arms. "You're astonishing," he murmured. "I'm so proud of you." He tilted up her chin. "Are you all right?"

"I'm fine," she replied. "A bit numb, but fine."

"Crompton," Damen repeated. "I never would have believed he had the presence of mind, much less the coldheartedness, to do this."

"I told you," Royce responded. "This killer is a master at deception. Crompton assumed you'd think him too eccentric to be the culprit. He was right. None of us guessed."

"I don't think I've ever seen him without his gloves," Anastasia commented. "Not before or after Breanna shot him. Then again, I'd have no reason to. The only times I've seen him have been at formal or sporting events."

"Shooting," Breanna clarified.

"Yes, shooting . . . no, wait. That's not true." Anastasia sat up abruptly.

"You've seen him without his gloves?"

"No, but I've seen him outside Medford. It was right around the time Damen and I were about to expose Uncle George. Crompton was at the House of Lockewood . . ." She turned to gaze at her husband. "Meeting with John Cunnings. I remember because Cunnings came to your office looking for the viscount's portfolio."

"He met with John often," Damen concurred. "In fact, most of the time. He sought me out for large investment decisions, but on a day-to-day basis, he dealt with Cunnings."

"Obviously, discussing more than finances," Royce modified caustically.

"So what do we do now?" Damen demanded. "We know who the killer is. Why don't we just ride over to his estate and grab him?"

"That would be the worst thing we could do," Royce refuted. "First of all, Crompton isn't spending much time at his estate these days. He's here, watching Breanna. And if he knew we were on our way to seize him, he'd simply vanish, the way he did last time." Royce paused, his worried gaze shifting from Breanna to Anastasia and back.

"Only to resurface Lord knows when to finish what he started." Breanna completed Royce's unvoiced thought aloud.

"Yes."

"I see your point." Damen swallowed. "Then, how do we stop him?"

"We lure *him* to *us*. We taunt him, anger him, and turn this little cat and mouse game around."

Stacie looked intrigued. "How?"

Royce's jaw set, that purposeful gleam returning to his eyes. "I'll have one more chat with Maurelle. Who knows? Maybe I can even unearth a few more details while her tongue is loose—which it will be, as long as it's Landow she thinks she's betraying. At the end of that time, I'll let her know just how badly she underestimated Breanna. I'll toss out Crompton's name, and let her choke on it. Then, I'll help myself to an article of her clothing—preferably something intimate—and I'll leave her in the guards' capable hands."

"You're going to send the clothing to Crompton," Breanna murmured. "Let him know we have Maurelle."

"You're damned right I am. I'm going to flaunt that fact as crudely as I can. Let him think I'm bedding his precious Maurelle, violating the one thing he cares about. He'll react. I guarantee it. He'll go berserk. All his precision, his brilliant strategy, will be cast to the wind. Gut emotion will take over. Even his hatred for you will be temporarily forsaken. He'll want to free Maurelle, slit my throat for having her. And I'll be ready for him when he tries."

Breanna raised her chin another notch, studied Royce's face. "It had to come down to this, didn't it?" she asked softly. "From the very beginning. It was going to end in a final battle between you and him. You'd have it no other way."

"No, I wouldn't." Royce met her gaze. "From the very beginning? Maybe. Maybe not. I don't know. But from the day I fell in love with you? Definitely. So if you're asking if I'm arranging things this way so I can meet him face to face, personally pull the trigger to end his wretched life, the answer is yes. I wanted to wait until the odds were with me. They finally are. And Crompton is a dead man."

"I understand," Breanna said in a tremulous voice. "But, Royce, I love you." She lay her palm against his jaw. "I can't lose you."

"You won't." He turned his lips to kiss her fingertips. "Sweetheart, I'm not doing this out of arrogance." His tone gentled as he gave voice to that which they already knew. "The truth is that you and Anastasia will never be safe as long as Crompton's alive."

"I know." Breanna wet her lips with the tip of her tongue, weighing her next words carefully. "Your letter has to be convincing. Maurelle's chemise, even

doused in her scent, won't be enough. Remember, he
sent me a bottle of that same perfume. We could be
using that to fake Maurelle's capture."

"True." Royce nodded, eying Breanna speculatively
as he realized she was leading him somewhere in particular. "I intended to include a lock of her hair. I'd
parade her across the front lawn so he could see her
for himself, if it weren't so risky. Given the frenzy
he'll likely be in, he might go off like a loose cannon,
firing blindly at everyone in sight. I won't take that
chance."

"You don't need to." Breanna spoke calmly, her decision made. "Send the chemise and the lock of hair.
Make the letter as provoking as you can. And when
you do, mention the birthmark on her right breast. It's
in a spot only a lover would know about." She
flushed. "I'll describe the exact location to you when
you write the letter. But that should get you the response you're looking for."

Royce stared at Breanna in amazement. "How did
you have the presence of mind to—?"

"I didn't. It just so happens that Maurelle used
undressing as a means to conceal the fact that she'd
been looking through the files. She changed into a
nightrobe while I was in the room. The birthmark is
very conspicuous."

"And you call me brilliant." Royce kissed her triumphantly, unbothered by their audience. "This is almost over," he said, raising his head to include
Anastasia in his assessment. "Hold on a little longer."

Royce strode into Maurelle's chambers and shut the
door behind him.

She smiled inwardly, seeing the victorious gleam in

his eye. Her ruse had worked. Chadwick now believed that Arthur Landow was her noble assassin.

Excellent.

"May I help you, monsieur?" she inquired, folding back the bedcovers. "I was just about to retire for the night."

Royce glanced at his pocket watch. "It's not even dinnertime."

"I'm fatigued." Maurelle smoothed her hand over the sheets. "Your friend Lady Breanna exhausted me."

His jaw tightened fractionally. "I heard that Lady Breanna had been in to see you. And while I wish she hadn't subjected herself to that, I can't deny I'm pleased by the results."

"I thought you would be."

"Funny, you didn't seem to me to be the type one could reach through compassion."

"People aren't always as they seem."

"No, they're not." Royce paused, rubbed his palms together. "In any case, I'm glad you relented. It will be easier on everyone."

"Is that why you're here?" Maurelle inquired, gripping the bedpost. "To ease my fears?"

"No. Frankly, I don't give a damn about your fears."

She smiled. "I appreciate your honesty, monsieur. So tell me, what can I do for you?"

"You can answer a few questions. I want as much evidence against Landow as I can get before I send Bow Street over to arrest him."

Warning bells sounded in her head, and her gaze turned wary. "What kind of evidence?"

"His relationship with Cunnings—what do you know of it?"

Ah, that. Inwardly, she relaxed. Cunnings was dead. He couldn't deny Landow's guilt. Therefore, the closer she stuck to the truth, the better.

"Arthur knew John Cunnings for quite some time," she replied.

"So Lady Breanna overheard Cunnings tell her father. He said he'd seen the assassin's . . . Landow's," Royce corrected himself, "accomplishments for years."

"That's true. From what Arthur explained, he needed a contact to arrange the jobs he took on."

"The executions, you mean."

"Yes. Cunnings was perfect. He knew scores of people through his position at the House of Lockewood. You'd be surprised to learn how eager some supposedly honorable men and women are to rid themselves of family members that stand between themselves and their fortunes."

"I don't doubt it."

"The bank itself made an ideal meeting place. No one suspected anything unscrupulous was going on during their meetings. After all, Arthur was a client—a good one." Her lips curved. "And a smart one. He eavesdropped on Cunnings's conversations enough times to realize he was willing to compromise himself for money. He confirmed that fact by keeping an ear to the ground and learning Cunnings was spending more than he had, courting women with expensive jewelry, buying homes he couldn't afford. In short, John Cunnings was willing to do anything to support his expensive habits. Arthur offered him that opportunity."

"Hmm." Royce stroked his jaw thoughtfully. "In other words, Cunnings got a percentage of Landow's fee on the clients he referred?"

"Exactly." Maurelle sighed. "I'm sorry Monsieur Cunnings had to die. I have a soft spot in my heart for him. After all, it was through him that Arthur came back into my life."

"So Landow did find you again through Cunnings's notes."

"*Oui*." Maurelle lowered her lashes, reminding herself that she was supposed to be feeling guilty, torn by her own betrayal. "Arthur didn't come directly to Paris. First, he went to Germany, to visit that brilliant Dr. Helmett. Wilkens, the gunsmith, met them there. Arthur had surgery." A thought struck her, and she eliminated the quickest and most logical way for Landow to prove his innocence. She had to buy Ansel time—time to finish his mission and vanish. "The surgery was so successful, his finger is as good as new."

"Is it?" Royce looked surprised. "Then why is he so eager for revenge?"

"Because it took some time to regain his muscle control. And being in control is more important to Arthur than anything else. He was at a disadvantage for months. He had to master the new weapon Wilkens crafted in order to shoot. Also, he can't bear the thought of being bested, especially by a woman."

"I see." Royce nodded, acknowledging the truth of her words. "Where is Helmett now?"

Maurelle swallowed. "Arthur killed him. He had no choice. He didn't expect Dr. Helmett to react so strongly when he heard Arthur boast of his plans to do away with Lady Breanna."

"Ah. The good physician threatened to alert the authorities?"

"Yes."

Royce inclined his head. "By the way, Wilkens is dead, too. Did you know that? Your lover killed him a few days ago."

"No, I didn't. But I'm not surprised."

"I didn't expect you would be. He seems very adept at eliminating anyone who might give him away."

"He is." She bit her lip. "That's why I'm so frightened. If he should learn I've betrayed him—"

"Oh, he will," Royce assured her cheerfully. He glanced at his timepiece again. "This very night, as a matter of fact." He stepped aside, yanked open the door. "Hibbert, I could use your help."

"My pleasure." Hibbert strolled in, walking over to jerk Maurelle's arms behind her back. "Go ahead, my lord."

Maurelle's eyes widened as she saw the razor appear in Royce's hand. "Are you mad? I've told you everything you want to know, and in return you're going to slit my throat?"

"No. You're not worth it." Royce crossed over, quickly shearing off a lock of her hair. Wrapping it in his handkerchief, he glanced about the room, spying the pile of clothing Maurelle had left on the chair near the wardrobe. He went over, rifled through it until he found her chemise. "This will do." He crumpled it up, tucked it beneath his arm. "Let her go, Hibbert."

Hibbert complied, shoving Maurelle away from him as if she were an odious insect. He headed to the door, Royce directly behind him.

"Oh, Maurelle." Royce paused on the threshold, arching a brow in her direction. "In case you're wondering, I'll be sending off your chemise and your strand of hair, together with a very provocative letter." His teeth gleamed. "Crompton should have it before midnight. That's Ansel Crompton, by the way, not Arthur Landow. Then again, you already know that. Your attempt to save him was valiant. Speaking of which, Lady Breanna asked me to thank you. She appreciated your switching those drawings. You played right into her hands and helped ensure Crompton's downfall."

If Royce needed any further proof, the look of sheer panic on Maurelle's face provided it.

Her anguished cry, "Ansel," echoed through the halls as Royce and Hibbert walked away.

Crompton was applying the final touches of red paint to the last porcelain figure when the messenger galloped up his drive.

He frowned, wondering who could be contacting him this late at night.

Ah, Maurelle, he thought, his frown vanishing. No doubt she was summoning him, eager to have him back in her arms, her bed.

Well, she hadn't long to wait. By tomorrow at this time, Lady Anastasia and Lady Breanna would be dead, and he'd be on his way to Paris.

He held the statue away from him, admired his own handiwork. The two women were leaning over a book, clutching it as they read together. And they were smiling—placid smiles that seemed incredibly out of place when one considered their fatal injuries and mutilated hands.

Satisfaction glinted in his eyes. He'd severed both women's right index fingers, trickled bloodlike paint over their hands and the book's binding, and added a final red splotch over their hearts.

His final gift to Lady Breanna. It would arrive in the dead of night.

Tomorrow morning, it would be time.

He'd planned it all very carefully. The guards changed shifts at 6 A.M. As always, that stout, uncouth sentry posted on the far side of the estate would have been drinking his secret cache of ale from sometime after midnight, and would have nodded off no later than half past 5 A.M. That left thirty minutes—more than enough time to climb the sturdy oak he'd been using for his comings and goings, and slip onto the premises. From there, he'd creep toward the manor, hide in the thick brush, and eventually ease his way around the house until he had a clear view of the sitting room.

Then, he'd wait.

Sometime between 10 and 10:20 A.M., both Lady Breanna and Lady Anastasia would appear—heavily guarded by Chadwick, Sheldrake, and those two old codgers, Hibbert and Wells.

Did any of them actually believe they could scare him off or—an even more ludicrous thought—block his shot?

If so, they were bigger fools than he'd realized. *They* weren't what had kept him from striking before now. His battle plan was. He'd devised it. He meant to carry it out.

The first step had been to terrorize Lady Breanna.

That step was complete.

Now, it was time for the second step. Lady Anastasia had to die—right at her cousin's feet. For that, he needed no more than fifteen seconds. And he'd get those seconds, the instant Sheldrake stepped away from his wife.

Lady Anastasia would be dead by ten thirty.

Then came the tricky part—step three.

He had to isolate Lady Breanna. It wasn't enough to kill her. If it was, he'd simply shoot her right after he did away with her cousin. No, he had to first ensure that she knew precisely who he was, what he intended to do to her. He had to close in on her like a tiger stalking its prey, see the stark terror in her eyes as she realized her life was about to end.

He needed to see her crawl, to hear her plead for her life, sob for mercy.

Then, he'd blast away her life with one long-awaited shot.

It wouldn't be that difficult to get her alone. The house would be in an uproar once Lady Anastasia fell down dead. People would scatter. Chadwick would rush outside, determined to find the killer.

Taking Lady Breanna with him to ensure her safety.

That's when he'd make his move. He'd grab her the instant Chadwick turned his back.

No, this wouldn't be difficult at all.

A knock on the front door broke into his thoughts, reminded him of the messenger's arrival.

Carefully, he lined his desk drawer with a handkerchief, then placed the statue upon it, sliding the drawer shut to conceal it. He'd write the note later. For now, he wanted to read Maurelle's words of love.

He left his study, made his way to the entranceway.

His butler had just accepted a small package from the messenger and was shutting the door. He looked up, saw the viscount approaching.

"For you, sir," he announced.

"Excellent. Thank you." Crompton took the parcel, glancing at it as he retreated to the privacy of his study. He'd expected a letter. Had Maurelle sent him a gift?

He locked his study door, lowered himself to the settee, and unwrapped the package. A carnal smile touched his lips as Maurelle's fragrance greeted his nostrils. He lifted out the perfume-scented chemise, amused by Maurelle's uncharacteristically girlish gesture. Evidently, she missed him as much as he missed her. But she needn't have gone to such extremes to tell him so. She, of all people, knew he needed no enticement. Not when it came to her. His desire for her was compulsive, a gnawing in his belly that seemed never to fade.

He brought the chemise to his face, inhaled deeply, and felt his body throb to life. Another day. That's all it would be. Then he'd be with her. And not just for a brief interlude. For the rest of their lives.

He lowered the garment, intending to restore it to the box.

A lock of hair tumbled out of the folds.

His brows arched in surprise. Maurelle's hair? Why on earth . . . ?

The note caught his eye. It was neatly penned, but not in Maurelle's hand.

A warning bell sounded in his head, and he tensed, snatched up the page.

Crompton, it read. *Your maneuvers were good. Mine were better. To the victor go the spoils. In this case, the spoils are the prisoner I've taken. And I do mean taken. Not once, but repeatedly. Her body is too lush to resist—especially that erotic birthmark just under her right nipple. I salute you for your taste in women. Maurelle Rouge is one woman I'd never sell. She's extraordinary. Insatiable, but extraordinary. She keeps begging for more, insisting that my charms exceed yours. Yet another victory, wouldn't you say?*

Crompton's skull was hammering so loud he could scarcely think, his body shaking with a rage like none he had ever known.

Chadwick had Maurelle. His intimate description left no room for doubt. That filthy bastard was bedding *his* Maurelle.

Damn him. Damn him to hell.

Crompton dragged his sleeve across his forehead, sweat trickling down the side of his face as he forced himself to read on.

Did you think I'd summon Bow Street? Think again. I want no intermediary. It's just you and me, Crompton. Except the roles have now reversed. You're the mouse and I'm the cat. I've hunted you down. Now I can torment you as you tormented Lady Breanna. I've already stripped you of everything—your anonymity, your unblemished success record, even your woman. Concede defeat. Or die by my hand. The war is over. The best man has won. — Chadwick

A roar of denial exploded from Crompton's chest. He bolted to his feet, crumpling the note into a ball and hurling it and the box across the room.

He raked both hands through his hair, pacing about in an effort to comprehend what had happened, *how* it had happened.

Chadwick knew who he was. He knew who Maurelle was. He'd called her Maurelle *Rouge*. Worse, he'd kidnapped her, forced her to act as his whore. She'd never have gone willingly. He had to have brutalized her.

Had he also brutalized her into revealing her lover's name?

No. Maurelle would never betray him. Not even if she were tortured.

Then how had Chadwick figured it out? How had he gotten his hands on Maurelle to begin with?

Hibbert.

That wretched old fool had been in Paris. He must have found Le Joyau, seized her there.

Which meant he'd found the women. *All* the women.

Emma Martin. *That's* who'd given him away. She was the only one who'd seen his face.

He'd kill her later. After he took care of the others.

He stopped pacing, forced air into his lungs. He had to think, to come up with a plan. Chadwick wasn't sending Bow Street here. He was too pompous, too cocky.

Too smart.

He knew bloody well that if Bow Street showed up here, the man they sought would find a way to elude them, to drop out of sight and, as a result, be back in a position of control. Instead, Chadwick was trying to lure him out, to goad him into showing himself.

Oh, he'd show himself, all right. But not in the reckless way Chadwick expected.

He'd rethink his strategy. He'd get into that house. He'd rescue Maurelle.

And then he'd kill every last one of them.

28

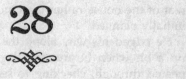

*H*e arrived at Medford as originally planned, at half past 5 A.M.

It had taken all his self-control to wait out the night, to restrain himself from rushing right over there and breaking down the front door, firing at everyone until he found Maurelle.

But that's what Chadwick assumed he'd do. The son of a bitch was lying in wait.

As a result, the only thing to do was to outmaneuver him.

Oh, the best man would win, all right.

And Chadwick would be dead.

Crompton jumped down lightly from the oak tree, glancing behind him at the sleeping guard. Scornfully, he noted the half-empty bottle clutched in the man's fist.

Pathetic fool.

Turning away, he crept across the grounds, his black clothes invisible in the darkness of night's final hours.

He reached the manor.

This was where his original strategy ended, and his modified one began.

He squatted down in the bushes, remaining in the rear of the house rather than inching around front, as initially planned.

He edged his way along the outside wall, raising up a bit when he reached the kitchen window. He peered through, checking to see if the staff had appeared to begin preparing breakfast.

A cook and two scullery maids were moving about, starting their morning routine.

Splendid. Just enough people to suit his purposes, not so many as to obstruct his entry.

Silently, he dropped to the ground, choosing a spot next to the rear entrance—one with just a spotty number of evergreen shrubs. It wouldn't do to choose a denser patch. His goal was to cause a disturbance, not to burn the whole manor to the ground.

He struck the match.

It took two minutes for the fire to leap high enough to be seen, and for the fumes to be smelled as they seeped beneath the windows and door.

The kitchen staff reacted.

One of the scullery maids shrieked and dropped a frying pan, pointing to the curling wisps of smoke.

The cook grabbed a kettle of water and doused the area, only to realize the source of the fire was outside.

She flung open the door, wringing her hands as she saw the flames.

She swung around, shooing the two maids away, and gesturing toward the inside hallway.

The three servants dashed off to alert the household.

Crompton waited ten seconds. No more, no less. Then, he slipped inside, making his way straight to the pantry and concealing himself in a dim, barren alcove within it.

He pulled up a stool, sank down on it. Alert yet unmoving, he settled himself for the long hours that lay ahead.

He was an expert at lying in wait. It was one of the skills that had made him the fine general he was. He knew how to outlast the enemy, to create the illusion that the danger was gone.

Only then would he strike.

By 7 A.M., the flames were doused.

By 10 A.M., the guards had given up patrolling the area. Having spied no one suspicious lurking about, they'd come to the conclusion that the fire was indeed an accident and bore no connection to the intruder they were guarding against.

Chadwick wasn't so certain.

He hovered at the scene, scrutinizing the shrubs and muttering to Hibbert, who had accompanied him outside to search the area.

Eventually, they let themselves in through the kitchen.

"Go back to Breanna," Chadwick instructed his manservant. "I don't want her left alone."

Hibbert frowned. "You suspect Crompton did this?"

"I don't know. It's winter. The air is cold and dry. A spark from the kitchen might have started the fire. So, it could be a coincidence. But I'm not taking any chances. If Crompton is behind this, he's on the grounds. I'm going to alert Mahoney's men, have them search every inch of the estate, not only this immediate area. After that, I'm heading down to the servants' quarters to see what Maurelle is up to. If Crompton did break into Medford, she's the reason why."

"I agree." Hibbert nodded briskly. "I'll watch Lady Breanna. Lord Sheldrake is with his wife. And Wells is standing guard outside Maurelle's room, just in case. He's been there since he awakened."

"Good. Putting Maurelle in the room next to his was wise. He can keep a close eye on her." Chadwick was already heading out. "I'll check in with you later."

"Fine."

The two men left. Quiet ensued.

The day wore on.

Slowly, the ordinary routine resumed, tension ebbing away as hour gave way to hour and no further incident occurred.

At last, the sun set.

Darkness fell, settling over the manor with the customary impatience of January.

The evening meal was served. The kitchen staff completed their work, washed the last of the evening dishes, and doused the lights.

The lower level fell silent.

Just above the pantry, the family chatted in the library, the distinct sounds of Lady Breanna's lilting tones and her cousin's more Americanized accent drifting to the floor below, interdispersed by comments issued in Sheldrake and Chadwick's deeper baritones.

It was time.

Inside the cramped alcove, Crompton stood, stretching his arms and legs to restore feeling. He winced at the throbbing pain that gripped his finger, which was raw and stiff after the prolonged day he'd spent in this chilly room.

Soon that pain would be vindicated. Then, he'd sail off to a warm climate where the sun would ease his physical torment.

But first, he had to rescue Maurelle.

She was alone now. He'd watched the house often enough to know the evening routine. Wells would be posted at the entranceway—especially at this point, when they were anticipating the delivery of the final statue—and Hibbert would be stationed in the hall between Wells and the family, adding his presence for extra security.

That was fine. They weren't his targets—yet.

Of course, there was always the chance that Chadwick had kept guards posted outside Maurelle's door. However, that prospect was unlikely, now that this morning's threat had been removed and there was no reason to believe the noble assassin was anywhere near Maurelle, much less on the verge of rescuing her. Chadwick wouldn't want to waste the men, not when they could be patrolling the perimeter of the estate, or standing guard over Lady Anastasia and Lady Breanna.

A bitter smile curved Crompton's lips.

Cautiously, he crept out of the pantry and through the kitchen, made his way to the servants' quarters.

The wing was deserted. Not a surprise, given that the staff was doubtless either retiring for the night or upstairs preparing their employers' chambers so that they might do the same.

Nonetheless, his fingers closed around his pistol to ready it, most particularly when he rounded the corner that led to the butler's quarters.

Wells's chambers were silent. Clearly, he was upstairs at his post.

Crompton relaxed his grip, moving to the door next to Wells's.

It was locked.

Ever so slightly, he jiggled the handle to make sure. Yes. Definitely locked.

He glanced about, ensured he was alone.

Then, he knocked—a hushed little rap.

No answer.

He tried again, this time louder.

"Have you lost your key, monsieur?" Maurelle's icy voice sounded from within. "Don't bother getting another. I have nothing more to say to you."

That was all Crompton needed.

He pulled out a blade, slipped it into the keyhole, and gave a hard flick of his wrist.

A telltale click told him he'd accomplished his goal.

He turned the door handle and stepped into the room.

Maurelle looked up from the chair, her features set in hard, unyielding lines. "I just said I'm finished speaking to . . ." Her mouth snapped shut, and she gave a start of surprise as she saw who her guest was. "Ansel." She rushed over, gripping his arms and peering wildly over his shoulder. "Are you insane? You're playing right into Chadwick's hands."

"No. He's playing into mine." Crompton shut the door, capturing Maurelle's chin in his gloved hand and tilting up her face so he could study it. "What methods did he use to force you? I'll prolong his death one painful minute for every time he took you."

Maurelle's brows drew together. "What are you talking about? He didn't bed me. Is that what his letter said? He was baiting you, Ansel. He cut a lock of my hair and took my chemise. But he never laid a hand on me."

Thunderclouds erupted on Crompton's face. "He described your birthmark. The one here." He touched her breast.

"My birthmark." Maurelle glanced down at herself in puzzlement. "How could he . . . ?" Abruptly, her head snapped up, and her eyes blazed with anger. "That bitch Lady Breanna. She was in here while I was changing. She must have given him a description." Worry supplanted rage. "Chadwick arranged this. So he must know you're here. He'll kill you."

"No. He doesn't know I'm here and, no, he won't kill me." Fury rippled through Crompton's body in violent currents, intensifying as he realized how Chadwick had duped him. "I have no intentions of letting him win."

"But he set this whole thing up so—"

"Yes." Crompton's confidence returned as he reevaluated the events of the day. "He managed to deceive me. But I've outmaneuvered him. This morning, he suspected I broke in. But I've since convinced him otherwise. He now thinks the household is safe and secure. Which gives me the advantage."

Crompton seized Maurelle's hand, led her to the door. "Chadwick's amateur tactics are over. I'm getting you out of here. Then, I'm coming back and completing things once and for all. I'll execute Lady Anastasia the way I should have in August. Then, I'll make her wretched cousin beg for mercy. And once I have, I'll fire a shot through her heart right in front of Chadwick, show him how pitifully he's failed in his attempts to protect her."

"And Chadwick?" Maurelle's eyes were glowing with smug anticipation.

"He'll die next," Crompton vowed, hatred etched on his features, pervading his tone. "I'll relish that moment. Then, I'll do away with Wells and Hibbert, and whoever else gets in my way, including Sheldrake." He paused, the taste of victory on his tongue. "I won't have further need of the House of Lockewood anyway. You and I will be sailing away this very night."

Maurelle nodded eagerly. "*Oui.* I can hardly wait."

Inside the next room, Wells stood, taut and ready, his fingers gripping the door handle.

He forced himself to wait, to follow Lord Royce's instructions to the letter.

He remained still, listening as Crompton exited with Maurelle, their footsteps moving toward the rear of the house, then fading into silence.

Instantly, he rushed from his room and upstairs to the library.

"He freed her, my lord," he announced breathlessly to Royce. "They just left the house. Through the back entrance, I think."

"Excellent." Royce checked his pistol, a fierce light glinting in his eyes. "Let's give them a minute. I want Crompton a healthy distance from the manor, for Breanna and Anastasia's sake. Then, the rest is up to me."

"No." Damen stood, snatching up his own gun. "It's up to *us*. I want him dead as much as you do. Besides, it's you who's been goading him. If he sees you, he'll go after you with a vengeance. You'll need help."

Royce gave a terse nod.

Breanna bit her lip, exchanging a quick, worried glance with Stacie.

Before either woman could speak up, Hibbert announced, "Wells and I are coming, too." He flourished his weapon.

"Definitely." Wells produced the pistol Hibbert had provided him. "This isn't a question of honor, my lord," he advised Royce. "The viscount could be anywhere. The grounds are vast. And I know them better than anyone."

"You're right," Royce concurred. He went to Breanna, gripped her shoulders. "You and Anastasia go upstairs to my chambers. Tell two of the guards to stand outside the door. Stay put. That's just to be on the safe side, since Crompton assumes you're in the library. But he's thinking of Maurelle right now, not you. So he'll be heading away from the manor, not toward it."

"Very well," Breanna murmured.

Stacie couldn't bear her passive role another instant. She jumped up from her chair. "But, Royce, I want to—"

"Stacie." Breanna's quiet admonishment silenced her. "Let the men do what they have to. Otherwise, Crompton will escape." She met her cousin's gaze, and a current of communication ran between them. "It's best this way."

"All right." Stacie ceased her protests.

Breanna rose up, kissed Royce gently. "Be careful."

"I will."

Soberly, Breanna watched her future husband walk away, along with three men who meant the world to her.

She waited only until she and Stacie were alone. Then, she whirled about to face her cousin.

"What are you planning?" Stacie hissed.

"I'm planning to stop Crompton and protect the men we love."

"How?"

"By doing what we do best." Breanna heard the front door shut, and she grasped Stacie's arm. "Come on. We must work quickly."

She hurried into the hall, snatching the two dark mantles that belonged to her and Stacie. "Put this on," she instructed Stacie, tossing her one of the wraps and shrugging into the other. "After that we'll . . ." Abruptly, she stopped, a self-deprecating expression darting across her face. "What was I thinking?" she murmured, her gaze falling to Stacie's abdomen. "Your babe. I won't endanger your child." She gave an adamant shake of her head. "I'll manage this alone." That done, she reached up, began tugging pins out of her hair, releasing the upswept knot and letting it tumble free.

"No, you won't." Stacie yanked on her own mantle, realization mingling with fierce determination. "We're switching places," she said, a statement of fact more than conjecture.

Breanna hesitated.

"Breanna, you need me for whatever it is you're planning. Besides . . ." Stacie laid a protective palm over her abdomen, "my going after Crompton won't mean endangering my babe. It will mean saving it. Destroying that man is the only true protection I can offer my child. Right now he—or she—is at risk. It's my responsibility to eliminate that risk. In short, you need me, and I need to do this. So, tell me, shall I put up my hair? We are switching places, right?"

"Yes and no," Breanna told her, relenting. "We're each being both of us."

Stacie paused in the midst of buttoning her mantle. "You've lost me."

Breanna faced her, drew a slow breath. "Crompton will never leave Medford for good. Not as long as we're alive. So if he flees with Maurelle, we'll go right back to living in perpetual fear and uncertainty. I can't bear that thought. Nor can I bear the thought of what he'll do to Royce and Damen if he finds them before they find him. We have to eliminate that possibility."

"How?"

Another pause. "Stacie, this plan borders on reckless."

"Not as reckless as letting Crompton escape. That would be akin to a death sentence—for us and my babe."

"You're sure you want to—?"

"I'm sure."

Breanna nodded, knowing there was no changing Stacie's mind, equally sure that, were it she who was pregnant, she would make the same choice—for her child's sake. "We're going to lure him back. We're going to provide the viscount with exactly what he wants: us. The only problem is, he won't know which of us is which. And that will pose a major obstacle to that consummate plan of his. Remember, he means to kill you first. With one bullet. No mistakes."

"True," Stacie concurred, understanding dawning on her face. "And he can't very well do that—not with utter certainty—unless he's sure it's me he's firing at. Why, he could be undermining his entire plan, killing you first. It would reverse his order *and* deny him the sick pleasure of torturing you further, making you watch me die. That would be unthinkable after all his meticulous planning."

"Exactly. To a man like Crompton, certainty is everything. And how can he be certain? He'll see two Anastasia's: you," Breanna altered her voice, dropped her clipped accent in favor of Stacie's Americanized tones, "and me." She finished shaking out her tresses, her hair tumbling over her shoulders, loose and uninhibited like Stacie's. "It's risky, but it's the only way we can protect the men we love, and be sure Crompton doesn't vanish, only to keep terrorizing us."

"I agree." Stacie nodded, her mind racing. "We'll have to stay far enough apart so Crompton believes we're each alone, yet nearby enough to appear at a moment's notice—so that whichever one of us Crompton spots first can be quickly joined by the other."

"Right." Breanna finished her preparations. "Once we've done that, we'll have to challenge his pride without pushing him over the edge. We'll simply remind him that if he were truly the master shot he claims to be, he'd know which of us was which. We'll point out that to fulfill his plan, he has to shoot Anastasia first with Breanna watching—and that he has to kill us with only one bullet apiece." She raised her chin. "We'll each take a pistol. The minute Crompton turns away from one of us and provides the other with a clear shot, that Anastasia will fire." Breanna's gaze grew intense. "Stacie, I asked myself this question days ago, and answered it. Now I'm asking you—can you shoot to kill? Because I can."

Stacie's palm strayed back to her abdomen, caressed her unborn child. "Oh, yes, Breanna. When it comes to the Viscount Crompton, I can shoot to kill."

29

*B*reanna walked slowly through the thatch of trees on the south side of the estate.

Her instincts told her that Crompton would use this avenue to escape. Stacie's had concurred.

If anyone knew the grounds of Medford Manor better than Wells, it was they. They were the ones who had played here as children, found hiding spots, climbed trees. And they were the ones who knew the densest areas in which to conceal oneself.

They'd intentionally left their hoods down. Their hair—a bright, burnished auburn—glittered in the moonlight, highly visible even in the darkness of night.

Gripping the handle of her pistol, Breanna placed one foot before the other, her heart hammering as she surveyed the deserted grounds. Every shivering leaf, every whoosh of wind made her jump, her stomach knotting as she contemplated what she was walking into.

Worse, what she'd talked Stacie into walking into.

Her cousin was with child. What if this plan went wrong? What if Crompton was no longer exacting, in control? What if he went wild, shot them both? What if . . . ?

No. She clenched her teeth, forced herself to stop thinking that way. Stacie's babe was in danger whether or not they enacted this plan, and it would continue to be in danger as long as Crompton lived.

They had to stop him.

A twig snapped behind her, and everything inside Breanna went numb. A sort of sickening, fatalistic awareness came over her, and she knew.

The moment of reckoning had arrived.

As if in a dream, she turned, not the least surprised to find the Viscount Crompton leaning against a tree, eyeing her calmly.

"You've made this far too easy," he commented, adjusting his gloves and watching dispassionately as she raised her pistol with a trembling hand. "Don't be absurd. You can scarcely hold that weapon, much less fire it." His arm snapped up, and the glint of his pistol flashed as he aimed it at her heart. "Whereas I . . ." A biting smile, and Breanna could see the madness in his eyes. "I'm a perfect shot."

He watched her frantically scrutinize the area beside him, and easily read her thoughts. "You're searching for Maurelle. Did you propose to hold her at gunpoint in the hopes of bringing me to my knees? Don't bother. You'd be dead before you finished aiming. Besides, she's off the estate. I made sure she was safely ensconced in my carriage before I came back to get you and Lady Breanna." His features hardened. "Now put down the pistol. Or I'll make your execution so painful, so prolonged, you'll beg for death."

His middle finger hovered over the trigger. "You can die quickly. Or you can die with agonizing slowness. The choice is yours. Make it."

Breanna sized up her options, which were nil. She could try to shoot him, but it would be suicide. He could elude her bullet by simply stepping behind the tree, whereas she was utterly exposed, and standing before an expert marksman. Her only hope was to throw down her gun and keep him talking until Stacie arrived.

"Very well." She tossed her pistol to the grass.

"A wise choice," Crompton informed her dryly. "You would have failed, and died a horrible death doing it. Whereas I never fail."

"You did last August," Breanna reminded him, careful to use Stacie's voice. "My uncle hired you to shoot me, and you didn't."

Hatred twisted Crompton's features. "That was because of your wretched cousin. By the way, where is she?" he added, his middle finger pressing closer to the trigger. "Wherever you are, she can't be far behind. And I'm determined she should watch this."

As if in answer to his own question, his head jerked around, and he stepped backward, shifting to aim his pistol to the left, while keeping Breanna in his sight. "Come out, Lady Breanna," he invited icily, angling his head to survey the area from which Stacie was obviously approaching. "I can hear you. Ah, now I can see you," he determined with great satisfaction. "Therefore, I'll coax you out in a more convincing manner." With that, he fired—one shot—and Breanna jumped, stifling her shriek. Dear God—Stacie.

What had he done?

A cry of surprise and a thud followed the shot, and

Crompton smiled cruelly, beckoning Stacie forward. "See?" he taunted with a vicious glare. "I can do it without mutilating your finger the way you did mine." His jaw clenched. "Now get out here and join your cousin."

Anastasia stepped out, her eyes wide with stunned apprehension, her hands unscathed, but devoid of a weapon.

Crompton's shot had sent it hurtling to the ground.

Which left both women unarmed.

Despite that fact, Breanna nearly collapsed with relief when she saw that Stacie was unharmed. They were in trouble. But they were alive.

Someone had to have heard that shot, she told herself. Wherever the men were, they would rush to Stacie's and her aid.

Crompton was too obsessed with killing them to consider that fact. So, it was up to them to keep him occupied until help arrived.

"Get over there where I can see you," Crompton was ordering Stacie. "Next to Lady Anastasia."

Breanna saw Stacie regain control, saw the flicker in her eyes as she reached the same realization Breanna had. She did as Crompton asked, walking slowly, her chin held high. "*Next to* Lady Anastasia? I *am* Lady Anastasia."

"Unless *I* am," Breanna challenged, boldly meeting his gaze.

For the first time, Crompton became aware of their identical appearances and voice inflections, and he hesitated, looking quickly from one of them to the other. "What kind of childish game are you playing?"

"No game, my lord." Breanna didn't know where

she found the strength to confront him. But she did—just as she'd confronted her father last summer.

"It's reality," she continued, hearing her own voice—no, Stacie's voice, but coming from her mouth. "We're just pointing out that either of us could be Anastasia. Or Breanna. And that presents you with a problem. You did boast you could kill each of us with one bullet—and that the first bullet was meant for Anastasia. Well, how do you intend to manage that without knowing which of us is she?"

Crompton's eyes narrowed. "I've been an expert marksman for more years than you've been alive. I've never been bested, not in or out of battle. Do you honestly believe you—two insignificant little chits—can outwit me?"

"We're not trying to outwit you," Breanna assured him, curtailing all signs of arrogance. "We're just curious. You've sent us note after note declaring your superiority, vowing your intentions and your capabilities. We're just curious how you would carry out your plan given this particular counterattack. Even if it is being launched by two insignificant chits."

A muscle pulsed in Crompton's cheek, and he turned his furious gaze on Breanna. "You've given yourself away. Breanna is a mouse. Medford made sure of it. Clearly, you're Anastasia." He paused, gauging her reaction.

"Maybe I am," Breanna agreed.

"On the other hand, maybe not," Stacie posed. "After all, my uncle has been in prison for months now. Breanna has come into her own during that time. So how can you be sure I'm not Anastasia? You disappoint us, my lord. You've never relied upon inferior tactics such as badgering people into providing you with answers. You've always found your own answers. Anyone can make a lucky guess. But you've always been so certain."

"You have us at your mercy," Breanna admitted with a sad shrug. "We know that. We realize we're both going to die. We only want to know how you're going to kill us without risking your entire reputation."

There was a wild light in Crompton's eyes now. "Damn you both. I won't forfeit my rank and position. I'm the ultimate marksman. I can outmaneuver anyone."

He broke off, sweat beading on his brow, the tension in his arm easing a bit as his deranged but brilliant mind raced for answers.

For an instant, Breanna thought they had won, that he was actually going to crumple before their eyes.

She was truly considering lunging for his gun, when he snapped back to attention. A sudden triumphant smile curved his lips, and his self-control reasserted itself, the wildness in his eyes dimming. His arm stiffened, his fingers gripping the pistol even more firmly than before.

"Very well," he said silkily. "Let's have it your way. I won't waste a bullet. I'll just designate a third—one per person. After all, there is a third person here to consider." He lowered his pistol a notch, aiming for Breanna's abdomen. "My first bullet will go to your child. Your unborn child." He jerked his wrist sideways, shifting to aim at Stacie's abdomen. "It will die before its mother. So bid it farewell." His arm lurched back and forth, alternating between the two women.

It was Stacie who acted, instinctively leaning over

to shield her unborn babe, covering her abdomen with both hands.

Crompton inclined his head in mock tribute. "A touching show of maternal protectiveness, Lady Sheldrake. And an ingenious approach on my part. Now I *am* certain." He turned his gun on her, gestured for her to straighten. "Now that we've established my superiority and resolved this amusing deception, I can finish my business and be gone."

He raised his arm a notch, aiming for her heart.

Without thinking, Breanna lurched to the left, planted herself in front of Stacie. "The only way you're going to kill my cousin is through me," she announced in a murderous tone that was totally foreign to her. She reached around behind her, held Stacie's arm so she remained firmly in place. "I can't stop you from killing us. But I won't give you the satisfaction of doing it the way you planned. You're going to fail, Lord Crompton. At least on some level. I'm going to die first. You won't rectify last summer's mistake beforehand. Nor will I watch Stacie die. So, once again, you'll be bested."

With a vile oath, Crompton strode over, grabbed Breanna by the throat, his fingers biting into her as he flung her aside. "No, you little bitch, I won't." He moved quickly, before she had an opportunity to catch her breath, much less rise. He lowered his booted foot to her chest and pressed, pinning her painfully to the ground. "Say good-bye to your cousin," he commanded, raising his pistol and pointing it at Anastasia. "She's about to die. And then I'll finally, *finally* have the ultimate pleasure of blasting away your life."

"Think again, Crompton."

Royce's voice rumbled out of nowhere, and Crompton whipped around, pistol raised.

He was still in motion when Royce's shot rang out.

The bullet pierced Crompton's chest, sent him jerking backwards from the impact.

A look of utter disbelief crossed his face.

Then, he slumped to the ground, less than a foot away from Breanna.

Royce walked over, his pistol still aimed and ready. He bent over Crompton's body to make sure he was indeed dead. Satisfied, he helped Breanna to her feet, held her tightly against him as he stared down at the blood seeping through Crompton's coat, soaking the fine wool.

"One bullet through the heart, you bastard," he muttered. "Now rot in hell."

30

Royce's bedcovers were a tangled, disheveled mess.

"Are you sure you don't want to sleep?" he murmured, balancing himself lightly on his elbows and kissing Breanna's flushed cheeks as she lay beneath him, limp and sated.

She sighed, a dreamlike smile her only reply.

They'd been making love for hours, ever since the guards had disposed of Crompton's body and seized Maurelle as she tried to flee in Crompton's carriage. The family had stumbled back into the manor, numb with relief, stared at each other in mutual understanding and bone-deep fatigue. Then, after a few emotional hugs between Breanna and Anastasia, everyone had retired for the night.

There would be time enough for discussion tomorrow.

For tonight, it was over. And it was time for recovery—recovery and renewal.

Breanna suspected Stacie and Damen had much the same sort of remedy in mind as she and Royce did:

each other. And not only out of desire. Out of a soul-deep need to reaffirm both their lives and their love.

Now, hours later, the need seemed no less pronounced.

"Would you like to sleep for a while?" Royce repeated, brushing her lips with his.

"Sleep?" Breanna echoed, as if the word were foreign to her.

"Um-hum. It's almost dawn."

"No."

"You're sure?"

"I'm sure," Breanna whispered. Her lashes lifted, and she shifted to take Royce more deeply inside her, looped her arms around his neck. "Why? Have I tired you out?"

He chuckled. "Not a chance. Not now, not ever."

"Ummm, I'm glad." She leaned up, kissed the damp hollow at his throat. "Have I told you how heroic you were tonight?"

"Yes." Royce frowned, despite the erotic pleasure shuddering through his body. "Have I told you how reckless you were tonight?"

"Repeatedly." Breanna arched her hips, eliciting an involuntary groan from the man she loved. "Can we stop rehashing it now? It's over. And thanks to you, I'm fine. We all are."

With fervent intensity, Royce tangled his hands in her hair, lifted her face to meet his burning gaze. "You have no idea how much I love you," he told her, his voice husky with emotion. "Or how terrified I was when I realized the danger you were in—the danger you'd put yourself in. God, Breanna . . ." He kissed her fiercely. "Don't ever do that to me again."

"I won't." She caressed his spine, traced the damp

planes of his back with her fingertips. "I'll go back to being self-contained and conventional. Later." Her eyes sparkled as she drew his mouth down to hers. "Much later."

Much later turned into much, *much* later, and the sun was climbing the sky when Breanna finally gave in to the need to rest.

She curled quietly in Royce's arms, watching the day unfold outside his window and thanking the heavens for the simple joy of knowing she could continue to do that, day after day, savoring each moment with the man she loved.

"Later this afternoon, we'll go visit that church you told me about," Royce announced, as if reading her mind. "I'll have the license within a week. How much time do you need to prepare for the wedding?"

Breanna smiled. "A fortnight," she decided abruptly. "Any invited guests who can't change their plans to accommodate us, will simply have to miss the occasion. The loss will be theirs. The union," she added softly, "and all the joy it promises to bring, will be ours."

Royce drew a sharp breath, then tilted up her chin so he could see her face. "You know what I want," he stated flatly. "I want you, as my wife, as soon as possible. But *I* also know what *you* want."

"Do you?"

"Yes. You want a formal wedding, something traditional and refined, something to make up for all you've been denied."

"I already have that—and more. I have you. No wedding celebration, no matter how grand, could enhance that joy."

A dubious look. "Sweetheart, are you sure?"

"Very sure." Breanna caressed his jaw. "I feel as if I've been given my life back. I want to begin it in the most perfect way imaginable—by becoming your wife. I want to be Mrs. Royce Chadwick the instant I can. As for guests, everyone I love is already under this roof. Including Grandfather, who's always with us. You and I will begin our life together surrounded by love. The rest is unimportant."

"Just what I wanted to hear." Royce kissed her fingertips, the delicate pulse at her wrist. "Now that I consider it, a fortnight sounds like forever. Maybe we should make it ten days."

Breanna laughed. "Stacie and Wells will be crushed if we give them *no* time to prepare. Besides, I think the prospect of a wedding is just what everyone needs to raise their spirits. Let's allow them a few weeks to savor it. Is a fortnight really that intolerable a waiting period?"

"Yes. But for your sake, I'll try to withstand it." Royce pressed her palm to his lips. "It won't be easy. I need you to belong to me in every way possible."

"I do. I will. And after that . . ." Breanna broke off, sobering as a sudden, worrisome thought intruded. "Royce, we haven't discussed our living arrangements."

He arched an amused brow. "We've certainly changed bedchambers often enough. Which room would you like to officially make ours?"

Breanna's eyes widened. "You really don't mind?"

"Mind what?"

"Living here. At Medford Manor. I know your memories here haven't exactly been pleasant ones. And you do have your house on Bond Street. I was afraid . . ."

Royce silenced her with a kiss. "Did you really think I'd take you away from your grandfather's dream?" he breathed into her lips. "Never. We'll use my house when we stay in Town. As for my memories of Medford—they're more than pleasurable. They're miraculous. This is where I met you, fell in love with you, made love to you for the first time. All that outweighs everything else, even Crompton. We'll start over right here, pick a section of the house that's new to us both. A private section, where we're assured of exquisite, utter seclusion. We'll wipe out all the ugly memories, keep only the spectacular ones. We'll redecorate, order all new furniture. You can provide brand-new sketches and needlepoints. And we'll move your porcelain figures, one by one, to our new chambers, designating a place of honor on our nightstand for the statue holding your silver coin. How would that be?"

Tears glistened on Breanna's lashes. "That would be wonderful."

"Anastasia and Damen's house will be ready by spring. Their babe will arrive not long after. And the family your grandfather prayed for will be well under way." Royce's midnight gaze darkened. "If I have my way, that family will be growing faster than even he expected."

Breanna smiled through her tears. "Perhaps that wish is already under way."

He started. "Breanna, are you saying—?"

"I don't know." She rolled over until she was lying atop him, her jade eyes filled with tender promise. "But given the daring man I'm marrying, and the unconventional woman I've become, I suspect our child won't comply with tradition. We've anticipated our wedding vows. Why wouldn't our babe?" She leaned over to kiss him, waves of auburn hair tumbling forward to encompass them in a shining cocoon. "Perhaps he or she was conceived this very night."

"Perhaps." Royce could scarcely speak. The very idea of Breanna carrying his child was almost too overwhelming to bear, and his body reacted instantly, hardening to almost painful proportions. He gripped Breanna's hips, lifted them so he could lower her onto his rigid shaft. "How would you feel about increasing our chances of that happening?" he asked, his voice rough with passion.

"Now?" she managed, her own words unsteady.

"Right now." He cupped her bottom, pushed deep inside her.

Breanna's breath caught, and she nodded, sinking into Royce's hypnotic spell. "Now would be ideal."

Epilogue

❧

Medford Manor
November 1824

*T*he two six-year-old girls peeked curiously into the dining room.

The table was set with fine china and silver, and pinpoints of light cast by the gilded chandelier danced off the crystal glasses as the seven adults raised them in a toast. Lord Ryder, the evening's sole guest, beamed from ear to ear, thanking his hosts—the Lockewoods and the Chadwicks—for all they'd done to make this day possible. Then he rose, pivoting toward the sideboard, where Hibbert and Wells stood, and offered a special thanks to Hibbert, murmuring something about the fact that without Hibbert, his Emma would never have been restored to him.

Hibbert replied in his customarily gracious manner. Then he and Wells drank, actually abandoning whatever subject they'd been heatedly debating tonight, to join in the festivities.

The footmen refilled everyone's glasses, and the chattering resumed. Royce muttered something that made everyone laugh, and turned teasing eyes on Breanna, whose cheeks were tinged with color, but who looked more pleased than embarrassed by whatever her husband had said. Tenderly, Royce pressed her gloved hand to his lips.

"It's not Christmas yet." Holly Lockewood twisted an auburn curl around her forefinger, studying the adults with curious jade-green eyes. "Are our parents celebrating something?"

"They must be. They're laughing." Her cousin, Joanna Chadwick, followed her gaze, took in the scene before them. "So's Lord Ryder. Even Wells and Hibbert are smiling between arguments. It must be an important celebration."

"Maybe. Maybe not. Our parents always laugh. And they kiss, too. A lot more than most grown-ups do." Holly gave her cousin a wise look. "Mama says it's a special kind of magic."

"Magic? What kind of magic?"

"I don't know. She says I'll understand when I'm older." Holly made a face. "Why do we always have to wait to get older? That leaves nothing to do till then."

"Maybe the magic comes from the coins great-grandfather gave our mamas," Joanna suggested, still pondering what her Aunt Anastasia had told Holly. "Maybe the coins have special powers."

"That makes sense." Now Holly looked intrigued, her fanciful mind dancing through the possibilities. "Gold for laughing and silver for kisses." Her brow furrowed. "We should test our idea on Cody, stick the gold coin in his fist when he's waiting for Mama to feed him," she muttered. "Maybe that will make him smile when he's hungry. He cries so loud it hurts my ears."

"That's true," Joanna agreed. "But you're still luckier than I am. At least your brother's too little to walk. Mine runs all over. And he scribbles on my drawings if Mama isn't looking."

Holly grinned. "Maybe we should wake up both Cody and Quinn and bring them down. Just to see what Lord Ryder would do with one squalling baby and one little boy tearing up the dining room."

"Holly." Joanna, the far more practical of the two, planted her hands on her hips, shook her head. "That would only get us in trouble."

"Well, I'm bored. We've been listening to Lord Ryder talk about his new granddaughter for an hour. That can't be what they're celebrating. She's a baby. And babies yell too much to celebrate. Besides, he already has two grandchildren. He visits them all the time in Paris."

"Maybe his daughter and her family are coming here for Christmas!" Joanna's face lit up. "I like when they come. Monsieur Girard and Papa tell exciting stories."

"Especially the one about when Monsieur Girard rescued his wife from that bad witch." Holly's eyes sparkled with her typical romantic excitement. "And then they got married and she found her papa, Lord Ryder. It's like a fairy tale."

"We can go in and ask if the Girards are coming."

"We could. But even if they are, we'll still be bored now." Holly's shoulders slumped. She paced around the hallway, her mind searching for something unique to do.

"There you are." Miss Carter, the Chadwick governess, appeared at their sides. "Joanna, it's bed time. You, too, Holly," she added, turning to face the other child, who happened not to be Holly, but Joanna. "Your parents said you could sleep here tonight since it's so late. Unless you'd rather go across the way and sleep in your own bed? I could ask Wells to walk you home."

Holly sighed, tugging at the governess's sleeve. "*I'm* Holly, Miss Carter," she informed her. "And I'd rather stay here. But Joanna and I aren't tired. We wanted to be with the grown-ups for a while."

"Oh." Miss Carter gazed from one child to the other, exasperated by the mistake she seemed perpetually to make. Then again, the entire staff made it—with the exception of Wells and Hibbert. It was virtually impossible to tell Joanna and Holly apart. With only four months separating them, the two girls could pass for twins, just as their mothers could.

With regard to Holly's request, Miss Carter knew that neither set of parents would object to having their children stay up later than usual. In fact, they enjoyed having them about. It was a pleasure seeing the genuine affection that existed between the Chadwicks and Lockewoods and their children.

"Well, perhaps a few more minutes then," she relented. "But only a few."

"Thank you, Miss Carter," Joanna agreed. "We'll come up in a little while." She sighed as the governess headed off. "She still mixes us up."

"Everyone does," Holly said with a shrug.

"Except Hibbert and Wells. They always know who's who. So do our parents."

Holly's entire face lit up. "That's it!"

"What's it?"

"What we can do for fun. Remember what Mama told us about the game she and Aunt Breanna used to play? Let's change dresses. Then let's go into the dining room and try to fool everyone. You be me and I'll be you. Just like our mamas used to."

"They even fooled Wells."

"We will, too. We'll fool everyone."

The girls rushed down the hall to the blue salon, where they quickly changed frocks, slippers, even hair ribbons.

"Make your hair messier," Holly instructed. "Mine never stays as neat as yours."

Joanna nodded, tying her ribbon, then tugging out a few strands of burnished hair, letting them topple to her cheeks. "How's that?"

"Perfect." Holly's eyes glowed. "Now let's go in there. Remember to keep twisting those loose strands of hair around your finger. Papa says I do that all the time."

"And you bring in that new sketch I made," Joanna urged. "The one of the pond. I promised Mama I'd show it to her tomorrow. But tonight would be even better."

Holly's nod was filled with enthusiasm. "You left it in the library for the ink to dry. We'll get it on our way to the dining room. C'mon."

Five minutes later, Joanna and Holly poked their heads into the dining room—a far different dining room than the one their mothers had crept into more than twenty years ago when they'd been desperate to protect Breanna from her father's wrath. Oh, the furnishings hadn't changed much from when Stacie and Breanna's grandfather had celebrated his sixtieth birthday. But the occupants had. So had the aura they exuded. Tonight there was no tension, no arguing, no resentment permeating the room.

Tonight, there was only love and laughter and contentment.

"May we come in and listen for a while before we say good-night?" Joanna asked.

Sipping at his coffee, Damen chuckled. "For a while? You've already been listening for an hour, only outside the door."

Across the table, Anastasia laughed, beckoned the girls in. "Of course. Come in and hear all about Lord Ryder's new granddaughter. She's only a few months old."

Joanna wrinkled her nose, remembering she was supposed to be Holly. "Is that what you're celebrating?"

Anastasia nodded, although she knew what was coming.

"Does that mean she yells as loud as Cody?" Joanna demanded, rather enjoying her role as her more outspoken cousin.

Lord Ryder coughed—a cough that sounded suspiciously like a smothered chuckle. "From what I experienced during my visit there last week, yes, I must say she does yell. But not often, and not terribly loud."

"Then that's different." Joanna gave Lord Ryder a reassuring look. "I don't think you should worry. She'll probably be okay. Cody's a boy. They're worse."

"Not always," Royce inserted dryly. "The entire staff was jolted out of sleep whenever Joanna bellowed."

"Funny, it was the same with Holly," Damen concurred. "I guess too many years have passed for our daughters to recall the din they created as infants."

The girls exchanged disbelieving glances.

Ryder's lips twitched, and he nodded his white head at the girl he thought to be Holly. "Thank you. I'm relieved to hear that the shouting will be minimal. I'm sure my Emma will be, too."

"Are they coming here for Christmas?" the real Holly inquired.

"As a matter of fact, yes." Ryder beamed. "The whole family will be arriving in three weeks."

"And we'll have them over for a long visit," Breanna inserted, anticipating her daughter's request. "I'm sure Monsieur Girard and your father will keep you both up until the wee hours of the morning, telling stories." She rolled her eyes. "And now that Quinn is almost three, he'll probably want to stay up, too, along with Emma's two older ones. It should be quite a gathering."

"Don't forget Damen and Wells," Anastasia added, grinning wryly at Breanna. "They hang on to every word, just like the children. And Hibbert's worse. He adds his own personal touches to each story."

She and Breanna laughed.

In the process of pouring himself and Hibbert a brandy, Wells gave a dignified sniff. "I thought you two had gone to bed," he questioned Joanna and Holly, striving for a measure of discipline. "Where is Miss Carter?"

"Upstairs. She said Holly and I could stay here for a little while." Holly flashed him a beatific smile, her cousin's drawing clutched in her hands. "Please don't be angry, Wells. We just wanted to see what you were celebrating. And to ask Lord Ryder if the Girards were coming to Kent for Christmas. Oh, and I wanted to show Mama this." She waved the sketch in the air.

Wells tried, and failed, to look stern. "Very well. But

it's late. You and Miss Holly can visit for ten minutes."

"Well, perhaps fifteen," Hibbert interjected, then glared defiantly at Wells, who scowled back, gearing up for another disagreement.

Royce rose from his seat at the head of the table. "We'd all like to see the sketch, moppet. Come in."

Beside him, Lord Ryder rose, as well, ruffling Holly's hair as she walked by. "Your daughter is delightful, Chadwick," he praised Royce. "As beautiful and talented as her mother." He turned to gaze fondly at Joanna. "And Holly is as dazzling and fiery as you, Anastasia. It's astonishing to have two sets of such enchanting women in one household."

"I have to agree." Royce caressed Holly's cheek. "Damen and I are lucky men. Our wives and daughters are incomparable treasures." He took the drawing, placed it on the table so that Breanna and everyone else could see.

"The pond," Breanna murmured, smiling. "It's lovely. You've captured it all, right down to the two ducklings we saw there last week. We'll have the drawing framed. You can hang it in the sitting room for everyone to admire."

Joanna's heart lurched with pride, but she was careful to let Holly act out her part.

"Thank you, Mama," Holly said with all her cousin's grace and presence. Joanna was a natural lady, just like her mama. Also like her mama, she was an incredibly talented artist. She took great pride in her drawings, as Holly well knew. Bearing that in mind, she received her Aunt Breanna's praise with all the pleasure Joanna was feeling. "It's one of my favorites, too. Can we go into Town this week and pick out a frame?"

"I don't see why not." Breanna glanced at Royce, who nodded.

"How does tomorrow sound?" he asked.

"Perfect." Holly beamed, but her mind was already elsewhere.

Joanna knew exactly where.

"Papa," she chimed in, addressing Damen. "Can I go with them? I haven't visited the House of Lockewood since Cody was born. Mr. Graff promised to show me how to count the money like you do at the end of the day," she added, referring to the head gatekeeper at the bank. "Now that I'm older I'll really appreciate it. Mama can come, too," she suggested, sweetening the pot. "She can bring Cody. He hasn't even seen where you work yet."

Damen couldn't hide his amusement. "I see your point. But, tell me, what if he decides to do some of that yelling you were referring to? How will my clients feel about that?"

"I'll accompany Miss Stacie and the children," Wells offered at once. He gave a conspiratorial wink to the girl he believed to be Holly. "I'm sure that between us, Miss Holly and I can keep Master Cody amused enough to limit his shouts."

"And I'll help Miss Joanna pick out a frame," Hibbert announced to Royce. "My taste is exceptional, and you and Lady Breanna will have your hands full keeping Master Quinn from turning the shop into a woodpile."

"A fine plan," Royce concluded. "Consider it done." He grinned as the two girls tried to restrain themselves from jumping up and down. "Now, I'd suggest you both go upstairs and get some rest. We don't want you falling asleep during your excursion."

Without a word of protest, the two girls hugged their parents—both sets, so as to avoid figuring out who was supposed to be hugging whom—and curtsied to Lord Ryder. Then, they started to the door.

Abruptly, Holly stopped, deciding that so grand an evening deserved an equally grand conclusion.

She touched Joanna's arm, then gestured for her to follow.

Joanna complied, and the two girls walked back to Hibbert and Wells.

"Would you take us up?" Holly asked, her expression innocent. "Miss Carter might not have waited up, and Holly and I can't fall asleep without a story."

Wells beamed. "Of course, Miss Joanna. I'd be delighted."

"You, too, Hibbert," Joanna piped up. "I want to hear all about how you and Uncle Royce met Monsieur Girard."

Hibbert stood up tall. "That's one of my favorite stories, as well. It would be my pleasure to share it with you, Miss Holly."

Holly placed her hand in Wells's, and Joanna did the same to Hibbert.

The small entourage left the room, the girls beaming secretly at each other.

Royce waited until they'd gone.

Then, he leaned back in his chair, his shoulders shaking with laughter. "That was amazing."

"An exceptional performance," Damen agreed, his own laughter rumbling from deep in his chest. He shot his wife a pointed grin. "I wonder who they could take after."

"We had nothing to do with this," Anastasia denied at once, trying to speak between peals of laughter.

"That's true." Mirth danced in Breanna's eyes. "They did this entirely on their own."

"With no tantalizing stories from you to encourage them," Royce teased.

Anastasia and Breanna exchanged glances, and dissolved into giggles.

"They're going to be unfit to live with," Anastasia said, dabbing at her eyes with a napkin. "They not only fooled Wells. They fooled Hibbert, too."

"Has anyone ever fooled Hibbert?" Breanna asked her husband.

"Now that you mention it, no." Royce rolled his eyes. "God help us."

Lord Ryder was gaping from one of them to the next. "May I ask what you're talking about?"

"Certainly," Royce supplied. "Forgive our rudeness. What you just witnessed was a clever impersonation. Two, actually. The girl you thought was Holly was, in fact, Joanna, and vice versa. They were very convincing, if I must say so myself."

Ryder blinked. "Are you saying your daughters just switched places? And that they actually had us . . . well, some of us fooled?"

"That's exactly what I'm saying." Royce grinned. "And if Hibbert ever finds out he was duped, he'll never be the same."

"I doubt the girls will tell him," Breanna pointed out. "They'll want to savor their secret."

"I agree," Anastasia said.

Royce arched a questioning brow. "Shall we tell them we figured them out?"

"No." Both women spoke simultaneously.

"I guess we have our answer," Damen replied with a smile.

"I guess we do," Royce acknowledged.

Breanna reached over to take her husband's hand. "Stacie and I had our dreams. We've realized them all. Let our daughters have the same. Dreams can carry you a long way. As our grandfather always knew."

Upstairs, the two girls giggled as they changed into their nightgowns. They kept their voices low, since Wells and Hibbert were positioned outside the door, waiting patiently to be summoned for storytelling.

"We did it," Holly hissed. "We even fooled Hibbert and Wells."

"That's even better than our mothers did," Joanna declared proudly. "*They* only had Wells to fool."

"Let's keep pretending until we go to sleep. That way it will *really* be an accomplishment. We'll have fooled Wells and Hibbert for an even longer time, and without a roomful of people they can say distracted them—*if* they ever find out about our game. Which they won't. But if we ever do decide to tell them . . ." Holly dimpled. "Think how smug we can be."

"Okay." Joanna's eyes sparkled, the notion of besting Wells and Hibbert as appealing to her as it was to Holly. Her self-satisfaction, however, was short-lived, as another, far less enticing, thought occurred to her. "We can pretend until we go to sleep," she clarified, wrinkling up her nose. "But tomorrow I'm being me. I don't want to spend the day at the bank."

"That's fine with me. I hate galleries, and I couldn't choose one frame from another." Holly responded without hesitation. "So we'll switch back by morning."

"Agreed."

Squirming into her nightgown, Joanna wandered

over to the window, staring out across the grounds that her mother had gazed at for so many years of her life. But what she saw held none of the fear and loneliness her mother had known as a child, nor the terror she'd known as a young woman of twenty-one.

What she saw was the true magic of Medford Manor, the magic her great-grandfather had hoped to convey to Anastasia and Breanna along with the coins, a magic he hoped they'd pass on to their children and their children's children.

High above, a silvery moon shimmered in the sky, and golden stars twinkled alongside it, the gold and silver hues dousing the world in light and love.

Holly came to stand beside her cousin, propping her elbows on the window sill and reveling in the same wonders as Joanna.

The two girls saw safety and security. They saw the place where they'd been born, the place in which they were growing up, the place they'd always come back to no matter what changes life wrought.

They saw exactly what their great-grandfather had always prayed they would see.

They saw home.

Author's Note

I finish the "coin series" with a myriad of emotions I hope you share: relief that the danger has finally been annihilated, joy that Anastasia and Breanna have found their hearts, and peace that their grandfather's dream has at last been realized and is being carried on by two new, equally precocious identical cousins. I'm certain the Colbys will endure, in heart and in fact.

I close *The Silver Coin* with the same wistful feeling I always experience when concluding a book and bidding its characters farewell. At the same time, I feel an incredible rush of adrenaline, this time more than ever, because I'm about to embark on a new, excitingly different journey—one my readers have been clamoring for me to take.

As of now, all my energies will be focused on creating my first contemporary romantic suspense for Pocket Books. *Run for Your Life* is a gripping novel set in the fast-paced world of New York City. It's the story of Victoria Kensington, who's desperate to save her sister's life, and Zachary Hamilton, who's hellbent on exposing those who destroyed his. Zach's investigation takes him on a collision course with Victoria's—the last thing either of them plans or wants. As luck (or fate) would have it, these two share a past together, one they're both determined, and unable, to forget.

Run for Your Life allows me the chance to blend the

rich characters and edge-of-your-seat suspense I love
to create with the challenge of setting a book in the
here and now. I'm already immersed in my research
and in carving out Victoria and Zach's story. The two
of them are wasting no time in coming alive for me as
I delve into their ardent past, the seeds of unrest that
doused their relationship and the life-threatening series of events that reignite it.

I think you'll find the characters and the story as
compelling as I do. Pocket Books will be releasing *Run
for Your Life* in the fall of 2000. I can't think of a more
exciting way for me to start the new millennium.

Until then, happy reading!

Andrea Kane

P.S. If you'd like a copy of my most recent newsletter,
just send a legal-sized stamped, self-addressed envelope to:

Andrea Kane
P.O. Box 5104
Parsippany, NJ 07054-6104

Or visit my Web site and read the newsletter electronically at:

http://www.andreakane.com

My e-mail address is:

WriteToMe@andreakane.com

Proof-of-Purchase

THE
SILVER
COIN

SONNET
BOOKS